GOLD STREET

Kathy T. Kale

Gold Street

Published by
Pollux Press,
Florida

ISBN 9780983686606

DISCLAIMER

This is a work of fiction. Names, characters, places, and incidents are either the product of the author's imagination or are used fictitiously. Any resemblance to actual persons, living or dead, events or locales is entirely coincidental.

Acknowledgments

Many thanks to those informed people who have tried to shed light on U.S. economic policy. Congressman Ron Paul (R-Tx) has led a protracted fight to expose, audit, and end the Federal Reserve Board. Senator Bernie Sanders (I-Vt) and Congressman Alan Grayson (D-Fl) have both tried to make public the covert operations of the Fed, and to tighten banking restrictions that have been continually weakened since their imposition after the Great Depression. Bloomberg News has also waged a lengthy and successful court battle to force the Fed to disclose those bailed out after the economic crash in 2008.

Many excellent and informative books have been written about the Fed and U.S. economic policy, and these include: *Web of Debt* by Ellen Brown; *The Creature From Jekyll Island*, by G. Edward Griffin; and *Griftopia*, by Matt Taibbi. Exceptional movies have also been produced and noteworthy documentaries include Michael Moore's *Capitalism: A Love Story*; and Charles H. Ferguson's *Inside Job*.

This book would not be possible without the support and encouragement of my husband. As always, my children, Will and Luc, now grown (and who in no way resemble some characters in this story) continue to inspire me to leave behind for them a better world. Thanks also to Jeanne Johansen for her creative insights and editorial comments; Robert Gover who was a continual source of information; Mark Springle for editing; Mimi Alonso for the cover design; Jan Dawson for copy-editing; Ray Farrell for his indefatigable, late hour assistance; and my parents who grew up in the depression and know the value of money. In memory of Renee Szlavnics Montminy who did call her mother on her birthday.

For Bill

It is well enough the people of the nation do not understand our banking and monetary system, for if they did, I believe there would be a revolution before tomorrow morning.

– Henry Ford

1

Let me issue and control a nation's money and I care not who writes its laws.

—Mayer Amschel Rothschild

SATURDAY OCTOBER 18

The call came before dawn, breaking the silence of the old house in the nation's capital where Jill Madison lay dreaming. "Happy Birthday Mommy," her daughter said, and in her sleep Jill smiled and pressed the receiver against her ear. Then the shrill second ring came and Jill was instantly alert.

Her husband snapped on the overhead light and answered the call. "Blaze Madison," he said, in the senatorial tone reserved for colleagues and constituents. "Good morning." It was five-forty.

Jill eyed her husband as he frowned at the phone. He was fifty-six, but looked younger, even though his hair and eyebrows were white. His eyes were dark brown and so shiny they looked liquid. He had a golden stubble and a perennial tan, but in the harsh light he looked pale. His brow was furrowed, showing deep lines that were seldom noticeable.

"Come again?" he said, as his voice broke and rose in tone.

Jill sat up and rearranged the blanket, feeling the mid-October chill.

Looking ten years older, Blaze said goodbye and folded the phone. "That was the police. Tyler's been hit by a car."

A weight fell on Jill's heart, which made it hard to breathe, hard to talk, hard to think of her vital and athletic twenty-four year old son run over by a car. "How is he?" she asked in a hoarse voice.

"Unconscious. He's in New York Downtown Hospital."

Jill was instantly cold, the room's autumn air now inside her bones.

"He was hit Thursday night." Blaze pulled at the stubble on his chin.

Today was Saturday. Tyler had been unconscious for two days and she hadn't known. "Why are they just telling us now?"

"They just learned who he was. His phone broke in the accident. He had no wallet, no ID, and no money."

Jill closed her eyes. She thought she had already lived through the worst possible nightmare.

"You have to go to New York." Blaze got out of bed pulling on his jockeys. He went to the north window and threw open the curtains. No light came in.

Jill didn't move. She wanted to go back to sleep, have *this* be the dream.

"I can't go," he said. "Not now, not with the vote. I've got to be in chambers at eight. If we don't fix this Vermont crisis, we'll lose the election." He sighed deeply, as if in contemplation of this. "I'm sorry this had to happen on your birthday."

Jill shivered and pulled the covers up over her shoulders. Today she turned fifty. The old boxer stared up from her doggie bed and looked worried, as if she sensed trouble. Tyler was unconscious and that meant a brain injury. He could be a vegetable, never able to walk or think again. Jill drew in a deep sharp breath. She wanted a drink; it would turn down the dial of her mind, dull the sharp edges of her thoughts, make things manageable.

"I'll drop you at the airport on my way downtown and come as soon as I can," Blaze said, as he strode to the closet.

Outside, a police siren wailed as it went screaming down Wisconsin heading toward the White House. The dog had gone back to sleep and Jill knew a drink would not change anything. Somehow, she had to find a way to deal with this straight and sober.

A crash from the closet got Jill out of bed. Cinching the belt on her robe, she crossed the floor, the bare wood cold on her feet. A pile of suitcases had fallen from the overhead shelf and lay on the closet floor. Blaze was rubbing his head. He picked up a black carry-on from the pile. "You'll have to fly standby. Don't check any luggage."

His cell phone rang and he rushed to get it. She stood in the closet doorway, clutching hangers and listening to his end of the conversation. He was evidently talking to the doctor, but doing more listening than talking. Jill hugged her clothes and held her breath. Let Tyler be awake, fully functional, cognitive, and miraculously recovered.

But Blaze said, "Let me know if there's any change." He gave the doctor two phone numbers where he could be reached and tossed the phone on the bed. "That was the neurologist, Dr. Patel. The prognosis is good. Tyler was hit close to the hospital and got there within ten minutes of the accident. They did an MRI and there was no swelling of the brain. He injured his shoulder, broke his clavicle, and has minor bruising. He's unconscious, but Patel thinks he'll snap out of it."

Jill knew with a brain injury there wasn't much you could do besides wait. It was like chemotherapy, when all you could do was hold your breath and hope. Nothing was in your control and you were as powerless as the doctors, who tried hard not to let it show.

"He's young," Blaze said, "he's healthy. He has that going for him." Her husband was a master of positive thinking.

He was on his way to the shower when the phone rang again. This time Jill couldn't tell who was on the other end, but it didn't sound like a doctor. Blaze listened intently, answering questions in terse reply, yes or no. He was staring out the window at the backyard, where the wind shrieked, shaking the trees. The melodic wind chime on the patio beneath them clanged and clattered.

Jill waited, clutching her clothes, numb and cold. The stone house was a hundred years old, solid but drafty. The bedroom was on the west side, with large windows on three walls and it often felt as if the wind blew right through. The room would be bright once the sun rose, but now it was dark, in spite of the white duvet, white bed sheets, white walls and oak furniture intended to lighten it.

Blaze closed the phone and turned around. He was still in his jockeys, not seeming to feel the cold. He could block parts of himself off. That was how he kept functional. She had done it by drinking, but not any more. Not for nine months, two weeks, and three days. She would need a miracle to get through this sober.

"That was the FBI," Blaze said. "They're looking into the accident."

"Why not the police?"

"It's routine."

Because he was a U.S. senator and there was power that came with being an elected official.

"He was hit on Gold Street. Down in the financial district. A hit and run."

Jill's mouth dropped open. "They just left him lying in the road?"

"He probably didn't look both ways when he crossed the street."

Jill looked at Blaze dubiously. "Are you kidding?"

He shrugged. "It's what the police thought."

Jill shook her head. Every fiber in her body fought that conclusion. From the time Tyler was young, she taught him to look three times before he crossed the street: first one way, then the other, and then the first again. And this on their quiet road! When he went to grade school, she walked with him every day. Even when he was too old for it, he held her hand tightly and always looked. Now he lived in New York where traffic was a nightmare. He ran marathons and didn't listen to music when he trained so he could hear the cars. So, no, she did not believe he would just step out into the path of a car without looking where he was going. It was unthinkable. "That's not possible. Maybe he was mugged and pushed into the road."

"He doesn't have any money."

"I know he didn't just step into the road without looking."

Blaze shrugged. "What's the alternative? He was hit on purpose?"

"He thought he was being followed."

Blaze dismissed that with a sweep of his hand. "He probably drank too much and stumbled into the street."

"He doesn't drink."

"Maybe not around you. Maybe he went to visit Julie."

Jill's older sister was a stock broker who lived near Wall Street, but her son and Julie lived in two different worlds. "I doubt it."

"It could be drugs. Face it, we don't know what he's into. He hasn't been home in months."

"Were you having him followed?"

"Me?" Blaze was taken aback. "Of course not."

"You did before."

"For a good reason. We agreed it was best."

No, Blaze thought it was best, and on the advice of his lawyer, he'd hired a private investigator.

"We'll leave at six-thirty." Blaze picked up his phone, dialed a number, and Jill knew who he was calling even though he identified himself only as, "It's me." He was calling Austin, and his ex-wife, rubbing salt in Jill's wound.

***

Reagan National Airport was a zoo even on Saturday at 6.45 A.M. Long lines snaked around the ticket counter with even longer lines at security. Flights were being canceled and delays were probable, thanks to an advancing front, the first one of the year, arriving early and bringing cold, blustery wind, gray skies and torrential rain.

Through security, Jill bought a disgusting cup of coffee and a *Washington Post* and sat near the window. Outside, the waiting plane was being shaken by the wind and drowned by the storm. The 8:00 A.M. departure time had already been delayed to 8:30.

She drank the weak coffee, as awful as it was, and read the paper, trying not to think about Tyler lying alone in the hospital with no visitors, no friends, and no family to show the medical staff he was loved and that people cared deeply about his progress and his treatment. Blaze had promised to call as soon as he heard anything, and she checked her phone again, but there were no calls. Phones weren't allowed to ring in chambers, but Chase, his top aide and campaign manager, was supposed to keep her posted. She put the phone on her lap within close reach.

The headline on the front page was: 'Vermont Near Bankruptcy'. According to the article, the trouble could be traced to a failing nuclear facility. Twenty-five million had been borrowed to get the plant fixed and modernized, only the job had been botched and the plant was still off-line, generating neither power nor revenue. The state needed the electricity and was currently buying power from New Hampshire. Short of cash, the government was unable to pay its employees and pensioners, or repay other debts. The state sought a paltry fifty million from Congress to fix the plant and keep the state afloat.

The crisis couldn't have come at a worse time. The presidential election was seventeen days away and Vermont had become the central issue. Blaze was up for re-election and did not need an economic crisis when he was already seen as a tax-and-spend liberal. At the moment, he was ahead of his Tea Party opponent, but just barely. During his twenty-four years in Congress, he'd never had an opponent this close. Privately, Blaze was musing about what they would do if he lost. They had a house in Austin, but Jill had no desire to go back there. They'd raised their family in D.C. Her memories were here.

Despite the advantage of incumbency, things had recently taken a bad turn for the Democratic President. Until the current emergency, he had been the favored candidate. Three months of positive employment and housing reports, and a robust stock market, showed a country in rebound and heading for prosperity.

Now, the crisis reminded voters of his fiscal irresponsibility. The President was calling for a bailout, and for Congress to immediately pass a bill to lend Vermont the money. Hence, the rare Saturday vote on the Hill.

It would be contentious because Republicans weren't going along with it. The Tea Party claimed the problem in the blue state of Vermont was emblematic of the problem facing the country; government just wanted to spend, spend, spend. The Republican presidential candidate, Rich Tumblin, a corpulent billionaire hedge fund CEO from Wall Street was also denouncing the bailout. Why should taxpayers in other states give away their hard-earned dollars to slackers in Vermont? The federal government couldn't solve everything. Vermont needed to grow up and fix its own problems. If it had to go bankrupt, so be it.

Which showed how much he knew about the law, for it was currently illegal for states to go bankrupt. So, today, the vote was for the bailout, and as usual, it was expected to split along party lines. The bill was expected to pass in the Democratic dominated Senate and fail in the Republican dominated House. With many members up for re-election, the response to the economic crisis would determine the fate of many political careers.

Jill read the positions outlined in the editorial pages as she waited to board. Take-off was delayed until 9:00, and she was sure it would be delayed again, but then the flight was called. Normally she flew business class and got to board first, but today she had a seat in economy and was lucky to have that for the flight was overbooked.

Her seat was in the last row of three and two overweight travelers sat on either side of her hogging the arm rests. She hugged her arms together, holding herself tight, phone close at hand. Soon she would have to turn it off, but would do so at the last moment. She was still trying to decide whether to call her daughter, Alexandria, who was a first year medical student at Harvard. She was in the midst of mid-terms and Jill was loath to worry her. Alexandria had wanted to come down for the weekend to celebrate Jill's birthday, but couldn't because of her exams. She had sent a nice card. Tyler, who could have come, said he was too busy. Doing what, he never said. Something that would cause him to be followed, mugged, and run over? Jill looked at her watch. He had been unconscious now for thirty-five hours.

She wanted a drink. She craned her neck looking for the flight attendant. Despite the overhead warning, Jill unclasped her seatbelt and stood up at a crouch. The aisle was empty. Just one small drink, a vodka with orange juice; no one would ever know. She would just have one, enough to calm her thoughts, sedate her fears. There was no sign of the drink cart or the stewardess and she sank back down.

The man on her right turned and peered at her. "Are you Jill Madison? The senator's wife?"

"Yes." Jill forced a smile. Since she had quit drinking, it was increasingly hard for her to be out in public and she preferred to be home, protected behind a big sturdy fence and a locked gate. Out here she was a walking target, a public figure through marriage. Without alcohol, she found this nearly intolerable. Her therapist said it would pass, but for the moment advised Jill to stay home, keep stress to a minimum, and not do anything new to invite temptation.

"Will they bail out Vermont?"

"Eventually," she said, wondering why people thought they could ask her anything they liked.

"Why should we bail them out?"

"It's the right thing to do," she said, without much conviction.

"No one bailed me out when I lost my house."

"Sorry."

"Will he be re-elected?"

"Yes." Jill nodded emphatically. Always exude confidence, she'd learned. You never knew who you could be talking to. She didn't want tomorrow's headline in the *Washington Post* to be: 'Senator's Wife Doubts Win'.

"You're the one with the daughter who died, aren't you?"

"Excuse me, I have to go to the bathroom." Jill stood up, hunched over, waiting for the man to move.

"You have to keep your seatbelt on." He pointed to the sign.

"I'm going." She spoke so stridently, he was quickly up on his feet and in the aisle.

There was no line for the bathroom and no flight attendant to shoo her back to her seat. Jill went into the stall and locked the door. She looked in the mirror and was appalled. She had got her hair cut for her birthday and it was horrible, a stupid unflattering cut that was too angled around her chin and chopped at the back. She combed it with her fingers. Her hair was light brown, thick and wavy, not suitable for this style. The gray was coming in quickly, but she let it come, too apathetic really to do too much about it. She had dark blue eyes, which had once been bright and shiny, but now looked dull and without luster. She was aging fast and didn't care. At least she still had her figure, not that she worked on it. She walked three miles with the dog every day and ate healthy food because Blaze had high blood pressure and needed to watch his weight. She had expected to feel healthy after she quit drinking, but after nine months of sobriety, she felt worse. She couldn't sleep, she worried incessantly, and grieved the loss of her younger daughter.

She returned to her seat, hoping her seatmate would have found something else to do in her absence, but he was at it again as soon as she sat down. "Is it right for the government to lend money that it doesn't have? To borrow money just to give it away?"

"It's a difficult situation." Jill reached for the in-flight magazine, reminding herself she had to be nice. Every person was a potential voter or a potential threat. Anyone could write anything and have it end up in the paper: 'Senator's Wife Tells Voter To Fuck Off'. She got out her reading glasses. "Excuse me."

The man nudged her with his elbow. "You're reading upside down."

"I can read upside down." She turned a page.

"You're kidding?"

"Yes." She turned the magazine around and stared at an ad for perfume and thought about her son. She knew he could be doing a number of things that would get him into trouble. Unlike Blaze, she didn't believe that Tyler was into the kinds of things that normal college age students were into, like drinking and dope, girls and sex. He wanted to make the world a better place.

He hadn't finished university, and so far he had been to three. He always wanted to be a doctor and had been enrolled in pre-med at

Georgetown. Then Hope got sick. It didn't take him long to decide he wanted no part of the health care system, but he stuck it out for a year. He transferred to the University of Maryland as a sophomore and enrolled in Computer Science. That lasted two semesters; the classes were too boring, the programming too juvenile. In his junior year he went to Howard University and took Economics and History. He liked the history – the black people's version – but he questioned the economics.

Some time during the year he applied to the Peace Corps and although they didn't normally accept volunteers without university degrees, he talked his way in. He was posted in West Africa, in a small town in a coastal country that had no oil. The country was poor, with an average per capita income of fifty cents a day. Tyler's job was teaching green agriculture to low income subsistence farmers. He'd been there fifteen months when the government arrested him for sedition.

Tyler's defense was that there'd been a serious drought and crops were ruined and food prices were rising, there were shortages and people were starving. Typically, at this point, the International Monetary Fund would come in with a loan, but the country was behind in its debt repayment and the IMF refused to lend more money. The government printed money, resulting in hyperinflation and the value of the country's currency plunged. The cost of imports, especially oil, skyrocketed. Business in the country came to a near standstill. People were starving. They died by the thousands.

Finally, the government agreed to a strict repayment plan and austerity measures for its people, and the IMF came back with new funding. Now, government services and workers' pay were cut. Taxes were raised. The people rebelled. Workers across the country went on strike. In the capital city an early curfew was imposed, stores were closed and university classes canceled. People marched in the streets and Tyler marched with them. He was quickly arrested, thrown in prison and could have been there for years had the ambassador not intervened.

Tyler was shipped home in time for Christmas and moved to New York in the new year. He lived with Jill's sister for two days and then got a room in a boarding house where he'd been now for ten months. He tried to get a job, but with official unemployment nearing ten percent, and unofficial unemployment over twenty percent, he couldn't find work. He didn't want to go back to school and had trained for the New York Marathon, was volunteering in a soup kitchen, learning Portuguese and advanced French, with a plan to return to Africa.

He would have already gone, but he was arrested in June for harboring two Zimbabwe dissidents who were wanted at home on felony charges. That was when Blaze had him followed. Their lawyer didn't want any surprises and there weren't any. Tyler didn't drink, didn't do drugs and didn't gamble. There was apparently a girl, but he never spoke of her, and in any case, she didn't last. Although the felony charges were bogus, the judge sent the Zimbabweans home and gave Tyler six months probation. He couldn't leave the country for another two months.

Maybe now he could never leave. This was what she had wanted, but not at this cost. *Be careful what you wish for, you might just get it*. Tyler might never wake up, never walk, never smile, never talk, never run another marathon or save the world.

Recognizing a downward spiral, Jill ordered herself to find good thoughts. Her therapist said that it was as easy to think good thoughts as it was to think bad ones. Jill told herself that Tyler would wake up, he would be fine. Thanks to spectacular medical treatment, he would return to university and become a doctor after all. The accident would shake him up, make him see what was important. He would fall in love, get married, have kids and get a normal life and forget about fixing the world.

The pilot came on over the loudspeaker. The plane was ready to depart. Jill applauded along with the other passengers. Her desire to drink was gone, until the pilot announced they were number thirty-seven in line for take-off.

2

Economics is a dry and forbidding subject that has been made intentionally complex by banking interests intent on concealing what is really going on.

—Ellen Brown, Web of Debt

New York, as always, was busy, crowded, noisy and frustrating. There were too many people, all wanting to be first, which caused a logjam that slowed everything and raised tempers. Under gray threatening skies, traffic was bumper to bumper along the freeway, and the taxi ride from the airport to lower Manhattan took Jill over an hour. Downtown Hospital was on the corner of William Street and Ann, but there was no way to get off Broadway and get to it. The side roads were closed, and no cars or people were allowed past police-taped intersections. The cab was stuck on Broadway, and the cabbie, who kept up with traffic reports, didn't know what was going on.

Jill ended up getting out at Maiden Lane and headed for the hospital on foot, pulling her suitcase behind her. Campaign signs were everywhere, tacked to electric poles, stapled to trees and on posts shoved in brown patches of dirt. The street was packed with pedestrians streaming in each direction, walking three abreast. The wind blew against her back, the storm on its way from Washington. No sun shone. She passed a tavern and slowed, wanting to stop in, but thoughts of Tyler spurred her on.

She reached Fulton and another barrier. She looked around, saw no police, and side-stepped the barrier. She was hurrying along the sidewalk when she heard from behind, "Ma'am, Ma'am. You with the suitcase."

She stopped and turned.

An officer marched toward her. "The road's closed."

"I've got to get to the hospital. It's just over there." She pointed vaguely to the northeast. "My son's been hit by a car. He's unconscious."

"What's in the suitcase?"

"My clothes." She tried to smile, to appeal with good looks that she knew were in short supply. "I just came from D.C. My son is only twenty-four. He was hit on Thursday night. We just found out this morning. I came as fast as I could. I don't know how to get to the hospital with the roads blocked off. I –"

Her long story was interrupted by a volley of three shots. The officer looked in the direction of the sound. His radio crackled, "Code 3, code 3." Sirens started screaming and he waved her on. He turned around and loped off in the opposite direction.

Inside the barricaded streets, the sidewalks were empty and it was a welcome relief. She followed the Maps app on her phone and got to the hospital in ten minutes. It was a long rectangular brick building that was undergoing renovations. Big panels of plywood blocked off the windows and doors. She went down a hallway and realized she'd gone in a back door. She passed a closed Starbucks and headed for the entrance. The reception desk was staffed by an ancient volunteer with blue hair and a hearing aid. There was no record of a Tyler Madison in the hospital.

Jill leaned forward and spelled out her last name one more time, wishing she had stopped at the bar. It was hard to hear herself speak over the ear-splitting pounding of loud hammering.

A glimmer brightened the old woman's eyes. "One moment." She picked up a phone and pushed a button.

The next thing Jill knew, a young, sharp-looking woman appeared and shook her hand. The director of the hospital was going to escort Jill up to Tyler's room personally. Ms. Jones explained that Tyler wasn't listed in the system at the suggestion of the FBI. "We don't need the press. I thought your husband concurred."

"Yes," Jill said, though it was news to her. She fell in step with the director.

"We have Tyler in ICU. Not that he needs to be there, just so we can keep a close eye on him."

"I'd like to talk to his doctor."

"I paged him. He's in surgery now, but he'll speak with you the moment he's finished."

"Thank you," Jill said, cognizant of and grateful for the special treatment. Despite the invasion of privacy that came with Blaze's position, it had its perks.

ICU was up on the 4th floor and the elevator doors opened onto a hallway covered with plywood. The director apologized for the construction and promised that it in no way hampered patient care. Jill wondered about patient comfort. All the banging and power tools were giving her a headache.

They followed a maze of corridors to a hallway that ended with double black doors and the letters ICU. The director pushed a large button the size of her palm and the doors sprang open.

ICU was a big square room with a nurses' station taking up a huge center block and rooms arranged along the perimeter. Nurses milling about the center snapped to attention when the director stopped. A heavy nurse in pink scrubs and black crocs hurried over. He was Vincent, Tyler's personal intensive care nurse.

The trio walked down a wide corridor. The doors to the rooms were open and glass windows offered no privacy. Jill saw sleeping patients surrounded by family members, while Tyler was alone. She quickened her pace.

They turned a corner and Vincent pushed ahead to lead the way. He stopped in a doorway and Jill rushed past him into the room. Tyler lay on his back in bed, looking pale and still. Tubes snaked across him. An IV fed the back of his wrist and he had a clamp on his thumb and a blood pressure cuff around his bicep. She bent over the rail and laid her cheek against his. His skin was cold and his lips were tight. He wore a blue checkered gown and his left shoulder was heavily taped. Other than that, he looked good. His face wasn't smashed and his skull was intact.

There was a flurry of activity behind her and Jill straightened. A tiny Asian man in starched baby blue scrubs swept into the room attended by a crowd, which turned out to be neurology residents and interns. The director made introductions and Jill met Dr. Patel fresh from surgery.

The director retreated, bidding a regretful goodbye. Dr. Patel tapped at a tablet and spoke in a happy voice, "Miraculously, there is no internal damage. He did break his clavicle, but other than his brain, there are no more injuries."

It was a huge *but*. Jill faced the neurologist. "He feels cold."

"I'll get him another blanket." Vincent hurried from the room.

"He's pale," Jill said.

"Actually, his color looks quite good," said the neurologist. "Much better than previously."

"Not for him," Jill said. She was used to seeing her son tanned and glowing with the good health that came from running ten to fifteen miles a day. She stared at the monitor by the bed. "His temperature is only ninety-six. Why is it so low?"

"It is being in the normal range."

"His blood pressure is only 110/60? Isn't that low?"

"Again, I am afraid it is normal. Considering. Your son actually is in very good condition."

Jill wanted the truth. She would not be appeased. She frowned at the monitor. "He could have low blood pressure if he was bleeding internally, right?" She had learned a thing or two about medicine when Hope was in the hospital.

"I can assure you he is not bleeding internally," the neurologist said, as Vincent returned with a cheery yellow blanket and draped it over the bed. "We are taking blood twice a day to monitor organ function and detect infection and his blood work is consistently good.

We are giving him fluid to keep him hydrated. As you can see, he is breathing on his own and that is a very good sign."

The neurologist took a penlight from his pocket, leaned over the bed and pried open one of Tyler's eyelids. He shone the light in his eye. He did the same to the other eye. "He has good pupilary reflex," Dr. Patel said. "Which means his pupils contract with the light. It is another positive sign."

"But that's just a reflex, right," Jill said. "It doesn't mean his brain is working."

The neurologist patted Jill's arm. "Trust me. It is a good sign."

"Please be straight with me," Jill said. "What are his chances of a full recovery?"

The neurologist was hesitant to name a figure.

"Fifty percent?" Jill said.

"At least."

"So there's a fifty percent chance he'll be a vegetable or will never wake up."

The students suddenly found something interesting to see out the window. Dr. Patel looked uncomfortable. He slipped the tablet under his arm and said, "He is young. Very healthy. His chances are very good." Then the neurologist had to go, there were other patients to see, but if she had any more questions she could page him.

"Where are Tyler's clothes?"

"I'll get them." Vincent pulled open the bottom drawer of the bedside dresser and grabbed a plastic bag.

"Where's the bar?" Jill asked.

The surgeon, nurse, and students gawked with surprise. There was an awkward moment until she realized her error and corrected herself. "I mean, the bathroom."

There was one in the corner of the room.

After everyone had gone, Jill drew the curtain across the front window for privacy. She dragged an armchair from the corner to the bed, dropped the side rail, sat down and took Tyler's hand. She wanted to climb into bed with him, like she did when he was small, back when she had the power to chase away monsters and make his world happy and safe. Now all she could do was hold his hand and hope his glass was half full instead of half empty.

There was a puff, and the blood pressure cuff automatically began to inflate as it recorded Tyler's blood pressure. She read the numbers off the monitor: 118/70. His blood pressure had gone up, inching toward normal. Did Tyler know she was there? She squeezed his hand, looking for a response, but there was none. He felt cold and far away.

Jill glanced around the room. As far as hospitals went, it wasn't bad and that was something. It didn't smell of antiseptic or sick people. The walls were forest green with a rainforest trim as if bright monkeys and parrots could make people happy. A row of windows flanked one wall and she could see the East River. She heard what sounded like loud drumming, a power saw, and the noise of heavy traffic. For an insomniac like her, it would be disturbing, but Tyler slept through it all. He had always slept well. It was Hope who'd had trouble sleeping.

Jill picked up the remote clipped to the side of the bed and turned on the TV. It was tuned to a local station and the weather report was on and rain was coming. No explanation was given for the closure of the streets near the hospital.

She got up, opened the plastic bag with Tyler's clothes and emptied it at the foot of the bed between Tyler's outstretched legs. There was a whooshing sound as the mattress redistributed air to account for new weight. She went through his things. There were jeans that had faded to white and were ripped in the knees. There was nothing in the pockets, no wallet, no money, no ID. He'd been wearing a thin gray henley, the color of a used dish rag that was frayed at the hem, along with a navy sweater that looked too small and had a hole in the elbow and knots in the wool. It was sticky and bloodied. She picked up a green Nike and turned it over in her hand. It was a specialized lightweight running shoe with cushioning air pockets and yellow stripes. She pushed the clothes aside. She couldn't find the other shoe. He had no jacket and no socks.

She picked up his cell phone. It was the smart phone she had bought him for Christmas. Wistfully, she remembered going with him to pick it out. The store was having a two-for-one sale and he picked one out for her too. He was excited about the advances in technology that had transpired when he was in Africa and the phone made him happy. It had been nice to see. He had come back from overseas depressed and disillusioned.

She slid the on button and nothing happened. The police thought the phone was damaged, but the battery could be dead. She wondered how the police finally identified him and why it had taken them so long. Was Tyler a low priority because of his clothes? Did he look poor, irrelevant, unloved? It couldn't be further from the truth. She put the phone in her purse, shoved his meager belongings back in the bag and returned it to the drawer.

She sat back down. Tyler hadn't moved. She tried to envision his last conscious movements on Thursday night. He lived in the South Bronx and had come downtown. He didn't have a car, so someone either drove him or he took the subway. What would he be doing in the financial district at nine o'clock at night? What had he planned this weekend that prevented him from coming home? Did he leave his wallet with his money and ID at home, or had he been robbed? Was the accident random or deliberate? Was someone really following him? Did they come after him? Did they think they got him, or were they after him still? Then there was the biggest question of all: what was he doing that could get him killed?

The afternoon passed slowly. Jill sat by Tyler's bed watching CNN. Rain came with thunder that sounded like gunshot, but didn't last. Vincent came every hour to check on Tyler, but nothing changed. Dr. Patel came at five on his last rounds of the day and reiterated his assessment that Tyler looked very good. Blaze called at five-thirty to tell her he was leaving chambers. "We voted for the bailout, but the House didn't. We're going to have to meet tomorrow. See if we can find a compromise."

"I know." CNN had already reported it. Blaze's vote for the bailout was on the record. His Tea Party opponent, Candy Turner, who had never held any elective office, considered it ill-conceived. She made it sound as if Blaze were personally responsible for giving away the money of hard working people to government loafers and lazy retirees in Vermont. Blaze was clearly a socialist, bent on turning the U.S. into a communist country.

It was incredible to Jill that Candy was doing so well. She was far right, an ultra-conservative, albeit attractive, but with questionable ideas. She didn't think carbon dioxide was harmful because it was a natural compound. She thought wolves were dangerous and therefore shouldn't be protected. She wanted to fence in the whooping cranes, thwart their annual migration, and build a theme park for them in the unspoiled wetlands of Aransas. And, she wanted to cut taxes and decrease government regulation. The Tea Party loved her, as did its Wall Street backers. In September, money had begun pouring in to her campaign and now Blaze had a tenth of what she had. It was amazing she wasn't further ahead in the polls instead of almost even.

"How is Tyler doing?" Blaze asked. "Patel called and said he looked good."

Jill glanced at her son "There's been no change all day. What if this is it? What if he doesn't wake up? If he doesn't get any better?"

"Did you ask for a second opinion?"

"Should I?"

"It can't hurt. What about the brain trauma center in Houston?"

"What about it? Is it better? Should we try to move him?"

"We need to consider all options."

Which was exactly why he needed to be here and not wasting his time in chambers. But it was always this way, whenever she needed him, he was elsewhere. "I'll talk to the doctor," Jill said. But it wouldn't be until morning when Dr. Patel returned.

"Have you called Alexandria?" Blaze asked.

"No, she's got midterms next week and I don't want to tell her. She'd drop everything and come."

"Did you call your sister?"

"I want to stay with Tyler. I don't want Julie to know I'm here." Jill's sister had a way of moving in, taking over, taking charge. But that wasn't all. Jill hadn't seen her since she quit drinking and wasn't sure how they'd get along now that she was sober. She changed the subject. "Have you talked with the FBI?"

"Not since this morning. Why?"

"I wondered if they found Tyler's wallet. He's also missing a shoe."

"They're going to call me with an update and I'll ask them."

In the background Jill heard noises, bells ringing and Blaze had to go. They said their goodbyes. He was heading home to their warm cozy house, while she was stuck in the hospital getting ready to settle in for an uncomfortable night. Though visiting hours ended at nine, she had permission from the director to spend the night. It would be unpleasant, that much was clear. The armchair was already hurting her back.

Night-time at the hospital was pretty much like the day-time only the bright overhead lights were dimmed and the curtains were closed. The staff thinned, though Vincent stayed on to work a double shift. Jill was settling into the hard chair, bracing herself for an endless night, when her phone rang. It was her sister.

"Why didn't you tell me you were in New York?" Julie demanded. "That my only nephew was in a coma?"

"He's unconscious."

"Is there a difference?"

"How did you find out?"

"Excuse the noise, I'm at a party. Blaze told me. I called your house to wish you happy birthday and he answered and said you couldn't come to the phone. Obviously, I asked, why not."

Even Blaze couldn't stand up to her.

"You're spending the night, I presume," Julie said.

"With Tyler, yes."

A phlebotomist came in pushing a blood cart and nodded to Jill.

"I meant with me. They won't let you stay overnight."

"I have permission." Jill got out of the chair to give the technician space.

He grabbed a tourniquet, wrapped it around Tyler's arm, tapped, then swabbed a vein and withdrew blood. Jill walked to the window, lifted the curtain and looked out.

"I'll come pick you up," Julie said. "Leave your phone number at the nurses' station. They'll call if anything happens. You can be back in ten minutes."

Jill stared out at the water. The bridge, sparkling with lights, looked surreal, like a painting. None of what was happening seemed remotely possible, and Julie would not give up.

"Blaze said Tyler's been out of it for two days and there's no change. He's not a baby. If he wakes up and you're not there, he won't start wailing."

The phlebotomist had his blood and was leaving. Jill nodded goodbye, as her sister continued.

"I haven't seen you in months. You haven't been to New York in over a year and when you come, you don't call and would rather sit with someone who doesn't know you're there, than with me, who does."

Jill exhaled loudly. Her older sister never married and had no children. She lived a free, but lonely life. Jill was the only family she had left. And Julie did have a point; her apartment was nearby, and she had comfortable guest rooms. Jill could be back quickly if there was any change. Besides, it was a long shot, but Julie might know how Tyler spent his days. "Okay, I'll come."

"Don't make it sound like torture. Meet me downstairs in half an hour."

***

At nine o'clock, Jill kissed her cold, still son and left ICU along with the other visitors. A crowd huddled at the elevator and when it finally came, there wasn't enough room for everyone. She didn't fight her way on. She and a burly man waited for the next one. He wore a beige trench coat and spoke on a cell phone in a thick accent that sounded German. He had dirty blond hair that might have been dyed. A long, ugly bulging scar ran from the corner of his eye down across his left cheek to his mouth. He seemed rough, out of place, more like a thug than a worried visitor.

He caught her eye and she looked away. He snapped his phone closed quickly; in mid-sentence it seemed. There was a loud uncomfortable silence. He was standing too close to her. She shifted her eyes to look at him askance. He was staring at her carry-on. Christ, could he read her name tag? She jerked her suitcase away, whirled around and hurried down the hallway. She wasn't getting on the elevator with him.

Her heart was pounding. Was he a foreign reporter looking for a scoop? It wouldn't be the first time she was followed, or had photos rudely snapped. Though sober, she did offer less fodder for the tabloids. Was he the man following Tyler? Her body stiffened and she sped up, hurrying through a doorway that led to a deserted corridor. She glanced down at her suitcase. There, in big letters, was her name and address in D.C. He would know who she was and where she lived.

She got lost in the construction. Each footstep echoed noisily. The wheels on her suitcase squeaked loudly. She had never been followed when she was sober, and drunk it seemed like a joke, but there was nothing funny about this.

She reached a different elevator, pushed the button and the doors opened and an elderly couple was there. She caught her breath and began to calm down. It could have just been a man with a scar. He hadn't come after her; he hadn't made any threatening advances. He could have been looking at the floor, not necessarily her suitcase. Jill's palms were sweating. Her therapist had warned that her emotions could overwhelm her without notice. She had spent years sedating them with booze and needed to learn how to handle them sober.

The elevator reached the ground floor and the elderly couple stayed put and Jill got out. The corridor was empty. She headed for the exit, passing the Starbucks and the information desk. There was no one hiding in dark corners or lurking in the shadows. She reached the exit and the automatic revolving doors wouldn't budge. Panic instantly rose until she turned to the side door, leaned on the bar and the door opened. She stepped out into a biting wind.

A voice cried out. "Wait!"

Her heart was slamming again. Three men in the shade of the building slunk out from the bushes. She froze. They came closer and she saw that they were ragged and dirty, down and out. She yanked her suitcase to her side and hugged her purse. One yelled, "Please hold the door."

They came into the light and she saw they were young, Tyler's age. And polite. She lunged for the door and caught it just before it closed.

"Thank you." Now, an arm's distance away, she saw the man in the middle was slouching, supported on each side by his friends. He had flip-flops, torn jeans and his head hung down. Long, bright blond hair hid his face. He wore a grimy unzipped jacket, and held his hand above his heart. Blood seeped through his fingers. Their eyes met as she stepped back and gave them room to pass.

From the street, a horn hooted and high beams flashed. Julie's Jaguar was idling at the curb. The car door opened and a squat, round man of about sixty stepped out and came toward her. "Good evening," he said in a strong British accent. "Did you actually just let that riff-raff in the door?"

Jill didn't answer. She extended her hand to Julie's new butler. "You must be Charles. I'm Jill Madison."

The balding expatriate was going gray and swept what hair he had across his crown. The whites of his small bland blue eyes were tinged with red. He wore tight black slacks, a navy silk shirt and a leather bomber jacket. Instead of shaking her hand, he wrestled away her suitcase, slammed the handle closed and picked it up. "And I'm Tea Party."

"You sound British."

"Thank God."

Jill was taken aback by his rudeness. Because of Blaze, strangers thought they knew her politics and where she stood on every issue, which obviously had to match her husband's. She already missed the respectful and hard-working Christophe who had retired in the summer after twenty years of service.

The back door flew open and Julie was there, arms open. The scent of booze assailed Jill as they hugged. Julie was five years older, though routine cosmetic touch-ups made her look younger and strangers always guessed Jill was older. Julie was taller, smarter, prettier and richer. Julie was six feet tall and at five-nine, Jill was the runt. They both had brown hair and blue eyes and similar facial features, but Julie's looks were cranked up a notch. She had blond highlights and wore her hair rakishly short and feathered to the back. Big diamonds hung in her ears and a larger diamond sparkled on her neck. She had a French manicure and wore a striking white designer pantsuit. She worked at Sandford-Gallagher, one of the top financial firms in the country and made millions. How she had complained when the backlash against bankers threatened her annual bonus. Growing up poor, having and flaunting money meant everything to her.

Now Julie was peering at the hospital. "Who the fuck were those guys? Why'd you let them in?"

"They asked me to hold the door."

"They could have gone around to the ER," Julie said. "There's no security here. With the cuts in the police force, crime is off the charts. There's no telling what they're up to."

"They were young," Jill said. "Not much older than Tyler."

"Well, how is he?" Julie asked, as she tapped the glass dividing the front and back seat. The butler was in the drivers' seat and the car shot forward.

Jill hurried to get on her seatbelt. "He's unconscious. The doctor hopes he'll wake up. There's nothing we can do but wait."

"Blaze said it was an accident. Tyler had too much to drink. By the way, he does drink."

That was another thing about her sister. Julie always had to be right. There was no compromise with her. Small wonder she never married, though she claimed it was by choice. "It was a hit and run," Jill said. "Tyler was being followed."

"Christ, he's not in trouble again, is he?"

"I don't know," Jill said. "Have you seen him recently?"

"We had a fight."

Which was not unusual, given Tyler's antibourgeois inclination, and Julie's tendency to live like she was blessed by the gods and beyond reproach. "What did you fight about?" Jill asked.

"I'll tell you upstairs."

They had reached Julie's building and the butler pulled up to the curb. She lived on White Street just off Broadway, and the butler had got them there in five minutes. He opened Julie's door and Jill got out on her own. He went to park the car.

"You got your hair cut," Julie said, as they crossed the sidewalk.

Jill raised a hand self-consciously. "Worst I ever had."

"It's horrific," Julie agreed. "Who could do such butchery? You'll have to see my stylist."

Jill let this go. Julie wanted Jill to see her cosmetic surgeon, her personal trainer, her dietician, her clothing designer, and now her hairdresser. It would never happen. A stench of garbage assailed her and Jill wrinkled her nose. "What's that smell? A sewage leak?"

"Garbage pick-up's late." Julie pointed down the street where rows of garbage bags and bins lined the sidewalk. "We only get pick-up once a week now. The city is cutting back. Saving money. It stinks."

They climbed the front steps to a glass building. A doorman in uniform opened the front door. The lobby was bright with crystal chandeliers and modern furniture artfully arranged. It smelled fresh, of floral baby powder. They went down a thickly carpeted hall to an elevator that rose swiftly up to the penthouse, then down another stretch of carpet to a steel door.

Julie hit the entrance code and they went in. If there was one thing worse than Jill's appalling haircut, it was her sister's apartment. It looked like a fishbowl. There was glass everywhere and nothing to look at; no nature in sight, no grass, no trees, unless you counted the astroturf and fake schefflera that filled a blind hallway. The penthouse was one-story, with floor to ceiling windows that were twenty feet high. The glass went on forever supported by thick steel beams. The lights of Broadway were visible from the dining room and ugly buildings spanned every direction. Even the ceiling was glass, which would have been good for star-gazing, except the city was so polluted the stars were hard to see.

If the architecture was awful, the furniture was worse. Julie liked modern furniture made out of steel and chrome with square straight lines and a minimum of color. The chairs and sofas were low and the coffee table looked as if it were laminate, though it cost more than ten thousand dollars. White pedestals of various heights and thicknesses were placed strategically throughout the rooms and held expensive sculpture and artwork of questionable taste.

They sat down in the living room on an uncomfortable beige sofa. Julie kicked off high pointy heels. "Drink?" She quickly corrected herself. "Sorry."

"What? I drink. I'll have orange juice."

"I couldn't imagine quitting. I'll never quit. I bet you go back."

"It's been over nine months."

"That long. Wow. I'm surprised you lasted a week. I'm going to have a martini. Work hard, play hard. That's my motto. You never had an excuse."

Jill said nothing, and Julie made no effort to go get the drinks. That was what a butler was for. Instead, she took out her phone and checked her messages. Jill looked out the window at a construction crane. How far they had come from Galveston, Texas, where they grew up. Their father, now dead, had worked on oil rigs out on the gulf. Their mother walked out when Jill was four and they had never seen her again. They were raised by babysitters, though Julie claimed the responsibility had fallen on her.

Of her childhood, Jill remembered Julie ordering her about, constantly telling her what to do, how to improve herself and 'be someone'. In Julie's mind, it was Jill's fault their mother had left.

In high school, Julie had been a star, the head cheerleader, the prom queen, the valedictorian. She got a full scholarship to Brown and made the dean's list every year. She graduated with an MBA and by the time she was twenty-three was working for the top investment bank in New York. In contrast, Jill received a partial scholarship from the University of Texas and worked in a book store to make up for the shortfall. Against Julie's advice that it was a 'stupid career', Jill majored in journalism. After graduation she landed a job at the *Austin Tribune* working at the political desk where she met Blaze, a Texas Congressman. He was already married.

There was a rap at the front door and Charles appeared with Jill's suitcase. "And in which room will madam be staying?" he asked, with obsequious politeness.

There were three guest rooms, each with their own bathroom and whirlpool tub. "The pink one," Julie said.

Charles nodded formally and Julie ordered the drinks. Soon, from the kitchen, Jill heard the tinkle of ice. Julie liked the open concept and the first thing she did when she bought the place was to tear down the walls so everything flowed. However, gone was privacy. Jill watched Charles shove strawberries into his mouth as he shook a stainless steel drink shaker.

Julie covered a big yawn. She'd had a busy day. She'd just come from the party on Park Avenue that had started at three. She ran through the list of people who attended and Jill didn't know any of them. Julie had slipped out after the fifth course, and Jill wasn't to feel guilty for dragging her away. Family came first.

"You were going to tell me about Tyler," Jill said, steering the conversation back to her son.

"Was I?" Julie looked longingly to the kitchen. "I was surprised when I called your house and got Blaze. Shouldn't he be in Texas campaigning?"

"He had to come back for the vote."

"You must have been happy about that."

A veiled reference to Blaze's ex-wife, still in Austin. She was a banker, a woman of means and power.

"You should campaign with him," Julie added. "Support him. She does."

Jill shook her head.

"You make it too easy for her."

Jill didn't say anything.

"I warned you she'd never let him go."

Jill stared out the window and said without conviction, "I trust him."

"I'll never know why."

Charles came in bearing a small tray with drinks. The martini came in an oversized triangular glass and the orange juice in a small shot glass. Julie took her drink and told Charles to go though it was evident he wanted to stay.

After he left, Jill turned the conversation back to her son. "You mentioned an argument. What was that about?"

"I said a fight. Don't be putting words into my mouth. As a journalist you should know better." Julie tilted her head back and took a healthy swallow. She cradled the glass in her fingers. "I had a computer problem and he came over and fixed it. To show my appreciation, I took him to Bok Choy. That's the sushi place on Warren, in case you're wondering. Usually you need to make a reservation two weeks in advance, but I know the owner, Chan, intimately."

Jill wasn't interested in any of these details. "How did he seem to you?"

"Horny, but what's past is past."

"I'm talking about Tyler."

"Oh. We ate dinner. He was starving."

Jill hated to think of her son hungry.

"He drank three cups of saké. For your information he was looped."

Jill did not begrudge her son a few drinks. "Is he working at the soup kitchen?"

"He didn't mention it." Julie was playing with the diamond on her necklace, sliding it back and forth along the chain. It was the size of an acorn and perfectly round.

"Is he seeing anybody?" Jill asked, with too much hope.

"Not that he said."

"Is he still running?"

"Not after the marathon. He's too busy."

"What's he doing?"

"He was planning a march outside the Federal Reserve to protest a non-existent meeting that was supposedly today. He's pissed that the Fed bailed out the banks and won't bail out Vermont and forty-two other states."

"And that's what you fought about," Jill said.

"Of course not. Obviously the Fed won't bail out the states. That's hardly its mandate." Julie took the last sip of her drink and stared longingly into her empty glass.

"Do you want a refill?" Jill asked.

Julie handed over her triangular glass.

Jill refilled the drinks and returned to the living room.

"If you want to know what he's up to, read his blog," Julie said. Her cheeks were flushed with two high spots of color.

He had a blog? That was news to Jill. "What's it about?"

"He wants to end the Fed. He doesn't believe in the value of trickle down wealth. He thinks the rich are immoral and don't deserve money for working hard. He thinks we should pay more tax, support every-one who doesn't want to work. He thinks economic science is wrong. Can you fucking believe that?" She paused to take a sip. "If you must know, that's what we fought about. I don't see his degree in economics hanging on the wall next to mine, yet he thinks he can tell me how to fix the economy."

"And that's it?" Jill said, thinking that a march was nothing to be run over for.

"That's enough." Julie threw back another healthy swallow and waxed on until midnight about how the rich were hated, unappreciated and misunderstood.

3

It's not a real choice, it's an apparent choice, like choosing a brand of detergent. Whether you buy Ivory Snow or Tide, they're both owned by Proctor and Gamble... Those in positions of real power, the bankers, the CEOs are not vulnerable to the vote, and in any case they fund both sides.

—Arundhati Roy, author

SUNDAY OCTOBER 19

The phone rang again before dawn, but Jill was not asleep and she answered before it could ring again. Blaze was calling.

"Tyler's awake."

Jill shot up in bed and snapped on the light.

"The doctors are checking him. He can answer questions, follow instructions. He looks good."

For the first time in twenty-four hours Jill was able to fully breathe, the weight on her heart instantly lifting. She smiled at nothing, staring at the sparse pink room, with its pink carpet, pink bedspread, pink cloth wall tiles, pink lounge chair and thankfully, pink curtains to shut out the world.

"Dr. Patel is waiting for you at the hospital."

"It's locked. I can't get in."

"He said to go through the ER. I love you."

"I love you too." Jill hung up and only then did it register that Blaze was the one who got called first and not her, despite the fervent assurances of the staff they would contact her the moment there was any change. She sighed. The bearer of power was always well known.

Jill called a taxi and dressed quickly. In the interest of time, she threw on the same clothes she had worn the day before. She brushed her horrible hair and tiptoed into the living room. The clouds had cleared and Venus was rising with Spica, the two shining brilliantly together in the predawn sky. She pushed the code on the alarm – 1212 – her mother's birthday – and stealthily lowered the handle and let herself out.

Downstairs, the exhaust from the waiting cab was thick and the air was cold. The cabbie was drinking coffee and it smelled good. The streets were clear and the world looked fine. Jill smiled as she gave directions. Her son was awake and doing well.

They reached the hospital quickly. She skipped across the sidewalk to the ER entrance and went up to ICU. The great square was subdued, the overhead lights dimmed in deference to the night. The nurses had their backs to her and paid her no mind. The patients' rooms were dark and she hurried down the hall to Tyler's.

She expected to find a team of doctors with him, but he was alone, sitting on the side of the bed, tapping at the keyboard of the hospital's computer, his face blue in the glow of the screen.

He looked up and smiled, pushing the computer table to one side. She swooped upon him and hugged him tightly until she heard him sigh, then let him go.

"Hey Mom."

He looked skinny and gaunt. At six-five, he weighed at most a hundred and fifty pounds. He had sandy blond hair that was softly curled and worn long. He had large dark blue eyes and shining skin. He was already dressed, wearing the too small blood-stained navy sweater. His feet were bare.

She took his hand and squeezed it tight. "I'm glad you're back."

He sunk down on the bed. "It was Hope. She was calling me. She said, 'Tyler wake up, it's time to wake up.'"

Jill sat down beside him as shivers climbed her spine and brought goosebumps to her skin. "I dreamed of her too." After she told him the dream, she asked how he felt.

"I've got a bad headache," Tyler said. "I broke my shoulder."

"Do you remember the accident?"

He shook his head slowly. "I remember leaving home. I don't know where I was going."

"You were hit on Gold Street. It's down in the financial district."

"I know where it is, Mom."

"Police think you stepped into the road without looking."

"No way. I always look three times."

"You had no wallet, no money, no ID. It took thirty-four hours for the police to figure out who you were." Just saying the words brought it all back, the helplessness, fear, worry. Such sloppy police work.

Tyler had other concerns. "My phone's gone."

"I've got it." She took it from her purse. "The police say it's broken." She handed it to him.

He tried to turn it on and nothing happened. "Maybe the battery is dead." He tucked it in his pocket.

"It was a hit and run," she said. "The car took off."

Tyler nodded, saying nothing.

"When you called last week, you thought you were being followed."

He narrowed his eyes and raised his finger to his mouth, chewing on a nail, a bad habit he'd had since he was young.

"Julie told me about your blog," Jill said, trying not to sound hurt or accusatory that he would tell his aunt and not her.

"Oh that." Tyler shrugged as if it were nothing. "I write under a fake name so I can't be traced."

"What's it about?"

"Just our economic decline and impending status as a Third World country, thanks to the Fed."

He could be extreme and she tried not to react. "Hmm. America as a Third World country."

"Look at it. A high level of poverty. Unfair distribution of wealth. High unemployment. A dysfunctional government and a ruling elite. Corrupt leaders. Election fraud. Bought elections. An idiotic and unfair justice system. The difference is only a matter of degree."

"We have freedom of speech," Jill said. "First amendment rights."

"In theory."

"What does the Federal Reserve have to do with it?"

"Only everything."

"Julie said you organized a march at the Fed yesterday to protest a secret meeting she said wasn't taking place."

Tyler's eyes opened wide, as did his mouth, but he had no opportunity to answer for they were interrupted by the intrusion of Dr. Patel and his team.

"You are arriving quickly Mrs. Madison," he said.

Jill stood up to shake his offered hand. "Thank you for calling me."

He ignored this, got out the penlight and shone the light in Tyler's eyes. "As you may plainly see, he is doing well. We would like to keep him for observation, but he is refusing."

"I'm fine," Tyler said.

"He can't remember the accident," Jill said.

"That is typical. It is quite common after a brain injury to have no memory of things at the time of the accident. It may come back to him. Perhaps again, not."

"He has a headache."

"Also quite normal. That is to be expected. There may be some confusion, some disconnect in the thought process. But do not worry, it will not last. I have requested a physical therapist in regards to his clavicle. He may begin therapy this afternoon."

"I'm leaving," Tyler said. "I don't need physical therapy." He tried to rotate his shoulder and winced.

Dr. Patel faced Jill. "We cannot keep him against his will. But he will have to sign forms to absolve us of all responsibility."

Jill wanted to insist he stay, but her son, who was of age, had other ideas. "Bring the forms."

The team left and Jill stood up, ready to argue, determined to do anything and everything it took to keep Tyler away from his boarding house and from danger.

He knew it was coming and preempted the first strike. "I'm fine, Mom, really. I've got to go home."

"Come to Julie's."

"I'd rather shoot myself."

"Come on Tyler, she's your only aunt. She means well."

He rolled his eyes and didn't answer.

"I'll make breakfast. Julie was up late. She'll sleep in, then go to church. You could have a hot shower. I brought my charger and you can try to charge your phone. I haven't seen you in months." Then she dealt a low blow. "Consider it a late birthday gift."

Tyler lowered his head and sighed, his shoulders slumped in acquiescence.

She had won the first round. Now, the challenge would be to keep him at Julie's or convince him to come home to D.C.

***

He left the hospital barefoot, in a wheelchair, with Jill carrying his one Nike shoe. He had signed the papers, initialed each problem that could possibly arise and for which he forgave the hospital of all responsibility: dizziness, memory loss, hemorrhage, stroke, mental incapacity, myocardial infarction and death. None of these were grave enough to make him reconsider his move. He was adamant. He'd been in the hospital too long.

The doorman in Julie's building recognized him and commiserated about his accident. While he and Tyler made jokes, Jill scrutinized her son. He was tall and gangly and his jeans were falling off. They were too short and exposed his bony ankles and long white feet. The navy sweater was too small and the splashes of blood shone in the bright artificial light. If the doorman wondered about his lack of shoes, he did not ask.

They went upstairs and let themselves into Julie's apartment. Tyler went to the window and gazed out. "Venus is brighter than Spica," he said. "She's at perigee, about to turn retrograde."

Jill stood by his side gazing out. Blaze had passed on to his children his love of the sky. Hope had been the most enamored and from the time she was a toddler would go out with him on sweltering, buggy summer nights and brutally cold dark winter evenings to see the planets and the stars. She loved the myths that went with the constellations, especially the native Indian myth that each star was a soul, placed in the sky for everlasting life. "That's where I'll go when I die," she had said. "You can always look up there and see me." Jill forbade her to talk like that and promised her she wouldn't die.

Tyler turned from the window. He wanted to charge his phone and she got her charger. In the kitchen, she surveyed the fridge to see what Julie had in the way of breakfast. Tyler was a vegetarian and she passed over the bacon and sausage in favor of eggs, croissants, bagels, smoked havarti cheese, melon, green grapes and mushrooms. As she sliced onions, he sat at the kitchen aisle on a stool slapping his phone. He had plugged it in, but it was not responding; it wouldn't turn on.

He got a paring knife and pried open the back. "Jesus Christ," he said.

Jill turned away from the stove. "What is it?"

"The SIM card's gone. No wonder it won't work." He showed Jill the empty space with the connectors where the card would go. "Someone took it."

"And put your phone back together?" Jill didn't buy that. "The phone could have fallen apart when you were hit and it came out and the police didn't notice."

"A SIM card just doesn't fall out." He looked troubled. "The phone had to be working after the accident. How else would the police know who I was?"

Jill considered this in silence as she stirred onions sizzling in olive oil. There were noises in the hall and Julie stumbled into the kitchen, rubbing her eyes.

"Tyler, is that you?" She blinked under the bright lights.

And there would be no omelet making or trying to figure out how to use the elaborate cappuccino machine. Jill wasn't allowed in the kitchen for this was Charles' domain and he'd be pissed at the intrusion. Jill and Tyler were ordered out.

Julie called Charles, who lived in a bachelor apartment that she rented for him on the first floor near the air conditioners. He appeared five minutes later, looking sullen and half-asleep and pissed nonetheless. He started breakfast with a big Bloody Mary for Julie.

She downed it quickly, then said she'd be sick if she had to stare at Tyler in his bloody clothes for one more minute. She had clothes she thought might fit him and they filed into her bedroom. Hers was white, with a white carpet, white cloth wall tiles, and white curtains. Mother and son stood by the closet while Julie went through hangers and pulled out clothes: oxford shirts, dinner jackets, pressed jeans.

"Where did you get them?" Jill asked.

"Where do you think?"

"From men who left naked?" Jill offered.

"Something like that," Julie said, with a wink at Tyler. She selected a white sweater, black dress pants, and a navy blazer, and sent him to the bathroom to shower. He went without protest. Julie always got what she wanted.

She found him a pair of black loafers and closed the closet door. "Guys leave clothes thinking they'll be back," she said, answering Jill's earlier question.

Soon the shower in the guest bathroom was running and the sisters went to the dining room. Charles had set the table with brightly colored china and crystal glasses. Though it faced north, the room was light, for three of the walls were glass. There was a pedestal by the south window that displayed an original and expensive black and white Dali sketch on which his famous painting *The Persistence of Memory* was based. Like the objects in the sketch, the print seemed out of place in the glass room. Jill would have put up a Renoir, a painting of nature, something to bring warmth and life to the space.

"Tyler looks pale," Julie said, as Charles came with two cups of cappuccino and a refill of the Bloody Mary. "I'm surprised they let him out."

"They didn't," Jill said. "He insisted."

"You should have made him stay."

"He's twenty-four. What could I do?"

Julie lifted her waxed arched eyebrows and made a face at Jill's seeming impotence. Julie, no doubt, would have the power to make him stay.

"Is it all right if we crash here for a couple of days?" Jill asked. "I want to keep my eye on him, until he recovers." What she meant was, she wanted to keep him out of sight and protected until the FBI found out who ran him over.

"That's fine, but I'm not going to baby-sit him."

Jill had finished her coffee by the time Tyler emerged from the shower. The clothes fit well, though the pants were a little short, as were the sleeves of the sweater. He wore the black loafers without socks. Still, the sisters agreed he looked good. He wanted to borrow Jill's smart phone and she got it for him and he went online.

Soon breakfast was ready and Charles brought the food to the dining room. He apparently followed his own menu and had fried sausage and bacon. At least he didn't put any meat in the omelet and there was lots of fruit, though Tyler only picked at the food. Two and a half days without eating hadn't given him an appetite.

"I know what I was doing downtown Thursday night," he said, as he pushed a grape around his plate.

Jill and Julie looked at each other and waited.

"We had fliers made up for the march to protest the Fed. I went down to the copy shop on Gold Street Thursday night to pick them up. There were two thousand. I got a carton. I don't know what happened to it."

Julie stabbed a sausage link with her knife. "I told you before and I'll tell you now, there was no meeting."

"That you know about."

"No meeting, period. End of story."

"See what the papers say," Jill said, trying to make peace.

After breakfast, while Charles cleared the table, they moved to the living room and Julie opened the big Sunday paper and went through it page by page, while Jill looked over her shoulder. There was nothing in the paper about any meeting.

Not trusting the newspaper, Tyler borrowed one of Julie's laptops and searched online. After a half an hour, with a look of grave defeat, he had to admit he couldn't find any mention of it. "I bet there was a news blackout. The meeting happened and no one could report it. The big corporations own the network stations and the major papers. They support the Fed and the Fed supports them and everything's hushed up. I bet all the online articles were taken down."

"That's the stupidest thing I've ever heard," Julie said.

Jill, the former journalist, rushed to her son's aid. If this debate continued, Tyler wasn't going to want to stay an hour, let alone a few days. "He's right about the mainstream news. The owners of the stations and papers control the content. Free speech doesn't extend to the news. The paper prints what the owners want printed."

"No one can criticize the Fed," Tyler said.

"Bull shit," Julie said. "People criticize the Fed all the time. They have no idea of the good it does, how it stabilizes the economy. A little protest from you, Tyler, isn't going to worry them." She turned on the TV and turned up the volume to end further conversation.

The Sunday morning talk shows were in full swing. With Congress hard at work on the Hill, the President and his opponent monopolized the air waves. The President looked charming, pleasant and presidential in his dark navy suit and royal blue tie. On the large screen in high def, his hair looked precisely cut and peppered with appropriate gray. His eyelashes were long and black, as if painted with mascara. Concealer under his eyes brightened the dark circles. He stared into the camera with conviction and vowed to fight for Vermont and provide any economic assistance it needed. By law, states were prohibited from declaring bankruptcy and for good reason. America's word meant something.

He got no hard questions and was allowed to move on gracefully to his platform of clean energy. He gleefully quoted statistics enumerating how many people would get jobs once the new sector got going. He was promising all over again to end the wars and to implement tax reform to help the middle class. He promised not to cut Social Security or Medicare, and, though it might be controversial, promised to revisit universal health care and this time give it teeth. He was against cutting union bargaining rights and had the backing of most unions.

On another network station, Rich Tumblin had his say. He was in his sixties and completely bald. Short and stout, he wore a well-fitting and obviously expensive midnight black suit with a crimson red tie. An American Flag was pinned to his lapel. Tumblin maintained that Vermont had to work out its own problems. They were talking about selling a parking lot and a toll road to pay their debt, and at least they were taking action on their own and not waiting for the government to step in and be their answer.

He suggested they go to the banks with an IOU like California did before them. The banks weren't hateful. Tumblin was sure they would help out. But the government had to stay out of it. Government had to be smaller, cost less, interfere less. As president, he would stimulate the private sector and help all business, big and small. He would lower corporate taxes and reduce government regulations, make the country business-friendly again. That was the way to create jobs. When elected, he would run the country like a business and make it prosperous once more.

Rich was lucky he wasn't a career politician. He had no voting record, no trail of broken campaign promises like his competitor. What he did have was a successful hedge fund, and this was a problem. He earned an annual salary in excess of one billion dollars, which made him one of the richest men in America. While the poor and middle class were awed by his success, they were certain he didn't understand them or their problems. The rich of course loved him.

According to recent polls by Gallup and ABC, the current crisis was hurting the President. He had lost his lead and now had a forty-six percent approval rating, compared to Rich Tumblin's forty-eight percent. Given a margin of error of six percent, nine days before the election the winner was too close to call.

A commercial came on, a political ad, and Julie muted the sound. "Rich is going to be our next president," she declared with confidence.

Tyler looked up from the laptop. "No he's not. Dennis Drake is going to win."

Julie sighed with exasperation. "Drake the Flake? Who wants to give everyone ten thousand dollars? You must be as high as he is. No one will vote for that dope smoking communist."

"He grew marijuana, he doesn't smoke it."

Julie just laughed.

"He's not mentioned in any of the polls," Jill said.

"Only because the mainstream news won't include him. The network and cable news won't cover him, so he's not on TV. They wouldn't let him participate in the debates. He's flying under the radar, which is what he wants. He's taken no corporation money, so he's beholden to no one. Once he starts running his commercials, he'll get name recognition and by then it will be too late for anyone to stop him. He's been campaigning on the internet for two years. He's got sixty million in small donations and he'll run a blitz of TV ads starting next week. His name's on the ballot in all fifty states. He's got a Hispanic running mate named Maria Rodriquez, which is great for the Hispanic vote and women's vote. He's married, has a two year old daughter and his wife is pregnant. He's unbeatable."

"In your dreams," Julie said.

Tyler ignored her. "He's on YouTube every day. Here, watch this."

Tyler hooked Julie's laptop to the TV and played a video of Dennis Drake at a recent campaign stop. Jill had heard the name, but had never seen the man before. He looked young, in his mid-thirties, though he would have to be over thirty-five to be president. His hair was blond, the color of wheat, and it was neither receding nor going gray. He looked tall, athletic, healthy, with good bones and nice teeth. He wore blue jeans and a t-shirt dressed up with a navy vest. He could have passed himself off as an actor, a Kevin Costner type, building his field of dreams.

Drake saw a third option for Vermont. Why didn't anyone mention the Oasis Nuclear Power Plant was privately owned? Why was the government bailing out a private company? He wanted to know who owned it. According to his inquiries, a Texas company sold it for a song soon after a radiation leak was discovered a year ago. The new company, called Green Energy Corp, was registered offshore and the identity of the owner was unknown. Who was this CEO who felt the country should rush to fix his broken property? If the businessman could afford to buy a nuclear power plant, why couldn't he fix it with his own money? In Drake's mind, this was typical of the current system. There was no help for the states, but the government couldn't bail out big business fast enough.

The video ended. With the push of a button, it could be played again.

"He's a communist kook," Julie said, grabbing the remote and turning off the TV. "He'd ruin the country. People love to hate the rich. They have no idea of the good we do."

"Do tell," Tyler said.

"The economy works because of us," Julie said piously.

"Ah, the trickle-down theory backed by no empirical data and a reality that shows the exact opposite. The trickle up theory. Only it's a flood. How else do you explain how one percent of the population ended up with fifty percent of the country's wealth?"

"One percent is willing to work hard," Julie said.

"Or, maybe one percent got enough money and bought the government which made it legal for the rich to steal from the poor."

"Okay," Jill said. "Anyone want coffee? Is Charles still here?" She peered into the kitchen and didn't see him, though she hadn't seen him leave.

"It's not my fault if the poor are lazy and don't want to work," Julie said, as if Jill hadn't spoken. "They get to watch TV all day and have welfare babies who I have to support."

"Maybe they want to work and can't find a job. You shipped the jobs overseas so you would make more profit. All they want is a fair chance."

"What's stopping them? It's not like God hates the poor. God helps those who help themselves."

"What does God have to do with it? It's our government which keeps the poor disadvantaged."

"Maybe they're meant to be poor," Julie said. "Which is why it's a sin to help them. It goes against God's will."

There was a vein in Tyler's forehead that ran from his left eyebrow up to his hairline that popped out when he got mad. The vein was raised now, and pulsing. "Read the bible," he thundered, and Jill wondered if he ever read it in his life. Her family was not religious, they had not pushed God on the children. "Jesus hated the money changers. He was against usury. You changed the definition to make it acceptable. God threw your kind out of the temple."

Julie stood up. "That's bull shit. I'm not listening to you any more. I'm going to get ready for church." She grabbed her Bloody Mary and stomped down the hall.

Jill and Tyler watched her go. Her door slammed and they exchanged glances. Jill shot her son a look of apology. "Feel like going to a movie?"

"That's all you have to say?"

"She thinks what she thinks. You're not going to change her mind."

"I, at least try."

Jill shook her head. She grew up with Julie and she knew futility when she saw it.

"I'm going home," Tyler said.

"Julie said you could stay. I'll stay too. We could go shopping. Your jeans look worn out."

"I said I'm going home."

***

An hour later they were in a cab heading north to the slums of the South Bronx. It was a gray day, the clouds were thick and the trees looked like they were dying. Jill had a ticket home on a 4:00 P.M. flight, for which she had paid full price and could cancel at the last minute if she managed to change Tyler's mind. If he didn't want to stay at Julie's, they could stay in a hotel, at least until the FBI concluded their investigation. Tyler was refusing to consider it. He had no faith in the corrupt FBI. He was sure they wouldn't find anything.

He was in a bad mood, which the doctor said they could expect after the injury. He was still seething at Julie, only now it had spilled over to Jill.

"You should stand up to her," he declared, as they sped past Central Park. "When you say nothing, she takes it as support for her ridiculous ideas she claims as economic truth."

"She does have an MBA," Jill said, aiming for delicacy.

"The economists make crap up. Low taxes create jobs. Oh really? Where is the evidence of that? When we had the highest tax rates, we had the most jobs. They swear the Fed stabilizes the economy when it obviously causes busts and booms. It stabilizes nothing. Then they say cutting spending will cut the debt. *Wrong*."

"It's an inexact science," Jill said gently.

"No, it's false science," Tyler said, as the vein on his forehead popped. "There's nothing scientific about it. Big business donates money to a university and gets to choose the curriculum and who to hire and pretty soon what big business wants taught as truth is what's being taught."

"There's academic freedom," Jill said. "I'm pretty sure people who make donations don't get to influence university policy."

"Is that right?" Tyler said. "Those two filthy rich pro-business brothers have given thirty million to George Mason University. They fund an economic center that promotes a government with less red tape and less corporate taxes. That's where George Bush went when he wanted to reduce government regulation. He made it sound like the ideas came from a smart, free thinking university, when it came from big business. The financial bill was even a bigger joke. The lobbyists wrote the legislation because our elected officials couldn't understand Wall Street investments."

Jill sank into the seat, determined to say nothing more. She didn't want to fight with him, not now, not when she was dropping him at his boarding house and flying home and didn't know when she would see him again.

Inching through Harlem, Jill registered Tyler's alert vigilance. He'd turn his head around every few minutes staring out the back window, then glance furtively out the side windows, first one and then the other. He strained his neck to peer through the rearview mirror.

"Do you think we're being followed?" Jill finally asked.

"I don't see anyone."

"Did you see who was following you before?"

Tyler turned and faced her. "I did. I took a picture of him. It was on my phone."

"Did you back it up?"

"If I did, I can't find it," Tyler said sadly. "It would be on the SIM card, which is gone."

Jill turned around and stared out the back window. They were driving through the bad side of town. She saw the odd person, African American or Latino, wearing ragged clothes and heading nowhere quickly in the cold. Jill remembered the man in the hospital waiting at the elevator. "Was he a blond man with a scar?"

Tyler shook his head. "He wasn't blond. He didn't have a scar. I think I knew him."

That came as a surprise. "Who was he?"

Tyler gave half a shrug, lifting his good shoulder. "I can't remember."

"Maybe it will come back to you."

"Or maybe I'll see him again." Tyler turned once more and peered out the window.

North of Harlem the housing got worse. The buildings were smaller, older, dirtier, more run down. Garbage blew in the streets. Every other house was for rent or for sale. In the yards of abandoned homes, the grass was long and fallen leaves were thick. Windows were either broken or boarded up. Even so, lawns were filled with campaign signs. The President was a clear favorite on this side of town.

The cabbie turned down Maple Street, stopped in front of a three-story brick home and Jill saw for the first time where her son was living. Only begrudgingly had he agreed to show her his room. He said she wouldn't like it, he'd rather she not see it, and though he was probably right, she still wanted to know where he lived so when she pictured him in her mind she knew the background in the frame.

Tyler got out of the cab and asked the driver to wait. Apparently arranging a pick-up in this neighborhood was unreliable, if not impossible. It also gave a reason to cut her visit short.

Leaving the meter running, they crossed a broken walkway, went up a cracked stoop and entered a crumbling house. The wooden floor in the vestibule had rotting boards, and there were more on the narrow staircase that creaked as they climbed. Paint was yellowing and peeling on the water-stained walls. A light bulb hanging by a string from the ceiling swung in a draft.

They reached the third floor and went down a narrow hallway. Tyler stopped in front of a wooden door and patted his pockets. He had no keys, but apparently they weren't necessary. The door was unlocked and Tyler turned the doorknob and went in.

There was a man sitting before a laptop at a small table on the opposite side of the room and Jill was taken aback. She didn't know Tyler shared this small room. The man looked older than Tyler, in his early thirties. He had straight black hair and dark eyes and looked either Arab or Latino. He stood up and said something to Tyler. Ali was slight and short and bowed in greeting. Jill bowed back.

"Hello, nice to meet you," he said, in a thick accent and formal English.

"Ali lives next door," Tyler explained. "He came over to borrow my computer."

A gray and white striped kitten sprang out from nowhere and leapt at Tyler and he caught it in his arms. This was Kitty, a four-month old cat who belonged to another friend who went unnamed.

Jill stayed in the doorway as Tyler spoke to Ali in a hushed voice. Though she couldn't hear what they said, she could guess its content: That's my mom, don't say anything.

She glanced around the room. A pulled shade covered the only window and the room was dark and cold. It was square, big enough for a double bed, a bureau, and a rectangular table for three. The bathroom was down the hall. The bed was unmade and dirty clothes were strewn across the floor. The room smelled of sweat. She thought of her son's bright, sunny bedroom in D.C. and hated his choice of residence when he could live at home. He could go to university and Blaze would happily pay for it. Yet, here he lived, refusing any money that would make his life easier.

She knew his reasons. Washington and his parents and his up-bringing represented everything he stood against. He lived like the poor to be one of them; to know how it felt to be hungry, to worry about the next dollar, about police harassment and what if felt like to be disenfranchised and forsaken. It reminded him of what he was fighting for.

Tyler offered her a chair and she sat down at the small table. Still standing, Ali was hunched over and looking uncomfortable. Tyler was looking for his wallet. Jill smiled at Ali. This was the first friend of Tyler's that she'd met in a long time. "Where are you from?" she asked.

"Cairo."

"Oh." Jill remembered the Zimbabwe refugees and the trouble they caused and wondered if Tyler had picked up another refugee. She looked around the room. The silence was so loud she heard her watch ticking. Tyler was on his hands and knees looking under the bed.

"Maybe your wallet was lost at the accident," Jill said, as the cat jumped in her lap and began kneading her stomach. She rubbed Kitty's head and the cat let out a long, rolling guttural purr.

"Accident?" Ali said, in a thick accent.

"I was hit by a car," Tyler said.

"He was in the hospital for two days," Jill said.

Ali's brown eyes opened wide. He said something and Jill heard the words: Layla, text, call. Her ears perked up. Layla was the name of the girl he had been seeing in the spring. Blaze's P.I. said she didn't last, but maybe they were back together. "Who's Layla?" Jill asked.

"No one," Tyler said sharply. His face turned bright red and he looked away. He stood up, shoved his hands in his pockets and faced Ali. "I didn't get any of your messages. My phone broke. The SIM card's gone."

Ali looked surprised. He said something else and Jill picked up the words: computer and confiscate.

In a run-on sentence that didn't sound like English he explained what happened. Jill heard: coffee, Patriot Act, arrest, and New Jersey. Then he and Tyler were walking to the door. Tyler said they'd be right back.

They stepped into the hallway and closed the door. Jill wondered what they weren't willing to say in front of her. Who was Ali? Had he been arrested? What had he done? Police didn't pick up people for no reason.

The door opened and they were back, Tyler biting a nail. "Mom, if it's okay with you, I'll come home for a few days."

Jill didn't ask him what made him change his mind. That would come later. Right now the important thing was that he would be safe. She had won round two. Now, the challenge would be to keep the peace at home and keep him there while the FBI found out who ran him over.

4

The surest way to ruin a promising career in economics, whether professional or academic, is to venture into the 'cranks and crackpots' world of suggestions for reform of the financial system.
—Michael Rowbotham, Economist

Tyler packed and Jill booked him a seat on her flight. He shoved clothes in a plastic grocery bag, grabbed his laptop and passport, and was ready to go. Ali was heading to Jersey to visit his sister and taking the cat. He would leave as soon as he got his laptop, which was at the police station for reasons left unsaid. Leaving him to lock up, Jill and Tyler returned to the cab and headed for the airport.

La Guardia was packed. There were long lines of weary looking travelers going nowhere fast. Police and their dogs were everywhere, and Tyler kept looking over his shoulder. Jill printed the boarding passes and they moved to the security line with ninety minutes to spare before their flight.

Tyler was taken for extra screening. It was no surprise to either of them, but Jill didn't like it all the same. Tyler was honest, ethical and moral, but because he had no job and carried his clothes in a plastic bag and wore loafers without socks and slacks that were too short, he was selected by security for additional scrutiny. She watched as they booted up his laptop and searched his measly grocery bag. They took him for a whole body x-ray and he went without complaint.

Soon they were in the business lounge, sitting at a small round table, eating smoked almonds, sipping ginger ale and watching football. Tyler was peeved they were flying first class, but they had no choice for the flight was full. They passed an easy hour watching the Giants, which reminded Jill of when he was small and they had season tickets to the Redskins and the family went to the games on Sunday afternoon. Hope had been going since she was an infant and after the dog, loved football the most. Now Jill couldn't watch a game without thinking about her, and hadn't gone to a game since she died, even though they still had season tickets.

The first half ended as the flight was called. They got to board first and had oversized comfortable leather seats up front in the safest part of the plane. Jill had the window seat and Tyler the aisle. They were offered pre-flight drinks and both took orange juice. While the rest of the passengers boarded, Jill flipped through the *Washington Post* and Tyler borrowed her cell phone, attacking it with his thumbs.

Before long, the sweet voice of a flight attendant came on the loudspeaker and reminded everyone to fasten their seatbelts; they were leaving the terminal and would take off immediately. Electronics had to be off and all carry-on luggage safely stowed.

Tyler closed her phone and returned it as the engines began to roar. Soon they were in the sky, flying low through wispy clouds. Tyler turned to her. "What do you think about the Fed?"

She shrugged. "I really don't know much about it."

"What is it?"

"A government agency that sets economic policy."

"Wrong," Tyler cried. "It's a central bank. A *for-profit* bank. It's not a part of the government. It gave itself the name federal so people would think that it was, and we'd assume it was on our side, when in fact it's against us. It's nothing but a commercial bank with stockholders and a mandate to make money."

Jill raised her hands in concession. She could see his passion for the subject and didn't want to upset him. "As I said, I don't know much about it. I assumed it was a part of the government, but apolitical and autonomous in order to prevent politics from influencing monetary policy."

"Ha," Tyler spat. "It set itself up that way to protect itself from the popular vote. The people get no say." He was excited. There was high color on his cheeks and his voice was loud, but muted by the drone of the engines. He leaned closer and continued. "It has more power than our elected officials. It controls the economy for its own purpose and profit. Tell me, how do banks make money?"

That was easy. "People make deposits and the bank uses the deposits to make loans. They charge more interest on the loans than they give for deposits and that's their profit."

"Wrong!" Tyler declared for the second time. "Well, you're a little right, but mostly wrong. Ever hear of the fractional reserve?"

"No."

"Of course not. Few have. It's the way banks get to print free money. When you take out a loan, you owe the bank the money, so that loan becomes a bank asset. Normally, when you lend someone money, you end up with less, but when the bank loans money, it ends up with more. Nice, huh?

"Only it's more insidious. The banks get to lend out a multiple of the amount that anyone borrows. Where do they get this money to lend? They create it. The money isn't in their vault, they don't shift it around, and they don't get it from another depositor or another bank. They make it. The money doesn't exist until someone borrows it."

Jill strove to maintain a stony expression. "Really. That's incredible."

"What's even more incredible is that it would be as easy for the government to print dollars, as it is to print the IOUs they use to borrow dollars, on which they have to pay interest."

"I didn't know the government printed IOUs."

"IOUs, bonds, bills, and notes, they're all the same thing. My point is, instead of printing the money itself, the government goes into debt getting the private, for-profit central bank, to print money for it."

"That doesn't seem right."

"You don't believe me, but it's true. If you want to know what I'm doing, I'm letting people know how our money system works. It's the point of my blog, my Facebook page, my tweets, and what the march was about. The Fed loans us fake money at high interest and it's bankrupting us. It's like the IMF that loans money to Third World countries at high interest to bankrupt them. Our country is deliberately being saddled with debt so it can be controlled. We're becoming a Third World country and we don't know it. The Fed caused this economic mess and things will only get worse until we shut it down."

Tyler was so mad his face was red and the vein in his forehead was pulsing. Jill was taken aback by his rancor and privately thought that blaming the Fed for the entire economic crisis was extreme. Given all the news she watched and read, she had never read or seen one indication that the Fed was in any way implicated. And, she was quite certain Tyler didn't understand how banks worked. She wondered if he got his information from some questionable conspiracy website.

"Do you want to read my flyer?" Tyler asked.

"I thought you lost them."

"I have my edited copy." Ignoring the seatbelt sign, he jumped up, opened the overhead bin, removed his plastic bag and pulled a folded piece of paper out of the pocket of a pair of jeans. He sat down and handed it to her.

She looked down at the page. It was filled with editing scribbles. She read:

FED UP

In 1910, seven men secretly conspired to establish control of the world's money supply and made plans for a central bank. While they wished to appear anything but a bank, their goal was to protect banks and policies that would enable them to concentrate wealth. They bought the 1912 election which sent their man to the Oval Office. The next year, two days before Christmas, when most officials were home for the holidays, the Federal Reserve Act was signed into law.

The Act gave the Federal Reserve control of the U.S. money supply. Now, instead of the government printing money, the Fed would print money, and lend it to the government for interest.

The Fed does not work for this money, the Fed does not earn it, the Fed merely makes it, and for this it receives interest, which the taxpayer must pay. After the creation of the Federal Reserve, Federal Income Tax became necessary to repay the interest on printed money.

The Federal Reserve also gave banks the power to print money. We have a system where money is created through debt. This system is the fractional reserve. According to the New York Fed website, if the reserve is ten percent and you go to the bank and deposit one hundred dollars, the bank must keep ten dollars. Say the bank lends the other ninety dollars to Ann. When Ann deposits the money, the bank receiving the ninety dollars can lend eighty-one dollars to Mary. At this point, you have a hundred dollars in your bank, Ann has ninety dollars in hers, and Mary has eighty-one dollars. As the process continues, the initial one hundred dollar deposit magically becomes one thousand ($100+$90+$81+72.90+...= $1,000)."

This is how banks create money from nothing. This is the source of inflation. Things don't cost more. The dollar is worth less.

Over the century, the Fed has only gained in power. To see how effective it is, one only has to observe what has happened since its inception. Money has been transferred from the poor and middle class to the rich.

Everything about the Fed is the opposite of what people think. It is not a government agency. It does not stabilize the economy. It does not care one bit about the well-being of the American people. It is a private bank, run by bankers, for bankers, in the interest of bankers. Very few realize this. Probably not even you.

Anyone who speaks out against it has been eliminated. Three presidents who stood against a central bank were shot. Andrew Jackson, Abe Lincoln, and JFK, all wanted to put an end to usury, the printing of money with interest, which, according to the Bible is a sin.

In short, the Fed is responsible for the:

- US national debt

- High inflation and loss of the value of the dollar

- Bank bailouts and stock market rallies

- Economic booms and busts

- American and world poverty.

The Fed is in violation of the Constitution. Our lawgivers gave their power away and then enacted laws to enforce their own impotency. Propped up and protected by the Fed, the big investment banks buy elected officials who pass laws that favor the Fed. When you look around and wonder how the country got so poor, look to the Fed. The money you used to have went somewhere. It went to the banks, thanks to the biggest bank of them all, the Federal Reserve.

To learn more, go to our blog at: www.@bncrupt.com or visit Ben Crupt on Facebook.

She reached the bottom and turned the page. Written on the back was:

According to the Declaration of Independence ... All people are created equal and are endowed with certain unalienable rights: Life, Liberty and the pursuit of Happiness. That to secure these rights, governments are instituted and derive power from the consent of the governed. But, when any form of government becomes destructive of these principles, it is the right of the people to alter or abolish it, and institute new government. Our present history is a history of repeated injuries and usur- pations, with a direct purpose of establishing absolute tyranny. It is the people's right, their duty to overthrow such govern- ment and to provide new guards for their future security...

She put the paper in her lap. He was looking at her carefully. "What do you think?" he asked.

She thought that this couldn't be right; banks couldn't just multi- ply deposits through subsequent loans, even if he did reference the New York Federal Reserve as his source. The idea was too absurd, fanciful, unbelievable; that was just making money out of nothing. It had to be wrong, yet he believed it and was calling for a revolt because of it.

The stewardess came with water and that bought her time. They each took a bottle.

"Well?" Tyler said, as he uncapped the top.

"It's well written," Jill said, carefully.

"You really think so? I could have written a hundred pages, but I wanted to keep it short," he said, his voice high with excitement. "To pique people's interest and outrage."

"I'd say you did that." She handed him back the flyer. "But ..." She wasn't sure how to proceed. He would certainly take offense if she questioned his facts. Finally she said, "I think the government referred to in the Declaration of Independence was the British government."

"You could say the same about our government today."

She tried a different tack. "Doesn't the treasury print the money?"

"Oh, they print it all right. At the Fed's request. Do you have a dol- lar?"

She got one from her purse. He pointed to the top of the bill and she saw words she had never noticed before: FEDERAL RESERVE NOTE.

"See, it's not the government's money. By magic and law it's the Fed's. But the Fed doesn't work for it. It just prints it and by law it becomes real. Then the Fed lends it to the government and charges us interest on it."

Jill lowered her eye glasses. "That can't be right."

"Well it is. Right now we owe the Fed one trillion dollars in capital, which costs us thirty billion a year in interest. We're paying off the interest but not the capital. Think about what we could do if we didn't have to pay interest. If the government printed its own money and owned its own debt."

"This can't be how it works," Jill said, unable to keep the skepticism from her voice.

"It's exactly how it works. You didn't know, did you? Because the government and the Fed don't want anyone to know. The mainstream news won't report it because the banks own the major newspapers and network news station. Universities teach what the bankers and big business pay to have taught. That the Fed and our banking system is the best thing in the world. That printing money stimulates the economy. It helps growth. The Fed is always taken as a given. This is what it is and how it works, and how great it is. Blah, blah, blah."

Jill found the notion that students would accept this hard to believe. "Why would the government go along with it? Especially when we're in such dire financial straits?"

"Because the Fed prints money for the government and the people don't have to know about it. If the government wants one billion to build a bridge, it goes to the Fed with an IOU for one billion. Call it a government bond. The Fed takes the bond and prints one billion and gives it to the government as a loan that has to be repaid with interest. The interest is the price we pay for not being told about it. That's why Congress won't end it. It's their secret source of funding."

"I can't believe it."

"The sad thing is, the government could print the money itself and owe no capital and no interest."

"Why doesn't it do that?"

"Yes. Why? That's a very good question."

"Does your father know?"

"He doesn't want to know. Congress couldn't end it if it wanted to. The Fed is too powerful. It's got money – it just prints it – and it doesn't answer to anyone. It doesn't have to worry about elections. Whoever's got the gold makes the rules. No one can speak out about it. Don't fight the Fed. Ever hear that? And why not? It fights back. One way or another it will shut you up."

Jill looked at her son. "You think the Fed went after you?"

He nodded emphatically. "It knew about my blog. It knew about the protest and shut it down. It had me run over. It stopped me, but not for long."

Jill sighed silently and turned to the window. They must have been losing altitude for they were flying through clouds and she could see nothing but gray skies as the plane hurtled onwards.

***

The plane landed at five and they were home by five-thirty. They lived in northwest D.C. across from Rock Creek Park, two miles north of Capitol Hill. They had an acre yard, fully fenced, and a small double-story house. Made of white sandstone bricks, it had a pitched roof with white shake shingles and second-floor dormers. It had been built in 1912, and the yard was dotted with mature towering trees: oaks, maples, poplar and fir. In the summer, azaleas of all colors bloomed, but they were going dormant now.

Tyler punched in the entry code to the gate and it slid silently to one side. The yard was completely fenced and had been for ten years, ever since Blaze received death threats after his unpopular vote in favor of women's reproductive rights. The gate closed automatically and the front door opened and Margo roared out, followed by Blaze, still in his suit, but minus a tie. Margo bounded down the drive and headed straight for Tyler. He bent down on one knee, dropped his plastic bag and laptop, and threw his arms around her.

Jill kissed Blaze hello. Despite the cold air, his skin was warm and his cheeks were ruddy. Tyler stood up, towering over his father. Blaze was over six feet tall when they met, but he'd lost almost an inch over the years. Blaze extended his arm and shook his son's hand heartily.

They went inside, father and son, side by side. They were too much alike; which was the reason they had trouble getting along. They both wanted to make the world a better place, yet had different ideas about how it should be done. Jill thought that if she could keep them away from politics, they would get along fine.

A fire blazed in the hearth and the living room was warm and bright in the long slanting sunlight. Tyler stopped at the staircase. "I'm going to get changed."

"Mars is at perigee conjunct Algol," Blaze said. "They'll rise as the moon sets. Should be quite a sight."

"Sweet," Tyler said, "the most malevolent star rising with the malevolent planet of war." Despite his shoulder, he bounded up the steps two at a time.

"If I only had half his energy," Blaze said wistfully, as Tyler disappeared around the landing.

Jill followed Blaze through the kitchen and out onto the back porch. A layer of leaves and fading flowers coated the surface of the lap pool. The sweet scent of wood smoke filled the air and the barbecue was smoking. Blaze threw a handful of twigs on the briquettes and fanned the fire with his palm. Jill saw the telescope on the lawn pointing east. She leaned against the porch railing and gathered her blazer about her. A light breeze blew and the glass wind chime tinkled. The sky was gray, it looked like rain, and she doubted if they would be seeing Mars or Algol that night.

Blaze picked up his tumbler of whiskey and took a slug. He came and stood beside her, swirling his drink. "How is he?"

Jill chose her words carefully. Just one night, that's all she wanted, for her husband and son to be together and enjoy a nice dinner. At the same time, without alerting him to Tyler's activities, she wanted to know Blaze's take on the Federal Reserve. Finally she said, "The doctor said there could be some mental confusion." She was hedging her bets. "But he seems good. He needs physio for his shoulder."

Blaze took a long swallow of his drink. "How long is he home for?"

"I don't know. He mentioned a few days."

"I could get him a job if he wanted."

Jill knew Tyler would never agree to work on the Hill. *You're not the boss of me*, was his favorite saying since he was three. More recently that had become, *I won't slave for no one.* "I wish he would go back to school," Jill said.

"Even better. It's a shame to waste three years of university and end up with nothing. Maybe the University of Texas."

"Or Harvard," Jill said.

Blaze took her hand, his fingers were warm. He wore a thick, heavy platinum wedding band. "Not Austin?"

Jill smiled at him. "It's a long way away," she said, but it wasn't the truth.

He released her hand, and went and poked the fire. He was a good cook and liked to barbecue. He had grown up in Austin, the only child of an oil magnate who at one time owned half the rigs in the gulf where Jill's father worked. His mother grew up in Houston, on the grounds of Baylor, the daughter of a university president. They had an unhappy marriage; his father ran around and his mother pretended not to notice. Blaze vowed to be nothing like him. They had great dreams for their son, named after the great scientist-philosopher, Blaise Pascal. Both parents were now dead.

Growing up, Blaze split his time between Lake Travis and Corpus Christi. He liked the outdoors and became an Eagle Scout. He went to Harvard and studied with preeminent evolutionary biologists. He did a Master's in Population Ecology and got married. He was in the first year of his Ph.D., on his way to becoming a university professor, when a seat in the Texas Legislature became free. Against his wishes, but with the approval of his wife and father, Blaze quit school and ran for office. His father had influential friends and money poured in and Blaze won handily. He served out his term and ran for the U.S. Congress. He won, and two years later, ran for the Senate. He was now the senior senator from Texas.

He was liberal in his views, yet conservative in his vote. He was no trail-blazer and would champion no sweeping reform. He tended to vote for the status quo and was on the side of legislation that maintained it. The only thing he was known to fight for was environmental protection, no matter what the cost. He sat on one committee and that was Environmental and Public Works. He spent all his energy fighting to protect ecosystems and wildlife populations, controlling pollutants and managing man-made disasters. He was no economist, but Jill knew he held no grudge against the Fed.

She met him when she was twenty-two, just out of college and working at the *Austin Tribune.* He was twenty-eight and running for the U.S. Congress when she scored an interview with him. From the instant they met, the course of her life changed forever. The following week he suggested a follow-up interview at the Pecan Street Café, the oldest and most romantic restaurant in all of Austin. He almost canceled. She almost didn't show. She knew he was married and had a daughter.

The next week he moved out of his home and filed for divorce. His father was furious: You slept with whores, you didn't marry them. He thought Blaze had blown the election.

Blaze's ex-wife and daughter were still in Austin and Jill didn't want Tyler anywhere near them. Rebecca, shocked and humiliated by the affair, did not want the divorce and had never remarried. Though she inherited a bank, Blaze still paid her alimony. Calista was thirty-four and vice president at the bank. Blaze paid for her to go to Yale for her undergraduate, and the London School of Economics for her Masters. She was six when Blaze left and her mother had full custody. Blaze saw them whenever he went to Austin.

He recently bought a house down the street from his ex-wife and around the corner from his daughter. In the darkest days of the housing market crash, Rebecca found a buyer for Jill and Blaze's 'love nest', and set them up with an ostentatious five bedroom house with two living rooms that her bank had repossessed. Blaze couldn't pass up the deal and while Hope was dying, they sold their house and bought the one Rebecca wanted him to have.

Blaze finished poking the coals and sat back down beside her.

"How did it go on the Hill?" she asked.

"It turns out letting Vermont sink isn't a good idea. Fitch, a top credit rating agency, has taken an interest in the vote. If Vermont falls, they're threatening to downgrade the triple-A rating of the state's debt *and* the country's debt. That would be catastrophic. Republicans know it, so they've agreed to a bailout, but to save face, we have to cut spending. I won't agree. I'm going to Austin in the morning."

Rebecca would pick him up at the airport. Besides running a bank, she was involved in his Political Action Committee, and in charge of serious fund-raising. There was no doubt about it, he owed her. How he repaid her was a question Jill was afraid to ask. Instead, she said, "Have you heard of Dennis Drake?"

"Dennis the Menace? Yes. Why?"

Tyler says he's got quite a following. In some polls he's running even with the President and Tumblin."

"Nonsense. Where did he hear that?"

"On the internet."

"Anyone can post anything they like on the web. Drake's a nobody. A pot farmer who wants to buy the presidency with a ten thousand dollar buyout for every homeowner who can vote. Everyone knows we can't afford three dollars, let alone ten thousand." Blaze shook his head in wonderment.

"What do you know about the Federal Reserve?"

Blaze stared at the barbecue. "It's a central bank. It controls the amount of money in circulation."

"Does it work for the benefit of the country?"

"Of course. It stabilizes the economy. Keeps politics from determining monetary policy."

The sun sank behind the house and Jill sat down at the picnic table and stared across the lawn. It sounded reasonable. If Congress was in charge, the economy could crash while they postured and dithered and worried about their voters and the next election. If it was really a bad system, surely economists would speak out against it. And Blaze was right, anyone could put anything on the internet. Tyler couldn't have his facts straight.

Blaze sat down beside her. The barbecue was going and the wood snapped and crackled. High in the trees, the birds called to each other and two black squirrels chased each other across the lawn. Blaze and Jill were comfortable not talking; they could listen to nature, sit in silence. It was so different from Jill's childhood when there was non-stop screaming. When her mother was still home, her parents fought all the time. She was only four and Jill still remembered it. After her mother left, Julie did the yelling. Jill had made a private promise never to be like that.

Through the kitchen window, Jill saw Tyler raiding the fridge and they joined him inside. They watched the end of the Redskins game, which the Skins barely won. But a win was a win and Blaze was happy. He hummed as he prepared shish-kabobs, skewering onions, green peppers, mushrooms, pineapples and baby potatoes. She made a large garden salad with cherry tomatoes and cubes of fresh mozzarella. Tyler made a dressing with olive oil, squeezed lime, salt, ground pepper and fresh crushed garlic. Blaze barbecued the kabobs along with salmon steaks. He opened a bottle of white wine and they sat down. Jill looked longingly at the bottle. The hardest thing about not drinking was getting through dinner without wine.

The dining room was off the kitchen and faced south, so that by dinnertime the room was dark. There were exposed beams on the ceiling and a wood plank floor. The heavy long mahogany table was scarred and the wooden chairs were wobbly from years of children leaning backwards and stressing legs. The room would be claustrophobic if not for the French doors that overlooked the back yard. Antique sconce lights cast a yellow hue on the white walls and a high chandelier over the table threw a spot light on the ceiling. Blaze sat at the end of the table, with Jill and Tyler beside him on opposite sides.

Blaze didn't like to drink alone and Tyler accepted a glass of wine. Jill, looking for a safe conversation to carry them through dinner, brought up football. "I heard the Skins are going to trade Mario."

"Best thing they could do," Blaze said. "Did you see that dropped pass?"

"They'll never get rid of him," Tyler said. "They paid too much for him."

"He's not worth much if he can't hold a ball," Blaze said.

'We watched a bit of the Giant game at the airport," Jill said. "They were winning at half time."

"They lost," Tyler said. "Fifty to fifteen."

"I don't remember them winning at half time," Blaze said.

Jill flaked a forkful of salmon. "The fish is moist and tender." She smiled at her husband. He was a great cook and not immune to compliments. She looked at Tyler for reinforcement.

"Is this salmon genetically engineered or wild?" he asked.

"There's no difference in taste," Blaze said.

"I'm referring to food quality," Tyler said.

"It's been studied and scientists have shown the quality is fine," Blaze said.

"Who paid for the studies?" Tyler asked. "The fish farmers?"

Jill cleared her throat and shot Tyler a warning glance. "The mushrooms are good too. They explode in your mouth."

Blaze smiled at her. "Thank you, honey."

"How's the election going, Dad?" Tyler asked, in a tone Jill didn't like.

"It all comes down to money," Blaze said. "I may have the support of National Geographic, the Audubon Society and Greenpeace, but they're not rolling in cash. Whereas Candy Turner can't accept donations fast enough."

"Where does she get her money?"

"Who knows? She doesn't have to disclose. She's got fifteen million in her war chest and I have two. You're not going to see much of me on TV."

Tyler whistled softly. "I bet only the big banks have money like that."

Jill didn't like where this was going and tried to head it off. "We don't talk politics at the table," she reminded them.

"I'm talking about the economy," Tyler said. He looked at his father. "The banks are buying her and you do nothing."

"What would you have me do?" Blaze asked benignly.

Tyler leaned toward his father. "Start screaming. We're supposed to have a government for the people, and it's become a government for big business and big banks. Why shouldn't we know who's giving money to elect idiots? No wonder we're bankrupt."

Blaze looked at his son. "We're not bankrupt. We have the strongest economy in the world."

"No, China's is stronger. And they have the monetary system we're supposed to have, the one Lincoln envisioned, where the government prints money without interest."

"I'll take more salmon," Jill said. "It is really good." But no one was listening to her or passed her the plate.

"This isn't China," Blaze said. "We borrow money, we pay it back."

"You mean, the working poor will pay it back. Let's raise their taxes, cut their services. And while we're at it, give tax breaks to the rich."

"Okay, I'll get it myself." Jill stood up and picked up the platter. "Salmon anyone?"

Blaze was chewing slowly and washed down his food with a swallow of wine. "The people who benefited from the money, will pay it back."

"With interest. Tell me, why do we have to pay interest?"

Blaze laughed heartily. When he got angry, he'd laugh, become sarcastic, or crack his knuckles, but he seldom lost his temper. This was a big difference between him and his son. The vein on Tyler's forehead was standing out. Blaze said, "We borrow money, we pay interest. That's the way it works."

"It's not real money we're paying interest on. It's made money. It's counterfeit. It's not like any bank worked for it. We're never going to get out of debt when the Fed and banks print money."

Jill put the platter down.

"Salad anyone?"

"Why go along with it?" Tyler demanded. "Why don't you do something? Evil is when good men do nothing."

Blaze leaned forward and put his elbows on the table. "I go along with it, because this is the way it is and has been for a hundred years. The Fed manages the money supply without political interference."

"Ha." Tyler threw down his utensils. He had barely touched his plate. "You mean it manages the money supply without worrying about voters."

"What do voters know about economics? The point is, our system works. The economy is growing. The Fed wouldn't benefit from a weak economy. It's in their best interest to keep it strong. I don't know where you get your ideas. That incomprehensible *Creature of Jekyll Island*? That offbeat magazine *Rolling Stone*? Or that cuckoo blogger, Ben Crupt."

The name hung in the silence of the room. Jill looked at her son.

He said, "That's me."

Blaze's light-hearted, easy-going manner vanished in an instant. He exhaled heavily, as if he'd been punched. "I should have known." He shook his head sadly. "If I were you, I'd check my facts."

Tyler's eyes opened wide and the vein on his forehead pulsed. "What facts?"

A long sip of wine helped Blaze recover his cool. "You think three presidents who stood against a central bank were shot," he said calmly. "Andrew Jackson was never shot."

"He was shot *at* twice. Both guns misfired. And Lincoln and Kennedy were certainly shot."

"By deranged lunatics."

"That's misinformation. Oswald worked for the CIA, and Lincoln was killed because the bankers hated his greenbacks."

Blaze put down his fork. He cracked a knuckle of his index finger. "You have no idea what you're talking about."

Tyler threw down his napkin. "Wrong. You're the one who has no idea." He stood up, kicked away his chair and marched from the room. A moment later the walls shook as the front door slammed.

***

Dinner was over. Blaze finished his wine and Jill put down her utensils, her appetite gone. They quietly cleared the plates. It was not the first fight for father and son, nor the first where Tyler walked out. From the time Tyler went to college, every political argument ended this way, with Blaze looking a little more haggard and Tyler storming away.

"He's lost his mind," Blaze said, as he washed dishes. "You should see that blog. He's promoting crackpot economics. He thinks JFK was killed because he wanted to do away with the Fed."

With Tyler not there to defend himself, Jill argued his side. "There's still a question mark around the assassination. The Warren Report was a lie. It made the government look untrustworthy."

"It was the oilmen if it was anyone," Blaze said sharply.

"How did you find his blog?" Jill asked, leading the subject away from government dishonesty, which was for Blaze a touchy subject, especially when his own ethics were above reproach.

"Hey, I keep up. I didn't know it was Tyler, but I should have guessed. I knew he'd been visiting conspiracy sites and looking at the Fed."

"You know what he looks at online?"

Blaze stopped the faucet with a lift of his elbow. "The investigator we hired did."

"He hacked into Tyler's computer?" Jill was outraged at this invasion of privacy.

"How else would we know what he was up to?" Blaze had finished the dishes and pulled the plug. "At least he has enough sense not to blog under his own name."

Jill took the J-cloth and wiped the tiled countertop of the center island. "He said that the Fed doesn't allow anyone to speak out against it."

"That's ridiculous. Look at Ron Paul."

Blaze had a point. Jill laid the cloth over the faucet, dried her hands on her slacks and faced her husband. "You don't think the Fed would go after Tyler on account of his blog?"

"Are you kidding me? Of course not. No one takes him seriously. I don't know where he gets his information, but his facts are wrong. The Fed is non-profit. At the end of every year it sends treasury a check for any money it has left over."

Jill was taken aback. Was Tyler visiting questionable websites and posting misinformation on his blog as truth? As a journalist, she took grave exception to this.

Blaze dried his hands on a tea towel. "Honey, Tyler's no threat to anyone but sensible people. What does he think? The Fed ran him over?" Blaze shook his head. "He crossed the road without looking. I'll show you the police report. The FBI sent me a copy."

In the den, Blaze booted up his laptop and opened an email from the FBI. Jill got her glasses and read the report: The 911 call came at 2102 hours on Thursday night from William Sharpe, who reported that a man had been hit by a white sedan at the intersection of Gold Street and John in lower Manhattan. The operator requested the man remain at the scene and wait for police, but he did not do so. When the police arrived at 2105 hours, a small crowd surrounded the victim, but William Sharpe had left. An ambulance arrived at 2108 hours and the victim was taken to New York Downtown Hospital.

Investigators found no skid marks at the scene, indicating the driver had not engaged the brakes. The victim was in the road when he was hit. He wore dark clothes on a dark evening. The light bulb in the nearest street lamp was out. It was possible the victim was not visible until it was too late. It was further possible the driver never saw the victim and did not know someone had been hit.

The victim had no ID, no wallet, and no money. A cell phone was non-functional. Given the clothes, the victim was assumed to be homeless. An investigation to find the vehicle and the driver was ongoing. The police had ruled out foul play and the incident was considered an accident.

The last notation of the police file was that at 0545 hours on Saturday, October 18, the file had been handed over to the New York branch of the FBI, which was taking over the investigation.

Jill lowered her glasses. "If his cell phone wasn't working, how did the police know to contact us? How did they know who Tyler was? The SIM card is missing from his phone."

Blaze sighed heavily. "The police likely took it out and forgot to put it back. The phone probably got broken in the accident and they used the SIM card to get his identity. That kid sees conspiracies everywhere."

That was true. If his favorite basketball team lost, the game was thrown. If his political candidate wasn't elected, there was obviously corruption. The fact was, accidents happened all the time. If there was anything untoward, the police and FBI would have found it. It was dark and Tyler was wearing dark clothing, and the driver never saw him and might not have known he hit anyone. It could have been an accident after all, Jill thought.

Blaze forwarded the email to her and turned on the TV. There was a special on Nat Geo about climate change and extreme weather. The show ended at eleven with Tyler still not home. They took Margo for her last walk of the day. The quiet streets were empty and the skies were cloudy, Mars deeply hidden from view. Not even the sparsely spaced street lights cast shadows. It was in the low forties and Jill worried about her son who was out wandering aimlessly in the cold without a sweater or jacket.

Back home, they left the alarm unarmed and went to bed. Jill was hardly in the mood for love but Blaze was leaving in the morning and would be gone all week, and it was not hard to turn her on. And though the open bedroom door distracted her, it didn't for long, and soon there were just the two of them, moving with each other. And later, as they lay together, Jill listened to the clock ticking as she waited for the front door to open and for her son to come home safely.

5

In the U.S. today, we have in effect two governments... We have the duly constituted government ... then we have an independent, uncontrolled and uncoordinated government in the Federal Reserve System, operating the money powers which are reserved to congress by the constitution.

—Wright Patman, D-TX

MONDAY, OCTOBER 20

Tyler finally came home just after 3:00 a.m. and Blaze was up at 5:30. He dressed in his favorite and best-fitting suit and a crisp white button down shirt that brought out his tan. He put on aftershave, gold cufflinks and black pointed cowboy boots. He packed a duffle bag and left to catch an early flight to Austin. Normally Jill would go back to sleep, but this morning she got up in the dark. She drank coffee and watched the dawn break and thought up ways to keep Tyler home. He liked his physical therapist, who helped him get back in shape after he broke his wrist in a high school basketball game. Perhaps the doctor would put him on an intensive regimen that would necessitate lengthy treatment.

Jill was drinking her second cup of coffee, surfing the web and checking Tyler's facts when she heard him screaming. She raced upstairs. He had started getting nightmares after Hope got sick and though he had stopped talking about them, they were obviously still bothering him. Jill tapped his good shoulder. "You're home," she said. "It's just a bad dream."

He gasped and opened his eyes, his face white.

He came downstairs fifteen minutes later and patted the dog. "It wasn't a nightmare," he said. "It was the accident. I relived the whole thing. Two men were chasing me. They followed me on the subway down to the print shop and waited as I got the flyers. They came after me. I ran at least two blocks carrying that heavy, awkward carton. The car came up behind me and drove onto the sidewalk. I threw the carton at the car and ran into the road. It was a black Plymouth-like car with dark tinted windows. It hit me from behind. It never tried to stop. It just ran me down."

Jill felt the morning's coffee turn in her stomach. "It sounds like the driver was drunk."

"No, it sounds like the driver deliberately ran me over."

"It was a dark night. You wore dark clothes and a street light was out. Maybe the driver didn't see you."

"I was caught in the glare of the headlights. He saw me all right."

She remembered the neurologist's caution. "How do you know you can trust your memory? Dr. Patel said that after a brain injury there could be some confusion. Maybe it was just a nightmare."

"Only it wasn't."

"I saw the FBI report. The car was white."

"Wrong. The car was black and it ran me over on purpose to stop the march. It had to be the Fed. It's a cartel, just like the mafia, and it's just as powerful. It would run over me to shut me up without a second thought."

Jill shook her head. "Tyler, I just don't think it would do that."

"What do you know?" he snapped. "You already admitted you don't know anything about it."

She drew back, away from his anger, and he raised his hands in surrender.

"I'm sorry, Mom, but it's true. How do you know what the Fed would or would not do?"

"I was online this morning. I looked for your reference on the fractional reserve on the New York Federal Reserve website and I couldn't find it."

"The Fed took it off the website. Can't be too transparent. But you can still find it online."

"Tyler, anyone can put anything they want online."

He fixed her with a cold stare. "What are you saying?"

"Your dad told me the Fed is non-profit. Every year it returns any money it has left over to the treasury."

"Is that so?" The vein in Tyler's forehead popped out like a thick blue chord. "First of all, it's not audited, so it can cook the books. Second, it may pay back the interest it prints on direct government loans, but it's not accountable for the money it creates through the fractional reserve. So, right there, it keeps most of the interest it gets, plus all the capital it prints, which it can give to anyone, all its friends, whoever it wants, and there goes money that would otherwise go to the treasury. Third, it's a bank with shareholders. You want to know who they are? The big bankers. They have one goal and that is to make money. Not give it back to taxpayers."

"It just doesn't sound right," Jill said. "I can't believe it works the way you think it does. It's preposterous."

He nodded. "Yes, it is. And, it works exactly the way I told you it works. Instead of telling me I'm wrong about something you know nothing about, why not learn about it first, and then we can talk about it."

Jill looked at her son. "You're right." She decided at that moment to learn everything she could about the Fed and the economy.

She got him breakfast, pouring him a big bowl of Special K cereal, as if he were five years old and getting ready to go to kindergarten. Except that was almost twenty years ago and now he was grown and miles away from the safety of grade school.

Tyler started to eat. Margo lay down in a square of bright sunlight and Jill poured herself another cup of coffee. He read the sports section of the *Post* and she picked up the business section. It was a part of the paper she never read. She deliberately didn't want to know about the stock market, or still falling real estate values, or big mergers, or banking bonuses or bankruptcies. To her, money was something she now had and was happy and grateful for having. She knew the country was in an economic mess, but there seemed no way out. The government had dug the country into a grave and was still digging. Unemployment was over ten percent. The retirement age had been raised to seventy and older people were working longer which wasn't helping employment. Retirement nest eggs had been decimated in the 2008 crisis and the recovery was slow, if not non-existent. Interest rates were still low, the deficit was rising, as were taxes, the debt and inflation. Food and gas had gone up thirty percent in five years. People were angry and had every right to be.

Yet, in the business section, the theme was about making money, where to invest, what tax laws had changed and to whose benefit. She saw that futures were up, the bulls were raging, regaining the lost ground of the previous week, now that Vermont was expected to get its bailout. The Dow and the NASDAQ were expected to skyrocket, and people who had their money in safe CD's were missing the rally and losing a windfall. The message was clear: get in now, before it's too late, prices will only keep rising, especially if the Republican candidate wins the presidential election.

Jill turned the page. A small headline in the bottom corner beneath a bold advertisement caught her eye: 'Bomb Scare Closes New York Financial District Saturday'. She read the article, which explained the closed streets and the cancellation of Tyler's march. She showed him the article and told him about the trouble she had getting to the hospital.

"Convenient," Tyler said. "The bomb turns out to be a hoax. The streets in the financial district get shut down, and the meeting at the Fed goes on in secret."

"There was no mention of a meeting of the Fed," Jill said.

"Look at this." Tyler got his laptop, opened an email and clicked on a link to a photograph showing five men sitting in a plush room at a round table. She recognized the Fed chairman and Rich Tumblin but not the other three men.

Tyler pointed out the New York Federal Reserve branch president, the Republican hopeful running for governor in the blue state of Vermont, and a vice president from Moody's, one of the nation's top credit rating agencies.

"Where did you get this?" Jill asked.

Tyler shrugged with his good shoulder. He'd rather not say. He quickly changed the subject. "I sent you an invitation to join my blog and friended you on Facebook." Now she could get his blog and keep up with the financial links he posted daily.

"How is your shoulder?" she asked. "It looks sore."

"It's fine."

"I could make you an appointment with Dr. Shultz."

"I'm going home."

Jill gasped. "You can't."

"Of course I can. David is there, Ali is coming back, and we have to plan our next move. There's not much time before the election."

"Time for what?"

"To raise awareness."

"If you're in danger, you need to stay out of sight, stay low."

"If they want me, they'll get me wherever I am. I'll take the train back this afternoon. I don't like flying. I hate all the security."

"You can't go now." Jill cast about wildly looking for a reason to make him stay and found one. "Your sister is coming on the weekend."

"Alexandria? She didn't tell me."

"Maybe she wanted to surprise you." Jill carried her coffee mug to the sink and rinsed it out.

Tyler sighed loudly, the air deflating out of him. "I guess I could stay until the weekend."

"Great. I'll call the physical therapist."

Tyler didn't protest and Jill went upstairs to make the call. She closed the bedroom door, sunk down on the bed in a swath of sunlight and called her daughter. It was five to nine and her first class started in five minutes. Alexandria picked up after the fourth ring.

"Hi honey, can you come home this weekend? Tyler's here."

"Is he all right? Where's he been? I've been trying to reach him for days."

"He was hit by a car."

"What?" Alexandria shrieked into the phone.

"He was in the hospital for two days."

"Why didn't you call me?"

Jill stared up at a portrait on the wall that was taken of her two oldest children when Alexandria was two and Tyler was four months. He was sitting in her lap and she had her arms around him, protecting him, keeping him safe. They were close as kids and close still. "He was unconscious. I didn't want you to worry. He got out of the hospital yesterday."

"Mom, I would have gone to New York."

"I know. You had midterms. Can you come home?"

"Of course. I gotta go. Love you."

"Tell him it was your idea," Jill said, before she realized she was speaking to a dial tone. Alexandria had hung up.

Next, Jill called the physical therapist who managed to squeeze Tyler in at ten. It was the same time as Jill's weekly appointment with her therapist and in the same medical complex. When things worked out, they worked out. Tyler was home, where he was safe, at least until the weekend, and she didn't have to worry about him.

Jill showered and dressed. She pulled on straight Levi's and a bright yellow long sleeve cotton sweater. Her therapist paid close attention to her clothes and she wanted to look happy. Downstairs, she told Tyler about their appointments. They would have to leave immediately to get there on time.

"You're still in therapy?" He sounded surprised.

"It's only been eight months."

"You still go every day?"

"That was the psychiatrist. I go to therapy once a week."

"Why?"

Jill walked to the doorway and grabbed her blazer. "I stopped drinking. Recovery is a long process. Let's go." But, in fact, she didn't go to therapy for sobriety. After her daughter died, nothing mattered any more. Medication never helped. Finding a reason to get up every morning was hard. Life had lost its meaning and its joy.

Out in the driveway, she saw a dark, four-door Pontiac with tinted windows driving slowly down the road, driving slower than most cars would go. Jill and Tyler stopped and looked at each other. The car was navy, not black, but with the dark windows, the occupants were hidden. She squinted, trying to read the license plate, but couldn't see it. For a moment she wondered if the car would turn into the drive, but it kept going at a snail's pace, then made the corner and continued on out of sight.

"Did you see the license plate?" Jill asked.

"No. Let's see if we can catch the car."

***

Jill drove a green Prius, and they sped down the street after the dark Pontiac, but the slow moving vehicle had vanished. It must have picked up speed, for if it had maintained its slow pace they would have overtaken it before reaching Wisconsin.

"That was a government issue car," Tyler said, as he scanned the busy street.

Jill agreed it might be, but perhaps it was innocent. "The FBI is investigating your accident. It could be FBI agents."

"Spying on me?"

"Watching out for you. Maybe they saw us leaving and that's why they didn't stop."

"Or maybe they're doubling back to search the house."

"I set the alarm."

Tyler laughed. "That won't stop them."

In Tyler's mind, the government had vast and unimaginable powers. "Let's assume they're on our side," she said.

"Humph."

"It's as easy to think that, as it is to think the opposite," Jill said, in line with her therapist's view of positive thinking.

They gave up the chase and headed for their appointments. The medical center was on M Street off Rock Creek Parkway, and they got there with minutes to spare. Jill parked in front of the physical therapy building, left Tyler, and walked across the parking lot to the Mental Health building.

Jill had been consulting with the Jungian therapist Petra Rey for eight months. She'd seen a psychiatrist the year before that, but all he wanted to do was prescribe increasing amounts of medication that was mixing badly with the ever increasing amounts of alcohol she was consuming. He thought a year was long enough to 'get over' the death of a child, and since she was obviously failing in this respect, he thought pills were the ticket. Then, on New Year's Day, after a particularly horrendous and embarrassing party at the Willard, she quit drinking, quit the shrink and checked into the Betty Ford clinic where she stayed thirty days. Back in D.C. she went to AA, and despite its anonymity, the press found her. After the headline: 'Soused Senator Spouse Seeks Serenity,' Jill stopped going. But not before she found Petra, who hailed from Switzerland and had a delightful European accent and could see the day when Jill's ennui ended and life had purpose again. In theory, Jill could tell her anything and it helped to have an objective observer on her side

Jill was the first patient of the day and Petra was waiting. She had a corner office on the second floor and the room had large windows facing north and west, which let in the light but no sunshine. There was a running fountain in the corner that sounded like a babbling brook, and large paintings on the walls that looked like ink blots. Jill sat in the middle of a couch facing the west window, and Petra sat kitty-corner to her. On the coffee table there was a Zen sand garden and Jill picked up the tiny rake and smoothed out the sand.

Petra was a year older than Jill and cheerfully plump. She looked like a gypsy. Thick dark black hair fell around her shoulders. She had bright, sea-blue eyes that missed nothing. She favored long skirts and chunky silver jewelry. Bangles clanked on her wrists and hoops weighed on her earlobes.

"You got your hair cut," Petra observed.

Jill raised her hand self-consciously. "I don't like it. I was hoping I'd get used to it."

"Get it re-cut. You won't get used to it."

One thing about Petra, she called a spade a spade.

"I haven't had time," Jill said. "I've been busy."

Petra's eyes opened wide with surprise. Jill's usual complaint was that she was bored, the days were too long. Since Hope died, she'd lost interest in everything and didn't do anything except garden without enthusiasm, and take the dog for long walks. Quitting drinking had only exacerbated her aimlessness. As Petra put it, her life needed pizzazz.

The therapist flipped open her steno pad and clicked the end of her pen, although she seldom took notes. She didn't need to, for her memory was spectacular.

Jill summarized the events of the past few days; about Tyler's accident, her trip to New York, his march, and his feeling the Fed was after him, all in contrast to Blaze's belief the Fed was respectable and great for the economy by keeping political influence at bay. "Tyler insists they're a for-profit bank that has ruined our economy. He thinks he remembers the accident. The car ran him off the sidewalk and in to the road."

Petra bit her lip and stared out the window. The leaves on a maple tree were beginning to yellow. Finally, she said, "What does your gut tell you?"

"I think what he's writing is outrageous. I don't see how it can be true. I think maybe someone could be trying to stop his misinformation."

"I didn't ask what you thought. I asked what you felt." Petra tapped her heart.

Jill thought for a moment.

Petra was shaking her head. "Don't think. What do your instincts tell you? What's the first thing that comes to you? Tyler is safe. Tyler is in trouble. What resonates?"

"He's in trouble."

"There you go." Petra sat back in her chair, as if exhausted from the effort of getting Jill to pay attention to her intuition. For Petra, the logic of the gut always trumped the logic of the mind. "What are you going to do about it?"

"I'm going to learn more about the Fed," Jill said.

Petra nodded with approval. "Information is power."

"And, I'm going to do whatever it takes to keep him here, out of harm's way."

"At least until you understand the situation," Petra said.

Jill smiled at her. Much of the therapy seemed to involve Petra validating what she felt, which others, like Blaze and Julie, dismissed.

"How is Blaze doing?" Petra asked. "I read he was back in town for the special session."

"He flew to Austin this morning."

"How do you feel about that?"

Jill took a deep breath. She knew what Petra was really asking. He would see his ex-wife and his daughter. Rebecca couldn't say enough good things about Blaze. He was a worthy, upstanding man, fit to be a senator and good for the state. She was a power broker in Austin and won him votes. She helped out at his campaign headquarters. A twenty-six year long divorce had not dampened her enthusiasm for him, nor his enthusiasm for her, which seemed to Jill, had only intensified since Hope's diagnosis.

The Austin press routinely made much of his good divorce and his close relationship with his ex-wife. The voters liked the magnanimous man who could share a stage with a current and ex-wife; how civilized they all were. It came up every election, every six years, the great support of Rebecca and Calista. Over time, Jill had campaigned less and less, and now she didn't campaign at all. Reporters, she knew, were talking.

"I don't think I like it," Jill said. "But I can't change it." Just thinking about it made her sweat. She felt damp perspiration under her arms and mopped her forehead.

Petra made a note. "Is he sleeping with her?"

Jill shrugged. "He didn't say."

"Maybe you can ask. Perhaps tell him how you feel."

"He knows."

Petra made another note. "How was New York? Did you stay with your sister?"

Jill nodded. "She has a new butler who's rude and unpleasant."

"And your sister?" Petra asked.

"She's making money, so she's happy."

"Any criticism?"

"Just the usual. I don't work, I don't make money, I baby my son who doesn't know anything about economics. Best I shut up and stop talking."

"She's been telling you that your whole life. Do you see, that in fact, you do what she says? You keep quiet when you should speak up."

Jill turned her attention to the Zen garden and picked up the rake. Petra made another note.

"Did she mention your mother's abandonment?"

"No." Jill drew the rake across the sand.

"A four year old doesn't cause her mother to leave," Petra said. "You know that, right?"

"I know." They had spent six months going over it. Jill wasn't to blame for her mother's unhappiness. It was her marriage and money. They were poor. Coming from a rich background, her mother couldn't take it. She didn't leave because of Jill, no matter what Julie said.

"At least you didn't drink," Petra said. "That must have been hard. Frankly, had I known you were going, I would have advised against it."

Jill drew another line in the sand. "I had a dream. Hope called me."

Petra leaned forward. This was her territory. She loved to hear about Jill's dreams. "What did she say?"

"Hi Mommy, happy birthday. She called me on the phone."

"And?"

"That was it. The phone was really ringing. The police were calling to tell us about Tyler's accident."

"I'd say Hope was calling."

Jill smiled. "I thought so too. It gives me – well – hope. I'll see her again."

"You named her aptly."

Hope had been named after the town where she was conceived. They had been at a fund raiser for a former president. Alexandria was conceived on an illicit weekend in Virginia on the campaign trail, soon after Blaze was separated, and before they were married. Tyler was conceived outside of Dallas at a victory celebration for a Texas governor.

As for naming Hope aptly, Jill wasn't so sure. If anything, there was too much hope, too much denial. It kept the chemotherapy treatments going longer than was helpful. Hope was getting worse and worse and the doctors were upping her dose of chemo, trying to stop the aggressive cells, even though Hope said she'd had enough and just wanted to go home. Jill told her she had to fight, she wasn't going to die, she'd make it. Hope knew better, but Jill didn't listen.

The night she died, Blaze was in Austin, meeting with constituents and the older two were away at university. Jill was home alone. Thinking about it now brought an inward shudder and she closed her eyes. She couldn't let her thoughts continue.

"Everything all right?" Petra brought her back.

Jill opened her eyes. "Yes, fine."

Petra looked skeptical. "You can tell me anything."

"I know."

Petra made a note. She was making an inordinate number of notes today. "Well, whenever you're ready." She returned to the phone call. "Happy birthday. That's an interesting thing to say."

"Well it *was* my birthday."

"Look at it symbolically. A birthday is a new beginning. Your own personal new year. The old you is dying and you get to start over. I think it's a good sign."

Petra always read a lot into the littlest thing.

"And this accident," Petra added. "Of course it's not really an accident."

"You mean, he *was* run over deliberately?"

"I'm speaking generally. What looks like an accident is always a fork in the road. For him, but also for you. You think of the word, accident, and think it's something that happens for no reason. You couldn't be more wrong. Accidents always have meaning."

A non sequitur if there ever was one, but Jill was used to it, for Petra often talked in riddles. "Why did it happen?"

"It will become clear in time. Look at the effect on you. Since I've known you, this is the first time you've worn bright colored clothing. You didn't yawn ten times in the hour. You didn't complain you didn't know what you would do with the day after you left. You didn't spend half our time talking about wanting to drink. And, you're finally showing interest in something. You're going to learn about the Federal Reserve. Tyler's accident shook you out of your lethargy. This is the day we've been waiting for."

Jill wasn't so sure, but Petra seemed so certain at the purported breakthrough Jill felt compelled to agree. Then Petra looked at her watch, her signal the hour was up. That was enough enlightenment and progress for one day.

"Keep a close eye on Tyler," Petra said, as she walked Jill to the door. "I get the sense he hasn't told you everything. Given his history, he may be up to something that has put his life in danger."

Jill left the office and found Tyler in the parking lot, leaning against the car, wind-milling his left arm. He'd scheduled another appointment for Friday, but none after that, for he doubted he would be in town. Jill smiled and said nothing, determined, one way or another to change his mind.

They drove to the V Communications store in Foggy Bottom to buy Tyler a new phone. The store was just east of George Washington University in a building made of gleaming glass, which reminded Jill of Julie's. Inside, rows of electronic gadgets lined see-through cabinets. The store was well-staffed and not busy. They were served by a kid with a crew cut and thick glasses who looked fifteen but was likely a university student. In a second he had the broken phone apart, a new SIM card in, and the phone hooked up to a computer. Nothing. The problem was more significant than a missing card.

The kid unplugged the charger, opened the back of the phone, removed the SIM card and peered inside. He grabbed a pair of pliers and teased out a small round metal chip. "Did you put this in here?"

Tyler picked it up, a small silver dot on the tip of his finger. "Is it a transmitter?

Jill snapped to attention. She got out her glasses. Whatever it was, it was round, the size of a match head, and etched with electronic circuitry.

The kid had never seen anything like it.

Tyler raised the chip to his eye. "I bet it transmits GPS location, sound and data."

The kid popped the SIM card back in, plugged in the charger, and the phone was still dead. "Whatever it is, it didn't interfere with the phone. Which is shot."

"It was in an accident," Jill said. "Could that piece have broken off?"

The kid dismissed this immediately. "Nope."

Tyler dropped the transmitter in the small pocket of his jeans.

With the old phone dead, and a year left on the contract, there would be no deals, and the full price would have to be paid on the replacement phone. "Get whatever you want," Jill said.

Normally that would fuel his excitement, but as they left the salesman and wandered around the store, Tyler fumed about the transmitter. "I've been electronically tailed," he said, under his breath. "I bet every one of my phone calls, text messages and tweets have been hacked. Someone has my whole phone directory. All my contacts. Even my internet search history. I can't believe it."

Jill remembered Blaze's hired P.I. and couldn't discount the possibility that it was his bug. "You don't know how long it's been there. It might have been there for a while."

Tyler shook his head. He would have none of it. "Whoever ran me over and took the SIM card, bugged my phone. It's a sophisticated piece of hardware. You can't buy it off the shelf at Best Buy. It's got to be FBI or NSA. But now it's mine."

Jill looked at him with alarm. "What are you going to do with it?"

"Find out who it belongs to."

He busied himself looking at phones, while Jill resumed her worry, which Petra had flamed, that there was more to the story than she knew; he was involved in something more sinister than just planning a protest. At least he was in D.C. and she would do everything she could to keep him here, where she could look out for him and protect him.

It took him thirty minutes to select a new phone. He chose one with high resolution graphics, a texting keyboard, 6G broadband capable of heavy traffic and high speed downloads, crisp sound and a good camera.

They headed back to the counter, the tracking device seemingly forgotten. Tyler looked happy, his cheeks flushed with excitement. Though he disdained all trappings of wealth, for technology he made an exception.

"This is a great phone," the kid told him, as he took it out of the box and set about activating it.

Tyler wanted his old contacts transferred and the kid took the new phone to the back to make the transfer. He was gone only a moment before he returned. "There's a problem with your file. I'm getting an error message."

"What does it say?" Tyler asked.

"The file is corrupt. There could have been a glitch, a power surge. It happens."

Tyler was chewing his fingers. "Could someone with unauthorized access hack into my account?"

The kid shook his head. "Our firewall is second to none. I can assure you V-Comm offers the latest and best protection and security. I'm sorry." He handed Tyler the new phone. "Do you have your contacts backed up online?"

Tyler sighed wearily. "It's set for monthly transfers."

"You'll have your contacts, text and pics up to then," the kid said, as if something was better than nothing, which was usually true.

They left the store. Tyler walked slowly, dispirited, hunched over like an old man, weighed down with his oversized plastic shopping bag. "I'm going to find out what happened to my account. See if I can restore it."

"How?"

"Hack through the firewall. If someone else did it, so can I."

"Is that legal?"

"It wasn't for them. And it's my account." Tyler kicked a rock out of his path that shot into the gutter. "You know what else was stolen? Besides all my contacts and texts? That photo of the guy who was following me, and who chased me into the road."

6

The bank is trying to kill me, but I will kill it ... You are a den of vipers and thieves. I intend to rout you out, and by the eternal God I will rout you out.

-President Andrew Jackson,
speaking against the Second National Bank

Tyler nixed lunch at his favorite vegetarian restaurant in Georgetown in favor of hurrying home to start hacking. After gulping down a bowl of soup and a grilled cheese sandwich, he ensconced himself in Jill's office and closed the door. She walked the dog in the park, came back and stared at the lawn. Leaves were drifting off trees and shrubs, and the lawn needed to be raked, but she didn't feel like doing yard work. Many more leaves would fall.

She went inside, made a pot of coffee and sat down with her laptop at the kitchen counter and pulled up Tyler's blog. Occasionally she heard him curse, and hoped he wouldn't get too far in his hacking and find the P.I. that would lead him to his father.

Over the summer, Tyler had thought he was being followed, but he certainly didn't know his father had hired the tail, or that his mother knew about it and didn't tell him. She didn't know how he would react if he found out now, but it would be extreme. He abhorred dishonesty, below board tactics and hidden agendas. He would see it as a conspiracy – people unbeknownst to him – even if they were his parents – secretly colluding against him. He demanded people deal with him fairly and honestly, and would not take kindly to any breach of privacy.

She distracted herself with the blog. In his introduction he wrote:

This blog is about the Federal Reserve and how it has bankrupted the country. When you think of the Fed, with its dot-gov website, you probably think it's a part of the government. That assumption is incorrect. If you look it up in the phone book, you won't find the Federal Reserve Board in the blue pages under government listings. You'll find it in the business section along with the banks. If you took economics you were taught the Fed stabilized and grew the economy. This too is wrong. You probably know the Fed has the power to set interest rates and control the amount of dollars in circulation, all for the betterment of the people. Wrong again.

In actual fact, the Fed is a private commercial banking corporation. Its stockholders are bankers. You know who they are. The ones that got bailed out in 2008. The purpose of the Fed is to make lots of money and protect the banks. Although, by law, Congress must control the money supply, Congress gave this power away. Since the dark day the Fed took control of the money, the value of a dollar has dropped to five cents. The Fed has stolen ninety-five cents of every dollar.

How has it done this? Why is it allowed to operate? Why doesn't Congress or the President put an end to it? If we can surely prove our economic woes are due to a grossly inaccurate economic science and flawed economic policy promoted by the Fed to enrich itself and its powerful friends, why is it allowed to continue?

Think of it this way. Say you had the power to print all the money you wanted, for any reason, and give it to anyone you wanted, and buy with it anything you chose, including elected officials. Say you could operate behind a curtain of secrecy. No one could ever audit you. No one could ever find out how much money you're making or what you're doing with it.

Would you give up those powers? Of course not. Well, so it is with the Fed.

If you did what the Fed did, it would be called counterfeiting and you'd be thrown in jail. When the Fed does it, it's protected by law.

Look around you, and when you see the poverty, the bankruptcy, the loss of real dollars, of middle class wealth, ask yourself where the money went. What happened to it? Who's got it? And at what consequence? Poverty! Look at any Third World country and the effect of crushing debt, and you'll see where we're headed.

In this blog, to be written daily, you will learn what the Fed wants kept secret. Before long you will know how we have been robbed and by whom and for what purpose. Information breeds awareness and compels action. Only when we know what is happening, will we have the power to end it. Peace and Freedom through Prosperity, B. N. Crupt.

She was reading through old blogs when he came into the kitchen and opened the fridge.

"Has the Fed really taken ninety-five cents of every dollar?" Jill said. "That's hard to believe."

He closed the fridge. "Just a minute." He left the room and came back thirty seconds later with an armful of books and laid them on the counter. The top book was *End the Fed,* by Congressman Ron Paul. "Look at page twenty-five."

"Where did you get this book?" Jill knew he hadn't brought it with him on the plane.

"From Dad's library. I gave it to him. And this." Tyler passed Jill a tome called: *The Creature of Jekyll Island.* "He hasn't read it either. He doesn't want to know how the economy works. As long as the polar bears have enough ice, that's all he cares about."

Jill always found herself defending Blaze to Tyler. "He cares as passionately as you do. He just has different interests."

"If he learned something about economics, he might actually have some money to save the whooping cranes." Tyler opened the fridge and pulled out a bottle of water.

Jill looked at the rest of the books. There was *The Big Short, Griftopia*, and *Web of Debt*. Tyler took his water and returned to her office and Jill grabbed the stack of books and went to the living room.

She read all afternoon, first one source, then another, all confirming the Fed was not the panacea it was reported to be. It caused inflation. It had unlimited powers to print money. When the dollar was tied to the gold standard, there was a limit to how much money could be printed, but now that the dollar wasn't backed by anything but the taxpayer, the sky was the limit.

The practice of fractional reserve banking created money out of thin air that the banks got to keep. Small wonder they were so rich. The practice had begun in the 17th century. Basically, the term meant that a bank had to keep only a fraction of its deposits. In the old days, when gold and silver coins were the standard currency, people brought their gold to the goldsmith for safe keeping. In return, the goldsmith gave out paper receipts, which was the origin of paper money. The people could bring back the receipt at any time and get their gold.

Goldsmiths also lent money. It didn't take them long to realize that all their customers who had deposits wouldn't return at the same time to demand their gold. So the goldsmiths started writing out more receipts than they had gold. To keep solvent, they had to maintain ten to twenty percent of their gold deposits. This was the fraction needed to be kept in reserve, in order to stay in the black. Now, thanks to fractional reserve banking, it was the way the money supply grew. Every bank did it; all they needed were people to borrow money.

The problem was inflation. Printed money diminished the value of existing money. It was like taking Monopoly money out of the game and saying, now by law, this is real. While the money supply might grow, the value of the money was decreased by the same amount that had been added. If banks print the same amount of money already in circulation, they would double the supply; but now the value of the money would be half of what it had been, because half the dollars were fake. Prices would immediately double in compensation. This was the cause of inflation. Things cost more, because the value of the dollar was less.

The Fed also created money, but its primary borrower was the government. Getting the Fed to print money was how the government covertly financed itself when it didn't want to raise taxes or cut programs. No one had to know because the Fed didn't have to report it. So, the government had a reason to keep the workings of the Fed a secret. No wonder the screams to fully audit and investigate the Fed weren't louder. The government was in on the scam. They put up with the interest to get free money.

Only it wasn't free. The Fed charged the government a high interest rate and that was another problem. The Fed and the banks didn't print the interest that accompanied the loans. The interest had to come from somewhere, and it came from new loans, which generated more interest, requiring another loan, which came with more interest, and on and on, until infinity, putting the country deeper and deeper in debt with no end in sight.

Despite the screaming about the deficit and the debt, the U.S. would never, ever, be able to pay off its debt. If the U.S. took every last penny, nickel, dime, and dollar in the country, it would still owe more than it had, all because the Fed didn't print the interest along with the principal. This would keep the country always in debt. There was no way out.

At one time, though it seemed long ago, people used to know how the economic system worked, and they would debate about it, fight over it. Not since JFK had any president questioned the country's economic policy. Now the central bank was taken as a given.

It had not always been that way. In the whole history of the country, there had been only three central banks. The first two banks each lasted twenty years, while the third and current one had lasted more than a devastating hundred.

She was surprised to learn that George Washington chartered the First American Bank in 1791. Way back then, the country saw it was corrupt and it lasted only twenty years.

Five years after it went out of business, the Second American Bank was chartered. That bank also lasted twenty years, but it did not go as easily. Andrew Jackson ran for president on a platform to 'End the Bank'. The chairman, a man named Biddle, went all out to keep his bank. Biddle had Congress in his pocket and paid members' salaries when cash was tight and Congress consistently voted to keep the bank.

Jackson won the election and his first order was to the treasury to stop all federal deposits to the bank. From then on, government deposits were to be sent to out-of-state banks. In addition, all government bills were to be paid through the Second American Bank. Jackson's plan was to deplete the government's account.

Only, the Secretary of the Treasury refused to go along with the plan. Jackson fired him. The next secretary also refused, and he was fired as well. The third secretary did as he was told, and that was how Jackson wrested power from the bank.

Biddle wasn't happy. He began calling in loans and refused to make new loans. The economy crashed and he blamed it on Jackson for not using his bank. The people turned against the president. Congress censured him for ruining the economy.

Biddle boasted to his friends about what he had done. People heard about it and the tide turned in favor of Jackson. The censure was reversed and the bank's charter expired and the bank went out of business.

Without a central bank, there came fifty years of American prosperity. With the bank gone, the debt was repaid and the economy grew. Then came the Civil War. Lincoln needed money to finance it and went to New York seeking loans. Bankers offered him an interest rate of twenty-four to twenty-six percent and he knew what that interest would do to the country and he couldn't comply. He returned to Washington and ordered the treasury to print federal notes without interest, to finance the war. Printed on green paper, the currency was called the greenback and was used alongside the dollar.

The war came to an end, and Lincoln was re-elected. Within weeks he was killed and soon after, so were his interest-free greenbacks.

Another fifty years passed before the Federal Reserve Board was born. These bankers were more careful. To make it seem as if they weren't a bank, they didn't call themselves a bank. They got a law passed that gave them control over the U.S. money supply and embarked on a PR campaign claiming they would save the economy. The press, owned by the big banks, raved about the bill. Economic departments in universities supported by grants from the big banks, crowed that the economy would flourish once it was no longer run by fickle politicians.

Although practical experience clearly refuted these claims, the operations of the current economic system were never questioned. In Jill's mind it was a crime and a well-orchestrated cover-up.

At 6:00 o'clock, she stood up and went and gazed out the window. The sun had come around to the west side of the house and sent long rays of illuminating light through the windows. There wasn't anything difficult to understand about how the economy worked. What was so difficult for Jill to understand was why it had taken her so long to learn about it.

The answers to the problems of the economy were quite clear, but no one was talking about them. Jill was awed by the outrageous silence, the blatant repression, the utter omission of the source of economic trouble in the country. In the space of four hours, her world view had changed, been flipped upside down. Before lunch, she thought that elected officials did their best under difficult circumstances to serve in their highest capacity to improve society. But now, come dinnertime, she saw a more sinister alternative. The whole system was set up to transfer money from the working poor and middle class to the entitled rich. The proof was empirical: the sheer amount of wealth that had already been shunted. In her view, Blaze was too ethical to go along with it and didn't know it was happening. Still, it had transpired on his watch. And Julie, with her MBA and seven figure salary and investment banking experience, probably didn't see it either. It was hard to fix something when you didn't know it was happening.

Jill turned away from the window, still in a state of shock. She went to the kitchen and opened the fridge. After a while she realized she was looking for a bottle of wine. She was so astonished at what she had read, her automatic response was to have a drink. She closed the door and put on the kettle. Mint tea would calm her nerves.

She made a cup, carried it to the living room and turned on the TV. There was no sound from Tyler and she let him be. She sat down on the couch, took a sip of tea, then choked on it as Blaze's colleague, Lisa Harper, the Independent senator from Vermont, was slammed in the face with a pie. Jill spilled tea on her lap and turned up the sound for the replay.

Lisa Harper, who was not up for re-election, was defending her state's economy when the pie came. She was dressed in a stylish red suit and standing in front of a microphone on the steps of the Capitol talking about her state. "Vermont is not the only state in trouble. More than forty states are in danger of bankruptcy, as are countless local governments. And that's not all. Given our current deficit and debt, the federal government is also near bankruptcy. We need to get real on taxes. Continuing to give tax cuts to the wealthy is simply not tenable."

Then the pie came. A protester dressed up as a clown – no, Uncle Sam – ran up the stairs and hurled his pie. It hit Lisa in the face, momentarily plastering her features with the tin pan. Then the pie fell, as if in slow motion, and streaked down her face leaving a wake of white cream. It dropped to her chest with a splat of yellow, then fell quickly, hitting the point of a stylish red pump.

Lisa wiped cream from her face. It was on her eyelashes and in her bangs, on the reporter's microphone and on his face. The station cut to a commercial.

The phone rang and Blaze was calling. "Did you see what happened to Lisa?"

"Who would do that?"

"Someone from a far-right organization called the Coalition for Fiscal Responsibility. It's a Tea-Party branch that wants to stop all spending that's not military. They don't want to bail out Vermont."

"Why go after Lisa?"

"She's from Vermont. She wants to raise taxes and won't cut spending. That clown wanted to shut her up and he did. He warned her the next time she opens her mouth about raising taxes, she'll be hit with something and it won't be a pie."

"You can't be serious."

"After the shooting last month in Nevada, the FBI and Secret Service have no choice but to take the threat seriously."

Jill swallowed hard. In September, the Nevada Democratic representative was shot by an irate voter who was upside down on his mortgage and about to lose his home.

"There's a list of shame and I'm on it," Blaze said. "Lisa sits on my committee. I vote for her projects and she votes for mine. The Coalition has said they're not only going after her, but those like her."

"You?"

"Us. Not only elected officials, but their families."

Jill inhaled sharply. The hairs on the back of her neck were standing up on end.

"Don't worry," said the man who never worried. "They have twenty-five names on their list. They can't get us all. Just be careful."

Jill went to the living room window and looked out at the street. "Be careful, how?"

"Lock the doors and windows. Keep the alarm armed, even when you're home and especially at night. Keep the front gate shut. Don't walk Margo by yourself. Keep your cell phone close. They know where we live. People could picket the house. You might get phone threats. If that happens, call the police. They'll get the FBI."

They'd had threats before. The one time there had been a serious threat, they'd fenced the yard and got FBI protection around the clock. "Could we get a bodyguard?" Jill thought this might be the best thing to protect Tyler.

"There's no money. We're on our own."

Jill sighed heavily. "When are you coming home?"

"Thursday at the earliest. I've got six town hall meetings in the next three days."

A car came down the road. Jill heard it before she saw it. It had a loud motor and was driving slowly. It came past the tree line from the east and into view. An old jeep with no doors, puffing smoke.

"I'm sorry," Blaze said, into the silence. "If you want, you could come down here."

Right, and stay down the street from Rebecca and around the corner from Calista, and maybe sit with them at a town hall meeting. "I'll be okay." Besides, she knew Tyler would never go, and under the circumstances, she would not leave him alone.

The jeep went choking by. There was a young couple in it, a guy driving, and a girl in the passenger seat with long hair blowing in the wind.

"How is Tyler?" Blaze asked.

"He went to physical therapy this morning and then to the phone store." Jill paused and looked down the hallway. The door to her office was still closed. She lowered her voice. "There was a transmitter in his phone. The salesman had never seen anything like it. Tyler thinks it's a GPS that can track his movements, a listening device that can record his calls, and a receiver that can intercept his text messages and tweets, and monitor his internet activity. Would your investigator have done that?"

"Our investigator? I don't know. He was looking at Tyler's internet usage, but he never mentioned the phone. The transmitter is probably his. I mean, who else would it belong to?"

Jill didn't say anything.

"Hey," Blaze said, addressing the silence. "Are you really going to be okay? I'll come home if you want. It's what the American people want. Their elected officials in D.C. doing country business instead of out looking for votes."

"I'll be fine." Then Jill asked the question that had been foremost in her mind. "Have you read Ron Paul's book, *End the Fed*?"

"Can't say I did. Why?"

"I skimmed through most of it. Blaze, the Fed *is* a for-profit central bank. Everything in Tyler's blog is true. The Fed has ruined the economy so banks can make gross profits."

This was met with a long, stony silence. Then, finally, "Jill, Ron Paul is fringe. A crackpot. He's extreme. No one takes him seriously."

"That's what you said about Tyler. It's a knee jerk reaction to anyone speaking against the Fed, when no reasonable person could support it."

"I see." More cold silence.

"Will you read the book?"

"I will not. If you haven't noticed I'm in the midst of a campaign. I'm very busy. I have no time for that nonsense."

Jill said nothing more. Talking to him was like talking to Julie. He would learn what he wanted to learn and that was that. She left it for now, tried to get the conversation on a lighter track. "Did I tell you Alexandria is coming on the weekend?"

"Excellent." He gave a little laugh. It wasn't in his nature to hold a grudge or to stay mad. "Kids. I asked her to come last weekend for your birthday and she swore the earliest she could come was Thanksgiving."

Suddenly Jill felt bad for guilting Alexandria into coming. "Should I tell her not to come? At least in Boston she'll be safe."

"You're safe," Blaze said. He listed the reasons: she had a dog, Tyler, fences, a gate, locks, alarms and phones. The FBI was on alert and the police were minutes away. "You'll be fine," he said. "I'll talk to you later."

He hung up without saying "I love you". Jill slowly closed her phone and placed it down on the table. She regretted not saying more about the Fed, or pointing out the inflationary folly of the fractional reserve, the unfairness of printing money out of thin air and getting interest on it, as well as the lunacy of not printing the interest that went with a loan. Even more though, she regretted not asking about Rebecca, not asking what they had planned, or where he slept when he was in Austin.

She went to her office. She had the corner room on the northeast side of the house. It was one-half its original size, for back when they bought the house, they divided her office in two in order to install a downstairs bathroom. Back in those days, Jill envisioned writing a novel. She thought she'd have all day by herself to write when the kids were in school, but it never panned out. The kids took too much of her time. She'd been happy to give it to them, and she had no regrets. Perhaps part of her knew how fast the time would go, how quickly they would grow and be gone, or taken from her.

She knocked on the door of her office and was invited in and found Tyler hard at work at her U-shaped desk. He had already heard about the pie throwing incident and the threats. He had big news too. "The stock market crashed," he said. "Aunt Julie will be pulling out her hair. Moody's is going to audit Vermont. Take a closer look at their books. Get a clearer picture of solvency for investors."

Jill sat down on the edge of her book table. The three front windows were open and the room was cold and growing dark as the sun went down. She reached up and turned on a standing lamp. "You were right about the Fed. The country can never prosper as long as it's in control."

Tyler beamed at her. When he was happy, a light came on in his eyes that intensified their hue and brightened his pupils. "What made you see it?" he asked. "Specifically."

She had been reading in *Web of Debt* about mortgages. Three years ago they had bought the new ugly house in Austin for three hundred thousand with a thirty year mortgage at five percent interest.

Because of the interest, once they owned the house outright, they would have paid a total of five hundred and eighty thousand to the bank, almost double what the house was worth, and what they had originally borrowed. And this, given to a bank for money it didn't have, on a house it didn't own. No wonder Rebecca pushed so hard for the deal. "It's an outrage," Jill said, "how banks make out like bandits selling mortgages."

"Now you know why the banks couldn't lend money fast enough. Especially when they weren't holding on to the loans. They didn't care who they lent money to."

"I can't believe it's allowed."

"Actually, paying interest on printed money is illegal in the eyes of the law," Tyler said. He showed her a recent blog about a court case in the late sixties in Minnesota, where a lawyer refused to pay his mortgage on the grounds the bank didn't own the money it had loaned him. The bank started foreclosure and ended up in court. The banker took the stand and admitted the money didn't exist before the mortgage was approved: the money wasn't in the bank, it didn't come from anyone, it was created out of nothing. The judge said it sounded like fraud, the jury agreed and the lawyer kept his house. "To this day, that judgment has never been overturned, but it's never addressed."

"It's a travesty," Jill said, searching for and unable to find the right word to describe her indignation.

"Now you know why they hide it. If people knew, they'd never go along with it. I took economics for one year, and no one ever talked about it. People used to know how the system worked, but there's been a conspiracy to keep it quiet and no one knows any more."

"I don't think your dad knows."

"Ignorance is no excuse, especially for those who make the law."

"I don't think Julie knows."

"She doesn't want to know."

"I don't get the why. Why isn't interest enough? Why do banks get to print endless money for themselves? It's like an addiction. There's never enough, they always want more." It was like her own addiction.

She couldn't drink enough wine. One more glass was always necessary. Once she started, she couldn't stop.

"Or," Tyler said, "it's more sinister than that. Money is power. If you want to eat, you'll do whatever those with the money say. The point isn't only having money. They take away your money."

A cold breeze wafted into the room and Jill stared out the window. Night had fallen. She resisted an urge to get up and close the windows.

"We're being enslaved, Mom."

It was here she drew a line. She thought that even the bankers didn't realize the devastation they caused.

"Think about it," Tyler said. "What separates us from a Third World country? In theory, we care for the disenfranchised, we have good medicine, good hospitals, clean water, dependable electricity, good universities, good roads, solid bridges, clean air, and respectable and available employment. In a developing country, you get none of these things. All the money that would go for them, goes to pay off debt. No money is put into the country, its infrastructure, or its people. We're becoming more and more like that. The banker-kings rule the country; they've taken all the money and hold our debt. The money that should go into building the country goes to Wall Street banks in interest. Meanwhile more and more people fall below the poverty line. I can't stand by and watch this and do nothing."

"I'm going to write my congressman," Jill said, with a smile.

"You give up on Dad?"

"Not yet."

Her computer dinged and Tyler scooted toward it, skating across the protective wood floor mat in the rolling armchair. He tapped at the keyboard rapidly, peering at the screen. With his back to her he said, "Do you mind if I link my laptop to your computers? It will speed everything up for both of us."

It seemed like a done deal, but he didn't have to ask, she would do anything for him. "Of course. How is it going?"

He pointed to his new phone that he had wired to his laptop. "I put the transmitter in my new phone and I'm trying to find the computer that's receiving the information. If I'm lucky, I'll find out who bugged me and get back my phone records, along with the photo of whoever was following me."

Jill stiffened. "You'll be able to find out who bugged the phone?"

"Once I get the IP address, I'll know." He must have seen her look of concern, for he added, "Don't worry, I've set up a firewall. No one can trace it back to me."

"You'll get a name?" she asked. A name wouldn't necessarily tie Blaze to the P.I.

"I doubt it," Tyler said. "I'm pretty sure it will be the FBI or NSA. I bet they hacked into my V-Comm file as well."

"Will you get the file back?"

"I'm trying, but the salesman was right. They've got a good firewall."

She headed for the door to go start dinner, worried about the legality of it all. "Would you keep your eye on the gate? There could be picketers."

"Oh no, not picketers." Tyler shivered with mock horror.

***

That night they had more than picketers. Jill and Tyler were in the den at the back of the house with the windows closed. The front door was triple locked and the alarm was armed. Tyler was going through photo albums that Jill hadn't opened in three years. He wasn't looking at recent photos, but pictures taken when he was twelve or thirteen and going through a growth spurt that left him gangly and awkward. All he wanted to do then was play basketball. In every picture of him, except for their annual Christmas photo sent to Blaze's supporters, he was with a ball, shooting hoops or dribbling. He played in three inches of snow, in spring torrents, in the boggy summer swelter.

Alexandria looked about fifteen and was either reading a book or playing soccer. She played defense, but wanted to play forward and was known to get out of position and score. Hope was two, chubby and blond, with light curls and a happy smile that Jill found hard to look at. There she was, riding her trike, sleeping with Margo who was just a puppy, or waving a big fat foam finger at a football game. She was on the sidelines at Tyler's basketball games, at the soccer games, and sitting beside Alexandria pretending she could read. There were pictures of her in the kitchen with Jill making cookies and out in the backyard with Blaze staring up at the sky. Who knew that eight years down the road she would weigh fifty pounds, be bald, unable to eat, and too weak to walk.

Jill couldn't look at any more pictures. She watched TV. Vermont was still in the headlines. The banks had come to the rescue and agreed to accept IOU's from the state legislature. There was no need to sell a turnpike or a parking lot.

Both the President and his opponent were claiming victory. The President assured the public the country wasn't bankrupt and in fact had the strongest economy on the globe. Auditors for the state had assured him they would pass Moody's inspection with flying colors. As a backup, Congress had approved the emergency loan. The money was available if Vermont needed it. The crisis had been averted.

Au contraire, said Rich Tumblin. While Congress dickered, the banks bailed out the state, thanks to a few phone calls from him. And while the state had weathered the crisis, the solution was akin to putting a band-aid on an amputated limb. Policy had to change and he was the one who knew how to change it and get the country working again. There was no reason the country could not be managed like a business in a fiscally responsible manner.

The most recent polls showed Rich Tumblin gaining in favor. He had forty-nine percent of the vote, while the President fell further behind with forty-five. The current economic crisis was not favoring the incumbent.

There was no mention on the network station of Denny Drake. Tyler paid no attention to the talking heads or the polls. He was still going through albums. Jill changed the station to a crime show.

Suddenly Tyler shrieked and jabbed his finger at the photo album.

Jill craned her neck to see what he was pointing at. He removed a picture from the cellophane protector and brought it close to his face. It was a picture of him playing basketball with the FBI agent who had watched their house back when Blaze had received the death threat and there was money for protection.

The FBI's agent's name was Jared. Jill couldn't remember his last name but he worked the day shift, and unlike the night and weekend detail, he didn't sit in his car and play computer games or talk on his phone all the time. He patrolled the yard, supervised the building of the fence, and opened the gate for the family, which at that time was opened manually. He carried in groceries, pushed Hope on her trike, kicked a soccer ball with Alexandria, and shot hoops with Tyler. He liked the sky and used to stay late and lug Blaze's telescope around the yard. He was tall and good looking, about her age, which was late thirties at the time. Julie had come for a weekend visit and was smitten with him, but he was one of the few people she couldn't seduce. He had left abruptly. One day Jared was there, the next he was gone. He was replaced, but no one would say what happened to him. Soon after the FBI arrested the right-wing grandfather who issued the death threat, and the protection was pulled.

"That's him," Tyler said.

"Jared?"

"That's his name. He's the one who's been following me. I knew I recognized him. He was chasing me the night I was hit. He was one of the two men."

Jill's jaw literally dropped open. She finally found the words to object. "He's an FBI agent. You must be mistaken."

"It's him. He didn't even try to disguise himself."

"Tyler, he wouldn't do that."

"Well he did. And I got a picture of him. I know it's him. The FBI ran me down. They changed the color of the car to throw off suspicion. The FBI must work for the Fed."

All Jill could do was shake her head. She knew Jared, she had watched him with her children and he could no more do this to Tyler than she could. He was wrong.

"I'll get you the photo," Tyler said. "I'll prove it."

Tyler returned to the album and Jill returned to the TV show. Legal or not, she was now rooting for Tyler to recover his phone records and get the photo. He would see he was wrong. Maybe there would be a resemblance, but it wouldn't be Jared, of that she was certain.

She focused on the show. There was a shoot-out, with sirens wailing, guns popping and people screaming. Even Margo was affected, the ridge on her back, raised. She started to growl. Jill hit the mute button. Margo barked so sharply that Tyler jumped and dropped the album.

He shot up and went gliding into the hall. Jill heard a strange noise. *Thwack, thwack, thwack.* A dozen or so times.

Tyler was at the front door. He snapped on the porch light. There was the sound of screeching tires and an engine gunning. He lifted the drape.

"Don't go out," Jill said. "Make sure the door's locked."

Tyler undid the three locks, turned the handle and opened the door. The alarm began to beep. He stepped outside. "Oh shit."

A cold wind blew in and the night air brought goosebumps to her skin. "What?" she asked breathlessly.

"Eggs." He pointed to the stone façade, the arched door, and the columns by the entrance way. The house had been pelted with eggs. The yolks and egg white streaming down. "I get cars," he said. "Dad gets eggs."

Jill unarmed the alarm and turned on the perimeter security lights and the yard blazed in artificial light. There were no cars on the road, no people on the street. Margo stayed with them on the porch.

Jill called the police and within two minutes a squad car came down the road, siren screaming, lights flashing. The officer pulled up in front of the gate. Tyler, who was against calling the police, went down and let the officer in.

The police officer took notes and decided it was an early Halloween prank and told them not to worry. "Kids will be kids," he said. He stayed two minutes before speeding off into the night.

"Told you," Tyler said, as they watched him drive away. "Worse than useless."

7

Capital must protect itself in every way, through combination [monopoly] and through legislation. Debts must be collected and loans and mortgages foreclosed upon as soon as possible. When through a process of law, the common people have lost their homes, they will be more tractable and more easily governed by the strong arm of the law applied by the central power of wealth, under control of leading financiers. People without homes will not quarrel with their leaders. This is well known ... in The Bankers Manifesto, 1934

THURSDAY OCTOBER 23

The work week progressed. There were no more egg-throwing incidents, no more mysterious drive-bys. Blaze campaigned, Alexandria took midterms, Tyler did shoulder exercises and tried to trace the origins of the transmitter and hack into V-Comm, while Jill learned about the economy. The stock market held steady while the country awaited Moody's verdict on Vermont.

Unreported by the mainstream media, but racing like the wind across the internet, were details of the President's meeting with the Federal Reserve Board chairman. The President wanted the Fed to issue low interest loans to cities and states in fiscal difficulty. He was asking no more than what the Fed was already giving to the banks, but the chairman had to think about it.

Twenty-four hours later the Fed came back with an answer. Sorry, but the Fed had no plans to get involved in the affairs of local and state governments.

Tyler followed this on his blog and twitter, and was livid. The Fed was practically giving away money to the banks, whose risky gambles had caused the problems for local and state governments, especially in regard to pensions, but the Fed wouldn't help the states out and buy their bonds at the same low interest rate they gave the banks. Although outrage flew across the internet, the story received no coverage on the network or cable news, or in the *Washington Post*.

On Thursday, Dennis Drake came to Washington, and Jill and Tyler went down to the National Mall to hear him speak. Initially the campaign stop was supposed to be in the auditorium at Howard University, but when thousands announced on Facebook that they would attend, the venue was changed at the last minute to the Lincoln Memorial.

It was a beautiful Indian summer day and the sun was shining brightly on the nation's capital. After a week of unseasonably cold weather, the temperature was in the low seventies and trees were awash with fall color. Around the Lincoln Memorial and Reflecting Pool, a crowd was gathering. Vendors did a brisk business selling t-shirts, caps and buttons. Tyler bought a bright yellow t-shirt and although Jill saw no photographers or news cameras, she bought a cap to go with her oversized sunglasses to protect her anonymity. Her presence here would not sit well with Blaze's supporters.

There were tables staffed by volunteers handing out brochures and pamphlets and Tyler picked up one of each. There were sign-in sheets for street addresses and email addresses and instructions on how to friend Dennis Drake on Facebook and find him on Twitter. Volunteers were waiting and ready to accept donations and no amount was too small or insignificant for the cause. Tyler gave ten dollars.

They got a place on a low marble step of the Lincoln Memorial facing the Reflecting Pool. Organizers were setting up speakers and a microphone on a table in front of the pool. Soon the steps were filled and police directed the overflow around the sides, where people would have a view of the speaker's back. Many in the crowd waved placards in support of Dennis Drake.

The crowd was shoulder to shoulder down both sides of the pool when three school buses came down 23rd Street and discharged a throng of people wearing Tea Party t-shirts and bearing their own signs: Let's Have a Tea Party; Tea Partiers for Reduced Gov; and more confrontationally: Drake the Flake; and Go Home, Dennis the Menace.

There were a lot of police, as if trouble was expected. Their guns were plainly visible, as were batons, but Jill was glad for their presence. In a crowd like this, it would be easy for someone to take a shot. There was no general security, any thug could bring a gun, hide it in a jacket or a sock, and whip it out and shoot. Jill cast a vigilant eye at the crowd, but saw nothing untoward.

She tried to estimate the size of the crowd, dividing people into sections, but soon gave up. There could as easily have been five thousand as ten thousand in attendance. Tyler thought there were twenty thousand, and they would learn later that almost forty thousand people had come to hear the candidate speak.

At 2:00 P.M. the student president of Howard University strode to the podium. The meeting was jointly sponsored by students at George Washington University, Howard University, and George Mason University, which explained the young crowd.

The student president thanked Drake for coming, for providing an alternative that Americans could ethically vote for. This was booed by the Tea Party, but loud clapping drowned them out. "The current President has shown that the best intent in the world isn't enough to stand up to Wall Street. With business interests corrupting both the Democratic and Republican candidates, the country's only hope is Dennis Drake."

With a wave of his arm, Drake was welcomed to the podium amidst thunderous applause. He was as good looking in person as he was on YouTube. Tall and husky, he looked tanned and relaxed, as if he was enjoying himself. He wore no tie, no jacket, just a yellow dress shirt rolled to the elbows, well-fitting blue jeans and boat shoes. He surveyed the crowd as if surveying an empty field and hearing: *if you build it, they will come.*

The clapping stopped. He cleared his throat and began. He thanked everyone for coming. It proved they had an interest in securing a prosperous future. "We used to be a country governed by the people, for the people. That was the vision this country was founded on. We've lost that vision.

"Big business has taken over the country. Now it's a government for the rich. Our President sold out. He moved Wall Street into his office. He's raised an unprecedented amount of campaign funds. The only candidate with more money is his hedge fund CEO opponent. They've both spent a billion dollars on the election already. Where is the money coming from? Well, the only people who have any money. Big business."

He talked about the changes he would make. It had to start with campaign reform. Right now the rich were buying elections. They were getting themselves or their people into office and passing laws to enrich themselves. Government no longer answered to the people, but to the rich who bought the politicians.

The second problem was lobbyists. The time had come to end special interest peddling in Washington. We couldn't subsidize corn growers or build dams in Asia or give oil explorers huge tax breaks. The playing field had to be leveled. The power of Wall Street had to be cut. No one was looking out for the little guy, who was taxed to the hilt and got nothing in return.

To a loud raucous cheer, he said it was time to throw the tea overboard. No taxation without representation.

If elected president, Drake would end the wars that served corporate interests and pocketbooks. He would raise taxes on the rich and restore cuts in services to the poor. He would increase Social Security payments and work on Medicare. He would revamp the universal health care bill and lower health care costs. He wanted non-profit health insurance. He didn't think big business should benefit from the misfortune of the sick. He would lower the retirement age, make it sixty, and free up jobs.

He spoke about the current economic crisis and the 2008 housing market crash that nearly took down the banks and Wall Street. "How did it happen?" he asked. "The answer is simple. Banks gave people mortgages they couldn't afford. It was a lucrative business, especially because there was no risk. The banks weren't keeping the loans, they were selling them. Thanks to Clinton, the mortgages were bundled together and traded on Wall Street.

"Moody's, that illustrious rating agency now investigating Vermont, was so confident workers making minimum wage could afford million dollar homes that they rated these mortgage-backed securities as triple-A. The banks knew the mortgages were toxic and got rid of them as fast as they could. They bundled them together and sold them on the stock exchange. Because they had the highest rating possible, pension funds, insurance companies, and other conservative investors bought the stocks, thinking they were safe.

"We all know what happened. Everyone who could sign their name had a mortgage. With empty homes on the market and no new buyers, home prices stopped rising. People couldn't take second and third mortgages out on their homes any more and began to default. Now there was an ever bigger housing surplus. With supply high and demand low, prices plummeted further. The economic downturn began to snowball. People lost their homes. I lost my farm."

For him, it was personal. No longer able to farm, he had turned to politics. "Is this fight against the banks personal?" he asked. "You bet it is! But I'll fight for you, I'll fight for everyone who got screwed in the crash, which is everyone but the big bankers.

"In 2008, this country lost ten trillion dollars thanks to Wall Street's greed. The stock market lost seven trillion and three trillion was lost in housing equity. Across the globe, the total loss was fifty trillion. There were so many losers in this game, yet the people who caused the problem not only got off scot-free, they got bailed out.

Taxpayers who lost half their wealth were called upon to save the banks."

He shook his head in wonderment. Heads were shaking in the crowd.

"The reason cities and states are in such trouble today is that they lost their employees' pension funds. No one talks about it. All we hear is how states over-spend. Hogwash. States lost their pension money making bets on Wall Street that were rated safe, but weren't.

"Since 2008, nothing has changed. No new laws have been passed that would prevent the same thing from happening all over again. Wall Street likes the way the system works, so that's the way it works.

"Now the country is broke. Instead of the big banks and big business taking a moral and righteous stance and fixing the damage they caused, they're hauling in bigger bonuses than ever and paying no tax.

"With so little corporate tax coming in, social programs have to be cut. Social Security needs to be taxed twice. Thanks again Mr. Clinton. There are no cost of living increases to help those on fixed incomes. There's no money to help the poor heat their homes or feed their kids. There's no money for education. No funding for colleges and universities. We're being dumbed down," Drake declared.

He paused and looked into the crowd. "Right now, all the government cares about is the wealthy. The government protects the big guy at the expense of everyone else. In the government's mind, we can work longer and harder, make less money, and retire much later. Slavery has returned to America.

"As president, I will kick Wall Street out of the White House. The days of buying an elected official will be over. As president, I will break up banks that are too big to fail. I will bring back laws enacted in the depression designed to protect Main Street. My financial reforms will have teeth. Lobbyists will not write my financial bills and the market will not rally when I sign them into law.

"I will protect the little guy. I will increase and actually collect corporate taxes. To jump start the economy I will pay every homeowner ten thousand dollars in compensation for what they have lost."

He had to pause as a cheer rose through the crowd.

When the clamor finally fell, he went on. "It should be a million dollars. That was the amount the government could have given to every homeowner in 2008, but instead it gave this money to the banks. Well, we're going to get it back. We're going to make this country great again. We'll empower the majority, instead of the wealthy one percent that now controls Washington.

"As president, I'll support the middle class. The economists have it wrong. Wealth doesn't trickle down. The most prosperous years this country has ever known was when we had a strong middle class, when the country was working for most people. I will invest in people. The true wealth in America is her human resources and people have been ignored for far too long. We may not have much power, but we have numbers. We can change the status quo. We can end the plutocracy that has bought a government that enslaves its people. We can put an end to it."

Drake raised his fist. "We can vote wisely. We can build a country that works for the majority. That is what will make the country great. It is in your hands. It is up to you. You can make this right. We can save this country. Make your vote count."

He ended with roaring cheers. People swarmed around him and he began signing autographs. Police and organizers directed the formation of a line and Tyler artfully slipped in place not far from the front. Soon the line snaked down the length of the Reflecting Pool and back up the other side. At this rate, Drake would be here until midnight. Tyler said he would stay until every last hand had been shaken.

The sun was going down. The air felt energized, the crowd around them buzzing. People were happy, smiling, joking. Laughter and light chatter filled the air.

Drake seemed indefatigable. Like Blaze on a campaign stop, he posed for photos, hugged supporters, held babies. Only Drake looked like a natural. He may have grown some pot and lost his farm, but he looked like he belonged in a way Blaze never did. A part of Blaze always wanted to be elsewhere and it showed.

Jill agreed with everything Drake said. It was what she believed, and what Blaze had believed, before he became part of the system; before the establishment reeled him in and covertly appropriated his acquiescence to the business as usual status quo.

Drake had a presence, a quiet assumption of command. He not only calmed the tea-partiers, he may have switched them to his side, for many stood in line. He reminded Jill of JFK who inspired the nation to greatness.

They reached the front of the line. Jill and Tyler exchanged cell phones so they could get their photos with the candidate. Darkness had fallen but Drake stood under a spotlight. He took Tyler's hand and pumped it heartily. "I'm Denny Drake. I need your vote. Thank you for coming. And you are?"

Tyler introduced himself as Ben Crupt.

The two men stood together and Jill took a picture. Drake gazed up at the sky. He bit his lip, then stared at Tyler intently. "You write a financial blog."

Tyler straightened, looking a foot taller. "It's about the economy and the Fed."

"I've heard a lot of good things about it. Will you send me the link?"

Tyler couldn't stop grinning. "Sure."

Drake pulled a card out of his pocket. "Here's my personal email." He passed Tyler a business card.

"It was a nice speech, but you missed the point," Tyler said.

Drake snapped his fingers. "Damn it," he said, with a smile.

"The role of the Fed and an economic system that creates money from debt."

Drake wagged a finger at him. "Write me."

An aide shuffled Tyler along and Drake reached for Jill's hand. "I'm Denny Drake, thanks for coming. And you are?"

"Jill Madison."

Tyler raised her cell phone and she removed her sunglasses and cap, and Tyler snapped a picture. Denny looked at him, then back at

Jill. He had bright blue eyes that blazed with intensity. She could smell his sweat. Even so, he radiated a presence, charm, and power, which made her knees weak.

"Senator Madison's wife?" Drake was staring into her eyes.

She was taken aback, felt herself stiffen and she tried not to gasp.

"Your husband did a lot to help the gray wolf and willow flycatcher in my state. I look forward to working with him."

Jill nodded, as words escaped her.

"Congratulations on your recovery," Drake said, as if he had kept up with her life. "Don't believe in miracles, depend on them."

An aide moved Jill along and she shuffled away, feeling light on her feet and giddy in the head. Away from his presence, she felt as if the sun had gone behind a cloud. She looked back at him – a rising bright star who could actually win the presidency.

***

By the time dinner was over, and they were awaiting Blaze and Alexandria, Tyler was friends with Denny Drake on Facebook, and Denny had placed a link on his Facebook page to Tyler's blog. In the span of two hours, Tyler had five hundred new friends and as many new subscribers to his blog. By eight, traffic to his website was so high, it crashed his site. After a call to Ali, back in New York, the website was up again by nine, with nearly a thousand new readers.

If so much had gone wrong for Tyler over the past week, so much seemed to be going right now. With a thumbs-up on his Facebook page, Denny promoted the blog and a nation-wide audience suddenly opened up for Tyler. He was moving beyond the confines of New York, getting his message out to the nation, all thanks to a dynamic presidential contender.

Jill was happy for him, but her nervousness rose along with his numbers. As Tyler's influence grew, he would become more and more of a threat, and there would be more and more of an incentive to shut him up.

Jill worried about this until ten, when Blaze and Alexandria arrived home. Tyler engulfed his sister in a bear hug and Blaze pecked Jill's lips. Coming back from Texas was never easy for him. Perhaps the transition from one family to another was difficult. As always, Jill was on the alert for lipstick stains and the scent of perfume, as one or the other, or both, were often present, and always attributed to constituents in need of a hug. As for Blaze, he found her scrutiny distasteful and wished she'd accept his past and get over it. It had been easier when she was drinking.

She turned to Alexandria who seemed thinner and exhausted. Her pretty daughter carried a worn knapsack and wore an oversized gray sweater and baggy khaki cargo pants that dragged on the floor. She could have looked beautiful, but that was like saying Tyler could have been rich, for Alexandria, with her long sun-blond hair, dark brown eyes and shining complexion, dressed like a bag lady. She was almost six feet tall and weighted at most a hundred and twenty pounds. Her hair was pulled back in some kind of knot and she wore no make-up. But when Jill hugged her, she smelled great, clean and fresh, like baby powder. As always, her hands were scrubbed and her nails were immaculate.

In they came, she and her Dad, and Jill closed and triple locked the door and set the alarm. Margo was so happy she ran around in circles, chasing her tail, and running from Alexandria to Blaze and back, acting out the exuberance in the air.

They got drinks and sat in the living room, Jill, Tyler, and Alexandria with ginger ale and Blaze with a tumbler of whiskey. Tyler was still overflowing with excitement from the afternoon. With blazing eyes he gave a rapturous overview of the candidate's speech. "Denny knows the problem with Washington. He's going to turn things around. Throw out Wall Street. Help the poor and the middle class."

"I hate to put out your fire," Blaze said, pausing to sip his drink, "but he doesn't stand a chance."

"I bet you'd like him, Dad," Alexandria said. "He believes in climate change and wants to protect endangered species. He's an environmentalist and will help the poor. All your core beliefs."

Blaze took another gulp. "Don't get your hopes up. He won't win."

Tyler took offence. "How can you say that? He represents everything voters want. He's not a part of the establishment. He knows the playing field isn't level. He's against big business and the banks and the slaughter of the middle class."

"Look at the polls," Blaze said. "He barely registers."

"Because your poll samples are skewed," Tyler said. "Where do the people you poll come from? A phone book? Who has a landline these days? Your pollsters go to the malls, banks, and airports. Who do they find there? People with enough money to shop or take a trip. You need to check the online polls. Denny has the Hispanic vote and those eighteen to twenty-five."

"They never vote" Blaze said.

"We'll see," Tyler said.

"He looked pretty good," Jill said. "He reminded me of you, back in the day."

"The day of ignorance," Blaze said.

"He wants to work with you, Dad, he said so," Tyler said.

"You helped save the gray wolf and some bird," Jill said.

Blaze looked at her. "You talked to him?"

"After his speech. I told him who I was. I didn't think he'd know me."

Blaze scratched his head, and took another drink. "I can't believe you went to hear him stump. You never come hear me. What if someone saw you?"

"I wore sunglasses and a hat. No one saw me." She changed the subject. "Did you find out who threw the eggs?"

Blaze sighed. "Unfortunately not. And it wasn't just us. Lee Sanders got his fence painted with graffiti calling him a communist. Maurice Shackles had every one of his tires punctured. Whoever did it left the ice pick and a note telling him he was lucky only his tires got stabbed."

"I think I was followed," Alexandria said.

Jill snapped to attention.

"Nothing happened," Alexandria said, as if alert to her mother's unease. She twisted loose hair that had fallen from her knot. If Tyler's bad habit was chewing on his nails, Alexandria's was playing with her hair. She twisted a golden hank around a finger. "It was just a feeling I had, that someone was watching me."

"In Boston?" Jill said.

"He came the whole way," Alexandria said. "He got on the bus on campus with me. We both got off at the station, and he was on the same car on the train coming here. He was behind me on the stairs and then I saw Dad and didn't see him anymore."

"Did anyone follow you home?" Jill asked Blaze.

"Not that I noticed."

"I didn't either," Alexandria said.

"Did you get a good look at him?" Tyler asked. "Did you recognize him?"

Alexandria shook her head.

"Was he wearing a green baseball cap or a navy hoodie?" Tyler asked.

"No." Alexandria shook her head. "He had dirty blond hair. He was big." She hefted up her arms to indicate huge shoulders. "A hulk."

Alarm bells rang in Jill's head. She remembered the burly man with dirty blond hair and a German accent at the hospital. Her first impression was that he looked like a hulk. "Did he have a scar?"

Alexandria nodded. "It went down his cheek." She raised her hand to her face and traced the track down her left cheek.

Jill's stomach tightened. She had convinced herself the hulk was a journalist, but this was too much of a coincidence. Was someone following not only Tyler, but Alexandria too? Were both her living children in danger? "Was he German?" she asked.

"I never heard him speak. He never even looked at me. Not once. I just felt that he was watching me."

Jill turned to Blaze. "I saw the same man at the hospital in New York."

"The world is full of kooks," Blaze said. "I wish they would reserve their criticism for me and leave you all alone. Be careful."

Alexandria nodded and Tyler rolled his eyes dubiously. He did not mention his suspicion that he was being followed by an FBI agent, and Jill didn't either. That would come after they had proof.

She got up and went to the window and peered out. The street was dark, but anyone could be in the park, hiding in the trees, watching the house, eyeing the kids. She had almost decided that the Fed was innocent of running Tyler down; that perhaps a hundred years ago it may have had people killed, but in today's world where it held ultimate power, it had no one to fear. Maybe she was wrong.

8

There are two ways to conquer and enslave a nation. One is by sword. The other is by debt.

—President John Adams

FRIDAY OCTOBER 24

Friday morning Blaze was up before the sun and off to work. Tyler had a physical therapy appointment at ten, and Jill was taking Alexandria to the mall. She said she didn't need anything; she wore her clothes until they were rags, and gave away any nice things she got, but she finally agreed to shop for Tyler. Jill was hoping once in the stores, Alexandria would see clothes she liked and get something new. She was also hoping that away from Tyler, Alexandria would shed new light on his activities. They were close. If anyone knew what he was up to, it would be she.

They set off at nine-forty, fifteen minutes late, though this could not be blamed on the kids, for the dog disappeared. They searched the house and came up empty. There was a doggie door in the kitchen, but Margo seldom used it, preferring to have the door opened for her. They searched the house and finally the yard and found her by the front fence, standing in the bushes. She wouldn't come in and Tyler had to pick her up and lug her inside.

Unlike her younger brother whose driver's license had expired, Alexandria wanted to drive and took the wheel with Tyler stretched out in back. She drove quickly and managed to get Tyler to the medical complex just five minutes late. They dropped him off and kept going, crossing Key Bridge heading for Rosslyn and the mall.

Jill hadn't been at the mall in some time, but she had never seen it so deserted. True it was early, but there were few shoppers. Many stores had gone out of business and their front windows were covered in brown butcher paper and election signs. Back when the kids were young and she took them to the mall on rainy days, it used to be packed. As a teen, Alexandria liked shopping and they would leave with their arms laden with shopping bags. She used to care about her clothes and her hair and changed outfits all the time. Jill had done endless laundry. Then Hope got sick and Alexandria let herself go. She broke up with her long time high school sweetheart and in three years had not dated anyone. She lost herself when Hope died and had never gotten herself back.

Jill wanted to buy Alexandria new jeans and they went to the Gap. They were the only ones in the store and were pestered by salespeople fighting for a commission and Jill shooed them away. She went through a rack of guys' jeans. "Tyler was also followed," she said, as she pulled out a pair of baggy jeans.

Alexandria stopped rifling through slacks and looked at her.

"He thinks the FBI had him run over."

Alexandria stared at her intently. "What on earth would make him think it was the FBI?"

"He thinks he recognized an agent. It was the guy who watched our house back when you were in high school."

Alexandria's brown eyes opened wide. "Jared?"

Jill nodded.

"No way." Alexandria didn't believe it either. "The FBI might be reading his blog. I'm sure they are, but they would arrest him, they wouldn't run him over. Jared wouldn't."

"If you think you're being followed, you need to be careful," Jill said. "Call your father or the police immediately if you sense that someone is tailing you or something's not right."

Jill finished going through the selection of jeans and found nothing suitable. Alexandria refused to look at clothes for herself and decided Tyler needed new running shoes.

They left the store and headed for the sports shop. Foot traffic at the mall had picked up, but it looked more like retirees out for exercise than able buyers. "I don't think the FBI or the Fed would deliberately run Tyler over," Jill said, as they went down a sunny breezeway, "but someone did."

"I bet the big banks have a security force," Alexandria said. "They wouldn't like what he's writing. He's calling for oversight, regulation, new restrictive laws, an end to derivatives, and breaking up the investment banks. It's not only the Fed he's upsetting."

Great, something new to worry about. A security force now. "He needs to stay low," Jill said. "Will you tell him?"

"He's planning another march."

Jill stiffened and stopped walking.

"Next Saturday, before the election. He wants the Fed to be a campaign issue." Alexandria continued, "You won't be able to talk him out of it." She entered the sports shop.

"He doesn't learn," Jill said, hurrying after her daughter. "Not even after getting run over. His friend was arrested."

"I heard. His computer was taken."

"Who is Ali?"

"He's Egyptian. He was one of Tyler's first supporters. He and David helped Tyler set up his website."

"I didn't meet David. Is he the one with the cat?"

"That's him. He was shot." Alexandria was heading for the back of the store.

"What? Who shot him? When?"

"He doesn't know. He was on his way to the march. He was just grazed, but he needed a doctor."

"How do you know?"

At the back of the store, Alexandria scanned a wall of shoes. "He called me."

"Why would he call you?"

"He needed help. I met him in the spring. I spent a weekend at Tyler's. He knew I was a medical student and he wanted to know if I knew anybody."

It was getting worse and worse. "Why didn't he go to the hospital?"

"He did. I know an intern who helped him out. David didn't want to report it. He didn't want the police involved."

Jill looked at her daughter. "Stay out of it. Please. For me. You helped him and now you were followed. You could be in danger."

"I know. Tyler doesn't want me involved. He doesn't want anyone involved. That's why he stopped coming home."

Jill picked up a running shoe. It weighed about an ounce. It wasn't like Tyler to keep his distance. When he was at university, he was always coming home. "What about Layla? Did you meet her?"

Alexandria turned and stared at her. "He told you about her?"

Jill returned the shoe to the rack. It was bright purple. "Let's say, I asked him about her. Why did they break up? Where did they meet? How long did they go out? Who is she?"

Alexandria smiled. "That, Mom, is why he didn't tell you about her in the first place. You ask too many questions." Alexandria picked up a red striped Nike. "Layla's nice. They met at the planetarium. She's doing a Master's in astrophysics at Columbia. They met in January and broke up in the spring. I don't know what happened. I think she wanted too much too fast. She was very intense. I know Tyler was the one who broke it off, but he was upset about it. He came to Boston the weekend after. He looked like he did after … Well, you know."

After Hope died was what she couldn't say.

Alexandria gave Jill the running shoe. "I think he'd like this."

Jill turned around and a salesman appeared. She asked for a size twelve and he returned a few moments later with a box.

They bought Tyler the shoes and went to pick him up. He was waiting in front of the building, standing on the sidewalk, well back from the curb, talking on his phone while rotating his shoulder.

He agreed to an early lunch and they went to Frank's in Georgetown. The day was bright, the wind blowing from the south, and in honor of the nice weather, they took a table on the sidewalk. Tyler put his phone on vibrate and laid it on the table. It kept going off and he would check it and then silence it.

"Expecting a message?" Jill said, trying to work her way around to his march without giving Alexandria away.

"Yeah," he said, without explanation.

"Is it about the permit?" Alexandria asked, coming to her mother's aid.

"We got it," Tyler said, as his face broke into a grin. "David knows someone who knows the mayor. A permit for next Saturday was just canceled and it's ours." He frowned at his mother's obvious distress. "Don't worry, my name isn't associated with it."

"I'm not worried about your name, I'm worried about your safety. Especially after you were run over."

"If we get a permit, the police will be there. We need to do this. Keep up the momentum. I'll leave with Alexandria on the train."

He would be leaving on Sunday. "You won't have enough time to organize anything," Jill said, grasping at straws.

"We'll get it done. We don't have a choice."

Jill looked to her daughter for help. Alexandria raised her eyes and cast a glance skyward as if for inspiration. Finally she said, "The train might be booked."

"Then I'll run to New York in my new shoes. Thanks Mom." Tyler began eating, shoveling salad greens into his mouth, as his phone nearly buzzed off the table.

***

They arrived home to find the gate ajar and the front door wide open. Tyler let out a cry and sprang from the car, shoved open the gate and sprinted up the drive. Jill hurried up behind him, calling for caution.

Whoever un-powered the gate and breached the locks could still be inside.

Tyler entered the house. Margo who always greeted them at the door was nowhere to be seen. Jill went inside with her heart in her throat, afraid of what she would find.

She halted in the doorway and saw the couch overturned, lamps knocked off tables, and an empty frame over the fireplace where the flat screen TV once hung. The stereo was gone, as were the speakers. Down the hallway, Tyler was shrieking.

She ran to her office. Tyler stood by the desk, hands on his head. Her monitor was on the floor upside down, the keyboard in the chair. "They took my laptop, yours, and your tower."

"And the TV and stereo."

Tyler let out a yelp and kicked the wall.

Jill felt the same anger. Her home, her sanctuary, her haven had been violated. Thieves had breached her security, invaded her home, absconded with her things, and Margo was missing.

Jill left Tyler moaning and went to search for her. Blaze's office door was open and he always kept it closed. His monitor was upright, but the screen had been smashed. The keyboard was on the floor in a tangle of wires. The tower was gone, as was his short-wave radio that delivered direct overseas news. Every drawer in his desk was open and one row of books had been swept off a shelf and lay in a heap on the floor.

She went to the den. The door was closed and they always left it open. She turned the handle, opened the door and found Margo, panting heavily and shaking mightily. Jill bent down and threw her arms around her. At least Margo was all right.

Jill carefully checked the rest of the house; Alexandria and Margo creeping behind her. The upstairs appeared unscathed. The robbers may have run out of time, or got from downstairs all they could take. She got out her phone and called Blaze. "We've been robbed."

"Are you all right? The kids?"

"We were out. Margo was home. She seems okay. They shut her in the den." Jill listed what had been taken.

"My computer?" Blaze said.

"Just the tower."

She heard a long exhale. "I had confidential reports and private correspondence. I bet that's what they were after. The deals we cut in order to save Vermont." There was a long silence, and then he said, "Did you set the alarm?"

"Of course."

"It never went off. The company calls when it does."

Jill went to the front door and checked the control panel. The alarm was off. There was no indication it had been triggered. She thought back to that morning. They had left late. Margo was missing. Was someone waiting for them to leave? Distracted, had she not set the alarm? She couldn't remember doing it, but it was something she did automatically.

"I'm coming right home," Blaze said. "I'll call the FBI. Don't touch anything."

They waited outside on the front steps. Tyler wanted to hook up the electric arm of the gate, but Jill told him to wait.

"There won't be any fingerprints," Tyler said, wringing his hands. "These were professionals. They won't leave prints."

"Do you remember me setting the alarm?" Jill asked.

"You always do," he said.

"It never went off. It wasn't triggered," Jill said.

Tyler narrowed his eyes. "It was turned off remotely."

"How?"

"Someone hacked into the house security system software and deactivated the alarm."

"Who could do that?"

He looked at her. "I could. I've done it before. In high school. It's not hard."

"Would common thieves know how?"

"These weren't common thieves," Tyler said. "They wanted my computer."

"Your father had confidential reports and emails on his. He thinks that's what they wanted."

"It's a red herring," Tyler said. "They wanted my laptop." He stood up and kicked the step. "First they hacked into my phone file, and now they stole my laptop. I was getting too close to them."

"To who?"

"Whoever hacked into my phone records and put in that tracking device. Well they got it back. They stole it too."

"Why didn't they just hack into your laptop?" Someone had hacked in Jill's email before. "Why did they need your computer?"

"I set up a firewall. No one could hack in. Now that they've got the computer, they'll get everything. All my contacts, all the people who get my blog, my browsing history, the names and emails of people who write me privately and off the record." Tyler looked like he might be sick.

***

Five minutes later Blaze arrived home in a convoy of three dark cars with tinted windows and flashing red and blue lights. He came with six agents, all dressed in black and wearing jackets with the letters FBI emblazed in yellow. The oldest agent looked gray and stern and was evidently in charge. He ordered Jill and the kids to the back porch to wait, while Blaze showed the agents the house.

Margo, who hadn't been ordered about, came with Jill and the kids. They sat at the picnic table and Jill watched the agents through the windows. They wore blue gloves and were swiping surfaces and shining black lights. Jill wished she had vacuumed and dusted and cleaned the bathrooms, which she would have done today if the kids hadn't been home.

Blaze came out five minutes later and sank down on the bench next to Jill. "Looks like they were after my computer," he said. "My confidential files and correspondence."

"How do they know it wasn't just a robbery?" Alexandria asked.

"They didn't take your Mom's jewelry," Blaze said, as Margo went to him. He rubbed her ears and stroked her back. "They didn't touch the safe."

"They didn't take just *your* computer," Tyler said.

"They didn't know which one to take, so they took them all."

"Or, they were after *my* computer," Tyler said. "They took yours to hide their intent."

"What do you have on yours that's so important?"

"I *also* have confidential correspondence I promised to protect."

Blaze looked benignly at his son. "I'm afraid there are degrees of confidentiality. I have top secret reports, emails from heads of state, as well as private negotiations."

Tyler was sputtering, but didn't get a chance to speak. Three agents appeared on the porch, wanting statements. Tyler would stay where he was, Alexandria was to go to the kitchen, and Jill out front. Blaze took the dog and went to his office to call his colleagues and staff to warn them of the breach.

Standing on the front stoop, Jill faced the street and hugged her arms with her hands. Clouds had gathered and after a warm autumn day, she felt cold and suddenly tired.

The agent pulled out a small notebook, licked a fat finger, and turned a page. He was young, about thirty, and short, shorter than she. Heavy set, his face was fleshy and his cheeks were big and round. His black hair was shaved short and he wore sunglasses, although there was no sun. He seemed out of shape for an FBI agent.

He introduced himself as Special Agent Mark Biltmore. "I'm sorry for your loss," he said, as if there had been a death. "I need to ask you a few questions. I know you must be upset, so I'll keep it short." He smiled a tight smile that made his cheeks bulge. "You have a nice home."

"Thank you." Jill wondered if this was an attempt to put her at ease.

"Do you remember setting the alarm?"

"Not exactly. But I always do. Could someone deactivate it?"

Agent Biltmore lifted his sunglasses and crammed them on his forehead. He had small brown eyes, widely spaced. "What someone?"

"The robbers?"

"Possible."

"It can be done," Jill said.

"Uh-huh. You locked the front door?"

"Always. Could they have gone through the dog door?"

The agent smiled the small smile. It didn't really look like a smile; more like a grimace. "That only happens in the movies. These were professionals. They likely picked the lock."

"What about the gate?"

"They turned off the power switch, undid the hinge and came right in."

Jill stared at the gate, appalled that her fortress was so easily penetrable. She had thought Tyler was safe, but he was no better off here than he was in his boarding house with the open front door and unlocked room.

"My son and daughter were both followed recently," Jill said.

"Your husband mentioned that."

"Do you think it's related?"

"Probably. Your husband and your family are being harassed, plain and simple."

"You don't think it was just a robbery?"

"The robbers knew what they wanted. They were after your husband's computer. His monitor was smashed in a violent aggressive attack. It would appear the theft was directed towards him."

"Did you find any prints?" Jill asked.

"We'll have to take the family's to rule out yours. But really?" He shook his head. "I'm not optimistic."

"What if they were after my son's computer?" Jill asked quietly.

The agent frowned and turned a page in the pad. "And this would be Alexander?"

"Tyler. Could his computer be the target?"

"What did he have on his computer?"

Jill was going to stay clear of Tyler's firewall and his attempts to track his tracker and hack into V Communications. While she searched her mind for something to say, the agent spoke for her.

"Porn?" His fat cheeks turned red.

Jill tried not to smile. She wished it were only porn. "No."

"Then what?"

She guessed the blog would be a safe place to go. "He writes a blog. He has a lot of followers. What if someone didn't like his blog?"

"Ma'am, people are allowed to write what they want in this country."

"He's speaking out against the Federal Reserve. Do the FBI and Federal Reserve work together?"

"We protect elected officials, if that's what you're asking."

"They're not a part of the government."

"There's your answer."

"He's corresponding with Denny Drake."

"Who?"

"Never mind. If the FBI broke into our house, would you know?"

The agent offered his small tight smile once more. "Ma'am, the FBI did not break into your house. And yes, I would know." He seemed amused by the exchange.

"About ten years ago we had an FBI team provide security for our house for about a month. There was an agent named Jared. Is there any way I can find out if he's still with the FBI?"

"You could make a formal request through your husband's office."

Jill nodded. It would never happen; Blaze would have too many questions. "Do you have the technology to trace cell phone content?"

"What type of technology?"

"Like a little bug, an electronic chip the size of a match head, that would intercept cell phone information."

The small eyes widened and she saw that she had piqued the agent's interest. She took a step back, moving away from him. "Is your cell phone bugged?" he asked.

She smiled her best smile. "No, no. I was just wondering if the technology was available."

"Not to the general public." The FBI agent made another note, then repositioned his sunglasses. He thanked her for her time.

9

Behind the ostensible government sits enthroned an invisible government owing no allegiance and acknowledging no responsibility to the people. To destroy this invisible government, to befoul the unholy alliance between corrupt business and corrupt politics is the first task of the statesmanship of the day.

—Teddy Roosevelt

SATURDAY OCTOBER 25

On Saturday morning, Blaze and Alexandria went off to play tennis leaving Jill alone with her son for the first time since the break-in. They sat at the kitchen island with their cell phones. Tyler was ordering new computers. During breakfast the insurance company had called to inform them their claim had been approved and they would get full current replacement value of their stolen and damaged property. They were able to replace and upgrade their four stolen computers.

Tyler bent over his cell phone reeling off specs. "We'll get dual core two gigahertz processors, four gigabytes of ram, and a hard drive with one terabyte." He looked up. "What do you think?"

"I don't know what you're talking about."

"They'll be the fastest computers on the market."

"Speed is good," she said, as a fresh pot of coffee brewed.

"I'll network mine with yours and if you leave yours on, I'll have access from New York and we can chat anytime."

He was throwing her a bone and they both knew it. "I guess it will take a few days for the computers to come," Jill said, hoping.

"They'll ship overnight and be here first thing tomorrow." He looked her in the eye. "Mom, I'm leaving in the morning."

She poured a cup of coffee she didn't need and changed the subject. "Did the FBI agent ask about your computer?"

"Peripherally. He wanted to know what I used it for. I said games. The guy believed me."

"Who do you think broke in?"

He lowered his phone. "Who do you think? The FBI."

"The agent I spoke to said the FBI didn't break into houses."

"What do you think he's going to say? Your son's firewall is so effective we couldn't hack in so we had to physically steal his computer."

Jill took a small careful sip of coffee. "If they do manage to hack in, what would they find?"

"If they get in, they'll see the set up of my security system, everything on my hard drive, my browsing history, all my contacts and email addresses. But they won't get my encryption algorithms. Most of the software is in New York."

Jill cupped her mug. "How can that be?"

"It's called networking, Mom. It's one great big system."

She had to admit that she knew very little about computers. "Who do you network with?"

He was paying more attention to his phone than to her. "Friends."

"Ali and David?"

Tyler shot her a sidelong glance. "Yes."

"Where did you meet them?"

Tyler looked up. "They were the first readers of my blog. They liked it and offered free technical assistance. They're software engineers from M.I.T. They worked in Silicon Valley and lost their jobs in the downturn. They're geniuses," he added with pride. "When I first started my blog I was getting so many hits, my website was freezing. They helped me organize it."

"After what happened, aren't you worried about holding another march? You're putting yourself out in the open, making yourself an easy mark."

Tyler placed the phone on the counter and folded his arms. "There's no other way. The country can't take another year of the Fed and business as usual. We're being enslaved. We have to stop them. You know that."

She exhaled with frustration and concern. "There are other ways. You need to protect yourself."

He looked around the warm kitchen, brightened by a warm autumn sun. Outside, leaves drifted aimlessly in the air and in the blue waters of the pool. "For this?"

***

That evening they had dinner reservations at their favorite restaurant and everyone dressed up to comply with La Fleur's dress code, no exceptions. Blaze wore a black suit with a crisp white shirt and white silk tie. Tyler wore the clothes that Julie had given him. Since he wasn't wearing a button-down shirt, he didn't need a tie. Jill's pretty daughter, who could look beautiful in anything, wore what appeared to be a long brown sack that looked horrendous with ballet flats. She refused to do anything with her hair or put on makeup. Tyler thought she looked superb. Jill dressed in an old but never worn before Rudi Olin fitted knee-high navy dress with sheer black stockings and three inch high Perrero heels.

They didn't eat out much as a family anymore and Jill was looking forward to the meal, although she was apprehensive about facing happy hour without a real drink. But at least in public Blaze and Tyler would work to get along, and maybe, just maybe, Jill could find a reason to make Tyler change his mind and keep him home.

The restaurant was on Capitol Hill in a small white building on Independence Avenue, a busy street that was home to lobbyists, lawyers and financiers. Out front, three arched windows were lit by amber bulbs shining in carriage lanterns. Owned and managed by Guy La Fleur, the restaurant had opened the same year Blaze was elected to the Senate and the men had grown in stature together. Guy had come to Alexandria's graduation and Hope's funeral, and Jill and Blaze had attended his son's wedding.

Inside, there was more amber lighting and a maître d' standing by. Blaze handed him a folded twenty dollar bill. He always tipped in advance and tipped well, doing his part to keep money circulating.

Guy rushed over to greet them. He was in his seventies, a short, spry Frenchman from Nice who had been in the country fifty years but still spoke in a thick accent. "Good evening, good evening," he said, and then for Tyler's benefit, "*Comment tu vas?*"

"*Bien,*" Tyler said, "*Et toi?*" He had learned French in the Peace Corps in West Africa.

"*Très bien,*" said Guy. He took the menus from the maître d' and led them to their table.

There were only twenty in the room, and widely spaced for privacy. There was a piano near the kitchen and a fireplace on the far side that was ablaze. Their table was next to the hearth in the corner. This gave a view both of the street and the room. Lighting came from sconces on the wall and candles flickering on tables. The carpet was thick and soft music played. At times there was the sound of silverware scraping. A sweet aroma hung in the air.

Guy pulled out Jill's chair. There was white linen on the table and crystal, silver, and china gleamed in the candlelight. Jill sat down, with Tyler across from her and Alexandria beside him. Blaze hadn't made it to the table. He was in the middle of the restaurant, holding a child on his hip and flanked by her parents, all smiling for a waitress with flaming red hair, a color nowhere near natural.

Blaze stopped at a few other tables, before coming to theirs and sat down beaming. The waiter appeared. Jim was Jill's age and had worked at La Fleur since it opened and knew them well. Blaze shook his hand and discreetly palmed him a fold of money. Jim poured water and took their drink order. He remembered Jill no longer drank alcohol and suggested a juice cocktail with lime mixed with ginger ale, orange juice and grapefruit juice drizzled over crushed ice. "It sounds, good," Jill said, and Tyler thought so too. Blaze was having whiskey on the rocks and the medical student ordered a martini, dry, shaken not stirred, and hold the olives, in the manner of Aunt Julie.

Jill opened her menu and was immediately shocked by the prices. The cheapest appetizer was twenty dollars and the entrees were upwards of fifty. She decided on her usual and closed the menu.

Blaze had already closed his. "Is it me, or have prices doubled since the last time we were here?"

"I'd say by twenty-five percent at least," Alexandria said, as she put down her menu.

Jill agreed with the estimate. They had come on Labor Day weekend when Alexandria was leaving for med school.

"That's strange when inflation is only two percent," Blaze said.

Tyler snapped his menu closed with a clap. "What inflation are you talking about, Dad? The items that aren't included?"

Blaze screwed up his face in a frown.

"Oh, you didn't know the Fed no longer includes gas or food in its measure of inflation?"

"I find that hard to believe," Blaze said.

"It's true," Jill said. "According to the experts, food and gas prices are too volatile to be included."

"That makes sense," Blaze said.

"No it doesn't," Tyler said. "By removing the two items most people care about, the Fed can pretend that the banks' endless counterfeiting isn't harming prices."

"The consumer price index certainly includes the price of food," Blaze said.

"Yes, but we're talking about inflation, and Social Security is tied to inflation not the CPI. If food and gas go up twenty percent, the Fed can say, hey, there's no inflation, so guess what seniors, you don't need any increase in your Social Security."

The conversation paused as Jim arrived with their drinks and a basket of bread. He took their order. Alexandria decided on shrimp in a white wine sauce, Jill, the stuffed flounder, Tyler, the sole in a bag, and Blaze, the hard-shell crab. The restaurant was well known for its excellent seafood.

When Jim was gone, Tyler faced off against his father again. "Do you know what causes inflation?"

"The price of goods goes up," Blaze said, swirling ice.

"Why do they go up?"

"The cost of living rises." Blaze tore a slice of bread in half and eyed his son from across the table.

"Why does it rise?"

"It's the nature of life. Things grow."

"No, Dad, what happens is the money supply grows. Do you know how?"

"Yes, the evil Fed prints money."

"It should be called counterfeiting, except the government calls it legal tender."

"I know, and even though a judge calls it unconstitutional, the Fed still prints money."

Tyler was taken aback. "I wrote about that in a recent blog."

"I read it. The 1969 lawsuit in Minnesota where a lawyer refused to repay his mortgage on the grounds the bank hadn't lent him real money. I'm surprised you didn't mention the judge died under mysterious circumstances less than six months after the trial."

"He died?" Tyler said.

"Son, you're a good writer. I wish you would go back to school and do something constructive with your life."

"I wish *you* would do something constructive," Tyler said testily.

He was always touchy when the subject of getting his degree came up. "Try your drink," Jill said, hoping for a diversion.

But Tyler glared at his father. "Do you think it's fair you get an automatic raise every year when everyone else doesn't get one?"

"I always vote to raise the minimum wage."

"Why don't you support Ron Paul?"

"Not my party. Plus, I think the country needs our protection. I do my best. There are limits to what I can do."

Jim came with the salads. He passed them around, then ground fresh black pepper over the radicchio, and sprinkled fresh parmesan on the greens. With a slight bow, he backed away.

"We're never going to get out of debt," Tyler said. "Not when the Fed doesn't print the interest that goes with the loan. The sad thing is, the government could print the money itself and not owe anyone, not owe interest. Think about how the country would be if this was our economic policy. We'd actually have money and you wouldn't have to spend all your time fighting about it. You could actually save the Everglades and clean up the Gulf. Isn't that a reason to do something?"

Blaze picked up his napkin and calmly patted his mouth. "You have no idea what you're talking about."

Tyler laughed, but the vein on his forehead was raised and his speech was clipped. "It doesn't have to be this way, Dad. Did you know that in the 1930's, two thousand different economic systems were proposed, and somehow we kept the plan that enriches bankers and impoverishes the country."

"I suggest you go back to school and learn *real* economic science," Blaze said.

"You mean where I can learn *fake* economic science. Where I can be brainwashed into believing my bank account isn't being plundered and the day will come when, gosh, if I could only get my spending under control, I'd get out of debt."

Blaze laughed. "I didn't know you had a bank account. And you seem to be doing pretty well for yourself. Nice cashmere sweater."

Tyler looked like he wanted to rip it off, but luckily Jim arrived with the entrees. Blaze got a bib. There was a comic break while Jim tied it around his neck and a diner came to get a photo.

Jill took a bite of flounder. It was stuffed with crab and shrimp and seasoned breadcrumbs and melted in her mouth. It came with julienne carrots, string beans, small round potatoes, a radish carved like a flower and a sprig of cilantro. She was hoping for peace, at least while they ate.

Blaze whacked his crab with gusto, cracking the shell with pliers. There was an image of a crab on the bib. He was enthusiastic about food, passionate in his appetites.

"Denny Drake gets it," Tyler said, as he flaked his sole. "We're at the service of the wealthy masters. Working longer and longer for less and less. Forty years ago a family could get by on one wage, now two isn't enough. When will the kids be sent to work? What about great grandma? When is eighty going to be too young to retire?"

"Who is working?" Blaze said, as he teased a long strand of crab from its shell with a small sharp fork. He smiled at his daughter. "Keep in mind, going to school is work."

Tyler shoved a forkful of fish in his mouth and chewed quickly. He swallowed and said, "Read about it, Dad, just read about it. Please, I beg you. The Fed that is supposed to stabilize the economy is stealing our money. It's neither benign nor benevolent. It's a reverse Robin Hood. Banks throw you a few crumbs and you shut up. Here's a few million, go save the Everglades and vote for our next bailout."

Tyler paused to take another mouthful of fish. He chewed quickly, swallowed hard and continued. "Look at North Dakota. It's the only state that wasn't razed by the 2008 meltdown. What did it do that was so different?" Tyler didn't wait for an answer. "It's the only state that has a state bank. It has low unemployment, the state is prosperous, and state salaries are high. It's nowhere near bankrupt. And why? The bank doesn't charge itself interest on the money it makes. It has no debt. Every state could be that way. The country could be that way. You could make it happen." Tyler paused to take another bite of fish. He threw down his fork. "This fish is bad."

Blaze cracked another crab leg. "This is the best restaurant in town. They don't serve bad fish."

Tyler folded his hands together and placed them on the table cloth. "I don't care if it's the best. This fish is bad."

Blaze laid down his pliers, reached across the table and inched Tyler's plate toward him. He forked up a large heap of sole and plopped it in his mouth. "It's fine," he said, when he was done chewing.

"I'm not eating it," Tyler said.

"It cost me fifty dollars, I'll eat it," Blaze said. He moved the plate to his side of the table.

"Do you want some flounder?" Jill asked her son. "I can't eat it all."

"I'm not hungry," Tyler said. "I don't feel that good."

He didn't look that good. There was a greenish tinge to his skin and sweat had broken out on his forehead. Still, he wouldn't give up. "The government can buy out the Fed at any time. Then the government will own its own debt. That will solve the deficit and debt problems." He wiped his forehead with his napkin.

Alexandria took up his battle cry. "Tyler's right, Dad. I don't know why so few people understand how the economy works. You don't have to study it at university. It's not hard to understand. But so many have the idea that economics is too complicated. The truth is, banks don't want people to know. Because when you know, you know how unfair it is." She stopped talking abruptly and said, "Dad, Dad, are you okay?"

Jill turned and looked at Blaze. A line of blood trickled from the corner of his mouth. The whites of his eyes were ringed with crimson. He turned sideways, and violently vomited foaming blood. Then he rolled off his chair, holding his stomach.

"Call 911," Alexandria yelled. She was out of her seat and down on the floor, loosening Blaze's tie and collar. "We need an ambulance."

Jill looked at Tyler and started. Blood ran down from his nostrils. He gripped his stomach. "I'm going to throw up too."

Alexandria ordered him to vomit and purge his system, but he sat hunched over in the chair, elbows on his knees, hanging his head. Blaze lay curled on the floor, moaning as blood trickled from his mouth. Alexandria took his pulse and wiped his mouth with the hem of her dress. Jill opened the window, and patted Tyler's forehead with a napkin. His skin was green and shiny with sweat.

Guy cleared the restaurant. Outside a siren grew louder. Guy paced, wringing his hands, cringing with apology, muttering in

French, *"D'accord, d'accord."* Suddenly, red lights pulsed in the restaurant, the door burst open and medics rushed in. Outside more lights flashed and new sirens sounded as more police cars and fire engines arrived.

Blaze was unfolded and shifted to a stretcher. An oxygen mask was placed over his mouth and an IV needle shoved in the back of his wrist. Tyler refused a stretcher and hobbled to the door. Alexandria rode in the ambulance with her father and brother, and Jill followed in the car.

It was raining, the wipers slapped at the windshield. Jill was caught up in a convoy of ambulances and police cars that went speeding to Georgia Avenue heading for Capitol Hill Hospital.

The ambulance parked in the receiving bay and Jill drove to the parking lot. She dashed to the ER through the rain. The waiting room was packed with no sign of her family. "My husband and son were just brought in," she told a nurse.

Jill was taken to a cubicle in the back of the ER where she found Alexandria sitting on a gurney, chewing the ends of her hair.

Jill sat down beside her. "Where are they?"

"Having their stomachs pumped."

"Food poisoning?" Jill dragged her daughter's hand away from her mouth.

Alexandria dropped her hand. "It wasn't salmonella or *E. coli*. It was probably strychnine."

"Rat poison?"

"It stops the blood from clotting," Alexandria said. "It had to be in a high concentration to act so fast."

"Will they be okay? Is there a cure?"

"Vitamin K. They'll get it IV. They should be fine."

An hour later an orderly arrived pushing Tyler in a wheelchair. Jill leapt off the gurney, bent down and hugged him fiercely. His skin felt cold and clammy. "Are you okay?"

"They pumped my stomach. My throat's burning. It feels raw. I think it's stomach acid. I'll be okay. How's Dad?"

"He'll be fine," said the orderly, who turned out to be a fourth year resident specializing in internal medicine.

"Was it strychnine?" Alexandria asked.

The doctor nodded.

"You said the fish was bad," Jill reminded her son. "How did it taste?"

"Bitter. There was a chemical flavor."

Jill faced the doctor. "Where is my husband? Why isn't he here?"

"The doctors are still with him. He's older, not in such good shape."

"He takes aspirin," Alexandria said. "Ever since he had that blood clot. The aspirin thins his blood. It will exacerbate the effects of the strychnine."

The doctor smoothed his bangs to one side and shot Alexandria an eager gaze. "Are you a doctor?"

"Med student." Alexandria didn't give him a second glance. She looked at her brother. "You should lie down."

He refused. He pulled himself out of the wheelchair and stood up. He was wearing a light green hospital gown with blue stripes and held it together at the back with one hand. "Where are my clothes?"

"We're getting you a room," the doctor said.

Despite the situation, Jill's heart leapt. Tyler wouldn't be able to leave, he would be hospitalized where he would be safe and not out in the open where he could be poisoned, or run over, or in New York planning another march.

"I'm not staying," Tyler said. "I want my clothes."

"Sir, under the circumstances, you should spend the night for observation. There could be internal bleeding." The doctor turned to Jill. "It won't take long to get a room. Please bear with us. We're taking overflow from the VA hospital and we're rather full."

"I'm not taking a bed from a vet. I'm fine."

"You could have a stroke," Alexandria said.

"I'm not having a stroke." Tyler was so optimistic for himself, so pessimistic for the country and its leaders. "I'm not staying."

The doctor shrugged. "I can't force you."

Jill stiffened with objection. Somehow she had to convince this doctor Tyler *had* to be admitted. If Jill had her way she'd check Tyler in for a week, throw every test possible at him. Post an FBI agent at his door and keep him from leaving. She longed for the past, when he was younger and she could put her foot down, insist he stay, and he would have to do what she said; he wouldn't have a choice.

"Shouldn't he have an MRI?" she said at last. "He was in the hospital last week. He was hit by a car and was in a coma."

The doctor frowned deeply. "Coma?" He looked at Tyler quizzically. "I'm quite sure you didn't mention that in your medical history."

"I was unconscious," Tyler said, frowning at his mother.

"He was in the hospital over two days," Jill said. "He just got out on Sunday."

"Mr. Madison, I strongly advise you to stay."

But the nurse was there with a plastic bag and his clothes. Tyler took them from her. "I'm fine. I'm leaving."

And he did. He put on his clothes and Alexandria took the car keys and there was nothing Jill could do or say to stop them. She watched them leave, standing in the forecourt, shielding her head with an arm, as rain poured down and her two surviving children headed out into the storm.

***

Despite the overflow, Blaze was given a private room on the 5th floor where Jill was allowed to wait while he received further medical attention.

The room was bright with artificial light and the shades were drawn. Jill sank down in an old armchair with ripped fabric. The only good thing she could see to come out of all this was that at last Blaze would see the danger Tyler faced. Last week he had been run over, this week it was poison. Blaze had eaten off his plate and was poisoned too. He would see that Tyler needed protection, that his life was in jeopardy.

Waiting for Blaze, she passed the time watching TV. Fox News broke the story first. A pretty blond reporter holding a furry microphone stared intently into the camera. *"And this just in. Democratic Senator Blaze Madison from Texas has just been admitted to Capitol Hill Hospital after collapsing with an upset stomach while eating dinner."*

The camera cut to a still photo of Blaze curled on the restaurant floor, awash with vomit and blood. It must have been taken by someone in La Fleur with a cell phone.

The newscaster continued. *"Senator Madison recently voted for the Vermont bailout and has repeatedly voted to increase spending and raise taxes on hard-working Americans. The four-time senator is up for re-election and according to the latest Fox Poll, is running three points below his opponent, Tea Party candidate Candy Turner."*

Jill changed the channel. This was the first time she'd heard that Blaze was behind in the polls and she didn't believe it. She knew that polls could be statistically rigged to support anyone. The station could have walked around the news room and asked employees who they were more likely to vote for, Candy or Blaze. The sad thing was, surprisingly, no laws compelled anyone to tell the truth. Misinformation wasn't just spread over the internet. She was outraged on her husband's behalf. The Vermont bailout never happened and he didn't repeatedly vote to increase spending, just social spending, and spending to protect the environment. And, he didn't want to increase taxes on everyone, just the top two percent. She wondered who approved the picture of him crumpled on the floor. That was just wrong.

On CNN there was a different version of the same story. Here, a banner with the words BREAKING NEWS flashed. A handsome reporter outside the restaurant announced that Senator Madison had fallen ill at a family dinner. They showed a picture of her husband standing beside an American flag looking tall and proud, strong and dignified.

"*The FBI is treating the incident as a crime*," said the reporter. "*Senator Madison has received death threats and is under fire from Republicans for his desire to pull out of Afghanistan and cut military spending. Senator Madison has never voted in favor of any war and prefers domestic spending over the building of foreign nations. Up for re-election, the senator is three points ahead of his Tea Party opponent, Candy Turner.*"

Which was more like it, but proved how variable the polls could be, Jill thought, as the national weather report came on and moving cold fronts swirled across the screen.

Blaze came to the room just before midnight accompanied by a team of doctors. Unlike the green cast of Tyler's skin, Blaze's looked cherry red. But there were purple circles under his eyes and he seemed weary and weak as the doctors transferred him from the gurney to the bed.

"Will he be all right?" Jill asked the doctors crowding the room. She took Blaze's hand. It was clammy and cold. The head doctor introduced himself with a name she didn't catch. There were monitors near the head of the bed and an IV stand in the corner, but no one made an effort to hook anything up.

"He ingested strychnine," the head doctor declared. "We pumped his stomach and administered activated charcoal to stop absorption. We believe most of the poison is out of his system. His clotting time has decreased, which means his ability to clot blood has increased. It's a good sign. We've infused Vitamin K and temporarily taken him off aspirin. We'll observe him for a few days, but we expect a full recovery."

She had no questions and the team filed out. When they were gone she closed the door and climbed into bed beside her husband and slung her arm around his shoulder. "How do you feel?"

"My throat feels burned."

"Tyler felt the same."

"How is he?"

"He went home."

Blaze frowned and tried to sit up. "Christ, why are they keeping me?"

"They wanted to keep him. He refused to stay. I wish he had." Jill sat up and faced her husband. "Have you talked to the FBI?"

"My office has. The FBI will keep us informed. The same agents from yesterday are on the case. They think this is part of the same thing; the same people who robbed us, egged the house, and hit Lisa with the pie. I'm over-spending, I should be poisoned."

"But Tyler got sick too."

"The executioner was sloppy."

Jill didn't press it. Blaze was obviously tired and weak and in much worse shape than Tyler. Tomorrow, when Blaze was stronger, she would point out the facts. Surely the FBI would see the truth and Tyler would have to be protected.

The door opened. A nurse peered in. "Oh, excuse me." She seemed hesitant to interrupt their privacy. "Senator, I have sleeping pills." She held up a small paper cup. "If you're interested."

He wasn't.

"If you need anything, I'm just down the hall." She closed the door and left them alone.

Blaze shut his eyes, Jill lay against him. He stroked her awful hair. "Are you going to stay the night?"

At this hospital you could stay overnight if you wanted. They didn't throw you out at nine, like some. "I should go. The kids are alone."

"They're grown. They'll be fine. They don't need you."

"I know."

But still, she got out of bed and took a taxi home.

10

The Federal Reserve definitely caused the Great Depression by contracting the amount of currency in circulation by one-third from 1929-1933.

—Milton Friedman,
Nobel Prize winner in Economics

SUNDAY OCTOBER 26

The UPS delivery man honked at the front gate at eight A.M. waking the household. Tyler and Alexandria unpacked the boxes and Jill checked in with Blaze. He was waiting to be taken for an MRI. "It's just routine, nothing to worry about." The nurse told him it might take all morning. He said goodbye to the kids.

By nine the computers were running and networked and Tyler showed off how fast they ran. "Do me a favor and don't turn them off," he said. "They'll go to sleep, but don't shut them down. We can chat any time."

With no appetite, Jill made an omelet for breakfast, which Alexandria was devouring, but Tyler was still too much under the weather to eat. Jill didn't eat either and too much coffee sat uneasily in her stomach. She had failed. Her kids were leaving and far from home they were devoid of protection. Right now, her best hope was that the FBI would wake up and put them both on a watch list. They could alert the local police to look out for them. She would get Blaze to push the FBI to find out who ran Tyler over and who poisoned him. Arrests had to be made. They had to get these people off the streets.

In the meantime, all she could do was warn her children. "Look, you both have to be careful. You've both been followed, we've been robbed, Tyler's been run over, and now he's been poisoned. You have to watch out for yourself. I wish you would reconsider leaving."

"I've got to get back to school," Alexandria said.

"It's not like I'm safe here," Tyler said.

Jill's hand started to shake and she put down the coffee mug. He was right, she couldn't protect her children, not even when she was two feet away from them. The old feeling of helplessness that had been her companion during Hope's last days was back and clamped on her heart like a vise. Jill faced her son. "Don't you feel at least a little afraid?"

"I feel a lot afraid. But to do nothing would feel worse."

Jill exhaled deeply, humbled by her son's courage. He put himself in harm's way and despite his fear, kept going, because he believed in what he was doing, and to stop or give up would kill him in another way.

"What did the FBI say about the food?" Alexandria asked.

"They just started their investigation. Last night they thought your Dad was the target and that the same people who broke into our house, threw the eggs, and the pie at Lisa Harper, poisoned him."

"How did they explain Tyler?" Alexandria asked.

Tyler stopped pushing around his eggs and waited for an answer.

"Someone got sloppy," Jill said.

"It makes no sense," Alexandria said. "Dad ate Tyler's fish. Tyler didn't eat Dad's crab. It had to be Tyler's plate that was contaminated."

Jill picked up her coffee mug. Last night she had drawn the same conclusion.

"It had to be someone at the restaurant," Tyler said.

"When did you make the reservation?" Alexandria asked.

"Monday, after I talked to you."

"So they knew we were coming," Alexandria said.

"We know almost everybody who works there," Jill said.

"Jim wouldn't do it," Tyler said.

"It had to be someone new," Alexandria said.

"There was that red headed waitress that took the picture of Dad," Tyler said. "I've never seen her before."

Jill remembered the unnatural shade of hair. "I'll talk to the FBI."

***

Jill drove the kids to the train station at eleven and hugged them goodbye. She made them promise they would either call or text every day and they were to alert her immediately if anyone was following them. Then they said their goodbyes. Tyler held onto her, hugging her tight, as if he would never hug her again. They entered the station and left without looking back.

It was too early to go to the hospital. Blaze would be immobilized in a tube having his body scanned. Jill could go home, but then she would have to turn around and leave for the hospital. La Fleur was on the way and she could stop there. She was once an investigative reporter. She knew how to ask questions. There was no need to prod the FBI. She could do this herself.

Jill drove to La Fleur, which had a Sunday brunch that ran from ten until three. Instead of going to church, the family used to go for brunch on Sunday mornings. The restaurant had everything, from waffles to fried chicken, crepes to chocolate éclairs. Back when Hope could eat, she would have blueberry pancakes with a chocolate milkshake. They took her there when she was on chemo and she couldn't eat anything and still threw up.

The place was crowded and Guy was at the reception desk, looking florid and rushed. He hurried around the desk when she caught his eye and pumped her hand. "*Je suis très desolé.*"

"It's not your fault."

"Ugh. We have no rats. There is no strychnine here, I promise you."

"I came to pay. We left last night without paying."

"*C'est rien.* It is on the house. And a free meal, if you return with Blaze and I can take your photograph."

"As soon as he gets out."

"I am so sorry. How is Blaze?"

"He'll be okay."

"I do not know how it could happen." Guy shook his head, bewildered.

"Did the FBI come?"

The door opened and a crowd pushed in. Guy took her elbow. "Come with me, *s'il vous plaît*." Leaving the maitre d' in charge of the front desk, Guy took her to the back of the restaurant and a small office off the kitchen where she could see the ovens and the stoves, and the chefs hard at work creating aromas that made her think she might be hungry after all.

Guy stood where he could keep his eye on the kitchen. "The FBI was here all night. They think we destroy evidence. And for why? Because we clean up? We thought Blaze had a heart attack. We did not consider poison." Guy made the sign of the cross over his face and heart. "What would they have us do? Leave the food out? That would surely call the rats."

"What did the FBI find?"

"We scraped the leftovers into the same bag. That was not wise. There was one plate especially contaminated. It had your husband's fingerprints."

"How do they know that?"

"It was a chemical test. They swabbed each plate with a Q-tip. Then they dipped the Q-tip into a vial with clear liquid. If it is red it is positive. One plate was off the charts. They check that plate for fingerprints. They did the comparison right here on a small computer. They had your husband's fingerprints. I don't know from where. I saw the comparison myself. Fingerprint from one bad plate, fingerprint from your husband. Ninety-nine percent match. It was his plate."

Jill didn't like it. Most patrons didn't touch their plates, the server did. And, she remembered how Blaze had inched Tyler's plate across the table.

"Was there someone new working last night?" Jill asked.

"Just Helga Grosch," Guy said. "She was from Germany and attending culinary school. She had no work papers, but wished to volunteer at a high class restaurant. I could hardly refuse." He touched his heart. "*Très joli.*"

"Did she have bright red hair?"

"Yes. She was dazzling."

German. Jill remembered the blond hulk with the scar at the hospital in New York who was speaking on a cell phone in what sounded like German. "Was she alone?" Jill asked. "Did someone come with her? Drop her off?"

"I did not see anyone with her, no."

"Did you tell the FBI?"

"They wished to have the resume of every employee. Myself included. Twenty-six years, *alors*."

"Did Helga give you a resume?"

"She did not. I did not hire her. She wished to work for free."

"When did she start?"

"Friday. She was helping in the kitchen and also serving. She was very good."

"She just walked in Friday and you hired her?"

"I hired her midweek. I did not need her, but she was free and eager to work."

"Did the FBI talk to her?"

"I have given the FBI her name, but I have no address. She left in the catastrophe. She cannot stand to see blood and looked faint. I told her, go. She is not getting paid after all. She was going to work today, but she has not come. I cannot blame her."

Jill thanked him for his help.

***

She drove to the hospital where she found Blaze back from his MRI and his room filled with people. His aide, Chase, was there, as was his chief fundraiser, pollster, and secretary. He didn't have a large staff. He preferred to keep it small to keep costs down and oversight high.

Jill pushed her way through the crowd, shaking hands and kissing cheeks. Congresswoman Lisa Harper was there, wearing the same red shoes she had worn when she'd been hit by the pie. They commiserated about the dangerous elements who knew no boundaries. The Chairman of the Ways and Means Committee was there, as was the senator from Alaska who sat on Blaze's committee and worried about melting icebergs.

She got to Blaze's bed and he reached out his hand. He was lying on a stack of pillows and his complexion was still cherry red, but he looked healthy. She bent down and kissed his lips. "I wondered when you would get here," he said.

"I stopped off at La Fleur."

"Give us a moment," he told the room in a booming voice. Then he winked. "Conjugal visit."

There was polite, perhaps forced laughter, as the room cleared.

When everyone was gone, Jill closed the door, tossed an oversized teddy bear from the chair onto the floor and pulled the chair to the bed. A row of vases stuffed with flowers lined the windowsill and more covered the top of a rolling cart and the bedside table. Balloons bounced at the ceiling in unseen currents of air. The room smelled of roses.

"What did the MRI show?" she asked, as she sat down.

"I'm fine. There's no bleeding in the brain. They want to keep me a few days for observation and I guess I'll stay." He was smiling broadly. "Did you hear? I'm up five points in the polls. Can you believe it? I poll better after vomiting from food poisoning than twenty hours of campaigning. I'll take a poisoning any day."

"Have you talked to the FBI?"

"They're posting a guard at my door. They don't want to take any chances. Whoever did this is serious. They gave me enough strychnine to send me over."

There was a knock at the door and, speaking of the FBI, in came the elderly stern agent she met yesterday at the house. He ignored her and addressed Blaze directly. "I just wanted to let you know we'll have someone monitor the door 24/7."

Blaze nodded his acquiescence and the agent backed up toward the door.

Jill called out, "Excuse me."

The agent turned around.

"How is the investigation going?"

"We're taking the poisoning seriously, if that's what you're asking. No one will get close to your husband again."

"Do you know who broke into our house?"

"Not yet."

"How do you know my husband was the target of the poisoning?"

The agent frowned, his gray skin pinched. He looked perplexed and glanced at Blaze, then back to Jill. "Your husband's plate was contaminated. He was deathly ill."

"My son was also poisoned."

The agent looked at Blaze again and scratched his head. "We suspect cross contamination. The strychnine was a powder in high concentration. A breeze, a puff of air could have blown it from one plate to another."

"My daughter and I were fine. Blaze ate off his son's plate. Blaze pulled the plate toward him. That's why his fingerprints were on it, but it was Tyler's plate."

"Ma'am, we believe this is connected to the break-in at your home and the current budget crisis. Your husband has received credible threats. Some sick individual is very angry at your husband. His monitor was smashed violently in an act of unrestrained aggression. We are quite certain your husband is the target of the poisoning."

"Did you talk to the new waitress at the restaurant?" Jill asked. "Her name is Helga Grosch. She's German. She started work on Friday."

"We have been talking to the entire staff."

"She's not on the staff. She was a volunteer from a culinary school. Guy La Fleur didn't get her resume. She left as soon as Tyler and Blaze got sick and hasn't been back. She was supposed to work today and didn't show up."

The agent looked at her coldly. "Mrs. Madison, please let us do our job. If any questions need to be addressed, we will address them." He looked at Blaze bemused. "Now, if you'll excuse me." He marched to the door.

Blaze pushed himself up so he was sitting straight. A balloon bounced in front of him and he bashed it away. "Jesus, honey, what the hell was that?" He began to crack his knuckles. "I was the one who was poisoned."

Jill leaned toward him. "Don't you see, the poison was meant for Tyler. He said his fish tasted bad and you took his plate and ate his food."

"It was the crab," Blaze said, as his phone rang. He checked the screen and sent the caller to voice mail. "That's what the FBI concluded."

"They don't know for sure because the leftovers were dumped in the garbage together and everything was contaminated."

"I was poisoned. Me." Blaze tapped his heart.

"They're after Tyler. He was poisoned too. He was chased down in the street and hit by a car. His computer, with all his contacts and all his files, was stolen. The SIM card from his phone was taken. On it was a photo of an FBI agent who's been tailing him. Tyler recognized him. He worked at our house. Jared."

Blaze blinked through a frown. "Jared Slater? Who liked astronomy? Who watched our house after we had those death threats years ago?"

So that was his last name. "Yes. Jared Slater."

Blaze held up his hand. "The FBI is not following Tyler. If he was being followed I would know. The SIM card was lost in the accident. The thieves were after my computer. I was the one that was poisoned. I'm the one in the hospital. Not him. Me."

His phone went off again and this time he answered. "Becca, it's good of you to call."

Jill exhaled and stared out the window. *Becca*. A diminutive he seldom used, at least not in front of her.

"No, I'll be there," he said. "Don't worry. That sounds great. I'll be down as soon as I can." He hung up.

"What sounds great?" Jill asked.

"She's going to keep an eye on the office and make me some home-made soup." He screwed up his face in a frown. "Jesus, Jill. Are we back there? I can't talk to her or Calista without you getting jealous and suspicious that something's going on?" He shook his head sadly, looking like a tired old man. "You see things that aren't there. You're as bad as Tyler with these stupid conspiracy theories."

"I know he's in danger. If you cared about him, you would help him. You would do something. Instead of running off to see *Becca*."

"I'm not running off anywhere." Blaze cracked his knuckles. "I happen to be in the hospital. When I'm better, I'll return to the campaign. There is an election."

"Can we hire your P.I. to protect Tyler?"

Blaze exhaled loudly. He drew his hand across his forehead and looked at her quizzically. "Have you been drinking?"

Jill stood up.

"You need to see Dr. Wisner," Blaze said. "You're not well. This quack you're going to isn't helping. You need medication."

"I don't need a psychiatrist and I don't need to be drugged."

"Go home. Don't talk to anyone."

"I'm going to New York. If you won't help Tyler, I will."

"What are you going to do?"

"Find out who ran him over and who poisoned him."

Blaze rolled his eyes. "We both know you're not going to New York."

***

Jill went home and packed. She grabbed a handful of clothes and her laptop. She didn't shut it down, but knew she would have to do so on the plane. She drove the dog along with her food and bed down the street to the dog-sitter, a kindly old widow who had watched Margo since she was a pup and would have adopted her if she could. Then Jill took a taxi to Reagan National Airport and bought a standby ticket on American Airlines. The terminal was packed and every flight to New York was overbooked. At eight o'clock the Redskins were playing the Giants in New York, and fans were flying out. Jill was twenty-ninth in line.

She called Julie and there was no answer, not on her cell phone and not at home. Jill wandered the terminal, smelling pizza and sweet cinnabon rolls that made her hungry, though she didn't feel like eating. On high alert, she maintained a state of vigilance. She saw no blond man with a scar, no dazzling red head, no tall, good-looking FBI agent. And, no one seemed interested in her.

She began to have second thoughts. There were leaves to rake, soil to turn, a pool to clean, and dead plants to pull. This was the most crucial time of any election and ducking out to New York sent the wrong signal. Still, Blaze was going to Austin where Rebecca was making soup. No one was looking after Tyler. He was young, naïve, inexperienced, and had no idea of the danger he faced if professional killers were after him. She had once been an investigative reporter and a good one. She could find the facts, follow the trail, find out who was after him, and protect him. Denny Drake's words came back to her: don't believe in miracles, depend on them.

That reminded her of Petra and the Monday session she had to cancel. She called her therapist.

Petra wasn't happy that Jill was going back to New York. "Did you ask Blaze to go with you?"

"He's in the hospital. He's going to Austin."

"I read in the paper that he was poisoned."

"It was meant for Tyler. He's gone back to New York. I couldn't stop him. He's planning another march. I have to go."

Petra listened to her reasoning and reluctantly agreed. "Be on guard against Julie. It's all right to stand up to her. You have a right to speak your mind and to be heard. Julie can take it."

Jill hung up and wandered on. She went into a bookstore and scanned paperbacks and magazines, but felt too keyed up to read. She walked the concourse. A shoe-shine man looked too long at her Pizzano pumps, but they were new and shiny. There was a barber doing a good business, and a drug store with a perfumery that was not so busy.

Boarding for the first flight began at three-thirty and four lucky standby passengers were given the seats of flyers who didn't make the flight. Now she was twenty-fifth in line and the next plane was at seven-thirty.

She continued pacing, feeling like a senior getting exercise at a mall. Again she tried calling Julie without success. When her phone rang at six, she thought it was her sister, but it was Blaze.

"Where are you?" he asked crankily. "The doctor wants to talk to you."

"I told you, I'm going to New York."

"You weren't serious."

"I'm at the airport."

"What are you going to do that the FBI can't?"

"Find out who's after Tyler and protect him."

Blaze sighed. "The contents of my computer were leaked to the press."

Jill paused.

"I don't know what's been leaked, but Chase is trying to find out. That proves whose computer the thieves were after. The press will be all over it. I need you here."

"Tyler needs me."

"He's a grown kid. He's responsible for his own choices. You can't baby him forever."

"He's in danger. Call it a mother's intuition. He needs me."

"That's so irrational. I'm in the hospital. My computer contents were leaked. But Tyler's the one in danger. Okay fine. Suit yourself." He hung up.

Jill listened to the silence for a time and then closed her phone.

The leak made the six-thirty news. Jill stood against a wall and learned that Moody's had been satisfied with Vermont's books and would maintain its credit rating. However, it now had California in its sights.

According to an unnamed source, the seriousness of California's situation had only become clear after confidential emails belonging to Senator Blaze Madison were leaked to the press. Extensive accounting reports contained in the emails left no doubt that the state was in deep financial trouble. The documents revealed California had already requested a bailout from the federal government. Moody's was flying west to investigate. Chinese and Japanese markets were tanking in response to the news. When markets opened in Europe, they were expected to follow suit. Reporters were awaiting a comment from Senator Madison, currently under guard at Capitol Hill Hospital after an attempt on his life.

Jill started pacing again, trying to assess the seriousness of the latest development. Vermont was a small state, with a small population, a small budget and a relatively small financial problem. It could be bailed out for fifty million. California on the other hand was huge, and had been in financial trouble to the tune of billions, for years. No small amount of money would bail it out. If California went bankrupt, it could bring down the whole country.

Blaze's people would scramble to minimize his involvement. He was in the hospital, vulnerable, gaining sympathy votes. It was not his fault if people sent him confidential information and his computer was stolen. Surely the story was California and not Blaze.

Jill decided to stay the course. Blaze had twenty-four hour protection and Tyler was the target. They didn't know that the same people who did the poisoning had stolen the computers. There could be two different groups. If the group who stole the computers hacked into

Blaze's and got past his security, they might get into Tyler's and who knew what they would find. Jill had not been there when one child needed her and she would not make that mistake again. She looked at the flight board. The seven-thirty flight to New York was about to board. She went to see if she could get a seat.

Unfortunately not. There were no empty seats and no one on standby got to fly. The next plane was at eight.

She bought a slice of pizza and kept wandering. The shoe-shine man was gone. The barber shop was empty and the barber sat idly in his chair. Jill passed the shop, caught her reflection in the glass, saw her awful hair and paused. She looked at the barber and he looked back. She reversed her steps and went in.

"Still waiting for your flight?" The barber was young, in his late twenties. His dark hair was spiked in front and shiny with gel. He had a diamond stud in his ear.

"I'm flying standby," Jill said. "Do you cut women's hair?"

He jumped out of his chair and waved her to it. He swooshed a black cape over her and tied it at her neck. "Now who is responsible for this abomination?" He lifted a piece of hair and shook his head.

"Can you fix it?"

"Of course. If you don't mind it short."

"I like it long."

"It will grow."

He wet it down and started to cut, making small precise cuts in inch wide sections, stopping often to check his work. Before long he was finished and stood back to admire his work. With a flourish he swept off the cape. He ran his fingers under her hair, lifting it up. "It is no muss, no fuss. You don't even have to blow it dry."

It looked fabulous. The best haircut she ever had. The cost? Ten dollars. She gave him twenty and told him to keep the change. She left the shop feeling almost buoyant, a new person, or the old person reborn; the investigative reporter who could get to the bottom of things and find the truth.

Half an hour later, another plane was boarding, but now, new hope. An inbound connecting flight from Denver was delayed by a snow storm, and wouldn't arrive in time. All twenty-five standby passengers were given seats. Jill got a seat in first class with preferred boarding. The tide had turned. She was no longer going with the flow, she was forging her own way.

At five past eight, the plane lifted to the sky and once more she was airborne. Outside, the lights of the city glittered like jewels. Everything suddenly seemed manageable. For the first time she felt no need for the free champagne that was soon offered. "I'm an alcoholic," she informed the steward to ensure that he would not ask again. "I don't drink."

11

We have come to be one of the worst ruled, one of the most complete-ly controlled governments in the civilized world – no longer a gov-ernment of free opinion, no longer a government by ... a vote of the majority, but a government by the opinion and duress of a small group of dominant men.

–President Woodrow Wilson,
who signed the Federal Reserve Act into law

MONDAY OCTOBER 27

Monday morning in New York came with no sign of Julie or her butler. She hadn't been home when Jill came from the airport and hadn't arrived during the night. The doorman didn't know where she was or when she would return. Jill had decided she had enough to worry about without worrying about her sister. Julie was fifty-five and could take care of herself.

Not having a clue how to work the fancy coffee maker, Jill skipped breakfast and went to shower. There was no shampoo, but she found a bottle in the tan bedroom, along with Tyler's green Nike running shoe. She picked it up, a symbol of the missing pieces of his story, and took it to her bedroom.

She dressed and in the dark headed for Starbucks where she bought the *Times* and scanned the paper while drinking a dry venti cappuccino with an extra shot of espresso. The day's headline was the impending bankruptcy of California.

Despite the state's insistence they could meet their monthly obli-gations, Moody's and Fitch investigators were scrutinizing the books.

The President reminded the country that a state bankruptcy was illegal and appealed for calm. California was convinced it would pass the audit. There were no new developments. California had been in trouble for years and everyone knew it. They had nothing to hide. The Democratic governor decried the leaking of confidential documents, calling it shocking and irresponsible. He did not mention Blaze by name.

With futures predicted to plummet in triple digits, Rich Tumblin too was calling for calm. He wanted everyone to take a step back until the audit was complete and the situation was clear. One thing he did know was that the California governor, not up for re-election, was following the flawed Democratic playbook and had allowed rampant spending that decimated the economy. He did not mention the governor had been in office less than two years and had inherited a mess from the former Republican governor. Tumblin also slammed Blaze and his party for not publicly disclosing the leaked documents themselves. So much for incumbent transparency.

Blaze's opponent, Candy Turner, was running with the story as well. She made it sound as if Blaze himself and his wild spending sprees had directly caused California's bankruptcy.

Jill finished her coffee, left the paper and returned to Julie's apartment. Sitting at the dining room table in the light of the rising sun, she opened her laptop and checked her email. There was a lot of spam and two messages from Tyler. The first was personal, reminding her not to turn off her computer. She sent him a reply. "It won't happen again. Love Mom." She did not mention she was in New York.

The second was a notice of a blog update. He now had twenty thousand readers and there were twenty-seven pages of comments on his latest blog. He was getting notice.

She read the blog. The theme was the value of state banks, such as the one in North Dakota, which he had mentioned in La Fleur before he and his father were poisoned. She learned that in 1919, the state had chartered the bank to serve the people and local businesses. All state deposits went to the bank and all state obligations were paid from the bank. It was non-profit, and all excess proceeds went to the state. Because the bank received interest on its deposits, it was able to make low interest loans to worthy borrowers. And, because it was a bank, it got to create money through the fractional reserve, but it did not charge itself interest when doing so.

The results had been outstanding. North Dakota was the only state that didn't have a real estate bust in 2008. It had the lowest unemployment in the country and the lowest number of foreclosures. The bank hadn't made stupid mortgage loans. It hadn't invested wildly on Wall Street, hadn't invested in CDOs, interest rate swaps and God only knows what else. It hadn't lost state pensions. And it was solvent, in the black, and debt free. The bank had been running a surplus for years, which it returned annually to the state to fund projects, salaries and improvements. Because it was a state bank, it paid no state tax and no federal income tax on its proceeds. The bank was like a mini Federal Reserve.

Contrast that with a bankrupt state like Vermont. In Vermont, the state deposits were put in a national bank that was headquartered on Wall Street. Sure, the bank paid interest on its deposits, but the interest it charged on loaned money was much higher. At the moment, the small state of Vermont paid four hundred and fifty million dollars every year on interest, an amount which exceeded the annual deficit of the state.

To get on their feet, all states had to do was charter a state bank that could create money without creating interest. Then the money that would otherwise go to Wall Street as interest could go to the state. Spending wasn't the problem, no matter how much elected officials wanted you to believe that. The problem was an atrocious economic policy that allowed banks to create money and charge interest on it.

Jill read to the end, her outrage growing. She saw Denny Drake liked the blog and had given it a thumbs-up and Jill clicked on the button to indicate that she liked it too. Then she settled down to the work at hand.

She got out a notebook and planned her investigation. She decided to start at the police station and interview the officers who had responded to the 911 call the night of the accident. She would compare the police report to the FBI report. Tyler had already noted one discrepancy. If she couldn't get the FBI interested, perhaps the police would take notice.

She scrolled down her email list looking for the FBI report that Blaze had forwarded to her. She couldn't find it and reviewed her messages more slowly. When had she read it? Monday? Tuesday? She highlighted each message, but it wasn't there. She noticed other emails were missing as well, mostly personal messages from Tyler, Alexandria and Blaze. Gone too was the photo taken with Denny Drake that she'd emailed herself from her phone. Despite her awful looking hair, it was one of the best pictures she'd ever taken. At least it was still on her phone.

She leaned back in the hard chrome chair and exhaled slowly. Her email had been hacked. They were not only watching Tyler, they were watching her.

She closed the laptop and went to the great north window in the dining room that overlooked Broadway and stared out. She had let down her guard. They could be watching her now, staring through any glass window and following her every move. She had to be more careful.

She grabbed her notebook and jotted down what she remembered of the FBI report. There hadn't been much. The car was white. Tyler had no money, no wallet, no ID, and a broken phone. There was no mention of the missing SIM card or the missing Nike shoe. He was left in the gutter near the intersection of Gold Street and John just after 9:00 P.M. It took ten minutes to get him to the hospital.

Jill used the Maps app on her phone and typed in the street names and police station. The closest station to Gold Street was the Fifth Precinct on Elizabeth. Jill called a cab and grabbed her purse.

Downstairs, the lobby was empty except for the doorman. She stood at the front window waiting for the cab. It was the start of the work day and the sidewalks were crowded. She didn't see anyone lurking in the shadows.

The cab came, and no surprise, the disheveled cabbie was familiar with the police station. They drove east, with no sign of the sun. It was a gray, cold day with building clouds. According to a bank temperature gauge, it was forty-five degrees, cooler here than in D.C. On the last week of October, the leaves were at their height of color.

They drove a few blocks and reached Chinatown where the sidewalks bustled with Orientals and the red brick buildings had outdoor fire escapes. The store signs were written in a mixture of English and Chinese, with wares displayed on the sidewalk. The recession had hit hard here, and many stores were boarded up and sprayed with graffiti. Recovery from the 2008 housing meltdown had been slower than anyone forecast and real estate was still at rock bottom, a bottom that was getting lower with each succeeding year.

The cabbie pulled over to the curb behind a police car. The station was a white four-story building with darkened windows that housed protruding air conditioners. A police van pulled in behind them. A line of small motor bikes leaned against the side of the building. From an upper level, a large American flag blew in the breeze. Jill paid the cabbie and got out.

Inside the lobby there was an information booth and she stood at the end of a long line. When it was her turn at the window, she asked to see a police report.

"File number?"

"I'm not sure. It was a hit-and-run a week ago Thursday."

"You?" The officer looked at her. He was Chinese with a high, sing-songy voice.

"Not me, my son. Tyler Madison."

The office typed at a keyboard for a moment and then looked up. "The investigation is ongoing. The report is not available to the general public."

"I'm not the general public. I'm the victim's mother. I've already seen the FBI report." Jill leaned on the counter. The man was beyond a pane of glass. "He was left in the gutter."

The officer looked at her. "I'm sorry, but I can't help you. Next?"

Jill didn't move. "Please, can you tell me the police officer on the case?"

"Lucien Lee, but he's not in today."

"Tomorrow?"

"Early shift. Next?"

Jill left the station and threaded her way past a group of policemen. She would come back tomorrow, early.

On foot she headed for Fulton subway station, where Tyler had disembarked from the subway that Thursday night. Although ten days had passed since the accident and she doubted any evidence would remain, she wanted to see the crime scene for herself. She would retrace Tyler's steps.

According to the Maps app, PrintPro, where Tyler had his flyers printed, was off Maiden Lane. She walked down William Street facing traffic, occasionally glancing over her shoulder. She stopped to gaze in store front windows and watched the street through the reflection in the glass. Nothing seemed untoward. Someone may have hacked into her email, but no one seemed to be following her.

William was a one-way street, as were most streets in the neighborhood. The street was bordered by tall office buildings and the sidewalks were packed with pedestrians. Lone, forlorn looking trees in concrete casings were spaced along the sidewalk. If the sun had been shining, which it wasn't, she doubted that any sunlight would reach the trees.

She got to Maiden Lane and turned left, still walking facing traffic. Gold Street was one block over and she turned left again. The cars were still coming at her. Gold was also one way. There was no parking allowed on the street.

PrintPro was near the corner. It was a small shop with a sign in the window indicating it was open six days a week, from nine until nine.

Jill went in. A young college-aged girl with pigtails was working a photocopier. According to her nametag, she was Gail. "Can I help you?"

"My son was hit by a car up the street."

Gail winced. "Sorry."

"It was a week ago. Thursday night about nine. He came here to pick up flyers."

"I don't work Thursday nights." Gail was pretty with dark hair and blue eyes.

"I wondered if you knew when he picked up his order." Jill would verify his recollection of the evening.

The girl left the copier and headed for the counter. She wore impossibly tight blue jeans cut low at the waist. A band of flat belly showed. "What's his name?"

"Tyler Madison."

The girl nodded as she typed at a keyboard. "Tyler. He placed the order online and I filled it for him. I printed out two thousand flyers." She looked up from her computer. "He got hit? Is he okay?"

"For now," Jill said, wishing Tyler would find a nice girl like Gail to occupy his time and distract him from activities that could get him killed.

"He organized a march against the Fed," Gail said. "I tried to go, but police turned me away. I never saw the flyers."

"Did he pick them up?"

Gail turned back to the computer. "On Thursday, October 16th, at 8.55 P.M. It was just before closing."

"How many boxes?"

"One carton," said the girl.

Which was what Tyler had said. There was nothing wrong with his memory.

"It was that size." Gail pointed to a row of boxes lined up against the wall.

The carton was the dimension of a ream of regular sized paper, the height of about five stacked on top of each other. It would have been awkward to run with, but Tyler had run two blocks before throwing it at the car. Jill wondered if the police knew what happened to it. She got out her notebook and made a note.

Jill thanked the girl and left the store and continued up Gold. The one-way street had two lanes of traffic and parking was forbidden. Tyler would have been easy to see with the curb clear of cars.

There was also no need for Tyler to have crossed the road. The Fulton subway station was to the left. He didn't need to cross the street, and even if he wasn't going to the station and he did cross the road, he would have been facing on-coming traffic. Even if the driver was drunk, even if he had no headlights, Tyler would have seen the car. Again, the facts supported his story. What Jill couldn't understand was how the car was chasing him if it was coming his way, driving towards him.

She passed a government building, a spa, and a pizza place, and reached John Street. He had been hit just past this intersection. The light was yellow and she didn't race it. John Street was also one way, heading east. To her right and down the street she saw Habitat for Humanity. To her left and set off the road was Park Tower, framed by a diagonal expanse of grass, a mix of tall trees, low lying shrubs, a few park benches, and what looked like homeless people.

Oh no! An elderly and dirty lady with a shopping cart was determinedly coming her way. Jill averted her eyes, stared at the "No Walking" sign and willed it to change. She heard the rickety wheels of the cart coming closer and smelled the woman's presence beside her. The light changed and Jill advanced, the wheels of the cart clicking behind her.

Across the road, the lady caught up with her, running over Jill's heels with the cart. Jill stopped and turned. The old lady smiled, showing perfect white teeth. Jill shoved her hands in her pocket looking for change.

And then she saw it. The homeless lady wore a long oversized coat that came to her ankles. She wore no socks and her shoes were mismatched. She wore a red lace up boot-type sneaker on her right foot, and there on her left foot, an enormous green Nike. Tyler's missing size 12 shoe.

Jill stepped to the side, opening her purse. She pulled out her wallet and a fifty dollar bill. "Can I ask you a few questions?"

The bag lady's eyes were wide open and on the money. In close range, she didn't look that old. She was middle-aged, younger than Jill. Her skin was unlined, but her pallor was gray. She had long dirty blond hair that looked wet with grease.

"My son was hit by a car here ten days ago on a Thursday night. Around nine o'clock. I wonder if you saw anything?"

The bag lady was staring at the money and Jill slipped her hands in her pockets. "He's only twenty-four. My youngest son. Well, my youngest child now. I had a younger daughter but she died three years ago. Leukemia." Jill moved quickly on. "He's tall." She raised her free hand in the air and marked his height. "He's thin. He doesn't eat much and doesn't have much money. He was carrying a carton. He remembers running."

"He made it?"

Jill's skin broke out in goosebumps. Here was an eye-witness. Jill had to be careful not to say or do anything that would scare the witness away. "He was hospitalized. He had a concussion. He lost a shoe." Jill pointed to the woman's foot. "I think that's it."

The bag lady looked alarmed, as if she might flee.

"It's okay. You can keep it. I'll bring you the other one. Here, take this." Jill thrust the fifty dollar bill at the lady and it quickly disappeared down the front fold of her coat.

"He was running all right," the lady said. "Running fast. He was carrying a box on his hip. Two men were chasing him."

She had seen everything. Here was the proof Jill needed. The FBI would have to act. "Then what happened?" Jill asked breathlessly.

"Besides the men, there was a car. It came up John Street." She pointed to her right.

"Wait," Jill said. "The car was going the wrong way on the one-way street?"

The lady nodded. "Then it turned right on Gold, also going the wrong way. One man chasing your son was about ten yards behind him by then. The other man hadn't made it to the intersection. The car made the corner and rode up on the curb. Your son threw the box at the car and ran into the road. The car hit him from behind and threw him forward. I heard the slam as he hit the ground."

Jill didn't know what to say, but the lady kept talking.

"Then the car reversed. The first man picked up the box and got into the car. It backed up onto John Street and drove away the right way."

"What color was the car? Could you see it?"

"I could see it fine. It was black with black windows. It looked like an undercover cop car to me. Law enforcement. The type you don't want to see when you're speeding on the highway."

So the observant and well-spoken bag lady likely once had a car and had sped on the highway.

"Then the second man came," the lady said. "He was tall and thin and wore a navy sweatshirt with a hood. He bent over your son and took his pulse." The lady held up two fingers to the side of her neck. "He pulled out a phone and a couple of minutes later the cops came and then an ambulance."

"Did you tell this to the police?"

"Are you serious?"

"Where did you find his shoe?" Jill asked.

"On the sidewalk in front of the park." She pointed toward the grassy square. "I didn't know it was his."

"You've been a great help," Jill said. "Thank you, thank you very much."

"I'm glad your son's okay. Is he in trouble with the police?"

"I don't know."

"What's his name?"

"Tyler. What's your name?"

"Vivienne. It's been a long time since anyone asked."

Jill shook her hand. It was warm, a firm solid grip. "Thanks again for your help." She pointed to the Nike. "I'll bring you the other shoe tomorrow."

She left the lady with her shopping cart and went on, walking past the curb where Tyler was hit. In the gutter she saw an empty water bottle, a dirty plastic grocery bag, and a red blotchy stain. She kept going, not wanting to see what was likely her son's blood.

***

Jill wandered down the street, reviewing the conversation in her mind. Her phone rang and she was startled. Julie was calling. "Where are you?"

"I might ask you the same thing," Jill said.

"I just got off the phone with Blaze. He said you're here. He wants you to go home. He's in the hospital and says you abandoned him."

"He's fine," Jill said.

"Tell *him* that. I promised I'd talk some sense into you. Meet me for lunch. It's been one hell of a morning. The market closed at eleven to stop the free-fall and on top of that we've got a computer virus. The IT guys ordered everyone off-line. I'm heading for the tavern, meet me there." Then Julie sucked in air as if she'd made a mistake.

"It's fine. I can go to the tavern."

In her drinking days, Jill and her sister had sat through many long, liquid lunches. There were times when Christophe, Julie's former butler, had to be called to help them home. More than once Jill's public inebriation ended up in the tabloids with headlines like: 'Senator's Spouse Lets Loose,' and 'Jill Madison Smashed by Noon'. The pictures were eerily similar, bleary unfocused eyes and the smile of an intoxicated fool. Jill shuddered to think of those days and wondered how Denny Drake knew she had quit drinking. Her sobriety had not made as much of a stir as her drunken antics.

The wind blew against her as she went down Broadway toward the tavern. If Julie wanted to talk some sense into her, she planned to talk some sense into Julie. Her sister held a lot of sway with Blaze. He was impressed by her job, her bank account, her Jaguar, and especially her windowed apartment with its glass ceiling that showed the sky. If Jill could get Julie to see her side of the story, she would talk to Blaze, break through his denial and get him to see that Tyler was in danger and do something about it. And Julie would see the truth, her logic was flawless; she was the smart one who had scored perfect on the math SAT. Blaze would listen to her and take her seriously.

Julie's firm was on Wall Street and the tavern was on Pearl Street around the corner from her office. The bar was small and dark and always crowded, no matter what time of day. Jill blinked in the dark light, then saw Julie waving from a tiny table for two by the front window. She wasn't alone.

Jill approached the table. A good looking man of about thirty glanced up.

"Michael was just leaving," Julie said. A wide margarita goblet rimmed with salt sat before her and she picked it up and took a long sip. She looked imposing in a tailored black business suit with gold buttons.

Michael stood up. "I'll call you."

Julie ignored this. "Sis," she said enthusiastically, lifting up her arms. "I can't believe you're here. You look great by the way. Love the hair."

Jill bent down and hugged her. The subtle scent of floral musk and the not so subtle aroma of tequila assailed her. She sunk into the warmed leather armchair. "Who's the guy?"

Julie brushed him away with a wave. "Old."

Old for her could mean five minutes ago or five years. Jill said, "I called you a hundred times. Why didn't you call me back?"

"I didn't think it was important."

"I left you five voice messages."

"I didn't listen to them. I've been busy. Out of town. Vegas." Julie played with her diamond necklace. "After Vermont's scare and the crash last week, and days of placating clients, S-G chartered a plane and rented a floor for us at Caesar's Palace so we could kick back, gamble and screw. We went for the weekend. It was rather untimely." She took another slug of her drink. "When we left, the market was supposed to rally and regain what it lost, only now there's California. I'm losing millions. And that's for the company. I'm not talking about my clients."

"Aren't they one and the same?"

"Don't be stupid. The company is concerned about shareholder profits. My clients, about their own profits. One is often at the expense of the other." She sipped her drink. "Don't look so shocked. It's all legal. Christ, you're lucky you don't have to work for a living."

A waiter came, dressed in tight black pants and a button-down black shirt, the uniform of the wait staff. "I've already ordered lunch," Julie said. "A Texas grilled cheese. We can split it. Get a drink. I didn't know what you'd want." Her sister could be so bossy.

The waiter beamed down at Julie. "Is this your twin?"

Julie smiled. "That's my sister. My shorter sister. My younger sister."

The waiter, Patrick, took Jill's order. The margarita looked good. Jill could almost taste the punch of liquor in her throat, the warm burning in her gut, the salt on her lips. Then the memory of the tabloid photos came back. "I'll have tonic water."

"My sister doesn't drink," Julie said. She unabashedly watched him leave. "Isn't he a doll?"

"Yes," Jill said. "I'm staying at your house. I hope you don't mind."

"Fine. Great. But why leave Blaze when he's sick?"

Jill leaned forward across the small, dark wood table and whispered, "Tyler's in trouble."

"Blaze said you're paranoid. He thinks you should go back to the shrink."

Jill felt a heat flush her body. Blaze had already got to Julie.

Patrick was back, stealthily placing a tall thin glass on a coaster before wordlessly retreating.

"I don't need a shrink," Jill said. "Tyler's accident was no accident. There's an eye-witness. He was run down. Two men were after him." She picked up the glass and took a sip. The ice cubes clinked. It should have had gin. "He recognized one of the men. He's FBI. He worked for us ten years ago after Blaze had the death threat."

"That tall, sexy, dark-haired guy with the great eyebrows and dimples who walked with a swagger?"

"That guy," Jill said. "Jared Slater."

"He's a gentleman. He wouldn't do it."

"Tyler saw him at the scene."

"Before he blacked out in a coma, and as I recall, forgot everything about the accident."

"The eye-witness confirmed what he remembered."

"Who is this eye-witness?"

"Well, a bag lady. Her name is Vivienne." As if having a name gave her more credibility.

"She wasn't swigging from a whiskey bottle, was she?" Julie said, as she swilled her margarita.

"No, she wasn't."

"Did you pay her?"

Jill put down her glass and looked out the window. "Only fifty."

"Fifty cents? You cheap bitch."

Jill glanced at her sister. "Fifty dollars."

Julie laughed. "She would have told you anything you wanted to hear for that." She shook her head. "You can't explain away the fact that Blaze was poisoned."

"Because he ate Tyler's fish," Jill said. "Tyler got sick too."

"But Blaze's plate was contaminated."

It was apparent her sister and husband had had a lengthy conversation. Jill glanced at the bar. There was a stand up wooden counter with a brass shoe rod running its length. People standing there were shoulder to shoulder, though it was not yet noon. The bartender was busy, tipping bottles, pouring drafts. Patrick was teasing pickles out of a jar. Jill looked back at her sister. "Our house was broken into. Tyler's computer was stolen."

But Julie knew this too. "So was yours, as well as Blaze's. But the contents of *his* computer were leaked and someone aggressively smashed *his* monitor."

Jill leaned forward. "They were after Tyler's computer. He's right about the Fed. It's bankrupting the country; it's the cause of our debt. It only gets away with it because no one knows what it's doing. It wouldn't appreciate Tyler exposing its tricks. If it didn't run him over, it hired someone who did."

Julie reached for her glass. "Blaze is right. You're absolutely bonkers. The Federal Reserve Board is not in the business of murder. Would you listen to yourself?"

"Julie, you have an MBA. You must see what the Fed is doing to the country. In a debt based economy there's never enough money, just debt."

Gripping her glass, Julie fixed Jill with an icy stare. "You're right. *I* have an MBA, not you. That makes *me* the expert, not you." She leaned forward and said in a low voice, "So shut the fuck up. You don't know what you're talking about."

Jill turned back to the window and faced the despair of the gray day.

Julie guzzled her drink and put it down. "I'm trying to help you. Really, go back to the shrink. If you don't like him, find someone new. I'll find you someone if you want."

Jill exhaled loudly. "My therapist is fine."

"Go home. Blaze needs you."

Patrick was back with a plate of food and put it in front of Julie. He gave Jill an empty plate. "Anything else, ladies?"

Julie ordered another margarita and divided the food. She passed Jill half a golden grilled cheese sandwich on rye, half a dill pickle and a handful of potato chips. Jill took a bite of the sandwich and strings of Swiss cheese pulled away with the bread. She took a sip of her drink and wished it was stronger.

"He feels like you take him for granted," Julie said.

Jill put down her glass. "He told you that?"

"Not in so many words. But it's what he thinks."

"Well he's wrong. You're wrong."

"If you want my advice," said Julie, whose longest relationship had lasted all of a month, "leave Tyler to get on with his life and go home. There's a week before the election and Blaze needs you. Let Tyler go. Cut those apron strings. You baby him and he'll never grow up. Stop listening to him. He's no expert on the economy. God only knows what crank or crackpot he listens to. He doesn't know what he's talking about. Go to Austin and stand beside that bitch Rebecca and smile. You make things too easy for her."

Jill just looked at her sister. Julie might not have much experience in relationships, but she knew instinctively what Jill had never told her and what Blaze couldn't see.

"If he leaves, you'll have nothing," Julie said. "That's what she wants."

Jill heard the unspoken words: fifty years old, grown children, no husband, no money, and no job.

"Go home," Julie said. She took another bite of her sandwich as her phone buzzed. Her secretary was calling. Julie listened and then put down the phone. "We're back online. The problem's fixed. We've got the best computer jocks in the world." Julie patted her lips with her napkin. "I've got to get back, see how many millions I lost over lunch."

She threw the napkin on the table and sashayed from the tavern, with more than one man watching her go. And then Patrick was back with Julie's margarita. He put it on the table beside the other one that was not yet empty and left without a word.

Jill finished her sandwich, eyeing the margarita and wondering if she could leave the bar without drinking it.

12

Jill paid the bill and left the tavern with the margaritas sitting on the table untouched. Out in the fresh air, in a crowd of white collar workers on their way to or from lunch, she called Blaze. She was vindicated, she had proof, forget about the poisoning, an eye-witness had seen the black vehicle with dark tinted windows that ran Tyler over. Once they started looking for the right colored car, the FBI might actually find out who was responsible. And if the FBI were involved, an eye-witness might give them pause, a reason to step back and leave Senator Blaze Madison's son alone.

Blaze's cell phone rang and rang and went to voice mail. Jill called his office and got Betty, who said he was busy and would see if he had a minute. Looking for quiet, Jill ducked into a bus shelter and sat down on the bench. An ad on one side of the shelter promised the smooth taste of vodka, an ad on the other, refreshing cold beer. Jill stared ahead at the street and the cars inching past. She waited five minutes and finally Blaze came on the line.

"Can you resend the email with the FBI report? I found an eye-witness to Tyler's accident. I was –"

He interrupted her. "I don't have time for this. The economy's in freefall."

A black teen with dreadlocks and low hanging jeans that dragged on the ground ambled down the sidewalk. He entered the bus shelter and plopped himself down on the bench beside Jill, placing himself between her and the exit. He couldn't be following her, he wouldn't be that obvious. She shifted her weight away from him.

"The car that hit Tyler was black. In the FBI report, it was white. That proves –"

He didn't let her finish. "It proves nothing more than a mistake. Let the FBI investigate. For god's sake, just come home. I'm getting slammed. Somehow, the California crisis has become my fault. If my emails weren't leaked, none of this would have come out, and the market wouldn't be crashing, which is the last thing we need the week before the election."

"You didn't leak anything. California isn't in this mess because of over-spending. It has to pay interest on loans that it shouldn't have to pay."

Blaze sighed loudly. "Okay, I'll announce that everyone should just read Tyler's blog. Problem solved."

A bus stopped in front of the shelter, coughing black exhaust. The kid left the shelter and hopped on the bus.

"I'm leaving for Austin in an hour," Blaze said into the silence.

Jill felt her body tense. "Becca making soup?"

"At least someone cares about my well-being."

Jill closed her eyes while the words ran around her brain. Finally she said, "You're not going to do anything to help Tyler?"

"I am. I'm going to get out of the way and let the FBI do their job. I've got to go." He hung up.

Jill slowly closed her phone. This was what always happened. It was his M.O. He used Rebecca as a threat. Usually Jill would yield, give in, acquiesce, and do whatever he wanted to keep him away from his ex-wife who was always waiting. Jill left the shelter, mulling this over, when her phone rang. Her heart leapt, thinking it was Blaze calling back, but it was her son.

"Hey Mom, I got the photo."

"You got into the V-Comm server?" Jill asked cautiously.

He didn't answer her question. "My file wasn't corrupt. I got everything. I'll email you the photo."

"Don't. I think someone's hacked into my email. Messages are missing. Like the one your father sent with the FBI report."

There was a pause. Then Tyler said, "Are you in New York?"

She looked around. A black stretch limo three car lengths long went slowly past. "Maybe. How do you know where I am?"

"I can see the tower where the call is being routed. You're in Greenwich. You just talked to Dad. What are you doing here?"

Jill watched a dog walker with eight dogs of various sizes and colors go by. The dogs were well behaved, not pulling in all directions, but walking forward as if on a mission. "I came to see Julie. I found an eye-witness to your accident. She confirmed that the car that ran you down was black."

"Mom, don't say anything more, okay."

Jill was about to ask if her phone was bugged, but she stopped herself.

"Can you come over?" he said.

She said she'd be there in thirty minutes and asked if he wanted lunch and he did. She called ahead to the Big Tomato, a good pizza joint on Broadway and ordered an extra-large with tomatoes, onions, pineapple, green pepper, jalapeños and extra cheese. She hailed a cab and they stopped enroute to get the pizza.

Up on the top floor of the crumbling house, Tyler's door was wide open and two friends were visiting. They were all sitting at the small table in front of the window typing at laptops. The blind was down, the room was dark. It was a mess, with clothes and papers everywhere. The gray kitten came out from under the bed and hopped across the floor, rubbing against Jill's leg.

Tyler jumped up, bounded across the room, took the pizza, and kissed her cheek. "Did you do something with your hair?"

"I got it cut."

"Oh." She followed him across the room and he made introductions. "Mom, you remember Ali. And this is David."

Ali nodded and she shook hands with David, the friend who was recently shot and had called Alexandria for help. Like Ali, he was older than Tyler and looked about thirty. David was short and slight, probably five-seven. He had long, thin, straight, bright blond hair, the color of corn. His eyes were green and his nose, long and sharp. He was effeminate looking, with small delicate fingers and thin wrists. He seemed to be filled with nervous energy and drummed his fingers on the table, and shook his foot. He wore flip-flops, despite the season, revealing dainty white feet. He looked vaguely familiar. She wondered if he was the older brother of a high school friend of Tyler's. He was looking at her as curiously as she was looking at him.

Tyler cleared a space on the table for the pizza. He opened the box and offered Jill his chair. He took his slice and sat on the unmade bed and started eating.

They ate as if they hadn't eaten in days. Incredibly, Ali ate with one hand and worked the keyboard of his laptop with the other. No one spoke as the pizza disappeared. She was disheartened that these software computer jocks couldn't find jobs.

David threw down a crust and wiped his hands on his shirt. He wagged his finger at her. "I know where I know you from."

"Tyler's high school?"

The kitten leapt up on the table, grabbed the crust and took it to the bed and began chewing.

David tapped his slim fingers on the table. "You were at the hospital last week, pulling a little black suitcase. You were picked up by a Jag."

Jill remembered the three men at the hospital asking her to hold the door. The middle man had been shot and was bleeding heavily, his arms draped over the other two. His head was hanging down, long bright blond hair covering his face.

David patted a place below his shoulder. "Lucky it was just a flesh wound, but it had to be cleaned, or it would have been infected. So, thank you."

Jill nodded, and wondered if he had thanked Alexandria, but kept her mouth shut.

He turned his laptop in her direction. "You say someone hacked into your email?"

"I think so."

"Is this your file?"

She leaned closer. Those were her emails. She nodded. "How did you get them?"

"Your password, Mom," Tyler said. "Margo? Pet names are the most common passwords. Anybody who knew you, us, would go there first."

Ali said something that Jill didn't understand and Tyler asked for her phone and passed it to him. Ali stopped typing, unscrewed the phone and removed the battery and the SIM card. He ran his finger over the circuitry, re-inserted the battery and slapped the phone back together. He said something else and Tyler returned her phone.

"It's not bugged," Tyler said. "There's no tracking device."

Ali picked up a piece of pizza and his laptop, said something else incomprehensible, and left the room. Tyler wiped his hands on his jeans, then rifled through a stack of papers. He came up with a black and white photograph. "Here's the photo."

The kitty leapt on the table as if to take a look too. Tyler picked her up and stroked her head. The kitty mewed with pleasure as Jill studied the photograph.

It showed a tall, good-looking man leaning against a maple tree in full foliage. He was clean-shaven and wore a dark hooded sweatshirt with the hood up. It shadowed his face and hid what was likely a military hair cut. He had a jutting chin, wide lips, high cheek bones and a protruding forehead. His eyes were round and deep-set, and the eyebrows arched, as if they had been waxed. There were dimples on his chin and both cheeks.

Jill recognized Jared Slater immediately. "That's him," she said. "Can I have it?"

"What are you going to do with it?"

"Take it to the police."

"They won't care, Mom."

"They'll have to, now there's an eye-witness," Jill said. "A lady saw everything. It was just as you said. The car chased you down the street. It was black with tinted windows. It was going the wrong way. It went up on the curb and forced you into the road and ran you over. Two men were chasing you, one had a hood." Jill tapped the photograph. "They took the carton with the flyers. That proves the hit-and-run was connected to your march."

David had been listening intently. "I wouldn't go to the police," he said quietly.

Jill looked at him sharply.

He visibly shrunk back. "They're rarely helpful." He gazed at his laptop. "I changed your password and emailed it to you. No one will be able to hack in again."

"Thank you."

He closed the file and smiled at her.

A strong breeze blew, lifting the blind over the table. For a moment there was fresh air and light, before the blind fell again.

"I think the police can help," Jill said. "At least, they'll push the FBI to investigate. Maybe if they look for the right colored car, they'll find it. Get whoever did this off the street so it won't happen again."

"And if it was the FBI?" Tyler said.

"They might be more cautious if they know the police are watching."

Tyler and David looked at each other. Tyler shook his head. "Just leave it, Mom. It's over."

Jill didn't say anything, but it was far from over. Like it or not, she was going to press on. But they didn't have to know. She asked about the upcoming protest. "How is the planning for the march going?"

"It's a rally," David said.

"We've invited Denny Drake," Tyler added.

"Wow," Jill said. "Will he go?"

"It depends," Tyler said. "We're going to protest the Fed, but the big problem is that most people don't know about it. Denny gets it, but he's hesitant to talk about it because as soon as he mentions our lame economic policy, he'll be labeled a flake."

"We're going to try to educate people," David said. "If we make it personal and people get it, Denny will come."

Tyler opened his laptop, tapped a few keys and pulled up his blog. The subject was 'Booms and Busts'. "This explains how we ended up in this mess, thanks to the Fed."

Jill got out her reading glasses and pulled the laptop toward her. She read that depressions, recessions and high times were all responses to the Fed's manipulation of the money supply. Whenever the Fed had a printing party, there was a boom, with lots of free, cheap, easy money floating around. People were borrowing, banks were loaning, and thanks to the magic of the fractional reserve, banks were creating money. The price of everything went up. Not only because the money was worth less thanks to inflation, but because production didn't increase, there were too many dollars chasing a limited supply of goods, which drove prices up.

When there was too much inflation, the Fed would come in and impose a correction. If too much money was the problem, money was removed. Instead of selling government bonds, bills and notes, the Fed bought them, thereby taking money out of circulation. Most diabolically, at the same time it contracted the money supply, it raised interest rates, making money more valuable. People and businesses were no longer so eager to borrow. Unemployment went up and the risk of loan defaults increased. Now, banks were loath to lend. The overall effect was a tightened money supply with fewer dollars in circulation.

Jill realized this was how that central banker Biddle had crashed the economy, which led to President Jackson's censure. Biddle had stopped lending and called in loans to contract the money supply and cause a bust. Now she read the Fed did the same thing in the years just prior to the Great Depression by removing one-third of the total money supply from circulation.

According to the blog, it happened just before the 2008 housing crisis, when the Fed first raised interest rates. Those with sub-prime mortgages with high floating interest rates were screwed. After the crash, the loss of home equity was three trillion dollars. Real money lost on the stock market was seven trillion. The result was a huge contraction of the money supply.

To counteract the loss, the Fed started printing money. It loaned money to the banks for next to nothing in an attempt to get money back into circulation. Only the banks wouldn't lend the cheap money to Main Street. They made more of a profit lending to the government and investing on Wall Street.

Hence, a recovery without jobs. There was a lot of money available and the stock market was skyrocketing, but the banks had it. With so much printing, the dollar was losing value and prices were rising, while wages were stagnant, social programs were being cut, and unemployment and pension benefits were being slashed. People were poor, all thanks to the Fed, which stood back and pretended it had nothing to do with any of it.

Jill reached the end and Tyler was watching her closely. She looked at him. It was news to her that the Fed caused the Great Depression. "I thought it was the stock market crash."

Tyler shook his head. "Contracting the money supply made the market crash."

It made sense to Jill. When you had no money you were poor and couldn't spend. When you had lots of money, you felt rich and could afford to buy.

"Denny gave us his data base," Tyler said. "Now we don't have to wait for people to find us, we can go to his supporters directly."

Apparently that wasn't all they were doing. The kids were now also helping Denny with his polls.

"We're also emailing questionnaires and analyzing responses," David said proudly.

Tyler showed Jill a sample questionnaire. There were demographic questions, asking age, residence, occupation, and political affiliation. Then, how likely it was that you were going to vote, who you voted for in the last election, and who you were likely to vote for in this election. You were asked to rank your four top picks out of the field of eighteen presidential candidates. Denny's name was listed at the bottom. Then there were ten priorities you were asked to rank in terms of importance and they included: End the Fed, Wall Street reform, campaign reform, universal health care, tax reform, environmental protection, education, technology and computing innovation, foreign policy reform, and military intervention.

"We list the Fed first, but it always comes back ranked at the bottom," Tyler complained. "People just don't see the harm it causes."

"We'll be able to monitor how effective our mission against the Fed is going," David said. "We want "End the Fed" to be the number one priority."

"Then Denny will come to the rally," Tyler said.

Besides contacting supporters and polling, the kids were also fundraising. Along with the blog and questionnaires, they were asking for money. They needed a sound system for their rally, and wanted to buy t-shirts and baseball caps."

"How much money do you have?" Jill asked.

The kids looked at each other. "Sixty dollars," Tyler finally said. "We each pitched in twenty."

"Here." Jill gave them a hundred dollar bill. "You don't have a lot of time to fundraise," she said, "not with the election a week away."

That wasn't news to them. They had to get back to work. The kitten stretched out across the table and Jill left them in the dark, messy room, bent over their laptops.

***

That night, following a day where the Dow Jones lost over five hundred points, Charles sat at the dining room table polishing silver, while Julie was glued to Money, the cable station dedicated to following the ups and downs of the U.S. economy. Tonight, after her wild weekend, she was on the wagon, which for her meant she was only drinking wine and not hard liquor.

Dinner was over and they were in the living room. Clutching her wine glass, Julie leaned forward on the living room sofa, eyes fixed on the tube. Realizing the seriousness of the situation, Congress and the President put politics aside and for once had not dithered. Both houses immediately passed resolutions promising to bail out California and provide whatever aid was necessary to keep the state from going broke. Market watchers agreed: prepare for a rally and an opportunity to regain what had been lost.

The California governor looked weary as he faced the cameras and maintained that all was well. California's fiscal crisis was no grimmer than usual. He was confident that Moody's and Fitch would keep the state's credit rating unchanged. He thanked Congress for their support.

The Speaker of the House had reached out to the Fed chairman for help. He asked the chairman to address Congress and discuss ways to assist troubled states. Again, the chairman politely demurred. There was nothing he could do. He praised Congress for quickly agreeing to a bailout. He was leaving taxpayers on the hook.

Even Rich Tumblin praised the President and Congress for acting so quickly. "Some times you have to put politics aside for the good of the country," he said, before adding in a back-handed stab, "too bad the President didn't learn this sooner."

The station cut to an ad and there was Denny Drake, in what must have been his first TV commercial. Standing on a mound of dirt on a brown and barren farm, he announced, "I'm Denny Drake and I'm running for president."

The camera moved in for a close-up and Drake's head filled the screen. "Like most of you, I'm looking at the current economic crisis and wondering where it will end. Why won't the government and Wall Street address the real source of the crisis? The problem with state and local governments is they lost their pension funds. They made what they were told were safe bets on Wall Street, only the bets weren't safe. Although the pension funds were lost, pensions still have to be paid. The money has to come from somewhere. State and local governments didn't spend their way into this mess. That's blatantly untrue. This is Wall Street's mess.

"Why wasn't Wall Street held accountable? Because Wall Street runs the government. Wall Street buys elections. Then Wall Street elects its friends and Washington does what Wall Street wants. We no longer have a government for the people. We have a government for big business.

"There is an alternative vote in this election. I have not taken one cent from any corporation. Not one cent from any bank. I am not beholden to anyone but the common people. If elected, I will represent the people. I will bail out the people. Every home-owning taxpayer will see a ten thousand dollar rebate in compensation for their housing losses. In 2008, your government had a choice. To help the people or help the banks. We know what choice was made. It's time government worked for you."

The camera panned out, only now the background was verdant; lush and green. "I'm Denny Drake and I approve this message."

"Would you fucking look at him," Julie said, as she poured herself more wine. "As if that's what we need at the moment, some stoned hippy pointing a finger of blame and dredging up ancient history. What are we supposed to do? Bail out the country? Hey, we weren't the ones who let government employees retire at fifty-five with sweet pensions. That has nothing to do with us. And a ten thousand dollar give-away? He's trying to buy the election."

In another commercial, Drake made his case for state banks. "What California doesn't need is a bailout. It needs a state bank. California doesn't need to pay interest to Wall Street banks for printing money. California doesn't need to borrow money! Let the state print its own money. Every state should follow the model of North Dakota, which is prosperous, booming, and running an annual profit."

Here was clear evidence of Tyler's influence and it sounded so reasonable Jill couldn't understand why every state didn't have its own central bank.

Julie, on the other hand, was incensed. "What a load of crap. If we had fifty state banks our economy would crash. They'd be printing money like crazy."

"Unlike the current banks?" Jill said.

"Stop talking about things you know nothing about."

"I know if I lend myself money, I don't pay interest on it."

"You don't have any money," Julie said. She held up her hand for silence so she could listen to the reaction of overseas markets. Hooray, futures were up. In celebration, Julie guzzled the last of her wine.

Charles, the enabler, came into the living room with a new bottle. "Shall I open this?"

"Please."

Then he could go, though he clearly wasn't happy about it.

The front door closed. Jill said, "Where did you find him?"

"I won him in a poker game."

Jill looked at her sister.

"Don't ask. I was fucked up. I really don't remember."

"So, what, he just appeared at your door one day?"

"Something like that."

"Did you check his references?"

"Hmm. Well ..."

"You didn't? You don't know who he is?"

"Of course I do. His name is Charles Grande. He's fifty-six. He comes from Surrey. He can drive, cook, clean, and iron. He's honest, he's got a cute accent, and he looks out for me. What else do I need to know? You have no idea how hard good help is to come by."

Jill could only shake her head. "He could be a spy. He listens to everything."

Julie threw back her wine. "Blaze is right. You are paranoid. Or maybe you're like Tyler. Or he's like you. You see conspiracies everywhere. Charles is just a fucking butler. Maybe the real problem is that he doesn't like you."

Jill blinked. "The fucking butler gets to have this opinion?"

Julie just laughed.

"I don't care what he thinks," Jill said. "I don't like him."

"He thinks you're too tight. I agree. You worry about everything."

Maybe because Jill didn't have the luxury of drinking a bottle of wine and a pitcher of martinis and getting loose. She could go down a long list of all that she had to worry about, but she had already gone through it for Julie and wasn't going to go through it again.

"He thinks you have too much time on your hands."

"Oh, he does."

"He's a modern man. He thinks women should work."

"I don't see a ring on his finger."

Julie tossed back her drink. Her eyes were glassy. "I mean, look at your life. I'd switch with you any day. You've got a wealthy husband, you don't have to work. You've got no stress, no boss, no clients, no one to answer to."

"Yep, that's me," Jill said, thinking about her children, the effort to be publicly perfect; losing her privacy, her own self, to be with Blaze.

"You garden, walk the dog, read books, watch news. Never leave home. Never do anything productive."

"I raised children," Jill said.

And Julie would give her that. "You're a good mother. You just don't know when to stop."

13

History records that the money changers have used every form of abuse, intrigue, deceit and violent means possible to maintain their control over governments ...

—President James Madison

TUESDAY OCTOBER 28

Tuesday morning, under a sky full of stars and no moon, Jill had breakfast with her sister, who had slept well and woke up excited. "It's going to be a great day on Wall Street," she predicted, as she watched overseas market news, ate toast and sipped espresso. "I have a feeling I'm going to make some serious cash."

Taking advantage of her good mood, Jill brought up Tyler's fund raising.

"Christ, what does he want money for?"

"The same old thing."

"End the Fed? I'd rather shoot myself than give money for that."

"He's planning a rally. He wants to rent a sound system, sell t-shirts and caps. Dennis Drake might go."

"Tyler should pay him to stay away. This country will never elect a president who smokes dope."

"He never said he smoked it."

"How much?"

"Excuse me?"

"How much does Tyler want?"

"Up to you. It's your money."

Julie grabbed her purse. Despite her shortcomings, she was generous, even for causes she didn't support. Although she was single, family meant a lot to her. She pulled out her checkbook. "I gather you can't make a donation?"

In the kitchen, Charles had his sleeves rolled up, hands plunged in streaming bubbles, washing dishes. Even with the water running, Jill guessed he listened to every word.

"It would get out. Look bad for Blaze. Supporting the opposition."

"You've got to get him to give you your own account."

"I don't need one."

Julie clicked open her pen. "You will if he leaves you. You'll be screwed."

"He's not leaving."

"I don't see why he stays."

Jill looked at her sister, mouth open.

"That goes for you too. I don't get marriage. How can you be with one person so long?"

"You don't have to worry you'll sleep alone."

"Who worries about that?" Julie began writing the check. "Should I make it out to you or Tyler?"

"He doesn't have an account."

"Fine. I'll write it out to you. Five thousand. Here you go." Julie scribbled across the check and ripped it out.

"You're a great aunt," Jill said.

"You got that right." Julie shrugged. "I'll write it off. I'll need something to offset my profits."

She went to shower and change for work, and Jill watched the morning news. The President was going to California to see the governor, a personal friend. With so many electoral votes at stake, it was a state the President could not afford to lose. The cameras showed the President in the rain heading for his helicopter. Behind a cordoned off square, a crowd of reporters thrust out microphones as he hurried by. The President stopped and made a statement.

He was certain California would survive the audit. Its credit rating would remain solid. Congress was standing by and money was available if it were needed. The President was certain that the stock market would recover.

He took a few questions. The first, to Jill's surprise, was about creating state banks.

"The country probably has enough banks already," the President said, with a smile. Despite the personnel from Wall Street in his office, he tried to portray himself as a foe of big business.

The President moved on, but the reporter went with him. "No, state banks that don't charge themselves interest to print money."

Jill sat forward on her chair. Denny was speaking out and Tyler's message was being heard.

But not by the President who ignored the question and pointed to another reporter.

"When can we expect Moody's report?"

"That's why I'm going. To get them to hurry." That was all the time he had. With a wave and a smile, the President jauntily jogged towards the waiting helicopter.

Blaze's popularity tended to mirror the President's and Jill went online to her husband's site for an update. On the home page, there was a large photograph of him at a campaign stop in San Antonio. There was a five minute video of the event sponsored by SAVE THE RIVER COALITION. Jill did not watch it. She was transfixed by the photograph. Rebecca Madison was onstage with Blaze, standing behind him, staring at him, her hands joined together as if in rapture.

Jill magnified the photograph, blowing up Rebecca to fill the screen. Rebecca wore a sleeveless black dress and was obviously working out and showing off her upper arms. Her jet black hair was pulled back tightly to reveal a prominent widow's peak. She was fifty-eight and had alabaster skin, like smooth, cold stone. She had painted bright red lips and heavily made-up eyes that bore into Blaze, unnoticed, as he addressed his people. Jill wondered what he saw in her, how he could have married her and had a child with her. His two wives couldn't be any more different. Julie was back and Jill closed the laptop. She knew Rebecca would be with him, but it was always a shock to see them together.

Charles hurried to the foyer wiping his hands on his slacks. Julie liked to leave the apartment at 6:45 A.M. sharp. He grabbed the car keys and an umbrella. A glance through the glass ceiling showed the stars of Gemini and Leo were gone and clouds were moving in.

Jill sat at the dining room table waving goodbye and trying to look undisturbed at what she had seen online. The door closed and Jill jumped up. In the old days, she would have fretted about the photograph for hours, but today she had things to do. She grabbed her purse and went to Julie's office to photocopy the photograph of Special Agent Jared Slater.

Julie had four desktop computers, two laptops, a big printer, and a bigger fax machine that doubled as a photocopier. Jill turned on the photocopier, opened the cover and placed the photograph face down. She hit the print button and the copier kicked into action. She heard a noise from behind and turned.

"Ah-ah hem." Charles, clearing his throat. "May I ask what you're doing in here?"

"Printing something."

"Did Miss Julie give her permission?"

"I don't need her permission."

"No one is allowed in this room," Charles said.

"Maybe not you," Jill said. He was overstepping his bounds. Julie wouldn't have a problem with this.

"I have no choice but to inform her."

"You do that." The copier had stopped. Jill pushed the print button again to make another copy. She turned around. Charles was still in the doorway. "Don't you have to take someone to work?"

"I have my eye on you." Charles raised his hand and pointed a V with his fingers from his eyes to hers.

Jill turned away, watching the second photocopy slide out. She turned off the machine and grabbed the two copies. When she turned again, Charles was gone. She went to the door and saw him in the dining room picking up Julie's checkbook.

He left and Jill sighed with relief. Who did he think he was? What did he mean, he was watching her. Was he part of the gang that ran Tyler over, that followed Alexandria from Boston? Who was this man who had penetrated Julie's inner circle? Jill didn't know, but she would be keeping a close eye on him.

Jill gave them five minutes and then left the apartment in a borrowed brown tweed blazer she hoped gave her a professional look. She also borrowed a black shoe bag she hooked around her shoulder that held Tyler's green Nike running shoe.

Outside, under cold, gray and threatening skies, she headed east on White Street, the bag banging at her hip. The precinct on Elizabeth was a ten minute walk and Jill strode quickly, hoping to get there before the early shift ended, and Officer Lucien Lee left for the day. She reached the intersection at Canal Street and impatiently slammed the Walk button. She glanced over her shoulder to make sure Charles wasn't stuck in traffic. Down the road and across the street, a man hurriedly ducked into a drug store. Was he wearing a dark blue hooded sweatshirt?

The light changed and she went on, but now she was looking back. As far as she could tell, no one came out of the drug store wearing a hooded sweatshirt. She hurried on, the drug store out of sight, and no one was behind her. She began to breathe easier. Jared Slater wasn't the only man in the world who owned a navy sweatshirt.

She reached the police station, threaded her way past employees and officers smoking on the steps and went inside, where once again she waited in line at the information desk. When she reached the window, she announced she had come to see Lucien Lee. No, she didn't have an appointment, but the officer happened to be free and agreed to speak to her.

He was Chinese, short and trim and wearing an impeccable crisp uniform and polished shoes. He was young, in his early thirties, with longish dark hair and bangs that fell into his eyes. He shook her hand

and led her to a huge room filled with many desks and officers crammed next to one another. His desk was in the back corner and he pointed to a chair. He took the one behind the desk. "How can I help you, Mrs. Madison?" His English was perfect.

Jill explained who she was and why she had come. "I'd like to see your report of the accident."

Lucien remembered the incident, but he was afraid he couldn't help her. "I'm off the case. The FBI took over. They have the file."

"You don't have a copy of your own report?"

He shook his head, then repositioned his falling bangs. "I have only my written notes."

Jill cheered up at this. "You see my son's memory has come back and what he remembers is different from what's in the FBI report. He saw a black car and in the report it was white."

Lucien brushed this away. "It's likely an error. It doesn't really matter when there's no license plate. I wouldn't make too much of it."

"How did you find out who my son was?"

"Excuse me?"

"The police called us Saturday after the accident. Tyler's phone was broken. The SIM card was gone. Lost or taken, I don't know. He had no ID. How did you find out who he was?"

"We listed him as a John Doe. I don't know who identified him. Perhaps a friend when he went missing? In any event, as I mentioned, I was taken off the case."

"Did you find the SIM card at the scene?"

"I wasn't aware it was missing."

"It wasn't in his phone."

"Which would explain why the phone didn't work."

"Is that unusual?"

"Not really. Not after an accident. The phone wasn't in his pocket, I do remember that. It could have come apart in the accident."

"There's an eye-witness," Jill said.

Lucien looked at her intently.

"A bag lady saw the accident. Tyler was chased down. A black car with black windows went the wrong way down Gold Street and drove up on the curb and forced Tyler onto the road."

Lucien picked up his pad and a pen. "A bag lady. How did you find her?"

"Her name is Vivienne," Jill said. "My son lost a shoe in the chase. She was wearing it."

Lucien made a note. His desk phone rang three times and then stopped. He didn't pick up. "I'm sure if you found her, the FBI will."

"I'm not so sure."

Lucien put down his pen and stared into her eyes. "I see you're frustrated and believe me, we all are. With budget cuts and early prison releases, law enforcement is stretched thin. Cases that used to close in a month now take six. We're overwhelmed. Give the FBI time to do their job."

Jill removed the photocopy from her purse and passed it to him. "Do you recognize this man?"

Lucien unfolded the paper and raised it to his face. He studied it with narrowed eyes. "There was a man wearing a dark hooded sweat-shirt at the scene."

"Did you get the names of the bystanders?"

"I did." Lucien flipped through his notepad. He showed Jill the list of names.

She went down the list. There were eight people on it, but no Jared Slater. "Could a witness have given you a false name?"

"We don't check the ID of helpful witnesses. None of the bystand-ers admitted they saw the accident or called 911. I didn't see your bag lady."

"She was across the street in a park watching Tyler get chased down. There were two men after him. This was one of them." She tapped the photograph. "He's an FBI agent."

Lucien Lee's face darkened. He scratched the back of his neck and made a face at his desk. Before he spoke, he exhaled heavily. "I am sure the FBI is not involved. Frankly, the man in that photograph could be any one. Even me."

He was refusing to even consider the FBI might be involved and was clearly losing patience. Jill guessed all law enforcement officials stuck together and protected one another. She had seen that when she was a reporter. Still, when people got upset, she knew she was hitting a nerve. She pressed on. "Did you find out who made the 911 call?"

"Actually no. It came in as an unknown caller from a secure phone. There was no name, no telephone number."

"Is that strange?"

He lifted a shoulder.

"Who has that capability?"

"I have a secure phone, for example. As do elected officials. I'm sure as a senator your husband has one. FBI agents, of course. Also, hackers with enough programming skills to block caller ID function."

Jill sat back. She hadn't considered these possibilities.

There was a commotion at the door. A woman began sobbing. She was standing, but bent double, hands to her face, really howling. It was hard to watch and to hear.

Lucien didn't seem to notice. He leaned forward. "Mrs. Madison, what is your son up to that has got him into this much trouble? Why would someone want to chase him down and run him over?"

Jill leaned forward and put her elbows on the desk, trying to block out the screaming woman. "He organized a march against the Federal Reserve. It was a week ago Saturday. The police stopped it."

Lucien tapped at his keyboard. "I don't know anything about a march. There was a bomb threat. We closed off the roads around Wall Street."

"But there was no bomb."

Lucien leaned back in his chair. "Mrs. Madison, I can tell you that organizing a march is not enough to warrant such attention. There has to be something else." Lucien flicked his bangs once more. Mercifully, the screaming stopped.

"The Fed is a powerful organization. It needs secrecy to function. Tyler had flyers printed that explained how it's ruining the economy. Whoever ran him over took the flyers. That proves the two events are connected; his march and the hit-and-run."

Lucien looked pained. Bangs fell over his eyes and he left them. "The government doesn't kill people."

"Ha," Jill said. "The Fed is not a government agency. It's like the mafia. A legal mafia."

It seemed Lucien made an effort to not roll his eyes and she knew she had lost him. "Your son is allowed to speak his mind," he said. "And the Fed – or the Fed-mafia – can speak its mind. That's the way it works. There must be something else."

"There isn't."

"Drugs?"

Jill shook her head.

"Theft?"

"No."

"Bombs?"

"No."

Lucien shrugged his shoulders and cleared his bangs. "There's something you're missing. Something your son isn't telling you."

"You don't understand the power of the Fed."

"No. But I understand the power of the mafia. And they run people over for a reason. If your son was run over, and it's a very big if, I can assure you, the reason was not simply organizing a march."

That declared, Lucien looked at his watch and called it a morning. "I'll pass on your concerns to the FBI."

"I just want to find out who ran him over," Jill said. "My son is organizing a rally on Saturday."

"If he has a permit, the police will be there and we will protect him."

"Can I bring in Vivienne? Have her make a statement?" Jill said.

Lucien maintained a straight face. "If she comes in, we'll file a report and pass it on to the FBI."

"Thank you," Jill said. It was obvious the police weren't going to help her, but if the FBI knew they were in the loop, it might compel the FBI to play by the book, to speed up their investigation, to actually try to find the car and the people who ran Tyler down.

Jill left the police station and headed to Gold Street to find Vivienne. According to the Maps app it was two and a half miles away and a twenty-five minute walk. She had reached City Hall when her phone rang. Blaze was calling. She sat down on a park bench and answered the call.

"Have you seen the latest headline?" he asked, in what was for him, a most unpleasant voice.

"You speaking at the River Coalition?"

"No, you shaking hands with Drake the Flake."

"I didn't see that headline," Jill said.

"You told me no one saw you at his campaign rally. You wore sunglasses and a hat."

Jill stared at pigeons pecking at trash in an over-flowing bin. She had taken off her sunglasses and hat for the picture Tyler had snapped with her phone. She had sent the photo to her email that had been hacked.

"The rumor is you've bailed. You're backing him and you moved out after you poisoned me."

Jill let out a long slow breath. Whoever hacked into her email released the photograph. She wondered if it was Blaze's PI. "Are you having me followed?"

"Of course not. Why would you even ask?"

"I do support Denny. I can shake hands with him. It doesn't mean I don't support you."

"Thanks for all your support. I'm down three points."

"You agreed to bail out California. That should help."

"I'm taking the heat for starting this mess. Everyone is against me."

"Not everyone. The River Coalition likes you. Not to mention Rebecca."

"Jesus Christ, can you give it up? The voters appreciate her support. They'd appreciate you too, but apparently that doesn't matter."

Jill sighed heavily and said nothing. She heard the dial tone in her ear. Blaze had hung up. She got up from the bench and walked on, dragging her feet. Rain started to fall and she suddenly felt cold. The day suddenly seemed grayer.

She heard a chirping, a rhythmic beeping, and she stopped walking, and looked around to see where the noise was coming from. It was her purse. She pulled out her phone. It was flashing, but the ring tone was one she had never heard before. She brought the phone to her face and glanced at the caller ID. Unknown caller. She stood under a crimson maple and answered the phone.

"Mrs. Madison?"

It was a man's voice she didn't recognize. "Who is this?"

"Special Agent Mark Biltmore. We spoke on Friday. I'm investigating your home invasion."

She remembered the pudgy agent.

"I'd like to come talk to you."

"I'm not at home," Jill said. "What do you want?"

"I prefer not to talk over the phone. Can we talk in person?"

"I'm in New York."

"Yes. I could come tomorrow."

He knew where she was. Had he also hacked into V-Comm and was he watching the tower that picked up her signal? "What's this about?"

"We could discuss it tomorrow. I know you are worried about the safety of your son."

"Tyler?"

"I can be there by lunchtime," Biltmore said.

"Does Blaze know you're coming?"

"He does not. And if I might be so bold, I would request you not inform him."

"Why not?"

"We'll talk tomorrow." The agent hung up, though Jill had agreed to nothing.

She closed her phone and resumed walking. The rain had stopped, but the clouds in the south flashed with lightning. Had Mark Biltmore joined the dots and realized Tyler was in danger? The agent sounded urgent. It was serious enough to warrant the cost of his travel. Though her first impression of him wasn't good, Jill took it as a fortuitous turn of events. She had finally found an ally, someone who could help her, someone on her side.

The rain had started up again by the time Jill reached the grassy verge. Today the park was deserted. The homeless were no longer sitting on the benches, sprawling on the grass, or panhandling on the sidewalks. Vivienne with her one green Nike was gone.

There was probably a shelter where the homeless could go get a warm meal and wait out a storm, Jill thought, as she lowered her head and turned into the rain. She would come back later when the sun was out.

Back at the apartment, Jill changed out of her wet clothes. There was no sign of Charles and she wondered what he did during the day. She called Tyler, who was working on his blog and sounded busy. "I thought I'd bring lunch," she said. "I've got a surprise."

***

She brought Thai food, with spring rolls, salad, soup and juice to the small, smelly dark room Tyler called home. It was a good thing she had the five thousand dollar check from Julie, because the kids weren't so excited that an FBI agent was taking enough interest in the case to fly out from D.C.

"I wouldn't talk to him," Tyler said, as he took a container of food to the bed.

"He wants to know how much you know," David said, in between bites of pad Thai. Ali, who wasn't saying a word, ate with a fork as he typed with one hand.

"Don't tell the FBI anything," Tyler warned, as he dug into panang curry with steamed tofu. "I know who ran me down, I know who poisoned me, and who stole my computer. The FBI did." He broke off the end of his spring roll and gave it to the cat.

"I'm going to ask Vivienne to come to the police station with me and make a statement. If the FBI know the police are informed, they'll have to watch out."

"A bag lady won't go to the police station with you, Mom. They'd arrest her. Vagrancy is against the law."

Jill admitted she couldn't find her. "It was raining. She's probably at a rain shelter."

Tyler shook his head, lifted his eyes. "Mom, there are no rain shelters. There are half the number of cold weather shelters there used to be, thanks to cutbacks. You could be putting the lady in danger. Leave it alone."

Jill said nothing more, but she wasn't going to leave it alone. She got out the check and that immediately changed the ambience in the room. The kids' eyes opened wide with astonishment. It was like Christmas for them. The food was momentarily forgotten while they planned what they would do with the money. They were going to order Fed Up t-shirts, caps, and buttons. They'd put down a deposit on the sound system. It was agreed Jill would deposit the check and give Tyler a credit card. She was getting in deeper, and Blaze and his minders would protest, but at least the bills would not come due until after the election. She handed over a seldom used Visa.

"Thanks Mom. We'll keep an account of what we spend."

"You could get signs made for the rally," Jill suggested. There were election signs all over the place, on empty lots, store windows, front lawns. "They're cheap. You can get a thousand made for two hundred dollars."

"We'll slap sticks on them. Make them into placards." David rubbed his small hands together with anticipation.

"We have twenty-five thousand people confirmed on Facebook that they'll attend," Tyler said with pride.

"Is your permit for that many?" Jill asked.

"We guessed between five hundred and two thousand," Tyler said.

"Change the number," Jill said. "It should be accurate. It will determine how many police show up."

"The fewer the better," said her son.

"We're meeting Denny's aide later this week," David said, changing the subject.

She dropped her protest over the police. Surely Denny's staff would set the numbers straight.

"The latest crash is helping his polls," Tyler said.

"Crash?"

"Didn't you know? The market lost over a thousand points in an hour. It closed at ten-thirty, reopened at eleven and closed ten minutes later. It's still closed."

"I thought it was supposed to rally," Jill said. "What happened?"

"There are rumors China won't lend us any more money," David said.

"So much for Congress agreeing to bail out California," Tyler added. "Who are they going to get the money from?"

"The Fed wasn't prepared for this," David said. "It took them by surprise."

"If we can't borrow, we'll be as bankrupt as any Third World country," Tyler said, not without triumph. "Austerity measures will kick in. Services, government wages, pensions, Medicare, Social Security, it all will have to be cut to pay back our debt, appease our debtors. Worldwide, the dollar will lose value. The currency's been going down for four straight years and it will only get worse, making imports more expensive. Once we lose our good credit rating, interest rates will skyrocket, and everything will cost more. If we do find someone stupid enough to lend us money, it will cost us a fortune to borrow." He picked up the cat and put her in his lap. "Maybe it's what we need to get people to wake up."

"Won't the Fed just print more money?" Jill asked.

Tyler nodded. "It will, at least for a while."

"That will only weaken the dollar more," David said.

"And put us deeper in debt," Tyler said.

"The real danger is if China demands to be repaid in something other than dollars," David said. "What if it wants euros? The Fed can't print euros. What if the U.S. dollar was no longer the world's currency? Countries across the globe would trade in their dollars. With so much money flooding in, the value of the dollar would crash. It wouldn't be worth the paper it's printed on. We'll be burning money to keep ourselves warm."

"We could cash in our gold," Jill said.

Tyler laughed. "Only we don't have any. You didn't read yesterday's blog, did you?"

"Not yet."

Tyler put down his box of curry and chopsticks, grabbed his laptop and typed a few keys. He positioned the laptop in front of her. His blog was open and the title was: *Forget Gold*. Already, over one hundred people had left comments.

And so Jill read about the great gold confiscation of 1934, when every American turned in their gold at the government's going rate of twenty dollars an ounce. Those who failed to comply were fined ten thousand dollars or sentenced up to ten years in prison.

The confiscated gold was melted down and poured into gold bars that were taken to Fort Knox for safe keeping. In 1937, with all the gold confiscated, the vault held seven hundred and fifty million ounces of gold, which amounted to seventy percent of the world's total supply that wasn't in the ground.

Once the government had the gold, it turned around and increased the price, raising it from twenty dollars to thirty-five dollars an ounce. In so doing, the government had in effect halved the value of the dollar, since now, nearly twice as many dollars were needed to buy one ounce of gold.

Who was buying the gold? Since Americans were not allowed to own gold, it was bought by overseas investors. American corporations with off-shore accounts and addresses were also buying it.

Now Jill learned that in the stock market crash of 1929, the Federal Reserve Board warned its friends the crash was coming. It knew it was coming because it contracted the money supply and made it come. Forewarned, the big bankers got out before the crash. They bragged about their foresight, how they saw the crash coming. What did they do with their money once they got it out? Before the great confiscation, they bought gold and shipped it out of the country. Once FDR hoarded the gold and raised its price, the value of gold owned by the big American banks immediately almost doubled. They made a killing.

Back in the U.S., by law, the Department of the Treasury was ordered to visibly audit the gold stock in Fort Knox every year. Despite the law, the last time it was done was 1953. Treasury claimed it was too expensive. In the 70's, news was leaked that the gold in Fort Knox was gone. Who leaked the information? The secretary of the big banker, Nelson Rockefeller. She died three days later when she fell out of a tenth floor window of her apartment.

In 1982, Reagan wanted to go back on the gold standard, and learned the country had no gold. There was none in Fort Knox. Some had been sold off, and the rest was taken by the Federal Reserve as collateral against the U.S. debt. It was in the basement of the New York Federal Reserve building. What belonged to the people had been stolen. Tyler was demanding an immediate and thorough audit.

Jill reached the end of the blog and shook her head. Tyler was looking at her. "It just gets worse and worse," she said.

Tyler smiled. "The question of using gold to bail ourselves out is bound to arise. It will be interesting to hear what the President has to say."

"Denny is going to make it a campaign issue." David said. "It's a hot topic and it polls well. People across all demographics want to know about the gold. If we can show what the Fed has done, we might finally get people stirred up enough to protest."

The kids had finished eating and lunch was over. They seemed in a hurry to get back to work, and Jill called a cab. She had a sinking feeling that Tyler and his friends were turning up the heat. The blog about the state bank had not directly criticized the Fed, but the gold blog was another matter entirely. They were not only accusing the Fed of causing the Great Depression, but of insider trading and grand theft.

She had the cab detour to Gold Street. They drove slowly down the one way street and Jill asked the driver to wait at the park. The sun was out, the puddles had dried, but there were no homeless people. The park benches were empty, there was no sign of any of them.

***

That Black Tuesday, the New York stock market fell one thousand points in the worst crash in recent history. When Julie didn't come home after work, Jill guessed she was at the tavern, along with the rest of Wall Street drowning their losses. Alone, Jill watched the news unfold on TV. Out in California, the President was calling for calm. Right now there were only unsubstantiated rumors that China wasn't going to lend the U.S. any more money. It wasn't true. There was nothing to worry about. If necessary, the country would fall back on its gold reserves. The U.S. had the biggest stockpile of gold in the world. The country wasn't as destitute as the stock market believed.

Soon after the President spoke, the Secretary of the Treasury was asked about the wisdom of bailing out the country with the gold reserves. He shook his head and was quick to say that was the worst solution imaginable. It would send the wrong signal to the Chinese and other investors. It was sheer folly, akin to selling off assets to finance a spending spree. "I won't agree to it."

He couldn't very well agree if there was no gold, Jill thought, and wondered why he sounded as if he had the power to overrule the President.

Rich Tumblin was ignoring the question altogether. CNN showed a clip of him leaving the Chinese Embassy. He was a fat man in a hurry, waddling through the rain and holding up a hand to ward off questions as he ducked into his limousine.

The station cut to a commercial and there was Denny Drake. "What if there is no gold?" he said, as he faced his audience with troubled eyes. "What if the gold, confiscated from the American people on the pretext of stabilizing the economy, was stolen? What if the vault is empty? Why has there been no audit of Fort Knox? Why will the government not conduct a full visual audit as stipulated by law? Why can the people not see their own gold with their own eyes? Unless there's nothing to see." The camera panned out. Dark words on a white screen remained: WHERE IS THE GOLD?

At least someone was asking the right question, Jill thought as Julie arrived home. It was after eight and she was in surprisingly good spirits, although that was likely the booze.

"Hi honey, I'm home," she said, as she stumbled in, kicked off her high heels and tossed her fur.

"You're in a good mood," Jill said.

"Buying opportunity," she said with glee, as she settled in the living room to watch the money reports while Charles went to the kitchen and prepared a martini. That made, he brought her a glass and went down the hall to iron and eavesdrop.

"Isn't the country on the verge of bankruptcy?" Jill said. "We're about to dip into our gold. If we happen to have any."

"We don't need gold," Julie said. "The Chinese aren't going to stop lending. Futures are way up. The market is going to regain everything it lost and more. I'm going to make a killing. And look at the latest polls. Shush, shush," she said, though she was the one talking.

The latest Gallup poll showed the President was polling at forty-three percent and Tumblin at fifty-four. For the first time, Tumblin was winning beyond the margin of uncertainty. When likely voters were asked who could best solve the current economic crisis, Tumblin came in at nearly seventy percent and the President at twenty-eight.

Julie clapped her hands and celebrated by guzzling the martini.

Jill looked at her sister quizzically. "How do you know the Chinese will lend?"

"Think about it. They own billions of our debt. If they were to stop lending, the value of the dollar would plummet. The money we owe them would be worthless. That would crash their own economy. They'd never do that." She drained the dregs of her drink.

"Did you know Tumblin was going to the Chinese?" Jill asked.

Julie shrugged knowingly and smiled a sly smile.

"Isn't that insider trading?"

"Can I help it if I don't listen to rumors? The Chinese never said they weren't going to lend. I knew they'd be foolish not to." She raised her empty glass and Charles was there to whisk it away and replenish it. "The market can only go up, up, up."

Denny's commercial played again and once more the screen faded to white, leaving the bold question: WHERE IS THE GOLD?

Julie looked like she wanted to hurl her drink at the TV. "What the hell is he trying to do? Crash the market? He better shut the fuck up about the gold. Doesn't he understand the narrative has changed? Tumblin is talking to the Chinese. We've got a lender, we don't need gold."

"How can we be sure there is any, if there's no audit?" Jill asked.

"Every Tom, Dick, and Harry doesn't get to know everything," Julie said. "Let the world guess how much gold we've got."

"It's our gold," Jill said. "We have a right to know."

Julie looked at her sadly. "Thinking like that has no place in business. We're all lucky "Drake the flake" doesn't have a hope in hell."

"According to Tyler, he's doing well."

"Tumblin's our next president. That's what my astrologer says and she's never wrong."

Jill burst out laughing. Her sister threw her a hard glance and she composed herself. "Oh. You're serious."

"She's got every pick right for the last twenty years, so I'm guessing she's got this one right."

"Is she psychic?"

"For your information she looks at the alignment of the planets and makes predictions." Julie paused and threw back a healthy gulp. "Don't look so skeptical. She forecasts the stock market with an accuracy of eighty-four point two percent. She knows within a three day window whether the market will go up or down. She saw this dip coming and told me not to worry. J.P. Morgan said that millionaires don't have astrologers, billionaires do. She's correctly predicted the last five elections."

Jill stared out the window. A siren went screaming down the street, then another. "It's bunk," she said, over the noise.

"It's called bunk until you study it. Here you go again, having opinions on things you know nothing about." Julie put down her drink and grabbed her purse. "I'm making you an appointment with Layla."

Jill paused. That was the name of Tyler's old girlfriend. "Layla?"

"Maybe she can help you."

"Does Tyler know her?"

"He went to her after he came back from the Peace Corps. He seemed lost and I thought Layla could help."

Jill had the impression the astrologer was an older woman who had correctly predicted the last five presidential elections. "How old is she?"

"In her sixties."

Jill inhaled sharply. "And Tyler dated her?"

Julie sniggered. "Not her. Her daughter. Her name is also Layla."

The blood began to flow again in Jill's body.

"I don't know if she has time to see you, but I'll call her."

Jill shook her head. "What if someone saw me? It will look bad. Remember Nancy Reagan?"

"Take a chance for once in your life. Be open to something new. Have courage."

"Maybe another time," Jill said.

"I'm calling her."

"I'm not going."

14

We have in this country one of the most corrupt institutions the world has ever known. I refer to the Federal Reserve Board... This evil institution has impoverished the people of the U.S. ... and has practically bankrupted our government.

—Rep Louis T. McFadden

WEDNESDAY OCTOBER 29

First thing Wednesday morning, Jill was on her way to see the astrologer. Julie made her an appointment at seven and woke her up at five-thirty to make sure Jill was ready on time. Apparently, the astrologer didn't like to be kept waiting. Although Jill needed only twenty minutes to get ready, she was given over an hour. She took a long shower, drank too much coffee, and watched the morning news. Julie's information had been spot on – the overseas markets were booming.

The Chinese had issued an official statement from Beijing. Of course they would continue to lend money to the U.S. government. They had every confidence that the government was a good credit risk. Moody's and Fitch had also stepped forward and declared California sound. The state was not in need of a bailout, although it would immediately have to address its deficit, debt, and spending.

Out in California, in spite of his falling numbers, a jubilant looking President took credit for solving the crisis. His equally jubilant opponent was running commercials of himself coming and going from the Chinese Embassy, making clear who the closer really was.

At this early hour, there were no Denny Drake commercials. He ran his at prime time and on late night TV. This early in the morning, his demographic was fast asleep.

At six-forty-five, Julie was ready to go. Jill borrowed another blazer and grabbed the shoe bag and her purse. Charles got the keys. "What's in the bag?" he asked.

"None of your business," Jill said.

Julie practically ripped it off her shoulder and peered inside. She slapped it back in Jill's hand. "What are you doing with a shoe?"

"Giving it to the eye-witness, if you must know," Jill said sharply. "Not that it's any of his business."

"Why didn't you just say so?" Julie said. "Charles probably thought you were trying to steal something."

Charles looked at her and raised untidy eyebrows.

Jill said nothing. She wouldn't speak in the car. She turned away from Julie and stared out the window. It was a good thing it was a short ride. The astrologer worked on Broome Street in the Blue Nile Hotel, and when Charles pulled up to the curb, Jill got out without a word. She slammed the door so hard the car seemed to shake. Charles raced off, screeching the tires like a spoiled juvenile brat.

The hotel was a six-story brownstone with steep stairs, a front stoop and an entrance guarded by a pair of bronze lions. Jill wearily climbed the steps, already regretting she had agreed to come. She didn't believe that the planets were anything other than rocks and balls of gas, and that stars were anything other than products of hydrogen fusion. Jill's plan was to go in, sit politely, nod, say nothing, and leave as soon as possible. What a waste of time!

She wanted to go find Vivienne and get her to the police station to make a statement. At some point, Special Agent Mark Biltmore would call and she would learn what was so important that he had to speak to her in person.

Jill entered the building. It was cold outside, in the low forties, and a fire crackled in a hearth in the lobby. The worn couches and chairs looked comfortable. The clerk at the desk was nice. Jill could find Layla Star up on the second floor.

She took the elevator up and knocked on the door at the end of the hall. There was no answer. The ditzy astrologer had probably forgotten that she had agreed to open up early. Jill tried the handle and found the door unlocked. She went in.

It looked like a doctor's waiting room, with two couches and a desk with a computer. The walls were plastered with poster-sized pictures of outer space.

The inner door opened and a tall, sleek woman emerged. She looked closer to fifty than sixty. She had brown hair pulled back in a bun and sparkling green eyes. Layla wore a black slack suit over a crisp white blouse and dangling sapphire earrings. A pair of glasses hung on a chain around her neck. Jill didn't know what she was expecting, but it wasn't a woman who looked like a lawyer.

"Good, you're on time." Layla said, in a low, scratchy, almost breathless, baritone voice. She shook Jill's hand heartily and smiled a big smile, crinkling her sparkling eyes. With a wave of her arm, she invited Jill into her office. "Come in. Can I get you coffee? Water?"

Jill accepted a bottle of water. She wasn't going to stay long enough for a cup of coffee.

The inner room had an arched window overlooking Broome Street. A large desk dominated a third of the room, and behind it stood floor to ceiling bookshelves that took up the entire wall. There was no free space on the shelves where books were stacked horizontally on top of standing books. There was a love seat and two matching armchairs set around a polished wooden table that showed the rings of a tree trunk.

Jill was going to take a chair, but Layla directed her to the loveseat. "This way you can see what I'm doing."

Jill wondered what she was going to do.

Layla sat down, crossed her legs, picked up a file and pulled out stapled pages. She adjusted the stems of her glasses around her ears. "Let's get started."

Jill surveyed the room. There was a balcony with pots of geraniums that seemed to flourish even in the cold. Like the reception area, the free wall space was filled with blown-up photographs of the sky. Jill saw Saturn with its rings, Mars with its rocks, and the spirals of the Milky Way. Colorful magazines were fanned out on the end table; different issues of *The Mountain Astrologer*.

Layla held up a page with a big circle scattered with symbols. "This is your chart," she said. "A snapshot of the sky at the moment of your birth. Imagine you're standing at the center. You were born at 8.10 A.M. so the Sun was rising and here it is in the 12th house in Libra. A Libra Sun is looking for –"

Jill stopped her right there. "I didn't come for this."

Layla cast Jill a sidelong glance. "Pardon?" she said, in her deep scratchy voice. She lifted her glasses and peered directly into Jill's eyes.

"I came about Tyler. I think he's in danger."

"I'm sorry, but my discussions with other clients are confidential."

Great. An astrologer with ethics.

Layla repositioned her glasses and stared at a spoked-wheel and more symbols. "Did you have a fight this morning?"

"What?"

Layla pointed to the page. "I can see you're a little agitated. Mars in Taurus is rising, exact a few minutes ago, pointing to an argument. Is everything all right?"

"Yes. Fine."

"Is there a problem with your husband?"

"No."

"Mars usually points to a male. An issue with a domestic man?"

"What? Like a butler?"

"Exactly."

"Nope."

"In Taurus, Mars could be an aggressive woman."

"Oh."

"Julie?"

"It's nothing," Jill said at last.

Layla repositioned her eyeglasses and commenced to read Jill's chart. It was dominated by something called a T-square, though in Jill's chart the T was upside down. Mercury and the Moon occupied the arms, with Uranus and Pluto together pointing to the sky. On one hand, it was an aspect of heartbreak and trauma, compounded by a difficulty in emotional or verbal communication. Layla looked at her. "Does that make any sense?"

In a sentence, she had summed up Jill's life. "Maybe."

"On the other hand, looking at the bright side, it shows a unique writing ability that is both forward looking and transformative. Are you a writer?"

Jill eyed the astrologer. "Tyler told you I was a journalist."

"No, but I'm not surprised. A 12th house Sun shuns the spotlight, but a Leo Midheaven needs drama and brings you reluctantly into the public eye. The Moon represents the emotions and is in Gemini, the sign of the writer, opposite Mercury, the planet of writing and communication, in Sagittarius, the sign that seeks the truth. They're both square Uranus and Pluto in the 10th house of the career."

"I stopped writing when I got married."

"Tell me about your marriage."

"There's nothing to tell. Everything's fine."

Layla looked skeptical. "I know your husband is in the midst of a difficult election. Wasn't he hospitalized recently with food poisoning? I'm guessing this election is more burdensome than usual."

Jill chose her words carefully. "He's down in the polls. It's never happened before."

"The reason I ask is because Mars is hitting your T-square and so is Saturn. That's heavy energy. It's personal for you and for him. Things can't be easy at the moment."

Jill tried to look stoic. "A campaign is always difficult."

"Is someone on his campaign attacking you, upsetting you?"

"No."

"No aggressive campaign manager? A feisty aid? No one making you feel less than worthy?"

"No," Jill said, while she wondered what was going on in Texas.

Layla pursed her lips and seemed to pick her words carefully. "Transiting Venus is passing over your Sun. The Sun often represents the husband. Venus, a woman."

"Me?" Jill said.

Layla shook her head. "It's in the 12th house. Action behind the scene. It's possible that you don't know about it. It hasn't come to your attention, but it probably will at the Full Moon, which is Saturday. Whatever has been hidden will be revealed."

It was the day of Tyler's rally. Also, four days before the election. The woman behind the scenes, was of course, Rebecca.

Layla picked up her sheets and carried on. "What do you do now?"

"I garden."

Layla frowned at her paper. "Gardening. I'm afraid I don't see that. Perhaps your husband, with Taurus on your 7th house cusp, but not you."

"He likes to garden, he doesn't have time."

Layla moved on. "Is alcohol a problem?"

Jill tightened. "Did Tyler say something?"

Layla gazed at Jill over the rim of her spectacles. "Venus in the first square Neptune. Pleasure not knowing any boundary. Not knowing when to stop, when enough is enough."

"I have been sober –"

Layla raised a restraining hand. "Let me guess when you stopped drinking." She flipped a page, studied a circle. "I'd say five years ago you reached rock bottom."

"Wrong" Jill said, sounding more triumphant than she would have liked. "I quit drinking nine months ago."

"What happened five years ago?"

"It was opposite to what you said. It's when I really started to drink." Five years ago Hope was first diagnosed with leukemia and the drinking escalated. She hadn't quit drinking then. That was when it got out of control. The astrologer was wrong.

"My primary concern right now is Tyler," Jill said. She heard a kettle whistling and voices from the outer room. She regretted passing on the coffee and took a sip of water.

"Your son is grown. You have to let him go, be his own man."

"Is that what he thinks?"

"Moon square Pluto. A powerful, domineering, controlling mother, holding on at all costs."

Jill exhaled loudly. "I let him go. He went away to university. He went in the Peace Corps. He lived in Africa. I'm not holding him back."

Layla took off her glasses "You have to let him go in your heart." Then, as if as an afterthought, she said, "Oh. Moon square Uranus-Pluto. The sudden death of a child."

"He told you about Hope. You can't see that there."

"When did she die?"

"Three years ago. She was ten."

"A sickness?"

Jill nodded.

"When did she get sick?"

Jill sighed. "Two years before that."

The astrologer could probably do the math but Layla did not gloat. She put down her papers and turned sideways to face Jill squarely. "Moon square Pluto can also mean not owning your own power. When you don't own your own planets, you project them, and they come at you from the outside. But this Pluto is yours, the power belongs to you. You need to own it and claim it for yourself."

Jill stared out the window. A pigeon landed on the balcony and was walking on the railing.

"With Mercury involved, it's a double-edged sword. You don't feel free to say what you want and don't have the freedom to express how you feel. It's easy to lose touch with who you are."

"Hmm," was all Jill said.

The astrologer pressed on, not knowing how close she was getting. "The Moon also represents the mother. There must be something shocking, upsetting in regards to her."

Jill bit her lip and stared out the window.

There was a long silence. Jill was growing uncomfortable, and was about to break it, when Layla said, "In order to be happy, you have to be yourself, to speak your own truth. It's quite clear to me there's no correspondence between how you're living your life and the way it is meant to be lived. Something's holding you back. Guilt? With the Moon, Mercury and Pluto together with transiting Saturn, guilt can be crippling. It's a wasted emotion. The past is past. Whatever happened can't be undone, it can't be changed. You can only vow to do better in the future and move on."

"I wasn't there when Hope died," Jill said unexpectedly and surprising herself.

Layla nodded. "You had other children. You couldn't be there all the time."

"It's worse than that. I told Hope she was going to be fine. She wanted me to stay at the hospital and I left. I wanted a drink. I went home and got drunk. I left her alone to die."

Jill paused and Layla passed her a Kleenex and Jill turned to the window. She had promised herself that she would always be there for her children, that she would never abandon them, never leave them, never walk away from them like her own absent mother. And she had broken that promise, broken it at the worst possible time, and there was nothing she could ever do to make it right.

The pigeon flew away and Jill turned away from the window.

"It's something no one should have to go through," Layla said.

"So, yes, I feel guilty," Jill said, as if Layla had not spoken. "I never said goodbye."

"That's why you can't move on."

"I couldn't take it if anything happened to Tyler. I don't ever want him to feel abandoned."

Layla nodded. "It's a normal reaction. You have to forgive yourself. I'm sure Hope would forgive you."

The thought had never occurred to Jill before, and it struck her like a blast of nuclear light. Hope had been a happy, cheerful, forgiving child, so different from Tyler who could hold a grudge forever and was more like Jill than she cared to admit.

She felt Layla looking at her. "The opposite of asking for forgiveness, is being willing to forgive. You have to forgive your mother. Let go of resentment. It's like drinking poison and expecting the other person to die. You only harm yourself."

Jill was taken aback. She wasn't thinking about her mother, she was thinking about Rebecca and Calista. Only now did she realize the extent of her resentment toward them, except that it was more than resentment – it was hate.

Layla was still looking at her. She seemed to see everything, to know everything, all the deep secrets Jill was loath to say.

"Deal with your past and you can look forward to the future," Layla said. "I think you'll find your voice. You'll write what you need to write."

"I always wanted to write a novel."

Layla smiled. "No time like the present."

"I'm worried about Tyler."

Layla nodded. "As you know, I have a daughter. At some point you have to step back and let go."

"Do you know why they broke up?"

Layla frowned. "You should really talk to your son." She sighed loudly. "However, since this is not privileged information, nor anything we discussed, I will say, from one mother to another, it looked like love. For my daughter, it was. He broke it off suddenly. She was devastated. I wasn't happy either. I liked your son. I had never seen Layla so happy."

The astrologer's watch beeped and Jill knew her time was up. She had one more question. "Do you really think that Rich Tumblin is going to win the election?"

"Unfortunately, yes."

"What about Dennis Drake?"

"Ah, the newcomer. The young upstart." Layla shrugged. "I'm afraid I don't have his birth data, so I can't say. I do know that Tumblin is having favorable transits, unlike the President. In a two-way race, Tumblin wins."

"And a three-way?"

The astrologer stood up. "I'd need the birth data before I could say."

Jill followed her into the outer room where she saw a secretary and two waiting clients. One jumped up off the couch and came toward them. She was a petite dark-haired girl with dark eyes and dark hair pulled back in a pony tail. She picked a file up off the desk. "I ran the charts for you, Mom. I've got to go. I'll be late for class."

She spoke in the same deep, guttural, scratchy voice as her mother. As far as first impressions went, Jill liked her. Her eyes were big and bright and so dark they were almost black. She looked young, fresh, curious, and energetic. Jill could see her son with this girl.

The older Layla made introductions and Jill shook hands with Tyler's ex. They left the office together, each eyeing the other closely. "I'm sorry it didn't work out with Tyler," Jill said, as they walked down the hallway.

"Me too." Layla's face darkened and Jill knew she still had feelings for him.

It was a nosy thing to ask, but Jill asked anyway. "Why did you break up?"

They reached the elevator, but neither one of them made an effort to push the button. "We both got too busy. He was working in a soup kitchen and learning Portuguese and French, and I have research and classes."

"You met at the planetarium?" Jill said.

Layla seemed surprised she knew. "He joined the astronomy club in January. He'd already been to consult with my mother, which was unusual for that crowd, as you might imagine. We started going out. It was great. In April something happened. He started writing his blog.

He made new friends. A few weeks later he said it was in my best interest that we stop seeing each other."

"In your best interest?"

"I disagreed, but he wouldn't listen. I think he thought he was protecting me."

"From what?"

Layla shrugged. "He didn't say."

"He was run over."

Layla nodded. "I heard. He said he was all right."

"It wasn't an accident. He was run down."

Layla's big black eyes opened wide. "I didn't know."

"Maybe that's what he was protecting you from."

***

Outside, Layla caught a bus and Jill headed for Gold Street, deep in thought. Thanks to Julie, she had just spent the most illuminating hour of her life. Jill didn't know how it worked, but Layla had done in sixty minutes what the psychiatrist hadn't achieved in a year or Petra in nine months. It was astounding. There was no other word for it. How did it work? The world suddenly seemed magical.

She walked down Center Street with a smile on her face, feeling lighter than she had in years. She could not go back and redo the past, but she could move forward. Get on with her life.

Jill neared John Street and picked up her pace, her heart lifting when she saw the homeless were back. She crossed the street and headed for the grassy verge where the transients lounged. One man was sleeping face down in the grass. Another was sprawled on a bench with a newspaper over his head. But there was no sign of Vivienne. A man in a knit hat and navy sweater with holes that reminded her of Tyler's, shuffled her way. He had a grizzled gray beard and wore gloves without fingertips. "You lookin' for someone?"

Jill walked toward him. The scent of sour perspiration radiated off him. "Vivienne. She was here the other day."

The man, named James, embarked on a long and convoluted story of what had transpired the previous day. Everyone had been picked up by Immigration and driven to New Jersey. Sometimes it happened. If some big shot came to town, the homeless were rounded up and removed from the city. Yesterday, they were taken to an office and put in separate rooms. One by one they were interviewed. The officials wanted their papers: a birth certificate, a driver's license, a passport, anything. Of course no one had any papers. They wanted to know if anyone had seen anything unusual in the past couple of weeks, if anyone had bothered them, questioned them.

"And?" Jill said.

"We get bothered all the time. Timothy was beat up last month."

"Was Vivienne taken with you to Immigration?"

"She went with us, she never came back."

"What happened to her?"

"Maybe she had papers and got let out early and went somewhere else. The rest of us were held all day. Usually, we get money for our inconvenience, but yesterday all we got was a subway token."

"What time did Immigration come?"

James couldn't be sure. If he had to estimate, it might have been around nine, perhaps earlier, maybe later.

Jill gave James twenty dollars and thanked him for his time. He wanted the Nike shoe, which he promised to give to Vivienne, but Jill said she would come back.

She left him and walked on. She was reviewing the conversation and the timeline in her head, when she heard the sound of screeching brakes. She turned in time to see a tall man with a green baseball cap run in front of a car and cross the busy street. He reached the other side and looked her way.

Jared Slater. A bus temporarily cut him off from view and when the bus passed, the agent was gone, but Jill knew it was him. Though ten years had passed, she recognized his easy run, his straight profile, his fluid movement. There was no doubt whatsoever it was him. Was he trying to call attention to himself? Did he want her to see him? Was he sending her a message? A warning? He knew who she was talking to and now Vivienne had disappeared. Jill wondered who had the power to get Immigration to come out here to round up the homeless people.

Her phone rang. It was the strange ring tone and she knew who was calling without having to check the caller ID. Mark Biltmore was in New York and wanted to meet. "I'm free anytime," she said, "the sooner the better."

She suggested the Starbucks around the corner, but he wanted something more private and suggested Julie's. He said he'd be there in fifteen minutes and didn't ask for the address.

***

Jill returned to White Street and waited for the FBI agent in the lobby. No unknown guests were allowed in the building and all visitors had to be signed in by a resident or their representative. Jill waited only a few minutes before a taxi stopped at the curb and Biltmore emerged.

For someone so young, just a few years older than Alexandria, he labored across the sidewalk and trudged up the steps. He was the most out-of-shape FBI agent she had ever seen. He was dressed casually, wearing jeans and a gray collared t-shirt, but looked every bit the nerd. He was short and tubby, and the jeans didn't fit, and the t-shirt made him look pregnant and was stained with what looked like coffee. He leaned on the door and waddled inside. His skin was gray and his pudgy cheeks bulged when he smiled his tight smile. They shook hands. His was sweaty and small. Despite Tyler's previous words of caution, Jill was glad Biltmore was here. She needed someone on her side.

Jill signed him in and they went upstairs. He seemed awed by Julie's apartment and gawked out the big windows at a construction crane, touched the Dali print and gaped at the Mapplethorpe. He refused a drink. It wasn't a social call; he wanted to get down to business. They sat down in the living room on easy chairs on opposite sides of the coffee table.

"Why have you come?" Jill asked straight out.

Biltmore turned and looked out the window. Noisy construction was underway and a large crane lifted a long, heavy, steel beam that trembled in the wind. When he looked back at her, he said, "May we speak in confidence?"

"Of course."

"We have determined who leaked your husband's email."

Jill leaned forward.

"I'm afraid I'm not at liberty to disclose their identity. We know your husband's hard drive was sold on the black market. It was bought by the individual who leaked its contents. The other computers have not surfaced, which leads us to believe the thieves kept what they wanted and dumped what they did not. May I ask what was on your computer?"

"Nothing," Jill said. "Just email. Games. Photos. Nothing important to anyone but me. Maybe it was offered up for sale, but no one wanted it."

Biltmore looked unconvinced.

"Though someone did hack into my email," Jill said.

"What was in your email?"

"Personal notes, photos." Jill thought of the email with her picture with Denny Drake that had ended up on the internet. "Also, the FBI report of Tyler's accident."

Biltmore seemed to consider this and Jill did as well. The FBI wouldn't steal her computer to read their own file. Finally he said, "Whoever took your computer has your passwords. I would change them."

"I already have."

"Good. What about Tyler's computer? Was it hacked as well?"

Jill paused and chose her words with care, staying far away from Tyler's own successful infiltration into V-Comm. "It wasn't hacked," she said.

"What does he have on his computer?"

"Nothing he doesn't put online. He writes a blog."

"He took computer programming at university, correct?"

"Only for a year. He was also pre-med. He wanted to be a doctor his whole life. His sister is in medical school." Jill knew she was babbling. "Do you know who poisoned him?"

"We are quite certain he was the target. We suspect a hired waitress was responsible. She gave her name as Helga Grosch, but that was not her real name. She was a volunteer and gave no resume. There's no culinary school which she claimed to attend, and no street where she claimed to live. We drew up a sketch but there were no hits on our data base. She claimed to be German, but that could also be a lie. We don't know who she is or who she's working for."

"So, not you," Jill said.

Biltmore apparently thought she was joking and laughed.

"Did you tell Blaze?"

Biltmore stared out the window. "He would prefer, for political reasons, to believe he was the target." He slowly turned his gaze back to Jill. "What do you know about the car accident?"

Jill laid out her cards and told the agent everything, including the disappearance of the eye-witness Vivienne who vanished soon after Jill went to the police. "The homeless people were picked up by Immigration officials and taken for questioning. She never made it back."

Biltmore had taken out a small black notebook and was scribbling madly. Now he stopped, looked up, and said he would make inquiries at Immigration and get to the bottom of it.

She felt she could trust him, though she had no choice, there was no one else. She got out the printed photograph that Tyler had given her. "This is FBI agent Jared Slater. According to Vivienne, two men chased Tyler down and he's one of them. Tyler had two thousand flyers for his protest against the Federal Reserve and the agent took them. I saw him half an hour ago near the park where Vivienne was taken and where Tyler was run over."

Biltmore put down his pen, reached across the table and picked up the photograph. He peered at it closely. He didn't recognize Slater, but then he might be working for the New York branch.

"Can you find out?"

Biltmore would make some inquiries. He took a picture of the photograph with his phone. "You asked me at your house about technology to trace a cell phone. What were you talking about?"

Jill told him about the microchip in Tyler's phone.

Biltmore wanted to know everything about it, what it looked like, what color it was, where exactly it was in the phone. He took her phone apart so she could show him.

When her phone was reassembled, she asked if the bug belonged to the FBI.

Biltmore shook his head. "I've never seen anything like what you've described."

"Could it belong to a private investigator?"

He found this funny too. "If we don't have it, a P.I. wouldn't." He took a different tack. "What's Tyler's working on now?"

This was where Jill had to be careful. "He's planning another rally for Saturday."

"Does he have a permit?"

"He got one last week."

"How did he get the permit so fast?" Biltmore asked.

"There was a cancellation. Is that strange?"

"It depends on the circumstances. Usually these things take at minimum a month to arrange, and this gets pushed through in a matter of days. So, yes, I find it strange. In a crowd, he would be an open target, even with a police presence."

"I'm not sure I trust the police," Jill said. "Not after what happened to Vivienne. And I know the police report has been altered. According to the FBI, Tyler was hit by a white car, which according to both him and Vivienne was black."

"I have requested a copy of the report," Biltmore said. "I'm afraid these things take time. We have to go through channels, get permission. It's delicate. This is the New York branch's case and we don't want to step on anyone's toes, overstep our jurisdiction, that sort of thing." He paused to look at her. "But you say you have a copy of the report?"

"Not any more."

"You can request a copy from the New York branch. Better still, you might talk to the agents investigating the case."

"They'd talk to me?"

Biltmore extracted a business card from his pocket. "Agents Castonova and King are working the case. Their number's on the card. Call them. Mention your husband and they'll see you."

"Blaze doesn't want me involved."

Biltmore nodded. "It's up to you. I see how worried you are about your son. Frankly, you have a right to know what they've found. I'm certain they won't trouble your husband. He doesn't have to know." He handed her the card. "You could call them now."

Jill dialed the number and was patched through to Agent King. He listened to her request and said he would get back to her. She hung up and relayed this to Biltmore.

"He'll check you out. Make sure you are who you say you are. Then he'll call back and make an appointment. Would you agree to a wire?"

"Absolutely not."

Biltmore leaned back and held up his hands as if to ward off her vehement refusal. "We're on the same side. They probably won't give you a copy of their report, but they'll let you look at it. Will you tell me what it says?"

Jill nodded tentatively and Biltmore smiled his tight smile.

"The best thing would be to find Jared Slater and bring him in for questioning," Jill said.

"Let me look into it." Biltmore put away his notebook and pen and thanked Jill for her time.

She was walking him to the door, when it opened and Charles appeared, arms laden with grocery bags. She grabbed her purse and Julie's borrowed blazer, as Charles came in scowling.

"Good afternoon," he said, stiffly, as he eyed Biltmore, who eyed him back.

"We're leaving," Jill said.

Biltmore had to be signed out and they rode down in the elevator. "Well he was charming," Biltmore said. "Who was that?"

"My sister's butler." The elevator stopped and the doors opened. "Can you check him out?"

"I can." Biltmore extracted the notebook.

Jill gave him the details. "Charles Grande, fifty-six, from Surrey." She had one more question. "You said my husband doesn't know you're here. He's under the impression that he knows what the FBI is doing. That if, say, you were investigating Tyler, he would know. True or false?"

Biltmore opened his mouth and then closed it. Finally he said, "It's need to know. N2K."

"Are you investigating Tyler?"

Biltmore smiled his tight smile. "I want what you want. To get to the truth. To find out what's really going on." They reached the exit. "I'll be in touch."

15

The Fed is private, conducted for the sole purpose of obtaining the greatest possible profits from the use of other people's money. A purely profiteering group.

–Charles Lindbergh (R-MN)

Jill waited in the lobby while Biltmore caught a cab. By then it was almost one and she called Tyler who wondered where she was. "I'm on my way." She was glad she didn't have to invite herself over. She had no intention of returning to the apartment with Charles upstairs. "Japanese sound okay?"

She called in an order of sushi while awaiting a cab and picked it up on the way. Somehow she had to get the kids to wake up and realize the extent of the danger. An FBI agent had come out from D.C. to warn them. Out in the open, they were sitting ducks. If they wouldn't cancel their rally, they at least had to take a back seat.

The kids were too excited to listen. Their excitement was palpable, they were as animated as she had ever seen them. It didn't take long to learn the reason.

"Denny's coming to the rally," Tyler said, with a smile on his face as he passed out boxes of food.

"Maybe you can just let him talk."

Tyler shook his head. "He can't really mention the Fed, not without giving his critics a point of attack. But we can talk about it."

The kitty wound around her ankles and Jill picked her up and hugged her tightly. She sunk down in Tyler's chair. This was the worst possible news. Tyler and his friends were the ones who had to talk about the Fed. Denny wouldn't go there. Although he was getting them more attention, he was putting them more at risk.

Everyone began to eat. The cat stretched out on Jill's lap and she fed it pieces of shrimp. With one hand, Ali used chopsticks and chowed down, while typing with the other hand. He never had anything to say, and it was easy to forget that he was there.

In between bites, Jill told Tyler about her meeting with Special Agent Mark Biltmore. "He knows it was your computer the thieves were after. He thinks you were the one poisoned. He says it's strange you got your permit so quickly. Up on stage, in front of a crowd, you'll be an open target. And now, the eye-witness is gone. The homeless people got picked up by Immigration yesterday and everyone came back but her."

"Maybe she went home," Tyler said, from his perch on the edge of the bed, a plate in his lap.

"We've upped our numbers on the permit," David said, as if to appease her. "They'll increase the number of police. You don't have to worry."

"If Denny is recognized as a serious candidate by Saturday, he'll be given Secret Service protection," Tyler added.

"That's not going to help *you guys*," Jill said.

Tyler ran a sushi roll through a glob of green wasabi. "We'll be fine. Don't worry."

"We're finally getting somewhere," David said. "Denny's setting the agenda. He's ahead of the curve and the President and Tumblin are behind and scrambling to catch up. The media blitz is working."

"I loved the Secretary of the Treasury scrambling to explain why we wouldn't cash in our gold," Tyler said, with a chuckle. "Shows where the power really lies."

"Treasury is more Wall Street than Washington," David said.

Jill remembered President Jackson trying to wrestle control from the central bank by ordering his Secretary of the Treasury to stop making deposits to the bank, and two refused.

"Look where the secretary came from," Tyler said. "He was the senior vice president of Aunt Julie's firm. His under secretary is a former New York Federal Reserve chairman. The whole department works for the banks, not the people. All the President's economic advisors come from Wall Street. What kind of policy do you think they favor? You just have to look at the state of the country to know."

"Denny is going to focus on the gold," David said. "The President won't talk about it any more, but people are interested and it polls well. We all want to know what happened to it. How much we've got. Where it is."

"Denny will link it to the Fed," Tyler said. "Supposedly twenty billion dollars worth of gold is in the basement of the New York Federal Reserve. That gold belongs to the people, not the central bank. If it's been taken, that's robbery. Of course, we have to audit the Fed to find out if they've got it."

"And that's what the Fed's been fighting," David said. "It doesn't want an audit. It doesn't want people to know how much money it makes or who it gives it to."

"The Mayor and his news corporation sued the Fed to find out," Tyler said.

"The case went all the way to the Supreme Court," David added. "For the first time in history, the Fed had to disclose who exactly was 'too big to fail'. Besides the big banks, important friends and their wives got bailed out, and so did foreign countries. The Fed used our money to bail out the world."

"We're sending out another round of questionnaires, just on the Fed," Tyler said. He sprang from the bed, rooted around stacks of papers lying on the table, grabbed a page and gave it to Jill. There was a list of thirteen questions that required a true or false answer:

1. The Federal Reserve Board is not a government agency.
2. The Fed is a profiteering central bank that works for Wall Street.
3. The Fed uses taxpayer dollars but is never audited.
4. The Fed's economic policy serves the banks not the people.
5. The Fed prints money out of thin air and gets interest on it.

6.   The Fed printing money causes booms and busts and inflation.
7.   The Fed is the richest corporation in the U.S.
8.   The Fed was the cause of the Great Depression.
9.   The Fed was the cause of the 2008 housing crisis.
10.   The Fed plays the stock market and is guilty of insider trading.
11.   The Fed is more powerful than elected government officials.
12.   The Fed is the single reason for the country's uncontrollable debt.
13.   The Fed is turning America into a Third World country.

Jill read the questionnaire and it was obvious to her how Tyler thought the questions should be answered. "I'm guessing the correct answer to every question is true."

"You don't have to guess," Tyler said. "The answers are supported by facts."

"Does the Fed really play the stock market?" Jill asked.

"Absolutely," Tyler said. "If it wants the market to go up, it invests long in futures. If it wants the market to go down, it shorts the futures, betting against them. As for insider trading, since it gets to set interest rates, it always knows whether the market will go up or down. It tells its friends, lets them know in advance when to get in or out."

"The Fed can crash currencies," David added. "If it bets against them, their value goes down."

"The big banks have been accused of crashing the Czech economy by shorting the koruna," Tyler said.

"They're to blame for rising oil prices," David said. "When banks buy oil futures long, they're betting the price will increase and it does."

"Reagan set up a Plunge Protection Team," Tyler said. "If the market is in danger of crashing, the PPT rushes out and buys stock to prop it up. This gives the appearance the market is healthy when it really isn't. Every time the Fed chairman speaks, the PPT buys stock to make it look like the market sees his wisdom and likes what he said. Only it's all contrived."

"But the market fell one thousand points yesterday."

"And it already made it back. Wall Street is having a good day."

"How did you find out about the PPT?" Jill asked.

"The information is out there," Tyler said. "You can find it if you look. But it's buried. Who would announce it? The government? Banks? Stock brokers? They want people in the market. It's a zero sum game. You lose and someone else wins. It's pretty obvious who's winning and who's losing."

"We want people to know," David said.

"Denny wants people to know," Tyler added. "You can't change something if you don't know it's happening."

"The government can buy the Fed out anytime," David said.

Jill remembered Tyler had mentioned that at La Fleur, just before he and his father fell ill.

"We can buy it out for four hundred and fifty million," Tyler said. "Since we owe it one trillion, it's not a bad deal, until you consider they only printed the one trillion, they didn't earn it."

"Then the government will own its own debt," David said.

"Last year we paid thirty billion to the Fed in interest," Tyler added. "Think of what we could do if we had that money. If the government took over the Fed and printed a government dollar it didn't have to repay, or owe interest on. We would prosper. That's what Denny's fighting for. What we're fighting for."

Jill put down her chopsticks. Her nose was running and her sinuses were burning. While this sounded like utopia, the Fed would not sit back and allow itself to be bought out. It would fight for its life, fight to the death for its free money. "It won't go easily. It will fight back."

"It's already fighting back, Mom."

Lunch was over and Jill left soon after. Everything she learned about the Fed, every additional piece of information, only darkened the picture of corruption. And every piece of information Tyler and his friends broadcast, put their lives in more danger. And yet they pressed on, when every instinct they had should have been screaming: stop, turn around and run, they kept going. For everyone, the stakes were high. It was a literal fight to the death. While she agreed with what

Tyler and his friends were doing, it was too dangerous. Why couldn't someone else do it? Why did it have to be them?

***

Charles was gone when Jill got home. She sat in the living room while outside the glass windows the crane clattered and workmen shouted. She went online. Her computer was working slowly. It had been gradually getting slower and slower all week and she wondered if the crane and the construction were interfering with the Wi-Fi transmission signal. At first she had suspected Tyler, but Julie was experiencing similar problems.

She read Tyler's blog: 'One Trillion Reasons To Audit the Fed.' In the time it took her to read the three pages, her brand new laptop froze three times. The hard drive was always busy.

She went to Blaze's official website and the laptop behaved better. She learned he had stumped at Texas A&M University that morning. It was a conservative military university and the chief rival of her alma mater, the University of Texas. She realized he was desperate if he was campaigning in redneck territory.

He didn't list his poll numbers on his website but they were easy to find. According to both CNN and Gallup, Candy Turner was in the lead with forty-three percent of the vote. Blaze had thirty seven percent with sixteen percent undecided. He would find the numbers depressing, and in the spirit of forgiveness, Jill called him. The phone rang and rang. He didn't pick up. According to his schedule, he had the afternoon and evening off.

Jill called Alexandria. She and her father kept in close contact and if anyone – besides Rebecca and Calista – knew his whereabouts, it would be her. But she didn't know either, she hadn't talked to him in a few days. At least, all was well with her. No one had been following her, she had seen nothing suspicious. She had an anatomy exam on Monday and wouldn't be able to make it to the rally. She was registered to vote in Boston and was looking forward to the election on Tuesday. In every internet poll, Denny Drake was ahead.

Jill hung up and her phone rang immediately, again with the funny ring tone that made her think it was Mark Biltmore, only it was Special Agent King from the New York FBI. "We will be able to see you Friday morning at the FBI building at 7:30."

Jill started to say that she would be there, but the agent abruptly hung up. He probably felt he had to see her on account of Blaze and wasn't too happy about it. Well too bad, she had questions and wanted not only answers, but results. Why weren't they working harder to get criminals off the streets.

She turned on the TV. Before long, the President was shown arriving back home at the White House. He paused on the lawn to take questions from reporters. The first was about the gold. "Will we use it to pay down the debt?"

"It's not necessary," the President said. "We'll save it for a rainy day. We don't need money at the moment and the last thing we want to do is sell our gold on the cheap. That would send a bad signal to investors."

Which was parroting what his Secretary of the Treasury had said the night before.

"Why hasn't the gold been audited as required by law?" another reporter asked.

"It's in Fort Knox," said the President. "It's impenetrable, no one can get to it." He laughed as if he were making a joke.

The next question was about California, which was still in financial trouble and drowning in debt. "How can that not drag down the economy?"

"Look at the stock market," the President said. "Today, there was a gain of twelve hundred points. Today the market reached an all-time high. Despite the nay-sayers, we have a robust economy. We need to continue advancing alternative energy platforms, gain independence from foreign oil, keep those dollars here, put them in the pockets of the people, and we'll balance our books."

Those were all the questions he had time for. With a wave, he sauntered away from the crowd and toward his waiting wife.

A commercial came on and there was Denny Drake. "How much gold do we really have?" he asked, as he stared intently into the camera. "The American people have a right to know if the Fort Knox gold has been taken by the Federal Reserve as collateral for government debt. The gold reserves belong to the people. The law requires an audit every year. As president, I will uphold the law. I will demand a full audit of the gold. The American people deserve to know what has happened to their wealth."

Rich Tumblin wasn't addressing the question of the gold. He was back to his favored theme of running the government like a business. The current government had failed. It was all but bankrupt. In the real world, it would never survive. The books had to be balanced. As head of a multi-billion dollar investment firm, he could do this. Unlike the President, and the mysterious Mr. Drake, a man who admittedly had gone bankrupt himself.

Jill was startled by the mention of Denny on primetime news. This was the first time either presidential contender had mentioned him by name. On the one hand, they were giving him the recognition that was due, but on the other, he was being slammed. Jill questioned the wisdom of his plan to fly under the radar for so long and jump up at the last moment with serious baggage, like personal bankruptcy and farming medical marijuana. He would have to face those issues and put them to rest in order to win.

Julie arrived home earlier than usual. She kicked off her shoes, shrugged off her blazer and dropped her briefcase. Charles went to the kitchen to make a martini and Julie came into the living room and plopped on the couch "Best day ever in the history of the New York Stock Exchange," she said.

Jill put the TV on mute. "I heard. Up twelve hundred points."

"On a day the firm's server couldn't be worse. Everyone's having serious problems."

"My computer's working slowly too," Jill said. "I wonder if it's the construction."

"It's not. It must be your computer. We've got a virus. I don't know how it works, but it's like there's someone active behind the scene. The mouse bounces around for no reason. Files open and close by themselves. The hard drive freezes for no reason."

"Any money transfer out by itself?" Jill asked.

"Not yet. The IT guys are watching 24/7. We've got the best computer jocks in the world."

Charles handed her a martini and she took a gulp. "I'm going out to celebrate my turn of fortune. Care to come?"

Jill passed.

"You're so boring." Julie paused. "Unless you have other plans?"

"No."

"Seeing a man?"

"Pardon?"

"Charles told me about your young man. I'm not sure I like you entertaining strangers in my home when I'm at work."

"Who are you? My mother?" Jill glared at the butler who had his back turned and was busy picking up Julie's shoes.

"Who is he?" Julie asked.

Unable to tell her the truth, Jill thought quickly. "A friend of Tyler's."

"Where did you meet him?"

It was the third degree, just like when she was a kid. "In the park," Jill said, grabbing the first thing that came to mind. "I went there after I saw your astrologer. I liked her."

"Everyone does. Charles thought he was too young for you."

Charles, straightening the newspaper, ignored this.

"I'm married. I'm not looking for men," Jill said.

Julie just laughed. "I won't say a word." She raised a finger. "But I told you so. There's no such thing as monogamy. Not for you or for Blaze."

Jill was grateful when they left. Protected behind a steel door and armed doormen, she ate leftovers and watched mindless TV.

16

It is absurd to say that our country can issue $30 million in bonds and not $30 million in currency. Both are promises to pay, but one promise favors the usurers (lender) and the other helps the people.
—Thomas Edison

THURSDAY OCTOBER 30

On Thursday morning, Jill's phone rang at eight with the strange ring tone. Special Agent Mark Biltmore was on the line. "Good morning, Mrs. Madison," he said. "I hope this isn't too early to call. Are you busy? Could you come downstairs?"

Julie hadn't come home all night and Jill had already gone out for coffee in the darkness of the below-freezing morning and was back watching early news. She muted the sound. She had planned to wait until it warmed up and then head over to Gold Street to search for Vivienne, but she heard the urgency in Biltmore's tone and was immediately worried. "What's wrong? Is Tyler all right?"

"He's fine. Please. I prefer we not speak over the phone."

Jill hung up, turned off the TV, grabbed her purse, stepped into low pumps and rushed downstairs where Biltmore was pacing the sidewalk. She went outside. The cold air made her shiver and brought goosebumps to her skin. It was still freezing, the mercury hovering around thirty in unseasonable cold. The sun was rising in a cloudless sky and it looked like it was going to be one of those clear, frigid days.

"What's wrong?" she asked again.

Biltmore raised his hand and flagged a cab. He wore a black windbreaker, the same ill-fitting jeans with a collared t-shirt, which today was forest green. "There's a Jane Doe in the city morgue. I think it's your bag lady. Can you make an ID?"

A cab pulled up to the curb and Jill stood frozen in place. The last dead person she had seen had been her daughter.

Biltmore grabbed her elbow and steered her toward the cab. "Just give me half an hour, please."

She got into the car and Biltmore slid in beside her and slammed the door sharply. "New York City Morgue," he said, before he shut the sliding window.

Jill put on her seatbelt and wrapped her arms around each other. She wore a navy, long-sleeved cotton t-shirt and jeans and she was freezing.

Biltmore was pulling off his windbreaker. "According to the police report, an apparent homeless woman was pulled out of the river on Tuesday night. She drowned. Here, you look cold. Take my jacket." He tugged off a sleeve. "The woman had no ID, wore tattered clothes, a long overcoat and mismatched tennis shoes, one of which was a size 12 green Nike."

"Oh, God." Jill raised a hand to her forehead.

Biltmore adjusted his jacket around her shoulders and she slipped in her arms. "I want to get to the morgue and make the ID before we get shut out. The pathologist is expecting us."

Thirty minutes later they reached the morgue, a non-descript brown brick building without a sign in a busy section of town that Jill didn't recognize. Biltmore paid the driver and they climbed steep steps. Inside, he flashed his FBI badge and Jill showed her driver's license. They signed in and then passed through a metal detector. A security guard examined Jill's purse and pulled out the shoe bag and peered inside before waving them through.

Dr. Sedgwick arrived to take them downstairs. She was Biltmore's age and wore a white lab coat. Volumes of brown hair swirled at her shoulders. She had done the autopsy and had spoken with Biltmore over the phone.

They took an elevator to the basement and the doors opened into a long hallway. At the far end, the doctor punched in a code and two black doors swung open. They entered a freezing cold, gray concrete room that smelled of formaldehyde. Jill's head began to pound. In the far corner, another doctor was cutting into a body. A high-pitched metallic wail echoed off the walls. He was using what sounded like an electric saw. Jill turned, refusing to look.

The doctor's high heels clicked as she marched to a stainless steel wall lined with handles and pulled out a drawer. Jill stood behind Biltmore, her heart heavy and her knees weak. The body was covered in a sheet and the doctor pulled it back. Biltmore moved out of the way and Jill glanced quickly at the body and then away. She had seen enough.

Vivienne was naked, with a great scar up her torso branching to her shoulders. Her long dirty blond hair was tangled and still wet. No longer gray, her skin was green. Her mouth was wide open, revealing her nice teeth and a grimace. She died as if gasping for breath. Jill closed her eyes, leaned on an empty gurney and wondered if she was going to be sick.

"Well?" Biltmore said, coming into her line of sight.

"It's her." Jill turned away from the body.

"Where are her things?" Biltmore asked the pathologist.

Dr. Sedgwick opened a locker and pulled out a plastic bag and dumped the contents on a stainless steel table. Jill saw wet ragged clothes, a long sodden gray coat and two mismatched running shoes. There was the red high top and Tyler's green Nike. Jill reached into her purse, got out the shoe bag and removed the Nike. She put it alongside its match. The electric saw finally stopped screeching.

"Who was she?" asked the doctor.

Jill relayed what she knew. "Her name was Vivienne. She was picked up by Immigration officials on Tuesday morning."

"No," Biltmore said. "I checked with Immigration and they are not in the business of picking up homeless people."

"She has layers of skin under the fingernails of both hands," the pathologist said. "She did not simply drown. She went out fighting. She scratched someone. We'll get DNA."

Jill stared down at the gray cement floor and felt responsible. She had gone to the police about an eye-witness and here was the body. Now there was no corroboration as to what had happened the night of Tyler's accident. The drowning told Jill one more thing. The assassins were serious. They took people out. Maybe Jared Slater who shot hoops and carried groceries could kill after all. As could a blond hulk with a facial scar.

Biltmore finished talking to the pathologist, said goodbye, and steered Jill toward the elevator. They rode up, retrieved their IDs and went outside. Jill was thankful for the bright sunshine, but shivered in the cold.

Biltmore raised his hand for a cab.

"I've got to go," Jill said, shrugging off the jacket.

Biltmore lowered his hand and kept the jacket in place. "Did you want to look at bullet-proof vests? I can help you find something suitable. I don't think it would be a waste of time or money."

Jill paused. It could have been Tyler on that table, or her, with strangers gawking at big Y incisions on damaged flesh.

"This changes everything," Biltmore said. "We're dealing with a cold-blooded killer. Someone who can kill with their bare hands. Believe it or not, it's not a universal skill."

"Part of FBI training?"

"If we wanted to stop a bag lady, there are easier ways."

"If not you, then who?"

"CIA. Private mercenaries. The bigger banks all use security services, though mostly for internet security, not this."

Jill's phone rang. She yanked it from her purse. Finally, Blaze was calling. She held a finger to her lips to silence Biltmore, turned her back and started walking down the street. Blaze would see the seriousness of it. He would know what to do.

She opened her phone. "Thank God you called. I found an eyewitness to Tyler's accident. She was drowned. Killed. I just –"

He didn't let her continue. "*You're* killing me. Do you realize that? Do you want me to lose the election? How could you spend a thousand dollars on signs and t-shirts with the words: FED UP. I look like a hypocrite."

She stopped walking and took a deep breath, noticing that a cab was trailing her. The window in the back was down and Biltmore was inside.

"Do you have any idea how bad it looks for me to be bankrolling Tyler's protest?"

"You're not bankrolling it," Jill said, as she continued on and the cab kept pace. "Tyler has a donor. He doesn't have a bank account."

"So you use mine for a cause I don't believe in? I can't believe this. What will it look like when it gets out? When, not if. My accounts are transparent. I post them. You know that."

"Who will know what's on the signs or t-shirts?"

"I know," Blaze thundered. "It's not hard to find out. It's not like it's covered by privacy laws."

"The credit card bill won't be out until after the election."

"So it's okay if I look like a flaming hypocrite after the election?" On the other end, Blaze was sputtering. He said something like, "Agghh. I am not happy." He hung up without saying goodbye.

Jill walked on. It had happened again. She didn't have a chance to speak. Blaze was as bad as Julie, always shutting her down. More importantly, she couldn't depend on him for help. Murder left him unmoved. All that mattered were the charges on the credit card. Though he did have a point.

The cab stopped in the road and Biltmore threw open the door. "Ride?"

Jill was in over her head and right now her only help was in the cab and a man who didn't feel the cold. She got in. "I need to stop at a National Bank." She had to deposit Julie's check.

"There's one down the street from the gun shop." Biltmore stared out the front windshield. "If you wish to make purchases you prefer to keep private, you can always use a prepaid bank card."

Jill stared at the agent and he slowly turned her way. "Is my phone bugged? Am I wired?"

He smiled his tight smile. "I read lips. I'm sorry. I can't help it. Forgive me."

"What's a prepaid bank card?"

The agent's small eyes opened with surprise and he explained what it was. Jill never did the banking, had never heard of a prepaid bank card, but it sounded good to her. She could use a bank account or credit card to load a generic Visa that could be used to make purchases no one could trace.

They drove along the Avenue of the Americas and the cabbie let them out in front of the National Bank. With Biltmore waiting on the sidewalk, she went inside and deposited the check and got a five thousand dollar prepaid bank card. The gun shop was three doors down.

It had barred windows and a steel grate door that was folded to the side. A security guard opened the inner door and they went inside. The long, narrow shop smelled of sulfur and metal. Both sides of the store bore locked glass display cases filled with guns, pistols, and shotguns. Along the back wall was a long rack of vests.

Biltmore flashed his ID at the salesman and Jill wondered if you needed special ID to be in a gun shop. She followed Biltmore to the back. "You can order whatever you want," he said, "but there's not enough time before Saturday. I think you'll find what you're looking for here. Good material at a reasonable price."

She saw he had a vest picked out. He thrust his arm into the middle of a rack and pulled out a black vest. "You checked this place out," she said.

"I wanted to see what they had, if there was anything suitable. I didn't want to waste your time."

She smiled at him. He was the only one on her side. "You didn't have anything else to do? No big meetings? Strategy sessions?"

He looked ruefully at the vest. "To tell you the truth, I'm off the clock."

"You're doing this on your own time?"

"I think it's important. I took three days of leave. I'm supposed to be visiting family on Long Island." He made a face. "It's really why I need to keep a low profile."

Ah, the reason for the secrecy and why he couldn't call the New York FBI himself. No one knew he was here. No one saw the danger, but him. "Thank you for coming."

In response, he handed her the vest. It looked like it was made of down until she took it and her arm dropped with its weight. "If you put it on, the weight is distributed and it's not that bad," he said. "Here, try it on."

She pulled it over her head, over his bulky jacket. Velcro straps at the sides helped adjust the fit. It went below her hips, covering the genitals.

"It won't be as long on Tyler," Biltmore said, adjusting the straps. "It will be higher in the hip, but it should be fine. If he's a target and they're serious, they'll go for the heart. He can wear it over a t-shirt, under a sweater or a blazer. No one will know. It's made of Kevlar, tough but lightweight. A reasonable price." He helped Jill take it off.

"What happens if they drown him or run over him again?"

"That won't happen at the rally."

Jill bought three vests using her own Visa and barely looking at the total. When Blaze saw the charge he would have a fit, but this was their son's life and if he didn't recognize the danger, she did and so did this FBI agent. Tyler would never wear a vest if his friends weren't also protected, so there was no choice. With Biltmore holding the shopping bag, they went outside.

"What now?" he asked.

Though Jill was thankful he was on her side, there were limits to his involvement. "I have errands to run." She scanned the road for a cab.

"Keep in touch?"

"Sure."

"Did you make an appointment with the New York branch?"

"I set up a meeting on Friday morning."

"Will you reconsider wearing a wire?"

She shook her head. A free cab turned the corner, came their way and she raised her hand. The cab stopped at a light. "Did you check out Charles?"

"He's British, so it has to go through proper channels. It might take a while. I checked his license and he doesn't have an American driver's license. His must be international."

Jill looked at him. "Is that strange?"

"Not if he doesn't plan to be here long."

"What about the man with the scar?"

"Try and get a photo."

"What about Jared Slater?"

"I'm making inquiries. Under the circumstance, I need to be discreet."

He was going out on a limb for her and she was grateful.

***

Jill went straight to the Bronx, bringing the vests, but forgetting to bring any food. Traffic was heavy and slow, as sluggish and stuck as her thoughts. She couldn't get Vivienne out of her mind and Blaze was clueless to the danger, Tyler underestimated it, and her only hope was a vacationing FBI agent who was unable to get anyone to take him seriously. One way or another, she had to get the kids to realize they were in mortal danger.

She reached Maple Street and lugged the vests upstairs. She hadn't called in advance and the kids were surprised to see her. They were working at the table, all three of them typing quickly at their laptops when she opened the door. She saw them stiffen. Tyler and David stopped whatever they were doing and closed their laptops. Ali kept typing.

Tyler jumped up, crossed the room and took the oversized shopping bag. His arm fell towards the floor. "Is everything all right? What's in here?" He frowned into the bag.

"Bullet proof vests. The FBI agent thought it was a good idea. I went to the morgue this morning."

Tyler straightened and looked at her.

"The eye-witness is dead. Vivienne. The homeless lady who found your Nike. Who saw the hit-and-run. She was drowned. Murdered."

Tyler swallowed hard, his Adam's apple jumped. Ali coughed and smoothed down his cowlick. David drummed his fingertips on the table. "How do you know she didn't just drown?" Tyler asked.

"The pathologist said that she didn't go easily. She fought back. She scratched someone. There's DNA." Jill looked in her son's eyes. "These people are serious. They're killers."

"We know, Mom. We knew it two weeks ago when they ran me over, when Ali was arrested and David was shot. Denny knows that every speech he gives, he's out in the open. What are we supposed to do? Just shut up? Do nothing? Pretend our government isn't bankrupting us? It's not an option."

Jill looked at her son with mixed feelings. How proud she was of him; how appalled that he would take the life she treasured so lightly. "Take as much care as you can," she said.

He reached into the shopping bag and pulled out a vest. "I'm not wearing this. It weighs a hundred pounds."

"It doesn't," Jill said, as the cat, as if sensing her mood, scooted under the bed. "If you put it on, you'll distribute the weight and won't feel it."

"No way." He let the vest fall back into the bag.

"I'll wear it," David said, staring Tyler down. "Hey, I got shot. I don't want to go through that again."

"I got three," Jill said, as the cat batted a crumpled ball of paper out from under the bed. "One for each of you."

Tyler found the receipt and frowned. "I hope this isn't coming out of our budget."

"My gift."

"You mean Dad's. He won't like it."

That was the absolute truth, especially after their last conversation, but she would worry about it later. "Your safety matters to him."

Ali stood up and slid toward the door. He would go make some tea. He excused himself and went next door. The cat went with him. Tyler offered his seat and Jill went to the table and sat down.

She hugged her arms together. Without heating the room was cold. She looked around at the mess. The sheets were asunder and clothes littered the floor. The three drawers of the dresser were left open. Wads of paper were balled in a pile in the corner. There was chaos all around them.

"We're meeting with Denny's campaign manager later this afternoon," Tyler said.

"What for?" Jill asked.

"We've got to confirm who's going to say what at the rally."

"Denny can't attack the Fed himself," David said.

Of course not, Jill thought, Denny Drake was leaving the dirty work to the kids.

"He wants to focus on the future. David and I get to talk about the present." Her son smiled a wicked smile that did nothing to ease her anxiety.

"We're not supposed to swear," David added, not that she had ever heard him swear before.

"He's going on The Nightly Show on Friday." Tyler clapped his hands with excitement.

"It's his first appearance on TV," David said. "It will air tomorrow night and he'll plug the rally. We could have a hundred thousand show up."

More bad news, Jill thought. It would be a zoo, a mad house, a free-for-all, with who knew how many trained killers.

"Behind the scenes, the President and Tumblin are running scared," Tyler said. "They're pumping out attack ads. They've finally woken up."

Tyler pulled up a website and played a short commercial on his laptop. The President was slamming Denny Drake's youth, inexperience, and political ineptitude; much of the same criticism that had been levied against him four years before. Naturally, he was concerned about Drake's character. What kind of man grew drugs?

With so many of his potential voters bankrupt, or getting there, he did not mention that issue, but Rich Tumblin was running with it. Obviously, Drake couldn't stick to a budget. He had lost his farm, and that wasn't enough, now he was going after the country.

With money to burn, the Republican had done some investigating. Dennis Drake had gone to Russia in high school. He was a socialist, likely a communist. He took a hooker to the prom. His morals were obviously questionable. Clearly, his plan was to spread the wealth of hard-working people to the stoned unemployed who preferred to sit around and watch soap operas and eat Doritos. Well, Americans knew better; they would never vote for him.

Tyler paused the video. "They're going to play those ads tonight. Who dredges up high school trips and a date to a prom with a cheerleader who became a madam? They're desperate and all they have on him is his dope farm and his bankruptcy. Denny will use it against them. Here, watch this."

Tyler played another clip, a preliminary ad that had been sent out that morning to assess voters' response. Like most of his commercials, there was a headshot of Denny staring earnestly into the camera. "It's true, I grew medical marijuana for the suffering ill who were prescribed cannabis by their physicians. I am not a medical doctor, nor do I purport to know the medication required by the sick in order to be comfortable. I do know that every gram of product I produced was sold to the state dispensary. As you may imagine, there are strict rules,

oversight and guidelines to ensure compliance. I was never in violation of those regulations. I respect and abide by the law."

The camera came in from another angle. "I admit, I lost my farm. I
was duped. I listened to a slick banker who wanted to lend me money
so I could build greenhouses. I mortgaged my land to get the loan.
This was in 2007, just before the crash. I wasn't counting on it or on
the floods that drowned my crop. I missed one payment and the bank
began foreclosure. They refused to work with me. I lost my land and
my house. I was so mad, I'm here today. I know many of you were, or
are, as desperate as I was, and feel the way I felt. I can assure you, we
can fight back. We can get this country to work for the people. Wall
Street has bought Washington. The people can win it back. We may
not have much money, but we have a vote. You can vote for the banks,
or you can vote for yourselves. It's up to you."

The camera panned around to a full frontal head shot. "I'm Denny
Drake and I'm running for president and I approve this message."

Ali was back with the cat and four mugs of steaming tea and
passed them out. He took his laptop to the bed and sat down.

"Voters we've contacted love the ad," Tyler said. "Wait till tonight
and it airs back-to-back with the President's and Tumblin's attack
ads."

"Wait a minute." Jill said. "How do you know what commercials
the President and Tumblin are going to air tonight?"

"They have focus groups," Tyler said. "Like Denny, they send out
sample ads and see how people respond."

"And you're in their focus groups?" Jill said.

The kids exchanged glances. Jill looked at her son and he couldn't
maintain eye contact. He chewed a thumbnail. David examined a
frayed rip in his jeans. Ali typed on as if he heard nothing. Finally
Tyler said, "Not exactly." He bit his lip, pulled at the nail. "We put
ourselves on their list, unofficially."

Jill found it hard to breathe. "You hacked into their websites?"

"Just their campaign headquarters," Tyler said.

Jill raised a hand to her head.

"They weren't really protected," Tyler said, as if it mattered.

"It's illegal. You're breaking the law."

"We're just looking. We're not doing anything," he said, righteously. "It's not any different from hacking into V-Comm."

"It's very different. With V-Comm, you retrieved your own file." She paused. "Right?"

"Right, Mom."

"They could arrest you," Jill said.

"They don't know we're there," Tyler said. "Come on, the playing field is already so uneven. It helps to know what they're thinking."

"They're terrified of Denny," David said.

"They know he's coming and they're trying to stop him, but it's too late," Tyler said. "According to the internet polls, he's five points ahead of Tumblin, ten ahead of the President. They're freaking out. They can't believe it. Over at their campaign headquarters, heads are rolling."

"We leaked their private polls to the press," David said, slyly. "They won't be able to ignore them much longer."

Jill didn't know what to say. She sat silently, staring at the laptop. They had crossed a line, stepped on the other side of the law. Organizing a protest was one thing, but hacking was something else, especially when they were hacking into the presidential contenders' campaign sites. The kids might think they were unnoticed, but Jill found it unlikely. If someone wanted to shut them down, they could throw them in jail. There would be a valid reason.

"I don't like it," Jill said.

"I know," Tyler said. "That's why I didn't tell you." Tyler clicked on the mouse and closed the site.

A large photograph of Blaze eating a meal appeared on the screen. He was not alone. Tyler quickly closed the window.

"What was that?" Jill said sharply.

Tyler winced. Ali mumbled something and got up and left the room. David grabbed the cat and went after him. "Ali might have left the kettle on," he explained, as he closed the door.

"Let me see that," Jill said.

In obvious distress, Tyler pulled up the photo.

Jill stared at the screen. Blaze was dining with Rebecca. Their seats were pushed so close together that their elbows were touching. The room was dark and lit with candles. Jill recognized the gleaming bar behind them. They were at the Pecan Street Café. Blaze had his elbow on the fine linen, supporting his chin. They were gazing into each other's eyes.

"It's probably photoshopped," Tyler said. "It's going to run in the next issue of the *Enquirer*."

Jill felt as if she had been kicked in the gut. She ran her hand through her hair. "With what caption?"

"It's not written yet. There are two other photos."

"Can I see them?"

Tyler sighed, but clicked the mouse and another photograph appeared. They were at a campaign stop now. Blaze had his arm around Rebecca's bare shoulder. He was staring straight ahead into the camera, but she was staring at him with lust in her eyes.

Another click and another photograph. Jill recognized Rebecca's home. They were walking together down the front walk heading for the house. The stars were out and a big, bright moon was overhead. The leaves were off the trees. It was taken recently, the moon would be full on Saturday. Again, Blaze had his arm around her back, but his head was turned to face the camera, as if he knew he was being watched.

Tyler closed the site. "They're probably doctored. Their heads put on other bodies."

But if Tyler didn't recognize Rebecca's house, Jill did.

Tyler turned and looked at her. "He married you, Mom. If he wanted her, he would have never left her."

It was exactly what Petra often said. "You're right," Jill said, in what she hoped was an even, calm voice. Her ears were suddenly plugged as if there was a change in air pressure so she couldn't hear herself speak and didn't know how the words came out. Long ago, she had vowed never to bring her children into her marriage and she had nothing more to say.

She mumbled something about having to leave and Tyler walked her downstairs and waited for the cab with her. When it came, he kissed her goodbye. "We won't be here tomorrow," he said. "We've got tickets to The Nightly Show. Can you help out on Saturday? Sell t-shirts?"

"If you promise to wear your vest."

He smiled at her as he opened the cab door. "Don't worry about me. Don't worry about Dad."

17

Although the oppressor today is seen to be big government, what the nineteenth century Populists were trying to get off their backs was a darker, more malevolent force... They saw their antagonist rather as the private money power and the corporations it had spawned, which were threatening to take over the government unless the people intervened.

—Ellen Brown, Web of Debt

The cab drove slowly south through thick traffic. Jill stared out the window, watching garbage blow by. She saw a homeless man on a street corner and thought of Vivienne and looked away. There were winners and there were losers, and she always considered herself the former, but now she didn't know any more. She felt as if everything she had was slipping away. Blaze and Tyler both seemed beyond her reach.

She finally got to Julie's. Charles was dusting and vacuuming and she lasted five minutes in the living room under his caustic eye, as if his job was to spy on her and not clean and cook. She took her laptop to the bedroom and locked the door. She went online to look at the three photographs once more. She couldn't find them on the *Enquirer* site. According to their website, the most recent story they had on Blaze was from six months ago, when he was in Corpus soon after the last deep water oil spill. She went to his official website and glanced at his schedule.

Yesterday, he had spoken at Texas A&M and had taken the afternoon and evening off. Today, he was spending the afternoon at the Texas Banker's Association in Austin, which Rebecca would have arranged. He'd be there now, shaking hands and speaking, giving his view of the future, with not one word about the Fed.

Her phone beeped. It was a text message from Julie: *Dinner at 8. Dress up.* It was an order, not a request. Jill took it as a fortuitous invitation. She wanted to talk to her sister away from the prying ears of the nosy butler. Julie was always bragging about her primo computer jocks. Sandford-Gallagher had the latest firewalls, the top-of-the-line internet security. She might know if hackers could breach private sites without anyone knowing. Jill was also glad to get out, not to have to think about Blaze or wait for him not to call. On that front, she was in over her head, but she would never ask Julie for advice. Julie, of course, would be full of it anyway.

At six, Charles left and Jill showered and dressed in the best clothes she had brought, black slacks and a peach V-neck sweater. She turned on the news to wait for Julie. The Dennis Drake candidacy had finally made the network and cable stations.

He was the favored candidate of Independents, Hispanics, and many women, who liked Maria Rodriquez, his VP. AARP, a teachers union, and a nursing association, had changed their endorsements at the last minute and rallied to his side. The most recent polls by CNN, Gallup and Pews showed an unmistakable three-way race. The CNN poll had Tumblin on top, Gallup had the President, and Pews had Drake. With the margin of error six percentage points in each poll, the election was suddenly wide open. There was no telling how Drake's appearance would influence the results. Who would vote for him and whose votes would he steal?

The president of AARP, the league of retired persons, was on CNN to explain their endorsement. The organization had been following Drake for months and they were thrilled by his promise to protect Social Security and Medicare, when the other two candidates both admitted the sweet entitlements had to be addressed. Drake didn't buy it. He thought the word 'entitlement' was a misnomer. Retirees had paid into the system and deserved what they had paid for. It was a government obligation, not an elderly entitlement. AARP also liked his ten thousand dollar rebate for those who owned homes and had seen their housing equity tumble after 2008. They were also interested in finding out what happened to their gold. Some seniors remembered the confiscation and the immediate doubling in price that occurred once they turned in their gold. They were also concerned about the stock market. So many had been burned. They wanted oversight and regulation. They liked the fact that Drake wanted to audit the Fed. They were interested in a monetary system where the government printed its own money. Why did the government print IOU's? Some seniors remembered the question from the 1932 election, and the defeat of the candidate who proposed the government print dollars.

For Jill, it was an eye-opening interview. Denny was now publicly suggesting that the government take away from the Federal Reserve and the banks their exclusive and unfair 'right' to print money. It was Tyler and his friends' number one issue, and Denny had picked it up and was running with it.

The attack ads of the mainstream candidates were in full swing. Their commercials showed a teenage Denny Drake with red eyes, looking maniacal and stoned. In one photo, he was dancing with a slut in a short, low cut dress. The voice-over narrator warned of the harm of having someone with no experience or character in the White House. His opponents were united in their distaste for him.

Democratic and Republican strategists rushed to downplay the Drake candidacy. There were still four full days to go before the election. This was a diversion, a break in the monotony of a lengthy campaign. Here was a new kid on the block that no one knew about. They were certain once the newcomer was placed in the spotlight and scrutinized like their candidates, the polls would show a different story. At first glance, he seemed more communist than socialist, and VP choice aside, America might consider him, but would ultimately reject him and his crackpot economic schemes.

The markets had also spoken. Soon after the release of the latest polls, the Dow Jones Industrial Average fell two hundred points. The markets didn't like Denny either.

As expected, Julie arrived home in a surly mood. Jill wondered if dinner was off, but fortified with a martini, and pundits on Money who dismissed Drake summarily, Julie was revived and ready to step out.

She put down her glass, looked Jill up and down and told her to get dressed.

"I'm already dressed."

"Oh no." Julie shook her head.

Under Charles' disdainful eye, Jill followed her sister to her bedroom and plunked down on a cream colored comforter while Julie pulled clothes out of her closet. She was going to wear a navy pantsuit and decided Jill would look good in white. "Virginal," she said. "It will bring out your eyes. When did you stop wearing makeup?"

"I'll hardly look virginal and I didn't bring makeup. Can't I just wear this?"

"Nope." Julie thrust a white silk suit in her lap. "It's a short suit, but all my pants will be too long." She removed the hanger. "I know what you're doing."

"You want me to wear shorts in this weather?" Jill lifted the clothes from her lap. "What am I doing?"

"The shorts will be long on you. Add high heels and you'll look great. "You're trying to make Blaze jealous. That explains the friend you picked up in the park."

It took Jill a moment to realize the friend Julie referred to was Special Agent Mark Biltmore. "I'm not trying to make Blaze jealous."

"Well you should. Everyone in the world knows what Rebecca's up to except you."

Jill strove to maintain a look of neutrality. "What are you talking about?" She wondered if the *Enquirer* was out and the photos available for the whole world to see.

"The Bankers Association."

"It was just a fundraiser," Jill said, trying to minimize it. "Blaze needs money."

"How much did she net him and what did she get in return?"

Jill exhaled slowly. No matter how quiet she kept, her private business was always on the table. "Why do you care?"

"I told you from the start she was trouble. I told you she'd never give him up. I told you, you'd never keep him. She's got a bank and you've got nothing. He divorces you and you're screwed. I won't let that happen. I'm going to help you." Julie opened a dresser drawer and tossed Jill a black bra. "Take off your shirt. Just wear the blazer."

Jill did what her sister ordered, but only because she wanted to get out of the apartment and out of earshot of the eavesdropping butler. She put on the suit and the shorts flared below her knees, but looked as if they could have been designed that way. Though the black lace underwire bra was partially visible beneath the blazer, Julie declared Jill fit for an evening on the town. Jill wanted to wear flat pumps, but ended up in three inch strappy sandals studded with diamonds. She also got makeup: mascara, eyeliner, blue eye shadow, red rouge and pink lipstick. It took Jill back to their youth, when they tried on makeup and she looked as clownish now as she did then.

"I look hideous," she said, staring at her reflection in the mirror.

"Flash bulbs will wash out your skin. You look fine. Let's go save your marriage."

"Flash bulbs?" Jill said, getting a bad feeling about the evening.

Julie didn't answer and out in the living room, where he was sprawled on the couch reading the newspaper, Charles declared her, "Fetching."

"Agreed," Julie said.

"Are we expecting a flood?" he asked.

"Charles, you might know how to cook, but you don't know the first thing about fashion," Julie said.

Charles idly turned a page of the paper. "I recognize flood pants when I see them."

"They're shorts," Julie said. "Get the car."

Driving down Broadway toward the restaurant with the dividing window closed, Julie gave instructions. "Now, there'll be photographers, but don't look at them. If you try to hide they'll have to take your picture. They can't resist."

Jill stared out the front window where the lights of Broadway were shining. "I don't want my picture taken."

"He'll see you out having fun. You're not sitting home pining away for him as usual. Make him come to you. Rule number one. Don't chase him, attract him."

"He's not thinking about me. The election is four days away."

Julie ignored this. "I'm glad you didn't take my advice and go home. That would have been the worst thing. Don't make yourself available. Rule number two."

Charles slammed on the brakes as a jaywalker cut in front of him. Jill wondered if he even had a driver's license. He honked his horn loudly and the jaywalker turned and flashed him the finger.

"If we meet anybody, don't give away too much," Julie said, as they sped on. "Just smile and try to look interested."

"I thought just you and I were having dinner."

"I said, *if*. This is an exclusive restaurant. No riffraff. There's no telling who we'll meet."

It sounded ominous to Jill. "Let's keep a low profile, can we. I don't want to draw any attention to Blaze before the election."

The car stopped. Like a suitor, Charles opened the door and held out a hand for Julie. Surprisingly, he did the same for Jill. "Watch out for the puddles," he said, out of the corner of his mouth. She stepped onto the sidewalk, which of course was dry after a day of cold sunshine.

With a sister on each arm, he crossed the sidewalk. Photographers standing under the restaurant's marquee began snapping photos. Jill heard one of them say, "Is that someone?"

A doorman pulled open the door and Charles departed. The restaurant was small and dark and lit with candles. The maître d' wore a tux and welcomed Julie warmly. He led them to a table in the middle of the room and pulled out their chairs, with Julie facing the door. A waiter swooped in to take their drink order, which for Julie was a dry martini, shaken not stirred, and for Jill, Perrier.

Julie felt it necessary to explain. "My sister doesn't drink." She opened her menu and leaned forward. "Liz Smyth is at the next table. She's a gossip columnist. I'm going to have a drink and get her over. Remember, just smile, don't say anything."

Jill glared at her sister.

But Julie was surveying the room. Glancing over her shoulder, she gasped, then covered her mouth when she said, "Don't look, but Sly is at the next table. I'll get him over here first. Give Liz something to write about."

Jill peered into the darkness. It did look like him, eating with five companions. While Julie assessed the room, Jill straightened her silverware. It was heavy and there was a lot of it. There was a white linen tablecloth and thick white napkins fanned out on the plates. Too many unnecessary glasses reflected the candlelight. Jill put her napkin on her lap and counted silverware.

The waiter arrived with their drinks and took their order. Jill's Perrier came without ice in a tall narrow frosted glass and was ice-cold. Julie's martini came in a large triangular glass with a spear of three olives. She tossed the spear on her bread plate and the plate was quickly replaced.

"I can't believe you've been married twenty-four years," Julie said, apropos nothing.

"Twenty-six."

"I didn't give it one. I thought Rebecca would be more insistent."

"Maybe you don't know much about marriage."

Julie laughed. "I know enough to know I don't want it."

"Wasn't there ever anyone you wanted that you didn't want anyone else to have?"

"Perhaps once, but that was a long time ago. I learned my lesson."

"Which was?"

"If you don't want someone, they'll want you. And vice versa. Rule number three."

The waiter returned with salad plates and a basket of bread. He rearranged silverware and repositioned the candle and bowed as he walked away. Jill picked up her fork and speared a shred of lettuce. "What kind of security does S-G have?"

Julie tore a roll in half. "I assume you're talking about our computer jocks. We pay the best, we hire the best."

"Has anyone ever hacked in?"

"The worst we've had are viral attacks, like the one we had this week. Most of our security goes to protect the server." Julie slathered creamy herbed butter on the roll. "Why do you ask?"

"Could someone hack in and you wouldn't know?"

"Oh, we'd know. Nobody is going to hack in."

Jill smiled at her sister, who had answered a question that she hadn't dared ask. "Do you have any other security services?"

"What? You mean internal security? To keep check on the humans? Keep tabs on insider trading? Protect our trading floor? Our hardware?"

"Okay."

"As I said, when you've got money, you get the best. We've got ourselves covered in every direction. We've got the best security team in the business."

"Who are they? Security guards?"

"Are you fucking kidding me? We've got former FBI, CIA, and police officers. We protect our interests. People know not to screw with us. No one's going to break in and make off with so much as a pencil with these guys around."

Jill was astonished to hear this. "You've got the FBI and CIA working for you?"

"Ex-FBI and CIA. We pay better than the government." Julie took a bite of her roll. "Especially now with all the cuts."

"Do they ever arrest people?"

"Sure. We're all under high security. The boss doesn't want company secrets outsourced."

Jill took a sip of water. "Would they go after Tyler?"

The look of amusement vanished from Julie's face. "They don't give a fuck about Tyler. Why can't you see that?"

"What about Dennis Drake?"

"Him, they might get. He wants to rein us in, impose regulations that harm profits, break up the big firms, jack up taxes, stop bonuses, limit financial products, and give our proceeds away to the lazy poor when God doesn't want them to have money."

Jill leaned across the table. "They'd kill him?"

Julie swallowed a healthy swig and placed her glass down on the table. "They don't need to kill him. There are other ways to stop him." She wiped her mouth with her napkin and then threw it down. "Oh my God. There's my boss. Come on."

Julie was up and crossing the restaurant. Jill sighed and reluctantly got up and followed. She had only seen pictures of Stanton Sandford III, the CEO of Sandford-Gallagher. He was sitting with two women of model caliber, each in evening dresses and jewels bigger than the ones on Jill's shoes.

He stood up, a short, rotund man in an impeccable three piece pin-striped black silk suit, and round, gold, wire-rimmed glasses. He simultaneously pumped Julie's hand and kissed her check, already peering over her shoulder. His small bleary, beady eyes were on Jill and magnified through his glasses.

Julie made introductions and Jill smiled as previously ordered. He smiled back, a broad smile showing oversized square teeth that resembled Chiclets gum. He buttoned his blazer and they shook hands. His was small, damp and fleshy.

"Mrs. Madison, nice to meet you. I wish your husband the best of luck."

"Thank you."

"You're Tyler Madison's mother?"

Jill momentarily stopped breathing. "Yes."

"Send my regards."

"You know him?"

"Not directly."

Stanton unbuttoned his blazer and eased back into his chair. Julie draped a hand on Jill's shoulder and pulled her away. "See you tomorrow Sandy."

Back at the table, Julie said, "What the hell was that? Why were you gawking?"

"Did you know he was going to be here?" Jill took a hurried sip of water. She was suddenly hot, feverish.

"Maybe."

"Did you tell him about Tyler?"

Julie made a face. "Why would I?"

"How would your boss know him?"

"Beats me. Maybe he reads Tyler's blog. If Sandy wanted to meet you, it was because of Blaze."

"Tyler doesn't blog under his own name. It sounded like a warning."

"Because to you, everything that happens is a fucking warning to Tyler. Oh, shit."

"What?"

"Sly's leaving." Julie turned around. "And Liz has gone. Christ, I wasn't paying attention. Can you stop talking."

The food came. The salmon was pink, the asparagus was firm, the potatoes were soft, and the parsley was crisp, but Jill's appetite was gone. She was pushing the food around her plate with her fork when two men appeared at their table.

Julie's friend Malcolm and his friend Mathew just happened to come for dinner and couldn't leave two pretty ladies eating alone and had to join them. Jill was yanked up out of her seat for kisses and flash bulbs popped. Apparently Matt was some kind of actor.

They all sat down and Matt asked what she did.

Julie answered for her. "She doesn't do anything."

The conversation turned to tomorrow's Halloween parties and the latest movies. Jill glanced behind her at the corner table where Sandy was eating and staring back.

18

... Procuring the passage of the National Bank Act was the greatest financial mistake of my life. It has built up a monopoly that affects every interest in the country. It should be repealed. But before this can be accomplished, the people will be arrayed on one side and the banks on the other in a contest such as we have never seen in this country.

—Treasury Secretary Salmon P. Chase

FRIDAY OCTOBER 31

After a late night, Jill slept in, arising as Julie was finishing breakfast. Her sister was already dressed for work and sitting at the table leafing through a newspaper. "We didn't make the paper," she said sadly.

Charles appeared with the coffee pot and topped Julie up. "All set for another productive day, are we?"

Jill, wearing a guest housecoat, glanced out the window. Rain was pouring down, streaking the glass. A taxi would be hard to find. "I might not get dressed today." She wasn't going to tell them about her meeting at the FBI.

"Ah, to have a life of leisure," he said.

"I wish I didn't have to work," Julie said. "It's Halloween and I've got a hell of a hangover." She chugged her coffee. "Did I drink too much?"

"No more than usual," Jill said. "Do you remember coming home?"

"You wouldn't give Mathew a lap dance," Julie said.

"The guys called you the life of the party." This from Charles, said with a sneer.

Lightning flashed and more thunder boomed and Jill excused herself and went to her bedroom to call a taxi. The first available cab was at six-fifty, five minutes after Julie went to work. It gave Jill forty minutes to get uptown.

Julie left on schedule. When the front door closed, Jill leapt up, raced to her bedroom and quickly changed. She threw on the clothes she had wanted to wear to the restaurant last night and borrowed a raincoat from Julie that came to her knees. At ten to seven she was downstairs and the cab was waiting.

"Federal Plaza," Jill told the driver. "I have to be there by seven-thirty."

He charged ahead in traffic, ran a light and overtook the Jag. He cut Charles off and the butler blared his horn in protest. The cabbie raised his middle finger and ran another light.

Despite heavy traffic, Jill got to the Federal Plaza with fifteen minutes to spare. She paid the cabbie and stepped into the rain. She got soaked dashing down a long walkway on her way to the rectangular building, which was set far off the road. Rain was running down the back of her neck by the time she reached the entrance.

It was forty degrees outside and seemed colder inside. She shivered as she passed through security, signed in, and put her purse through X-ray, all reminiscent of the morgue and Vivienne lying there with her mouth wide open as if in a scream.

A secretary came down to take Jill upstairs. They rode a silent elevator up to the sixth floor and went down a windowless hallway with closed doors and gray carpeting. The secretary paused in front of a door and got out a key. She unlocked the door and threw it open. "Someone will be with you shortly."

Jill went in and the door closed behind her with a click.

There were no windows. The room was small, like a cell, with low ceilings and recessed lights. The furniture consisted of a rectangular steel table and three hard-backed chairs, one on the near side, two on the far side facing the door. Jill shrugged off her wet rain coat and laid it on the back of the chair on the near side. It dripped a puddle on the gray carpet.

She sat down and reviewed her questions. She wanted to know if Jared Slater was a New York FBI agent. Did the FBI cooperate with the Federal Reserve Board and provide information and security? Had they identified a blond man with a facial scar, and a waitress named Helga Grosch? She would ask about Tyler's accident. She wanted to see their report and the color of the car. Did they know who reported the accident to the police, and how the hospital learned Tyler's identity? What did they know about Vivienne and her murder?

Seven-thirty came and went. Then eight and eight-thirty. Jill was cold and wet and pissed off. Outside, thunder roared and the building seemed to shake. She tried calling Alexandria, but there was no reception in the room. She decided to leave, go downstairs and complain at security. She went to the door, pushed down on the handle, but the door was locked. She pounded on it with her fist. This was bullshit.

She paced, holding up her phone in hopes of a signal and weighing her options. Suddenly the door opened and two agents burst in.

Special Agent Castanova looked like a model and was tall with long blond hair. Special Agent King was older, taller, and except for a small paunch, appeared in good shape. They sat down on the far side of the table without shaking hands or offering an apology for their lateness or for locking her in.

"How can we help you?" Agent King asked, in a tone which suggested he would be anything but helpful.

"I'd like to see your report on my son's accident."

"It's classified," King said.

"I've already seen it," Jill countered.

"It's now classified at a higher level," King said.

"Why?"

"Sorry, that's classified."

"Your report is wrong," Jill said.

"How so?" Agent Castanova fixed Jill with blank, gray eyes.

"My son was hit by a black car, not a white one."

The agents looked at each other. Agent King said, "I don't recall a reference to the car color."

Agent Castanova shook her head.

"There was an eye-witness," Jill said.

Agent Castanova leaned back in her seat. "So we heard."

"She's dead," Jill said.

The agent held Jill's gaze. "The street's a hard place to live."

Jill looked at Agent Castanova's arms. She wore a short sleeve blouse with a gun in a holster over her left shoulder. There were no visible scratches. "She was murdered. She said my son was chased down and intentionally run over."

"We heard he was okay," said Agent King, as if that were relevant. He wore a blazer with long sleeves that hid his forearms.

Jill reached into her purse, pulled out the photo of Jared Slater and passed it across the table. "Does he work for you?"

They took cursory glances. "If he does, that's classified," said Agent King.

"He's an FBI agent," Jill said. "He's one of two men who ran my son off the sidewalk and into the path of the car."

"Hmm," Agent Castanova said, crossing her arms and leaning on the table. "Why would he do that?"

"He was planning a march," Jill said.

"You think the FBI ran over your son to stop a gay parade?" Agent King shook his head. "Sounds unlikely."

"It was a protest against the Federal Reserve. They don't appreciate exposure."

"Your son has been doing more than organizing gay parades," Agent King said.

Jill put on a poker face, attempting a blank stare. "What do you mean?"

"The NSA is keeping a close eye on your son. That's the National Security Agency. Among other things, they handle computer security."

King tapped his chin with his finger. "They are quite interested in your son."

Jill thought of V-Comm and presidential election campaigns and said nothing.

"Do you know what he's up to?" asked Agent Castanova.

"He's planning another rally."

"That wouldn't warrant NSA attention. I wonder what has."

Jill sat up straight. "If something happens to my son, I will hold you responsible."

The atmosphere in the room changed instantly and became more hostile as Agent Castanova took immediate offense. "Oh, I think something will happen to him," she snapped in a most unprofessional tone. "You can count on it. And there won't be anything you or your senator husband can do about it."

Dread brought goosebumps to Jill's skin. She took a deep breath and presented her case. "I know you changed the original police report. The car was black with dark tinted windows and looked like law enforcement. I know a secure phone was used to call 911. I know an eye-witness to the accident was murdered. I know the killer's DNA is under her fingernails and no one is doing anything to find him. You're not the only ones working on this case. An FBI agent from D.C. knows everything."

The agents looked at each other. "Are you referring to Mark Biltmore?" said Agent King. "He's here collecting evidence *against* your son. He might be helping the FBI, but he's NSA."

The dread settled in Jill's stomach, so heavy she could hardly breathe.

"Your son is breaking the law," said Agent Castanova.

"He's going down," said Agent King.

"We don't need to run him over to do it," added Agent Castanova.

"We'll bring you down too," Agent King said. "You obviously know more about what your son is up to than you're saying, which makes you an accomplice."

"So, if there are no more questions, you can see yourself out." Agent King said.

Jill could barely stand. Her legs felt weak.

"How was that astrologer?" Agent King asked. "Did she see your future? Looks rosy, does it? Husband getting re-elected? Son, happy and safe?"

It was all Jill could do to get to the door, where she had to wait for it to be unlocked.

***

Outside, rain fell unabated. Overhead, lightning flashed, thunder screamed and rain poured, as if the whole world were raging. Jill was drenched before she reached the sidewalk. There were no available taxis. She wandered down the street as if in a daze. She passed a subway station and a crowd emerged from underground. She was surrounded on every side and swept along as if she were floating.

There was a jab on her shoulder and she jumped. Her mouth dropped open and she was so shocked she stopped walking. The crowd pushed her on from behind. A man griped her arm.

Jared Slater. He wore the green baseball cap under the hood of the navy sweatshirt and rain dripped from the bill. "I'm not going to hurt you. We need to talk. Tyler is in trouble." He let go of her arm, matching his stride to hers. "There's a Starbucks on the next block. I'll meet you there."

Then he was gone. A class of manic high school students occupied the place where he had stood. Two wore Halloween masks, Frankenstein and a vampire. Jill was carried along with the crowd. She saw the Starbucks ahead and wondered if she should stop. What did Jared want? She didn't know if he was on her side or against her. If he wanted to hurt her, he could already have done so. He was close enough to shove a knife into her side and he had not. At one time, his job had been to protect them.

Her cell phone rang with the funny ring tone. The caller was unidentified, but she knew who it was and she turned off the phone. She reached Starbucks and went inside. Jared, in the far corner facing the door, was sitting at a small table and she sat down opposite him. Two venti cups of coffee sat on the table along with his baseball cap.

"Still drinking cappuccino?" he asked.

She nodded and he passed her a cup. "Are you still FBI?"

"No. A private hire."

"Are you after Tyler?"

"I've been hired to observe him."

"By whom?" She lifted the cap off the cup without taking her eyes off Jared.

"OSB. It stands for Offshore Bank that's based in the U.K. I'm not the only one watching him. Besides me, there are two other groups, one Turkish and one German, plus the FBI and NSA."

Jill slowly stirred coffee as she stared into the face of the agent she had not seen in ten years. He had aged. His hair was going gray and he looked tired and weary, as if he'd seen too much. There were deep frown lines by his mouth and sharp furrows on his forehead, though the perfectly arched eyebrows were the same, as were the deep dimples. "What has Tyler done?" she asked.

Jared sighed deeply and stared at the door. "He's a hacker. He's broken past significant firewalls in both the New York Stock Exchange and the Chicago Stock Exchange. Also, for reasons we don't understand, nuclear power plants. He's hacked into servers of the three big investment banks, as well as the Federal Reserve Board and three of their twelve branches. With a keystroke, he could transfer or destroy billions of dollars. If he alters bank, investment, and stock records, he could crash the economy. Each dollar he deletes or transfers would be seen as theft. He may view himself as a modern day Robin Hood, but in the eyes of the law, he's a thief."

Listening to him, Jill's whole body tightened. Her hands trembled and she put down the cup. Now this, this made horrifying sense.

Jared took a long pull of his coffee. "The people after him would kill him to stop him."

"You?"

"I'm only watching him." Jared took a sip of coffee and eyed her over the rim. "There are others."

"A blond man with a scar?"

"Dieter Von Heinz. He's working for a German bank."

"Who poisoned Tyler?"

"Ermine Talu. She's a Turk."

"The red headed waitress?"

"Brunette now. The most common hair color in the world. She's an expert marksman and has been keeping a close watch on you." Jared reached into his pocket and pulled out two photos and placed them on the table.

Jill moved her cup and stared into the sneering, scarred face of Dieter Von Heinz, the man she had encountered waiting for the elevator at the hospital. The other photo showed the smiling and seductive Ermine Talu from La Fleur. She had light brown eyes that were too close together and straight brown hair the color of rich mud. "Were they trying to kill Tyler?"

"They sent him an unmistakable warning. If they wished to take him out, they could have done so. They may need him to clean up the damage he has done. He's planted code in various servers."

Jill allowed herself to breathe. "So, he's safe. They won't kill him?"

"There are three of them. His friends are equally guilty. One will be enough to clean up the code. Ali Mohamed is the expert, the likely choice."

Tyler was in absolute danger. They all were. Jill gripped her cup to stop her hands from shaking. So this was what her son was doing that had put his life in danger. He was not only in physical danger, he was in deep, deep, legal trouble. Her hands started shaking again and she put down the cup. "What will happen to him?"

"Right now, the FBI and NSA are watching him. If he makes one financial transaction, he'll be arrested. That is, if the security firms don't get him first." Jared took a big gulp of smoking coffee while they discussed the murder of her son.

"Do you know Special Agent Mark Biltmore?"

"He's NSA. The FBI asked him for help." Jared drank more coffee.

"Who is Julie's butler?"

"Kenneth Eaton. He's M1-6."

"British Intelligence?"

"Precisely."

Jill looked down at her cup, shaking her head inwardly in wonderment. The servant was no buffoon.

"I gather Tyler didn't tell you what he was up to," Jared said.

"All I know was that he was trying to trace whoever bugged his cell phone. And he hacked into V-Comm to retrieve his own lost file." Jill exhaled and looked across the room. She decided not to mention his hacking of some presidential campaign headquarters. "I didn't know he hacked into the Federal Reserve and the banks, but I should have guessed. He knew stuff no one else knew."

"He likely doesn't want to implicate you, but you're helping him."

Jill remembered the threat of the New York FBI, that she was going down too. "I'm not helping him."

Jared put down his cup. "Of the computers stolen from your house, two were yours. Tyler has been transferring code and storing it on your computers."

Now she knew why she had to leave her computers on all the time. "Did you break into our house?"

The door opened and a crowd of people swarmed in and dutifully stood in line. The place was crowded now and there were no free tables or chairs.

Jared lowered his voice and spoke softly. "That was the Germans. Dieter broke in and I paid him to learn what he found." Jared looked around, surveying the scene, before going on. "Tyler and his friends have a complicated scheme going. They've been working on it for months. They randomly jump code from computer to computer, so that no one can track their programs. They've broken through firewalls thought to be invincible. At the moment, they haven't done anything except look at financial records, but understandably, people are very nervous."

Jill's hands were shaking again and she put them in her lap. "Why hasn't he been arrested already?"

"He hasn't done anything. The agency could arrest him, but if it went to trial, they'd be hard pressed to win a conviction. So far, he's caused no harm, but we don't know what comes next, what he's got planned." Jared gazed across the room. "You could stop him."

Jill started.

"You have access to his computer."

"No, he's never away from it."

"Well, your computer and laptop. Shut them down."

"The desktop is in D.C. If I shut down my laptop, he'll call and tell me to boot it up. He could probably boot it up remotely himself."

Jared leaned across the table and lowered his voice further. "You would have to uninstall Windows and reload it. Dell will do it over the phone. With luck, that will disrupt his program. It will over-write his code."

Jill tried to fathom how that would work and Jared tried to explain. Apparently, program files and operating system files were placed in different locations on a hard drive. In Tyler's case, he had placed these files on different hard drives. Shut down one hard drive, corrupt one part, and the whole system would cease to function.

"He would know it was me."

"Yes, he would."

Jill took a deep breath. It was getting harder and harder to breathe, as if air was at a minimum. "He would never forgive me."

Jared didn't answer. He stared into his coffee cup.

A couple was hovering nearby, looking for a table. Jill was looking for a way none of this could be true and her involvement wasn't needed or necessary. "Why should I listen to you? I don't know he's doing anything illegal." She reiterated Tyler's explanations. "He's conducting polls, he's sending out questionnaires and writing his blog. How do I know you're not trying to stop that?"

"I think you know the truth when you hear it."

Jill picked up the stirrer and dipped it in the coffee. She didn't want to think about any of this. She didn't want Tyler and his friends hacking into the stock exchange, nuclear power plants for God's sake, or the secretive Federal Reserve. If he hadn't done anything yet, maybe he wasn't going to do anything. And though Jared talked a good talk, how did she know she could trust him? He was always there when people were hurt. Jill put down the stir stick. "A bag lady saw Tyler being run over. She was murdered. Who killed her?"

"I don't know."

"Roll up your sleeves," Jill said.

He did as she asked. His arms were clean. "What are you looking for?"

"The bag lady drowned. She scratched someone before she died. There was flesh under her nails."

"She could have got my ankles."

Jill stared at him and he got up, bent down on one knee and pulled up his pant legs, first one and then the other. They were clean. He sat back down.

"Who called 911 the night of Tyler's accident?"

"That was me. I was there that night, but I did not run him over. That was the Germans."

"How did the hospital know who Tyler was?" Jill asked.

"I waited a day and called them. I thought he might get better care if they knew who he was and law enforcement seemed unable to ID him." Jared took another swig of coffee. "I liked your family. I was sorry to hear about Hope. That must have been devastating."

Jill gripped her cup. "Did you take the SIM card and bug the phone?"

He shook his head. "That was Dieter."

"What is your job exactly?"

"Same as it was when I worked for the FBI. Only now there are no rules."

Jill picked up her coffee cup, more to warm her hands than to drink, for she did not think she could stomach coffee at that moment. "In regards to Tyler?"

"I'm to observe him. See what he does, who he sees, where he goes."

"You weren't hard to spot."

"I didn't try too hard to hide. I wanted you to know you were being watched so you would be careful."

"Why did you leave the FBI?"

"I was in Afghanistan. I saw something I shouldn't have seen and wouldn't lie about it. I failed the psych exam and got fired."

It sounded to Jill as if he were telling the truth. "Ten years ago, you left our house suddenly and without warning. You never said goodbye. Why did you leave like that?"

Jared put down his coffee cup. "Something came up."

"At work?"

He rolled up his napkin and stuffed it in the cup, then broke his stir stick in half and shoved that in as well. "It was personal." He crammed the lid on the coffee cup. "I've got to go. They're watching me too." And then with dead-on aim, as if perfected ten years ago playing hoops with Tyler in the driveway, he tossed his cup at the garbage bin and scored. He stood up. "Whatever you decide, it's in your hands. You can stop him." He picked up the baseball cap, put it on his head and strolled from the café out into the rain.

Jill sat at the table, lost in thought as her coffee went cold. A new crowd came in, eyeing the empty seat and she called a cab. She gave up her table and stood by the front window waiting for the taxi. It took forty-five minutes for one to come.

She fought off three people trying to claim it and hopped in. The cabbie started the meter. "It's a crazy day," he said.

He pulled away from the curb. The back door opened and Agent Mark Biltmore hopped in, spraying rain. He thrust his FBI badge in the cabby's face and pointed a finger forward. "Drive."

The cabbie drove and Biltmore slammed the dividing window closed.

Jill looked at him coldly. Rain fell down his face, dripped from his hair. "What do you want?"

"You were going to call me after you met with the New York agents. I've been calling you and you haven't answered. What did they say?"

"That you were NSA."

There was no reaction. He continued to look at her accusingly. "They're crazy, they'd say anything."

"Who are you, really?"

"I'm on your side. I'm here to protect your son."

Jared was right when he said that she knew the truth. This wasn't it. "You don't look like a field agent. How fast can you run a mile?"

He answered without thinking. "Two minutes."

She shook her head. "You've never run a mile in your life. Even Olympians can't run that fast."

"So I can't run. So what?"

"You're not here to protect Tyler. You're here to arrest him."

Mark Biltmore's face changed in that moment. The easygoing nonchalance vanished. "Is that what your old pal Jared Slater told you? What did you two talk about? How to crash the market? Did he tell you he works for a bank? The FBI fired him, you know."

"Get out of the cab."

"I hit a nerve, didn't I? You like him? More your age? Buys you coffee when he's not running over your son?"

Jill leaned forward and rapped on the glass. "Stop the car," she told the cabbie.

"We could cut a deal," Mark said. "You help me, I'll help you."

The taxi stopped. Behind them, a horn honked loudly.

"If you don't get out right now, I'll scream." Jill opened her mouth and took a deep breath.

Mark opened his door. "From here on in, you're on your own."

19

(There were) two competing money schemes, one based on shared abundance, the other based on scarcity, greed and debt.
—Bernard Lietaer

Jill made up her mind in the taxi as it sluiced through the rain. If there was any chance she could save Tyler from the trouble he was in, she would do it. There were five teams watching him if you counted the FBI and NSA. He might consider himself a modern day Robin Hood, but what he was doing was illegal. If he planned to transfer money from accounts and manipulate stock portfolios, it would be over for him. The FBI and the banks would go after him, and if he was lucky he would live and go to prison, and if he was unlucky he would be killed. There wasn't an option to do nothing.

Upstairs, Julie's apartment was empty with no sign of the British agent. Outside, the rain fell on, pelting the glass ceiling and streaming down the windows. The clouds were low and hugged the building, shrouding it in endless gray. She changed into dry clothes and took her laptop to the dining room.

She went online to find the number for Dell. The laptop was working slowly. The hard drive was spinning, but any command made it freeze. The screen changed in blocks. She finally gave up and got the phone operator to give her the number for Dell and called them up.

She was transferred through their automatic voice system. Finally: press three for service. She was put on hold, subjected to elevator music while the hard drive whirred away, hard at work while she sat idle. She stared at the black and white Salvador Dali print propped on the south pedestal, where clocks fixed in time were laid out in preposterous positions. What point was Dali trying to make? The absurdity of it all?

Finally, an operator. His name was Barry, but he sounded Indian and it was probably Ramesh. Jill explained her problem. "I bought my laptop a week ago and it has a glitch or a virus. I want to reload Windows and don't have my disks. Can you reload it for me?" She held her breath.

"Very well. May I have your phone number?" They went through an interminable process where she gave her name and address and laptop serial number, until finally Barry said, "Are you working on the computer right now?"

"No."

"I see. Can you shut down the active program, please."

"There are no programs running."

"I see. I will take over your computer. You will watch the mouse move. Please do not touch anything until I tell you."

Jill watched the screen go black. Lines of code appeared in white in the top left corner. After three lines of type he stopped typing. "There is software on your computer refusing to be shut down. Do you have special security software installed?"

"Not that I know of. That could be the virus."

"I have not seen such a virus."

Jill heard her heartbeat in her ear. Now that she had decided to reload Windows, she was panicking that it couldn't be done; it was too late, Tyler had it so well protected, no one could disable it.

The typing resumed. Barry giving it his best shot. Line after line of instructions, while the laptop hummed loudly. Jill waited, watching the rain, as code streamed down her screen.

Barry was back. "I am very sorry, but I am unable to shut down your computer. I will see if my security officer is here. As it is Friday we may have to wait until Monday."

"I can't wait that long."

"I will find my supervisor. Please stay on the line."

Time passed. The spinning hard drive continued. As in Dali's black and white print, time seemed to stop. A lady finally came on. Her name was Cynthia and she also sounded Indian. She was the security supervisor and happy to help.

Jill took a deep breath of relief.

"Please do not touch the computer," Cynthia said. The screen went blank once more, Barry's code cleared, then new type appeared. A whole screen of it and then another. Finally, she said, "I am not knowing what kind of virus you have, but I am not able to override. I am afraid we will have to send out our technician."

"Can he come now?"

"I am afraid it will be next week. I will trans—"

"No," Jill interrupted. "I can't wait that long." She wanted to cry. Her mind raced. Tyler didn't want her turning off her computer. "What if I turn off the computer? Can you break in before it reboots?"

"I will try. You may go ahead and shut down your computer. Hold the ON/OFF button until I tell you to stop."

Jill pushed the button and the computer turned off. The silence after the constant running of the hard drive was jarring. From another room, she heard the rhythmic ticking of a clock.

"You may stop pressing the button."

Jill stopped and the computer came back on, the whirring beginning anew. The Windows logo flashed and the screen went blank. A warning came up on the screen in large letters. Existing files would be replaced. Back up all files before continuing.

"Keep going," Jill said.

The screen flashed and new text appeared. Windows was reloading. Cynthia had done it! She was copying over the existing programs. "I will now reload the software," she said. "Please do not touch your computer."

Jill slumped in the chair, elated and afraid. What would happen once Windows reloaded? Was the code gone? If the problem was corrected, was Tyler safe? Would the banks and FBI leave him alone?

But what if his program was protected to guard against this? Then nothing would have changed.

Cynthia's voice brought Jill back to the moment. "I will transfer control back to you. I believe the problem has been corrected." She thanked Jill for supporting the company. "Have a nice day."

***

Half an hour later, when the front door flew open and Tyler and David burst in, Jill guessed that reloading Windows had consequences. She was in the dining room, trying to figure out how to get the internet to work when they arrived. She closed the laptop and hurried to greet them. She didn't know what to say to them, and fell back on denial. "I was going to call you," she said cheerily, as if nothing was wrong.

"What did you do to your laptop?" Tyler peered at the dining room and pointed.

David made a beeline for the table and sat down. He crossed one knee over the other, began jiggling his foot and started typing. Tyler stood behind him, chewing at his nails. He turned and looked at her. "What did you do?"

She swallowed hard, not wanting to confront her son, or to admit what she had done. "It was working slowly. It was running all the time. I thought it had a virus."

"Running slow, how? What were you doing? Playing a card game? Online shopping?"

A mix of worry and anger tied up the real words that Jill wanted to say and she reiterated her line, "I thought it was infected. I reloaded Windows."

David stopped typing and looked up. The two guys exchanged glances. When Tyler looked back his face was white, as if all the blood had drained away. "You couldn't reload it. There's no way."

Whatever was constraining her words dissolved. "Well I did. What was on there? What did you put on my computer?"

"It was nothing." He was on the defensive. "I stored some files. I told you that." He lifted a shoulder as if to indicate it was nothing.

David was typing again, staying out of it, acting as if he were somewhere else, not hearing a word, his bright blond hair hiding his face.

She folded her arms over her heart. "Files enabling you to hack into the financial software of banks and investment companies? Or the New York and Chicago stock exchanges and the Federal Reserve?"

Tyler's eyes opened wide. She saw two dark pools of rage. "You did it on purpose? You wiped away six months of work."

"That could get you arrested or killed. That FBI agent Mark Biltmore is from the NSA. Three different security teams from three different banks in three different countries are watching your every move. They know what you're doing and they'll stop you one way or another." She realized she was yelling and paused to take a breath and calm down. She continued in a measured tone. "You still have time. You can fix it. Shut down your computers. Whatever you're doing, stop. You don't need to die or spend your life in prison to make your point. You have your rally. Denny Drake is on your side. You're legitimate. You don't have to break the law."

"It's too late," Tyler said.

"It's not. The banks will come after you. The FBI will put you away. How could you do this?"

"What about you?" Tyler spat. "What about what you did? You had me followed and you hacked into my email. Oh yes, I know it was you. You and Dad. You hired a P.I. and had me followed, watched my every move. You're not on my side, you never were. Just stay out of my life. You are dead to me."

His words hung in the air. David stood up, and said in a low voice, "Windows was reloaded. The code is gone."

Tyler stalked to the door, David at his heels. Tyler slammed it so hard, Jill jumped. The glass in the west window of the living room shook. A pigeon had flown into the glass. Its neck was bent and twisted, but its eyes were open as it slid down the glass, leaving a bloody smear. It dropped to the ledge and came to a stop, one wing flapping in the wind-driven rain.

***

Tyler had been gone for ten long minutes when the door opened and for an instant Jill's heart lifted with hope: he was back. But it was Julie and her butler who was not really a butler. She stormed into the apartment, her long coat open and flying out behind her like a cape. She stamped her foot and broke one of her high heeled shoes. She bent down, tore it off and hurled it across the room where it hit a wall with a thud. She yanked off the other one and flung it as well. "How fucking dare you," she said.

Jill thought Julie suspected Tyler had hacked into her firm's financial software and began to defend him, but she wasn't given the chance. Julie stalked toward her; six whole feet of seething umbrage. "After all I've done for you. I tried to save your stupid marriage while you've been fucking around. No wonder you wouldn't go home. All that crap about Tyler, when it was just about you."

Jill was taken aback, about to ask what Julie was talking about, when her sister's finger flew out, as it did when they were young, and Jill was silenced, forbidden to speak.

Julie dug in her purse, whipped out her phone, jabbed at the screen, and thrust it in Jill's face.

Jill gasped. It was a photo taken earlier in Starbucks, with Jared Slater down on one knee while she smiled upon him. Jill tightened and looked at her sister.

"What the fuck is this?" Julie yelled. "The one man I wanted. The one man I felt something for and you had to have him."

Jill was incredulous. "Jared? You want Jared?"

"I. *Had*. Jared."

Jill drew in a breath. Julie had been in D.C. the weekend he left unexpectedly −on account of his personal problem. Jill looked at her sister. "You slept with him while he was working for us?"

"You waited ten years to pay me back. You've been jealous of me my whole life. You're nothing but a short, fucking freak who got knocked up by the first man who would have you. You settled for nothing and wanted my life. And I didn't see it. I didn't fucking see it. After all I did for you. I looked out for you. I raised you. If not for you, I would have had a mother. She would have never left."

This was finally too much. "That's not true. She didn't leave on account of me. It wasn't my fault. It was never my fault. And I'm not jealous of you. I pity you. The only thing you've got is money."

"Ha ha ha." Julie laughed a small mean laugh. "You're the one who has nothing. Not even money. Likely not even a husband. Don't come crying to me when you're on the street. I've had it with you."

"What did you do? Did you send Blaze that photo?"

Julie straightened up to her full, towering height. "*He* sent it to me. He wanted to know what you were up to." Julie started to chuckle. "So I told him. You screwed me and now we're even."

"I never screwed you."

Julie whirled around. "Charles, we're done here." She marched to the door, and as Tyler had before her, slammed it solidly. Outside the window, the wing of the sodden bloodied pigeon flapped away.

Jill stood frozen in place, waiting for the windows to stop shaking. Blaze had sent the photo. Well, it could be explained and was nothing like his own photos, which were far more damaging.

Jill went to the kitchen, pulled a bottle of water from the fridge and took a long slow sip. She had taken outbursts like this from Julie for years without speaking out and it felt good to fight back. Julie had the authority of a five year advantage in age, and was never wrong. No matter what stupid things Julie said, Jill was always silenced, always shut down with a pointed finger, loud screaming and slamming doors.

Jill capped the bottle, wrenching the lid. Mark Biltmore must have taken the photo and sent it to Blaze. He didn't give her a chance to explain. He silenced her too. Instead of calling her, Blaze had called Julie. Jill closed the fridge and grabbed her phone.

She had forgotten that she had turned it off earlier. When she turned it back on she saw ten missed calls. Three were from Biltmore and the rest were from Blaze. The phone rang while she was looking at it. She opened the phone and said nothing.

"How could you?" Blaze said.

Jill felt the chill spanning the many miles that lay between them. Outside the window, a low black band of virulent clouds were advancing. "How could *you*?" she shot back.

"That photo with Slater will be in every paper tomorrow."

"What about you and Rebecca?"

"This has nothing to do with her. Why did you need a five thousand dollar prepaid Visa card?"

Jill was taken aback and momentarily speechless.

"What are you hiding? What did you spend that money on? A hotel room?"

"I gave it to Tyler. Julie gave it to Tyler."

"You really think I'm that stupid?"

"You took Rebecca to the Pecan Street Café."

There was a pause.

"And then you took her home."

"Are you having me followed?" His voice was dripping with outrage.

"I saw the pictures. They're going to be on the front page of the next *Enquirer*."

There was a long silence and she guessed that he had not known about this. Tyler knew because he'd hacked into the site.

"Rebecca supports me," Blaze said.

"And that makes it all right."

"This is not about Rebecca. It's about Slater."

"I have nothing to say about him. We were in a public coffee shop. Tyler is in trouble. He needs a lawyer. He was deliberately run down. An eye-witness saw everything and she was killed."

Blaze let out a long, loud expletive. "I won't listen to one more word. Either get psychiatric help or I'll get it for you. I'm going. I'm hanging up."

"No, you do not get to hang up. You do not get to turn your back on us. You were never there when Hope was sick. You're never around when we need you. You may be divorced, but it's this family you turned your back on."

"Do not bring up Hope. This is not about her. It's about you and Slater. Do you want me to lose the election?"

"You're doing that yourself. It might be for the best. You're helping bankrupt us all."

There was no response. Around her Jill heard teeming rain, but on the other end of the line, nothing. She looked at her phone. The call had ended. He had hung up.

She closed the phone. Petra was wrong. Getting it out had not been cathartic, it felt like hell. She went to the kitchen and opened the fridge. There was a juice bottle in the door and beside it, a bottle of red wine. She pulled out the bottle, it was heavy in her hand. She read the label. An aged Merlot with a price tag of ninety-five dollars. She would just smell it. She pulled out the cork and inhaled the rich aroma. She would have a glass. Just one. One little glass. And that was when the front door opened and Charles/Kenneth came home.

"Having a secret snort are we?"

Jill recorked the bottle and returned it to the fridge. She shoved the door closed. "You can go."

"I'm to stay. Someone has to guard the silver."

"I know who you are."

"And I know who you are. A drunken fool."

"How did you end up here, Kenneth? What did you think you would find?"

He did not react to the use of his real name. "Unfortunately, the most dysfunctional family this side of the pond."

"Leave Julie alone."

The British agent smiled. "Julie is not the point."

"I'm leaving," Jill said.

He clasped his hands together at his heart. "There is a God."

She went to the bedroom to pack. She gathered up the clothes she had borrowed and dumped them on Julie's bed. She threw her stuff into the carry-on and wheeled it out to the living room.

Charles/Kenneth was lounging on the couch, feet up on the coffee table, reading the paper as if he owned the place.

Jill went to the dining room, grabbed her laptop, slipped it into the front pocket of the suitcase and got her purse. She was still carrying around the empty shoe bag and placed it on the table. She opened the front door and paused. "There's a dead bird on the windowsill."

Charles/Kenneth lowered the paper. "Tell the servant." He raised the paper and continued reading.

***

Halloween night came early, with all the ghouls and goblins given free reign. Storm clouds brought a premature dusk and rain continued to fall. Down in the lobby, Jill called a cab and waited at the front window, watching costumed partiers pick their way through puddles.

The cab came and having nowhere to stay, Jill went to the Blue Nile Hotel. She liked the fireplace and the wood floors and the rooms with balconies and the astrologer who knew her so little, but well enough to know that by keeping quiet she had lost her true self.

It was a ten minute ride. The lobby was warm and cozy, and a fire blazed, and orange candles burned, but Jill still felt cold. The front desk clerk wore a Green Hornet's mask that failed to make her smile. A big bowl of finger-sized chocolate bars on the counter did not tempt her.

Jill got a room for a reasonable price. She headed for the elevator. The doors opened and the younger Layla stepped out wearing a short black dress and a tall pointed witches' hat. She wasn't alone. A burly football player stood by her side.

Layla smiled. "My mother's gone for the day. Did you have an appointment?"

"No, I'm getting a room for the night."

Layla glanced at the suitcase. "You're not staying with your sister?"

"No."

"Is everything okay?" She cocked her head, her black eyes bright as she looked at Jill curiously.

Jill put on her game face and smiled. "Everything's fine." She eyed the young man. Tyler's replacement? They weren't touching, they weren't holding hands, and Tyler was better looking.

"This is my friend, Devon," Layla said.

Jill and Devon shook hands. His was heavy and he gripped hers as if to break it.

"Devon's a football player," Layla said, as if apologizing for him.

Jill nodded.

"We're going to a Halloween party," Layla said, still explaining.

Jill nodded on, feeling awkward. The football player must have been feeling awkward too, for he was rocking back and forth on his heels and looking around.

Layla started walking away. "I'll be at the rally tomorrow. I'll see you there."

Jill went up to the room. It had a queen-sized bed, a writing table, and a balcony that overlooked a quiet street. There was no dead bird in the window and she took that as an improvement. She slid the chain on the door, turned off her phone, and went off the grid.

She turned on the TV, kicked off her shoes, stacked the pillows and stretched out on the bed. On CNN, pundits marveled at the unexpected three-way race. Chalking it up to a new age of internet campaigning, they could only guess at what the result of the election might be. The polls were skewed and unscientific and seemed determined by the manner of polling. Internet polls consistently showed Dennis Drake in the lead. Email questionnaires were mixed. Asked in person, more people than not said they would vote for Rich Tumblin, citing economic recovery as the number one reason for their choice.

At eleven, Denny Drake waltzed onto the Nightly Show for his first cable network appearance. Despite everything he knew about the economy and the Fed, he did not mention them once. He spoke about losing his farm, and his vision of the country he wished to leave for his daughter and his unborn child, a country that worked for everyone, not just a few. "We have a duty to the future," he said, "to make things right, to fix what is broken, unjust and unfair." He looked presidential and sounded optimistic, and the crowd loved him.

Jill fell asleep with the TV going and dreamed of Hope. They were at the airport and Hope was going home and Jill couldn't go, she had to work. "I'll watch for you, Mommy," Hope had said, and they hugged each other, and Jill said what she had not been able to say in real life. "Goodbye." Hope walked away, and the further she went, the smaller she got until only the clear blue sky remained.

20

If that mischievous financial policy which had its origin in the North American Republic during the late war in that country, should become indurate down to a fixture, then that Government will furnish its own money without cost. It will pay off its debts and be without debt. It will become prosperous beyond precedent in the history of the civilized governments of the world. The brains and wealth of all countries will go to North America. That government must be destroyed or it will destroy every monarchy on the globe.
–Editorial in the London Times
in reaction to Lincoln's debt-free greenbacks

SATURDAY NOVEMBER 1

During the night, the storm passed and the rain stopped and Jill woke early to a clear sky filled with stars and a full moon sinking in the sky. She remembered her dream and thought of Hope and for the first time her memory wasn't accompanied by crushing guilt. But when Jill thought of Tyler, the guilt came rushing back.

She turned on her phone, hoping someone had phoned, but there were no missed calls, no waiting messages. She dressed and went to the nearest coffee shop, where the toast was burned and the coffee gave her indigestion. The Fed Up rally made the front of the *New York Times* and Denny Drake was expected to speak to an audience of a hundred thousand. Jill knew that no number of Secret Service agents or police could control such a crowd.

She saw the date on the newspaper, November 1. She was sober now ten months. She needed every finger to count the months. It didn't matter if she had come close to slipping, the fact was that she had not. Ten months, that was something.

At nine o'clock, she left for the park. The sun was climbing and the day looked bright, the grass and trees were shining as if cleaned by the storm. The high was expected to be seventy, with a breeze coming in from the south and no chance of rain. According to the weatherman, it was a good day for an outdoor picnic.

She reached the river and people were gathering in the park. A hundred or so spectators formed a sparse crowd spread out on the grass before a raised platform. Up on the stage, the three computer hackers who stood on the verge of collapsing the financial world were stacking speakers. She moved into the shadow of a lamppost and wondered if they were wearing their vests.

A young girl meandered through the crowd with a large cloth shopping bag and Jill bought a navy FED UP t-shirt, a FED UP button, a DENNY DRAKE FOR PRESIDENT button, and a FED UP baseball cap, all for twenty bucks. She wondered if her days of having money were over.

Jill pulled the t-shirt on over her shirt, pinned on the buttons and put the cap on her head. Another girl with shopping bags bounded over and Jill saw that it was Layla.

"You're not helping out?" Layla said.

Jill made a small face. "How was your party?"

Layla lifted a shoulder as if to indicate not great. "Looks like there will be a big crowd," she said.

"I read a hundred thousand."

"Denny Drake's already here." Layla said. "Did Tyler tell you about the party at the hotel after? Can you come?"

Jill frowned as if she were considering attending the party she wasn't invited to. "I'll have to see."

"I hope you can make it."

Layla moved on and someone was testing the sound system. Ouch. Terrible feedback. Up on stage, adjustments were made. There were four great speakers stacked on each side of the stage. To the right stood a table in front of a row of folding chairs. There was a podium in center stage which would protect the speakers, force a shooter to aim high. Jill paused. Aim too high and the face was defenseless. Damn Mark Biltmore. He neglected to mention how to protect the vulnerability of the head. There was no sign of him in the crowd.

She saw news vans with huge satellites and camera people with big cameras. Comedy Central was airing the rally live and a crew was setting up large screen TVs. The crowd was growing thicker by the minute. Buses pulled up to the curb and discharged streams of passengers. They were met by the crew doling out t-shirts, buttons and signs. Soon, a sea of people waving signs and standing shoulder to shoulder were fanned out in all directions, as far as the eye could see. She thought that there might be more than the expected hundred thousand.

Jill was surveying the crowd and reading placards when she noticed a bald man looking at her. She stared ahead. Was he a member of a hit squad? He looked vaguely familiar, but she couldn't place him. She was certain no bald man had been following her. She looked back. His perfectly arched eyebrows and dimples gave him away. Jared Slater in a new disguise. She waved to him, but he turned his head, lowered his shoulder, and moved into the crowd.

A few minutes later she felt a jab to her side and started. Jared Slater stood beside her. "Look straight ahead," he said.

She stared at the stage, her heart racing. "I almost didn't recognize you."

"I think I'm going to get burned."

Jill took the cap off her head and handed it to him.

He took it from her. "I always liked you. Thanks." He put the cap on his head. "Did you do it?"

She turned to look at him and found him gazing at the stage. "I reloaded Windows. He lost his code."

"Eyes front. How do you know?"

"That's what he said. It's gone." She turned to look at Jared. "Why do you ask? Has something happened?"

"Face forward. Helga Grosch is here."

"Where?" Jill looked around, scanning the crowd.

"She's up near the stage."

"What about Dieter?"

"I'm sure he's here too."

"And the Secret Service?"

"They're supposed to be here. I don't see them."

"There's not many police," Jill said.

"The number is too low for this size of crowd."

"What does that mean?"

"Watch yourself."

"What about Tyler?"

There was no answer and Jill turned to Jared, but he was gone.

There was a loud roar and up ahead, Ali was crossing the stage. The man, who in the apartment was nearly incomprehensible, stepped up to start the show.

Ali reached the podium. He wore a black FED UP baseball cap, blue jeans, a black FED UP t-shirt under a navy blazer, and Jill hoped a bullet-proof vest under it all. He tapped the microphone tentatively and the noise from the crowd died down. He began hesitantly.

"I –I –I would like to th-th-thank you all for coming," he said slowly in his thick accent.

For no reason, the crowd broke out in thunderous applause. Whether it was because of his diffidence, or just the mood of the day, Jill didn't know, but he beamed a brilliant smile, leaned closer to the mike and continued with confidence. "After our national anthem we will hear from David Hooper."

There was more applause. A young lady in her early thirties stepped forward, adjusted the mike and began singing in a high clear voice. The anthem played and two gigantic flags rose behind the stage. Normally the song filled Jill with pride, but today she was so wound up, distracted, and unnerved, she could barely hear the music over the sound of her pounding heart. She knew the War of Independence was fought over the control of money, and the country's early founders would have been hanged had they been caught. They put their lives on the line to fight for economic freedom, as these three kids and a presidential candidate were doing now. The sitting ducks were all on stage. The risen flags flapped languorously in the clear blue sky.

The song came to a close and Jill clapped along with the rest of the crowd. She looked for Dieter, the waitress, and the pretend butler, but saw no one of their ilk. The singer left the stage and David headed for the podium.

Like Ali, he was decked out in FED UP garb, his baby fine bright blond hair blowing in the breeze. The clapping died and he began with confidence. "We're in economic trouble and it's not hard to trace the source of the problem. The finger is pointing directly at the Federal Reserve. Only there's nothing federal about it and it has no reserves. It's a central bank that runs our economy, controls the money supply, and determines the rise and fall of our fortunes. It's a for-profit bank. It makes billions, but pays no taxes and answers to no one."

Jill's heart was racing. He was not mincing his words, not candy-coating his message. She braced herself, wondering if guns would fire.

He went on. "The Fed does two destructive things that have to stop. First, it charges interest on printed money. We will never, ever, ever, be able to pay off this interest. Because of this, we will forever fall deeper and deeper into debt. Much of our budget goes to pay off this interest. It can't continue.

"The second practice is printing money. The Fed allows every bank to create money with a ledger entry. All a bank needs is a borrower and poof – a loan is created out of thin air. Banks also create money on deposits through the fractional reserve. They lend out fake money and get interest on it.

"Creating money causes inflation. Inflation makes prices go up. In the hundred years of the Fed's existence, the value of a dollar has fallen from one hundred cents to five cents. That is what printing money does. It dilutes the value of a dollar, the value of your paycheck, the wealth in our economy.

"What I want to know is why the government doesn't print money. Why did it give this power away? Why does it issue an IOU instead of a dollar? Why does it borrow money that it could make itself?

"This has to change." He held up two fingers, making a peace sign. "There are two things we can do, no, we must do." He held up one finger. "First, the government must issue its own currency. A United States note to replace the dollar. The government can print its own money and not charge itself interest."

He held up his second finger. "The second change we need to make is to stop the banks from printing money. That's how they got so rich and powerful. You'd be rich too if you got to print all the money you wanted. You could buy anything. Any elected official you wanted. Which is what happens."

He lowered his hand. "We do these two things and we get our economy on track. We won't need a Federal Reserve Board printing money and charging us interest on our debt. There won't be any debt. These two steps alone will solve the problem of the deficit. It's all we have to do to make our country prosperous again."

He paused and faced the crowd. "Ben Crupt will tell you what happens if we do nothing, if we continue along this course."

David moved offstage to loud applause. He was safe. He had made it through his speech unscathed and that would have brought relief, except now Tyler was coming out, heading for the podium, in a bright red FED UP t-shirt as big as a target. Jill scanned the crowd for the Secret Service, who normally wore tailored suits or collared t-shirts and sunglasses, but no one stood out. She was grateful David made it through his speech and as Tyler raised the mike, she hoped his would be as short.

Tyler bent forward toward the microphone and began. "I lived in West Africa for a year and a half. It was a small, poor country without material wealth, without oil. For years there was a drought. The corn crop failed. The IMF came in with loans. That was the beginning of the end. The loans came with interest compounded quarterly. It didn't matter if there were more droughts, more crop failures, the loan had to be repaid. Money that should have been spent inside the country on infrastructure, social services, government programs, education, national parks, was shipped out to foreign banks to pay off the debt. Taxes were raised, unemployment skyrocketed, as did crime, hunger, and sickness.

"Season after season, the interest was compounded, the level of debt grew and grew, until the country was so poor it had no more money to pay off its debts. The value of the currency began to fall even faster. The interest on new loans went through the roof. Lenders, worried about repayment, were loath to lend. Immediately the cost of imports, like oil, rose. There was hyperinflation. The price of everything went up. As did poverty and the numbers of those living below the poverty line. Those lucky enough to have jobs toiled to pay the government's debt. There was nothing the government could do to turn the country around. It was indebted to the foreign banks. The people of a sovereign country were slaving for foreign bankers.

"You probably think that Africa is a long way away and have pity for those poor people and thank God we're nothing like them."

He paused. "Wrong." He leaned forward.

"We're exactly like them. Every year, the number of poor in this country is rising. Right now, forty-five million people live below the poverty line. We're mired in debt. Only the people we owe aren't foreign bankers, they're our bankers. They're sitting right here, down the street." He paused again, lifted his arm and pointed in the direction of Wall Street. "They're taking our debt and redecorating their offices, buying another yacht, or an island in the Bahamas. While our elected officials can't jump through their hoops fast enough to pass the laws they want passed, to write the bills they want written, and to cut the taxes they want cut. While at the same time, services for the rest of the country are reduced, benefits are slashed, taxes raised, all so our bankers can buy a new Renoir or Picasso.

"How did we get in so much debt? We let the banks print money out of thin air and called it real. We let them charge interest on this fake money. They used the fake money to buy Washington. This is where our debt came from, rising over the years, compounded by interest, with never an end in sight. The more money we pay in interest, the less money we have for our people.

"Well, I don't think we owe this debt. I don't think banks should have the power to make money. I don't think the government needs to borrow money it can print itself. If you don't agree, then on Tuesday, cast your vote for the Washington lawyer or the Wall Street CEO. But if you're fed up, if you've had enough, cast your vote for economic freedom, for the well-being of your country. Vote for Denny Drake."

He stood up to his full height and raised his arm once more. "Ladies and gentlemen, I give you our next president."

The air thundered with applause. Jill had been too entranced by his speech to worry about him, and now he was done and heading off-stage, her relief and the lifting of dread was like a weight discarded and she felt lighter, taller, as Denny came out to a roaring ovation. She clapped louder, harder, finally able to breathe. The pounding in her chest died as Tyler took a seat beside his friends.

Denny silenced the crowd with a lowering of his hands and the applause simmered. He adjusted the microphone downwards, cleared his throat and began. "I have a vision for this country. I see a day when Washington isn't run by Wall Street and greedy bankers, when Washington doesn't spend its time squabbling over money and what programs to cut. I see a day when once again we can lead, take our place first in line, fund education, fund science, fund innovation, fund new technology, and take care of our people and our land.

"We don't need to be at war. What if we took the money we spend on war and spend it on peace, on environmental protection, on disease eradication, on crop science, on food programs. What if we work for a future that is brighter and better than today, a tomorrow that we can leave our children and their children with pride.

"I will work for this end. I will change our economic policy so it benefits the people and not the banks. I am not bought by Wall Street. I will take no money from Wall Street. As president, I will reform our economic system. I will reform campaign law. I will send the lobbyists home. I will throw out the laws that Wall Street has written to protect itself. I will enforce the intent of the Constitution and restore to Congress the power to control and print money. There will be no more drastic and crippling booms and busts. No more transfer of wealth from the middle class to the rich. No more banks which make free money for themselves. No more interest paid on printed money.

"It's time we invested in the well-being of our people. We can look after the disenfranchised, the down-trodden, and the sick. We can once again be a country run by the people, for the people. We are not broke. We are the wealthiest nation on earth. The problem is, the top one percent of the population has taken fifty percent of the wealth. This is what our current leaders have given us." He shook his head sadly. "There is nothing they can do to change this. They cannot speak out against those who have bought and paid for them. I have not been bought. As president, I can undo this travesty and I will."

A cheer rose through the crowd. Overhead, a formation of Canadian geese went flying by and when they were out of sight, he continued. "I can assure you the power-brokers will not go easily. They think money can buy them everything. But in this great country, there is one thing that is equal in measure to money and that is a vote. That vote gives us a voice. The voice of one person standing up and saying enough, no more, this is it. And then another and another and another, all shouting together: No more!"

He leaned forward and raised his fist. "Washington and Wall Street, you are on notice. We may have been in a slumber, but we are now awake and proclaiming loudly, vehemently, with one vote and one voice, "We are Fed Up, Fed Up, Fed Up!"

The crowd took up the chant. "Fed Up, Fed Up, Fed Up!" The words resounded, loud enough to scare away the birds. The chant ran through the crowd like music. The applause, loud enough to wake the world from its sleep. So much noise it sounded like gunfire.

No! It was gunfire! Bang! Bang! Bang!

The noise came from the area between Jill and the stage. People began to scream. They ran. With the river behind them, there was only one way to go and they fell over one another rushing to the street.

Jill stood frozen. People swarmed the stage. She couldn't see Tyler, Denny, David, or Ali. In the distance, she heard sirens. She smelled sulfur, gun powder. Before her, the crowd thinned. A space opened up. A tall burly man with blond hair turned. The man with the scar on his left cheek. Dieter. Only now his right cheek was inflamed with a rake of deep scratches. Their eyes met. He calmly shoved his hands in the pockets of his leather jacket and slipped into the crowd.

21

For progressive movements, the future does not lie with electoral politics. It lies in street warfare – protest movements and demonstrations, civil disobedience, strikes and boycotts – using all of the power consumers and workers have in direct action against the government and corporations.

–Howard Zinn, historian

TUESDAY NOVEMBER 4 – ELECTION DAY

The man who depended on miracles was shot three times and died instantly. Dennis Drake made the weekend news and then disappeared from public consciousness as quickly as he had come. There was no elaborate funeral and the public's outcry went unheard. The press said little and after two days, stopped talking about him altogether. Both Facebook and Twitter were experiencing multiple technical failures and were off-line.

The police had no suspects. They admitted a number of missteps impaired their investigation. Due to an unfortunate mix-up, the Secret Service, which should have been at the fatal venue, was not in attendance. As a result of a permitting error, the police presence was inadequate given the size of the crowd. While the cameras were rolling during the shooting, the film showed events on stage and not suspects in the crowd.

In the melee that followed the rally, six people were trampled and an elderly man suffered a heart attack. Tyler and his friends were missing. They could have been killed, kidnapped, or run away. No one knew. The police were hesitant to consider Tyler a 'missing person', and were hopeful he was on the lam and would come home of his own volition.

For three days, Jill and her family were in a state of heightened anxiety. Hurtful words were forgotten and all energy was directed toward tracking down Tyler and his friends. Blaze ended his campaign on Sunday and flew to New York to help in the search. He was out of money and, uncharacteristically accepted premature defeat. He announced he was stepping down to spend more time with family. His priority at the moment was locating his son. With his political capital gone, he was not expecting help from old friends.

Alexandria took the bus on Saturday night from Boston and refused to return until Tyler was found. She sacrificed her vote, but since there was no one she cared to vote for, it didn't matter to her.

Charles/Kenneth, the British Secret Service agent went AWOL and Julie rehired her retired butler and set Christophe to work. Her apartment became the hub of the search party. Jill and Blaze moved in, as did Alexandria, the younger Layla, and Kitty the cat.

Jared Slater was also assisting in the search for Tyler. He ascertained that hours after the shooting, a badly scratched Dieter Von Heinz left New York on a Lufthansa flight bound for Frankfurt. He could not locate Kenneth Eaton, the missing butler, or Ermine Talu, the Turkish sharpshooter.

On the political scene, it was, once again, a two-way presidential race. Rich Tumblin was the front-runner, though the President was making a strong final push. The market had already made its call and the Dow Jones was surging in anticipation of having a hedge fund CEO as president.

At lunchtime, Jill and Blaze were alone in the apartment. Julie had gone to the astrologer, and Layla was in class. Christophe was ferrying Jared and Alexandria around town. They were visiting police stations and hospitals throughout the city and suburbs. Jill and Blaze were awaiting a call, something, anything to signal a break in the case. As it had been for days, the unspoken words in the room left the air so tense, it was hard to breathe. They sat in the living room, phones on the table, the TV on low. Blaze had his laptop and was checking his email. Jill was flipping through *People* magazine.

Just after one o'clock, Blaze's phone rang, but it was not the call Jill was hoping for. Rebecca was on the line wanting an update. Jill listened to Blaze's side of the conversation with bated breath. When he said, "I don't know if that's a good idea," she looked at him with raised eyebrows. He lowered the phone. "Rebecca and Calista want to come help look for Tyler. I don't know if it's a good idea."

Jill heard the weariness in his voice, saw the haggard expression on his face and the worry in his eyes and would do anything to make things easier for him. "They can come if they want."

Blaze blinked. It was not the response he was expecting. A smile crossed his face and he made arrangements for the pair to come. When he hung up, he looked at her.

"They're a part of your life," she said. "I might as well accept them." And then, though the words were hard to say, she added, "It's thoughtful they want to help."

"Calista thinks of Tyler as her brother."

Jill doubted if that were true. "It's nice they're coming even though you're out of office."

"I'm not out yet."

"You sure you want to quit?"

"The offer from Georgetown University is tempting. We could stay in D.C."

"What about the whooping cranes and their amusement park?"

He sighed deeply. "As we learned from Tyler, there are ways to protest."

"You won't be able to travel so much."

"Maybe I traveled too much."

"What about Rebecca?"

"What about her?"

At last, Jill asked the question that had haunted her for years. "If it wasn't for Alexandria, would you have left her?"

Blaze frowned. "What are you talking about? I left her the week we met. I never looked back."

"What about the *Enquirer* pictures?"

"They were photoshopped. Calista was out for dinner with us. She went back to her mother's house afterwards. She was between Rebecca and me and was cut out."

Jill felt an opening up of her heart. "I should have known." She looked into his eyes. "I do trust you."

"I trust you too. It's just–" He paused, as if searching for words.

"Let me guess. Something Julie said."

"You know your sister."

Jill moved down the couch, closing the space between them. "It will be nice to have you home. In the last three years, you've been gone a lot."

"I know. That wasn't fair to you." He shook his head back and forth. "I couldn't watch Hope."

"It was like you lost two daughters."

Blaze moved toward her until they were touching. "No. I can still see Calista. I can tell her goodbye. I can't tell Hope."

Jill swallowed with difficulty. "I never said goodbye either. I left the hospital and she wanted me to stay. I left her alone. I wanted to go home and drink. I got drunk."

He had nothing to say. He took her hand.

"I think she'd forgive me," Jill said.

Blaze nodded. "She would. She had a big heart. She'd forgive anybody." He draped his arm around her shoulder. "Maybe even me."

"I don't know what I'll do if something happened to Tyler."

"We'll find him. We'll fix this."

She leaned into him. "Waiting is hell."

"I know what we could do."

They went to the bedroom. The sun was high and the sky was blue with wispy clouds dancing by. For now, they pushed away the weight of their anxiety and their burden of fear and made love as the sunlight streamed down across them, and what was broken became whole, and what was once split, became one, and what was wound up, came undone with shuddering light.

When it was over, and their hearts stopped racing, and their breath slowed, and the sweat dried, the worry that had abated, returned, as did the load of anxiety and dread, but also hope.

It was Layla's mother who found him. Using astrology, she decided he was with the authorities, somewhere underground, near water, southeast of Manhattan. The clues were sufficient for the former FBI agent to pinpoint the Federal Detention Center near Gowanus Bay in Brooklyn.

Late in the afternoon on election day, Jill, Blaze, Alexandria, Julie, Jared and the young Layla, descended on the prison. Although the Patriot Act allowed the police and FBI to hold Tyler indefinitely without charges, there was no ruling he could not have visitors. A lawyer was quickly hired and a hearing before a judge cleared the way.

Blaze and the lawyer spoke to Tyler first. They were gone five minutes, the court imposed limit. Next, Layla went to see him, giving Jill an opportunity to be brought up to speed.

The FBI wanted a deal. No harm, no foul. In exchange for Tyler's silence, the government would drop all charges against him and set him free. He could never, ever, disclose his activities for the past six months, and never, ever, hack into servers or software again. Furthermore, he had to help clean up and remove code inserted into the servers he had hacked.

His friends had agreed to the conditions and were being processed for release. Tyler had refused the deal. He had until morning, at which time the government would charge him with multiple counts of cybercrime and seek the maximum penalty, life in prison.

"He's got to agree to the deal," Jill said.

"He says he'd rather go to prison."

Layla came out, shaking her head and Julie jumped up. "I'll talk some sense into him."

Jill stood up. "Sit down, I'm going."

Her sister did not object.

Tyler was waiting in an interrogation room ensconced behind a guarded steel door which required three different keys. Jill went inside, the heavy door closing behind her.

Tyler sat in the cold bright room on a hard-backed chair at a steel table. He wore an orange prison jumpsuit and his wrists were chained together. His ankles were shackled and the chain was bolted to a ring on the floor. His eyes were red and he looked exhausted and rough in a three-day stubble. His nails were raw and bleeding, chewed down to the quick.

Jill went around the table, leaned down and hugged him. He smelled sour, of adrenalin and fear, and days of unbrushed teeth and unshowered sweat. Tears streamed down his cheeks. "They killed him, Mom. They just killed him." He swatted his eyes and the chains rattled.

Jill sat down at the table across from him.

"They did this. The government or the banks. I don't know which is which anymore. It's hard to tell them apart. They pulled out the Secret Service. There was a quarter of the number of police there should have been. Denny never had a chance. They let the murderers go. I saw them at FBI headquarters. The waitress from the restaurant and the blond man with the scar. His face was scratched on one side. I think they wanted me to see them. Because I can't talk about it. If I agree to their terms, I can't say anything." The vein on his forehead was raised and pulsing.

"If you go to prison you won't be able to say anything either. If you agree, you'll get out and you can still protest, just in a more legitimate way."

"Don't you get it? They don't let you protest. There is no free speech. Those with money have power and call the shots. They're killers. They would imprison someone for life without a second thought. And Denny would have won. He could have changed it. Now Rich Tumblin wins. Wall Street will be in charge. We'll be a Third World country by next summer." Tyler pounded the table with his fists and the chains clattered. "Did you know he owns the Oasis Nuclear Power Plant?"

Jill was taken aback. Oasis was the power plant in Vermont that needed fifty million and had instigated the latest economic crisis.

"It's owned by Green Energy, incorporated in the Cayman Islands, but the trail of owners lead to Tumblin."

Jill didn't ask how he knew. Of course, they'd hacked into the software at the nuclear power plant.

"Calista told me," Tyler said, as if he sensed Jill's thoughts.

"Calista? Your Dad's daughter? That Calista?"

"My half-sister, yes. She was a good source. She knows a lot about off-shore banking."

Jill looked at her son. "You talk to her?"

"Of course. You're the one who doesn't like her."

Jill took offense. "She doesn't like me."

"Because you're mean to her."

And Jill knew it was true. "I'm going to try harder to be nicer."

"Denny always thought there was something fishy about the plant," Tyler said. "No one knew who owned it, who was supposed to fix it, and why it wasn't fixed. So we checked it out."

Jill shook her head.

"The sad thing is, there's no problem with the plant. It's a software issue that can be rectified in five minutes. The state didn't need fifty million to fix it. It was just a ruse to make the Democratic governor look bad, get Rich's Republican buddy elected, and take fifty million away from the government and put it in Rich's pocket."

Jill could only continue to shake her head.

"He deliberately caused the crisis. The Fed was in on it too. They set it up at that private meeting we tried to protest. Tumblin, the Fed chairman, the New York Fed president, the wanna-be governor of Vermont, and the VP of Moody's, planned the whole thing. The Fed promised not to come to the state's rescue and Moody's promised to threaten to cut the U.S. credit rating."

"You know what they spoke about at their meeting?"

"It's just a guess. We hacked into the Fed's server and learned about the meeting, but we don't know what was said, only who was invited. Given what happened, we know their intent was to influence the election. Only they weren't counting on California. The mess was bigger than they imagined, thanks to the information on Dad's computer. They didn't plan those leaks. California going bankrupt could have crashed the economy, but that wasn't their goal." Tyler took a breath before he went on.

"It turned out all right for Tumblin. The market fell and Tumblin's rich friends got to buy stock on sale. The Chinese agreed to lend and Tumblin was credited with brokering the deal that saved the economy. He looked good, his poll numbers rose, and he seemed like a shoe-in. But then along came Denny. Denny had to be stopped. It was a coup d'état and I can't say anything."

"Either way, you won't be able to. Either way, they'll shut you up."

Tyler lashed out his leg and the chain on his ankle rattled. His eyes began watering.

"I didn't sign anything," Jill said. "I don't have to keep quiet."

Tyler stopped fighting his chains. He looked up and their eyes met.

She shrugged. "I always wanted to write a book."

A slow smile broke on Tyler's face and the light came back on in his eyes.

Four hours later, near midnight, with the sun at the nadir, and the country in its darkest hour, the election was called in favor of the Wall Street CEO. Once the legal work was done, they left the detention center. Tyler and Layla were holding hands. Outside, the stars shone brightly and the night sky was alive with fireworks. In Brooklyn, horns honked and people danced in the streets, celebrating the hope and promise of a new president.

The End